Behold a comatose human guy in a dystasis tank, hooked to a psychotronic apparatus that plays the same lovely dream over and over and over. He is being genetically engineered. . . .

The wakeful bits, when he manages to force open his eyes and peer myopically through the perfluorocarbon liquid, are fuzzy and surreal and punctuated by stabs of fear and helpless anger. During them, the floater recalls one vivid short-term memory snippet. . . .

He sits in a smoke-filled bar in a hollow asteroid in the distant Sagittarius Whorl, and the Haluk smiles at him as his consciousness starts to drain away. He remembers his despairing certainty, in the final instant before oblivion, that the aliens are probably going to subject him to something outrageously weird this time around, having failed to finish him off during their previous assaults and batteries. . . .

By Julian May
Published by Ballantine Books:

The Saga of Pliocene Exile
The Many-Colored Land
The Golden Torc
The Nonborn King
The Adversary

A PLIOCENE COMPANION

Intervention
The Surveillance
The Metaconcert

The Galactic Milieu Trilogy
Jack the Bodiless
Diamond Mask
Magnificat

BLACK TRILLIUM (With Marion Zimmer Bradley and
André Norton)
BLOOD TRILLIUM
SKY TRILLIUM

The Rampart Worlds Trilogy
Orion Arm
Perseus Spur
Sagittarius Whorl

SAGITTARIUS WHORL

An Adventure of the Rampart Worlds

Julian May

A Del Rey® Book
THE BALLANTINE PUBLISHING GROUP
NEW YORK

A Del Rey® Book
Published by The Ballantine Publishing Group
Copyright © 2001 by Starykon Productions, Inc.

www.randomhouse.com/delrey/

Library of Congress Catalog Card Number: 00-110291

ISBN 0-345-39518-2

Manufactured in the United States of America

First Edition: January 2001

10 9 8 7 6 5 4 3 2 1

Chapter 1

Behold a comatose human guy in a dystasis tank, hooked to a psychotronic apparatus that plays the same lovely dream over and over and over. He is being genetically engineered.

That much he knows, because he's been in one of the damned vats before—sometime, somewhere. The details are a mystery. He drifts in the glass coffin of bubbly oxygen-charged goo, too stoned by the drugs and REMory dream-programming to react rationally during his brief interludes of semiconsciousness.

The wakeful bits, when he manages to force open his eyes and peer myopically through the perfluorocarbon liquid, are fuzzy and surreal and punctuated by stabs of fear and help-less anger. During them, the floater recalls one vivid short-term memory snippet . . .

He sits in a smoke-filled bar in a hollow asteroid in the distant Sagittarius Whorl, and the Haluk smiles at him as his consciousness starts to drain away. He remembers his de-spairing certainty, in the final instant before oblivion, that the aliens are probably going to subject him to something outrageously weird this time around, having failed to finish him off during their previous assaults and batteries.

He squirms in the dystasis tank, making a futile attempt to swim up, push off the lid, and break free. But his limbs and trunk are firmly clamped in an upright frame. Only his head, gripped less tightly, is able to move a little.

He remembers a few more things.

He can swim. He can cook. He can pilot a starship. He can ride a horse.

He's a disgrace. He's a lawyer. He's a scuba diver. He's a zillionaire.

He was a cop. He was a suicidal drunk. He was a political gadfly. He was . . . doing something that got him in deepest shit.

When he finishes wrenching his head around uselessly, he sees another transparent-walled container next to his own. Inside it another body is dimly visible in reddish womb-light, a companion in dystasis. Straining, he tries to get a better view of the other person, but finds it impossible.

His mouth opens in a silent roar of frustration. With his lungs and the rest of his respiratory tract full of liquid, his vocal cords are as impotent as those of an unborn baby. The dystasis monitoring equipment detects his frantic muscle contractions and the hormonal flood that indicates an agitated mental state.

Naughty, naughty! His struggles are disrupting the genetic engineering procedure. The apparatus programs deeper anesthesia. He plummets back into slumber mode and the umpteenth dream replay begins.

He's always with his wife, whose name he can't recall any more than he can remember his own. There is background music—Scott Hamilton playing " 'Round Midnight" on a tenor saxophone. The bedroom is very large and of a rustic southwestern ranch style, with a high-beamed ceiling and walls of whitewashed adobe, adorned with antique Native American weavings and artwork featuring elegantly lewd pastel flower shapes. Double-glazed sliding doors with parted curtains reveal that it's night and snowing hard outside. The sound of the blizzard wind occasionally breaks through cascades of gentle jazz. White drifts are piling up outside on the patio.

He and his wife, young newlyweds, sit side by side on a shearling rug before a blazing fire. They're naked, propped happily against each other, sipping Roederer Cristal while they watch the dancing flames. Her hair is ash-blond, rippling after being released from its braided chignon, and reaches halfway down her back. Her eyes are the color of deep ocean waters beyond the reef. She is striking rather than pretty, and her features in repose are solemn until he caresses her and makes her smile.

Time to make love again.

And again and again, as the psychotronic machine endlessly loops his most exquisite memory to facilitate the dystasis procedure.

The poor happy schmuck in the tank is me.

Drifting and dreaming.

Tap tap tap.

Someone spoke, an alien voice filtered through a translator device. "How interesting. It looks as though he is waking up."

Someone else: "This is the template individual, Servant of Servants. The original. The transformed human subject is recovering in another room, attended by one's technicians. We will interview him shortly, just as soon as he is lucid."

"Let's see if this creature recognizes one."

Tap tap tap.

I slowly opened my eyes. The room outside was dimly lit, as always, with most of the illumination coming from a bank of alien equipment some distance away. The dark floor was intricately veined with a glowing red web that converged on my tank and the one beside mine, which was now empty.

Three Haluk stood looking at me, two males and a female, all wearing translator pendants. The tallest of the aliens knocked on the glass wall to get my attention as though I were a sulky specimen in an aquarium.

Tap tap tap. "Wah! Can you hear one, Earth life-form?"

Of course I could. My ears worked just fine while submerged in the oxygenated glop, and he must have known it.

He pursed his lips in the racial smile-equivalent and twid-
dled his four-fingered hand in mock playfulness. "Do you
recall this one's identity?"

With difficulty, I focused my eyes and concentrated.

Well, sure. The last time I'd seen him, he was wearing a
conservative human-style business suit of dark green with
faint white pinstripes, tailored to set off his wasp waist and
accessorized by a scarlet foulard scarf and a diamond stick-
pin. He was now attired in exotic haberdashery appropriate
to his high station: bronze-purple robes with glittering jew-
eled trim, an elaborate spiked diadem of platinum, and a
matching necklace inset with large fossil cabochons. But
that ugly blue face was unmistakable, and so were the oddly
beautiful eyes with their sardonic, hyperintelligent glint.

The perfluorocarbon bath had rendered me mute, but I
snarl-mouthed: *You friggin' xeno bastard! Damned right I
know you. You're the Servant of the Servants of Luk, the head
honcho of the Sovereign Haluk Confederation.*

"Bravo," he said dryly. The Haluk aren't telepathic, but
my response had evidently been clear enough. "Please accept the profound gratitude of this one and of the Council of
Nine. Thanks to you"—he nodded toward the tenantless second tank—"and to the turncoat rascal with whom you shared
your vital substance, one has high hopes of an accelerated
schedule for our Grand Design."

Suddenly, a surprisingly concrete recollection popped
into my skull. The alien leader and I had had a nasty confrontation a couple of years ago outside the Assembly
Chamber of the Commonwealth of Human Worlds in
Toronto. At the invitation of Liberal Party members sympathetic to Reversionist principles, I had finally testified
about . . . something important having to do with the Haluk
and their trade treaty with humanity. My speech had really
pissed off the Servant of Servants and the members of his
alien entourage, as well as a sizable percentage of the Assembly Delegates.

But what had I said? And who the hell was I?

I hadn't a clue.

The Servant said, "Feeling all right, are you? Archiator Malotuwak assures one that you came through the human-to-human genetic exchange in fine fettle. Unfortunately, we can't let you out of the dystasis tank just yet. We require a second demiclone."

Demiclone? ... What the hell are you talking about, huckleberry balls?

"Take one's advice, human. Cooperate willingly when you're called upon later for tutorial duties. Extracting the pertinent information by means of psychotronic interrogation machines is so uncomfortable. Who knows? If you do well, one might even allow you to live. Common laborers are always in demand on our newly colonized planets."

Screw you. With a magnum drill press!

The second male Haluk spoke up. Short and stocky, he wore a plain mustard-colored smock tightly cinched about his slender middle and carried an elaborate Macrodur mag-slate of the type favored by hotshot human scientists. "He's becoming excited, Servant of Servants. This is not a good thing for a dystasis subject. It could delay initiation of the second demiclone procedure. One will program a calming medication for him."

He prodded the slate and a warm woozy feeling began to seep into my body, dulling anxiety and slowing my thoughts. I fought the desire to relapse into sleep.

Demiclone! I should know what that meant. I *did* know. It was a highly illegal genetic engineering procedure. The Haluk had stolen some of my DNA and used it to—to—

To duplicate me. To morph some other guy into a replica of my precious person. I mouthed helpless obscenities. The Servant of Servants had already lost interest in me and turned his attention to the Haluk woman standing beside him.

She was elderly, her skin faded to the color of well-washed denim, and she wore robes of glistening black with a hood that nearly concealed her mane of pale hair. A very important-looking polished fossil on a long chain hung about her neck.

"Is it certain, Archiator Malotuwak," she inquired of Mustard Smock, "that the newly created duplicate of this individual retains his own mentality? It would be disastrous to the Servant's Grand Design if the demiclone were to be . . . contaminated, as it were, by the mind-set of this template life-form."

"That is quite impossible, Council Locutor Ru Kamik. Only the physical aspect of the demiclone has been altered." A grimace of distaste. "That other human's mind—such as it is—remains his own. One might mention that he was most uncooperative during the preliminary procedures, insulting one's assistants and behaving in an arrogant and offensive manner."

The Servant of Servants uttered the grotesque laugh of his species, which sounded like a miniature poodle choking to death. "Fortunately for us, the rascal's usefulness to the Sovereign Haluk Confederation does not require a congenial disposition."

"Yes," the Locutor said. "However, his usefulness *does* require that his true identity not be detected. One was somewhat disconcerted to learn that the demiclone is not, after all, an essentially perfect replica of this original."

"True enough," Mustard Smock conceded. "The restricted time frame we were allowed precluded optimal DNA transfer. It was necessary to use an abbreviated genetic engineering procedure. One made this quite clear to the Servant of Servants and to the demiclone subject himself at the outset. Even using the most advanced human equipment and techniques, along with broad-spectrum PD32:C2 transferase agents, four weeks in the dystasis tank is inadequate for complete chromosomal transformation, given the relatively large amount of intron material in the human genome. Introns are more difficult to exchange than exons—"

The Servant of Servants interrupted, addressing the female. "Nobody's going to test him, Ru Kamik. They'll have no reason to doubt his identity. He will be carefully coached in his role."

"Nevertheless," said the Locutor firmly, "please explain to this one the circumstances under which the demicloned person might be differentiated from the original subject by expert investigators of the Commonwealth of Human Worlds."

The Haluk scientist made the gesture signifying self-abasement. "You'll forgive if one gets a bit technical, Great Lady?"

The Locutor steepled her four-fingered hands in a gesture of condescending assent. "Continue. One is by no means completely ignorant of genetics."

"As you may know, not all of the DNA within body cells acts as a blueprint for life processes. Those segments that are active are often called exons. They trigger protein production—build the body and keep it in operation. The other DNA segments, those with no known function, are called introns. The noncoding introns are intermingled with the exons. In the human genome, about ninety percent of the DNA is noncoding. By comparison, we Haluk have a smaller percentage of introns, even though our total number of exons is close to the human complement."

"I understand."

"Because one was commanded to perform this procedure in the shortest possible time, one transferred only the exon DNA and about one-tenth of the introns from the donor to the recipient. As a consequence, even though the recipient exhibits the physical characteristics of the template as perfectly as an identical twin, he nevertheless retains a large part of his original intron DNA—the genetic material that seems redundant."

"And this can be detected by forensic analysis?"

"Readily, Council Locutor. Most of the genetic variation among human individuals is in the introns. Even a rough comparison of the demiclone's DNA with that of the original will reveal the fake. If one had only been allowed more time—"

"It was not practical," the Servant of Servants said dismissively. "And one must repeat: the chance of the demiclone undergoing DNA testing during his mission are vanishingly small."

The Locutor spoke in a neutral tone to the Servant of Servants. "Certain members of the Council of Nine have very grave misgivings about this stratagem. Using the human demiclone, that is, rather than one of our own race."

"Their doubts are groundless, Ru Kamik," the leader insisted. "The revised Grand Design is going to succeed! Almighty Luk will shower his beneficence upon us and shatter the spines of the human despots."

"There is still great danger," she said softly. "And this one is not speaking only of the possibility that the turncoat agent's identity may be detected. He himself is a traitor to his race and perhaps not entirely sane. One has seen his personality analysis—"

"Yes, yes, curse it for a wad of odoriferous lepido nose wax! One knows all about that. But the scheme he proposed is brilliant. If it succeeds, our grand expansion strategy will be accomplished in years, rather than centuries or even millennia."

"If the scheme succeeds."

"Wah! Would you have us abandon our great hopes, crawl back to the cluster, embrace our fatal allomorphic heritage, and go down to extinction as we exhaust the balance of our dwindling resources? Or shall we continue to submit to humanity's tyranny here in the Milky Way? . . . No! This one has promised the people that all will be freed from allomorphy—that our children will live on new, uncrowded worlds. If the Grand Design succeeds, this goal will be achieved peacefully. If it fails, we will use force to seize the planets we require from the loathsome humans. Curse their arrogance up a necrotic copulatory orifice!"

"Be tranquil, Servant of Servants," Ru Kamik advised. "This one has a duty to examine contingencies. Even unpleasant ones. Why would it not be possible to use a Haluk demiclone rather than the disguised turncoat to fulfill the Grand Design?"

"The scheme was conceived by him," the Servant pointed out, simmering down a bit. "And he alone is in a unique position to carry off the deception—at least in its initial stages. No Haluk demiclone would be able to worm his way into the confidence of the Frost family and Rampart Concern quite so readily, or so quickly, as the rogue human life-form. Once he is well-established, however, the situation changes. Taking his place, a trained Haluk demiclone will be able to maneuver freely, inserting other demiclones into positions of power and influence. Humanity will find itself in thrall to us before it realizes its peril."

"But how can we be certain that the turncoat will not fly out of control?"

"One has made the personal decision that the risk is acceptable. One is aware of the individual's limitations, and they have been factored into the operational equation. He will be carefully monitored by our other demiclone operatives in the Earth capital city. The rogue's personal agenda, vengeful and perfidious though it may be from the point of view of his own race, coincides with ours. At least for the time being."

"As you say, Servant of Servants." She lowered her head so that her eyes were momentarily concealed by the hood of her black garment.

"Don't worry, Ru Kamik," the Servant reassured her. "As soon as possible, the wretched human creature will be replaced by one whose loyalty is above suspicion. Our own esteemed agent, Ru Balakalak, will carry the mission to its successful completion. Meanwhile, the turncoat will have laid the groundwork for the coup. Needless to say, the rogue human knows nothing of our intention to eliminate him when his services are no longer required."

She made a noncommittal gesture and turned to address the scientist. "Is it true, then, Archiator Malotuwak, that the more lengthy demiclone procedure performed upon Ru Balakalak will create a totally undetectable duplicate?"

Mustard Smock hesitated. "That is the theory, Great Lady, according to the reassurances of the late Scientist Milik, who introduced the genetic procedure to us. Of course, there exists no validation. So far as we know, no Haluk-human demiclone has ever been subjected to DNA analysis by the Commonwealth Criminal Investigation Department."

"Milik!" huffed the Lady in Black. "Can one rely upon *her* word? She was a flaming idealist and an egregious fool, claiming she was ready to die if it would advance the cause of interspecific friendship."

"Milik was a selfless benefactor of our race," said the Servant with dangerous emphasis. "A martyr canonized by the Priesthood of Luk."

"But one that we in the Council of Nine did not fully trust—no more than you did, Servant of Servants. In truth, she was another human turncoat of unstable temperament and cloudy motivation . . . and one who may have secretly meddled with our racial heritage, if certain rumors are to be given credence. This one has recently heard that some of Milik's work on the eradication of allomorphism has come under scrutiny."

"Nonsense," retorted the Servant of Servants. "Those rumors are quite devoid of truth. It's ridiculous to think that Milik would have tinkered maliciously with the trait-eradication treatment. Or lied about the flawlessness of the demiclone procedure."

"As you say," the Locutor murmured. There was a brief silence. Then she asked, "When will the second demiclone be ready?"

"Ru Balakalak is preparing to enter the dystasis tank immediately. As I understand it, the unabbreviated procedure takes about twenty-six weeks. Is that correct, Archiator?"

"Approximately," said Mustard Smock. "In interspecific DNA exchange, there is a necessary preliminary operation, a sort of inoculation of the human template individual to preclude rejection of exotic DNA by the nonhuman recipient. This is followed by the phase during which the actual gene transfer and bodily transformation of the recipient is accomplished."

"Twenty-six weeks is a long time to wait," said the Locutor.

The Servant said, "Additional time will be required to tutor Ru Balakalak in details of the mission once he emerges from dystasis. It is estimated that he will be ready after thirty weeks."

"Thirty!"

"Meanwhile, one will keep the Council of Nine fully informed concerning operations on Earth. Needless to say, one expects that you, Ru Kamik, will be zealous in supporting the revised Grand Design."

She lowered her head again. "As you say, Servant of Servants."

"Excellent." He turned to the scientist. "And now one believes it is time for this one and the Council Locutor to interview the human demiclone."

"He awaits in the recovery room," Archiator Malotuwak said. "Please follow this one."

The three Haluk went away and I was left suspended in dopey horror, boggled by the technobabble and at a loss to understand the kind of espionage my duplicate was about to undertake. Questions swirled in my brain like terrified bait minnows in a bucket.

Who was the human traitor who now wore my face, who had hatched some ploy that was deemed vital to the Haluk Grand Design?

Whatever the hell *that* was.

How could a demiclone of me help put the Commonwealth of Human Worlds in thrall to an alien race?

Dammit—who am I, anyway?

A disgrace. A former cop. A diver. A zillionaire. Aside from the useless fragments of memory, my drugged brain had no answers.

So after a while I slept again and dreamed of falling snow, the roaring fire, the champagne, and my nameless wife's loving arms. Dreamed over and over again, to the accompaniment of Scott Hamilton's ancient, peerless saxophone.

At long last the dreaming stopped.

I realized instantly that my situation had changed. Some instinct warned me not to open my eyes and not to move. I had sense enough to obey.

I was out of the tank, breathing ambient air, lying on my back on a firm, slightly inclined surface, head cradled in a comfortable pillow. Warm and dry, not hurting—and surprisingly alert, even though I still had no notion of my identity or what had happened to me.

Alien voices were speaking and I felt gentle pokes and prods in different parts of my anatomy. Two Haluk individuals who called each other Miruviak and Avilik were right beside me, performing some sort of physical examination. The suffixes of their names indicated that one was male and one female. They were not wearing translators. My knowledge of the Haluk language is imperfect and I could understand only part of their conversation, which seemed to refer to my condition. I was apparently in satisfactory shape, and after a few minutes they covered me to the chin with a soft blanket and moved off, still talking.

I heard one of them say: "The *blah blah* authority figure is soul-glowing about the *blah* of the dystasis *blah blah*."

I understood that to mean that a Haluk VIP, perhaps my old chum the Servant of Servants of Luk, was happy about the results of some sort of dystasis procedure. "Dystasis" was the same word in English and Halukese because a human had illegally introduced it to the aliens.

The remarks that followed were spoken some distance away, couched in medical jargon almost totally incomprehensible to me. I risked cracking open my eyelids.

I could see most of the room. It was at least six meters square and looked like an accommodation in a superior Haluk hotel catering to humans, situated on one of their long-settled colonial planets. With the human-Haluk rapprochement in place in the Perseus Spur, I'd once stayed in a similar place.

Good. You remembered that. Now try to remember something essential—like who you are!

The furnishings, except for scattered pieces of mysterious technical apparatus with blinking telltales, were an eclectic mix of alien and Earth designs. On my right, where the wall was completely shrouded in opaque draperies, were exotic chairs, a low table, stands holding Haluk bioluminescent lamps with quaint shades, and an elaborate human-style infomedia credenza. To the left, in an open-plan adjacent room, was a wet bar—no booze visible—and a compact kitchen, also human in design. An alcove held a tall case full of e-books and slates, plus a collection of anonymous small cabinets constructed of exotic materials. The head of my bed was against one wall. Another bed stood on the opposite side of the room, flanked by an open bathroom door with a human-type sink visible. A second door in that wall was closed.

The two Haluk medical technicians, wearing human-style pale green hospital scrubs and murmuring quiet comments, hovered over the occupant of the other bed, who lay motionless while the aliens studied him. I didn't have a very good view of the patient, but I could tell that he was a good-sized human male with a fairly powerful build. A small console with what looked like medical monitoring equipment stood at his bedside.

I caught the question: "If a third demiclone is not required, then why not discard the *blah?*"

The female Haluk said, "This is a very *blah* demiclone, Miruviak. He must be taught *blah blah blah* and *blah* before *blah* his mission. Some of the teaching will be done by the human *blah* who taught *blah blah*. But *blah* from the *blah* over there is also needed. Our orders are to keep him alive until the *blah* decides he is *blah blah*."

Not very enlightening. In fact, ominous.

"This demiclone will wake up soon," said the male medic. "Listen, Avilik: one thinks we should *blah blah blah*. Just in case *blah blah blah*. Did you bring them with you?"

"Yes."

The meditechs had finished their examination of the other patient and replaced his blanket. Now they came across the room toward me again. I quickly shut my eyes, relaxed, tried to think Zen thoughts, and prayed that my bed wasn't equipped with a built-in vital signs monitor that would betray the fact that I was fully conscious. Somebody drew the covering away from my naked body. They rolled me over and I felt a sharp prick in the back of my neck.

"It is best that we wait to insert the second *blah*," Avilik decided. "But it is not really needed yet. He's still very weak."

Miruviak grunted something that might have been "That will take care of it," and then they rolled me over again and tucked me in.

"The dystasis turned him a most beautiful color," the female medic remarked, uttering the squelched barking sound that represented Haluk laughter. "His *blah blah* are certainly of an imposing size and *blah.* Later, one hopes to know him better before we must *blah blah.*"

"Disgusting," hissed her colleague, clearly miffed. "You women only *blah* one thing."

I heard more alien snickering. Then both of the medical technicians went out of the room. I lay still, cold dread seeping into my soul along with a growing comprehension. My memory was coming back on-line—parts of it, at any rate—and I didn't like what I recalled.

I'd been in a dystasis tank for at least seven months. The Haluk had made two demiclones of me. The first evil triplet had been a human traitor, imperfectly morphed at the cell-nucleus level but otherwise my physical duplicate. I had no notion what his mission might be, but it boded no good for humanity. The second demiclone was a transformed Haluk, destined to replace Agent Number One, who possessed certain talents but also had the potential to become uncontrollable. Number Two had been more expertly engineered and was perhaps a perfect genetic replica. I presumed that he now occupied the bed opposite mine. He was going to be tutored before going out to fulfill his mission, and some of the briefings were to come from me, whether I chose to cooperate or not.

The suite's mishmash of Haluk and human decor made more sense now. It was a schoolroom where my shadow and I would live and work together until he had his act down pat.

Interspecific genetic engineering . . . there was something peculiar about it. I tried to retrieve what I knew from my cerebral database. My sister—what was her name?—had once been targeted for demicloning. She was rescued before a duplicate of her could be made, but she'd still suffered certain dramatic side effects from the procedure.

As I would have.

Turning an alien into a human being was trickier than the usual total-spectrum biological refit job and even more illegal under CHW law. It required that the human DNA donor—in this case, me—first be modified with an infusion of critical alien genes so the demiclone subject wouldn't reject the human material. The preliminary genen procedure superficially transformed the DNA donor—

Rats!

I lifted my right hand and drew it out from beneath the covers. The skin was very firm and tinted a rich sky-blue. There were no fingernails on the four abnormally elongated digits. The bones of the pinkie and ring fingers were partially fused now, enclosed in a single fleshy envelope. My lower arm, quite hairless, was decorated with a dramatic pattern of ridges that sported faintly drawn golden patterns, almost like delicate enamelwork.

I touched my altered face and cursed more eloquently. Weird bulges and a Haluk-style flattened nose. Eye sockets of normal human diameter, slightly smaller than Haluk orbits. It seemed that I'd kept my human-sized eyeballs, just as my older sister Eve had when the Haluk tried to demiclone her.

Eve! Her name was Eve. And my name was . . .

On the tip of my tongue, which felt strange, as though it were too large for my mouth. My teeth seemed peculiar, too. The spaces between them were wider than normal.

Under the blanket, my hands explored a body that was humanoid but not human. Externally, the preliminary genen procedure had turned me into a facsimile of a Haluk, complete with a wasp waist that was only about 70 centimeters in circumference. But inside my ridged blue skin were human muscles and human guts and human bones, plus a discombobulated but swiftly recuperating human brain. I lacked the Haluk elongated neck and overall slender build. My alien hands groped lower on their inspection tour until they reached my crotch—

Oh, God! Holy blazing bloody shit! No! Not that!

It was all I could do not to scream my lungs out. Those fucking xeno fiends . . .

For a few minutes I felt drowned in a black tide of self-loathing and despair. Then I remembered that my partially morphed sister Eve—who hadn't experienced this particular indignity—had been restored to her normal human physiology by another sojourn in the dystasis tank. At the time, it seemed to be a miracle of modern science.

I, too, could be made good as new. The ghastly transformation of my genitals could be reversed, as could the other changes. Provided that I managed to live long enough, and escaped from whatever exotic planet the Haluk had stashed me on.

Very slowly I sat up, experiencing nausea and a fleeting dizziness. I was weak as a new-hatched chick and there was a curious itching sensation at the back of my neck. I touched it and felt a tiny lump right at the base of my skull. The damned Haluk meditechs had given me an implant, and odds were it had to do with keeping me under control.

Maybe it was signaling them at this very moment.

My weird blue feet settled onto the floor—wood parquet laid out in a minuscule herringbone pattern, coated with ice-clear "skating rink" glaze a full centimeter in thickness. It was a labor-intensive human interior design style, ultra-trendy. Just the sort of thing the fad-conscious Haluk were likely to borrow. I judged that I was being held in a very upscale alien establishment—certainly nothing resembling the godforsaken outpost in the Sagittarius Whorl where I'd gone on the Barky Hunt. Perhaps my captors had taken me to the planet Artiuk, their colonial capital in the Milky Way . . .

Which was situated in the Perseus Spur sector of the galaxy, fourteen thousand light-years from Earth. More memories data-dumped. I'd lived in the Spur myself, on a pretty little freesoil world called Kedge-Lockaby. Had a house on a tropical island, a yellow submarine named *Pernio II*, and a bunch of rascally friends. Once upon a time I'd been a disenfranchised Throwaway, an ex-cop, a happy-go-lucky charterboat skipper who ran a sport-diving service for tourists.

But not lately.

Something momentous had happened to me. I had returned to Earth and stayed there for some years, doing . . .

What?

Something to do with politics. Something to do with lawyering. Whatever it was had keenly interested the Haluk, given my double demicloning and the secrecy attending it. Unfortunately, the exact nature of my recent terrestrial activities still eluded me, along with my name.

My name! If I could just remember that, all the rest of it would come back.

Wrapping the blanket around my dainty middle to hide the disgusting alien sex organs that had captivated the female medical technician, I struggled to stand up. Exerted long-unused muscles and shuffled creakily across the room to the other bed. Stared down at the guy who lay there, asleep or unconscious, with tiny alien-type medical sensors stuck to his forehead, temples, and neck.

Recognized him.

I inhaled sharply, found myself pitching forward in a sudden fit of vertigo, shocked to the depths of my being. My blue fingers caught at the bedclothes and I saved myself from falling, pushed my trembling body upright and stood there swaying and gasping for breath.

The man was tall and heavy-boned, with a physique less well-developed than it should have been—although that flaw could be mitigated through appropriate clothing or even judicious doses of steroids. The face would need work, too. The skin was pasty from his long sojourn in the tank, and the features were too fresh and regular. He lacked a certain distinctive scar at the top of his left cheekbone. His nose had never been broken in a Big Beach brawl and coaxed back into shape by a defrocked Throwaway plastic surgeon suffering a cosmic-class hangover from Danaëan rotgut. His hair was pretty authentic, the color of bread crust, springing from his forehead in a distinctive widow's peak. It was a little too long, but a barber would fix that. When his eyes opened, I was positive they'd be cold green with an inner ring of amber.

I knew him, all right.

He was me.

My demiclone, the alien imposter who was going to take my place—or rather the place of Demiclone Number One, already secretly machinating. We would help conquer humanity on behalf of the Haluk race.

My name was Asahel Ethan Frost. Called Asa by my family, Helly by my friends, and Helmut Icicle by assorted crooks, ne'er-do-wells, and disenfranchised wretches of the Perseus Spur. My father was Simon Frost, the founder of Rampart Interstellar Corporation, which had now become Rampart Amalgamated Concern. My mother was the late Katje Vanderpost, gentle philanthropist, whose murder I had yet to avenge. Her gift had made me a zillionaire. My siblings were Eve, Bethany, and the matricidal Daniel. My wife—my former wife, for we had been divorced for nearly eight years—was Joanna DeVet, Morehouse Professor of Political Science at Commonwealth University, Toronto Campus.

I remembered it all, including details of my anti-Haluk political activities, my legal triumph for Rampart Concern, and the ill-advised escapade in the Sagittarius Whorl that had brought me to this pretty pass.

So, what are you going to do about it, you sorry Halukoid piece of shit?

The back of my neck tingled as a wave of fury washed over me, and I jumped as if I'd been goosed. Whatever I did, I knew I'd better do it mighty damned fast.

Fake Helly looked so peaceful, lying there. For an instant I wondered what kind of sweet alien dream they'd programmed for him while he was in dystasis. Then I twitched the pillow out from under his head, pressed it over his face, and held it down while he writhed feebly under me and uttered muffled cries.

The medical monitor standing beside the bed let out a shriek of alarm. Simultaneously, the gizmo implanted in my neck began to administer a series of increasingly severe shocks at intervals of about five seconds. If they were intended to deter me from homicidal rage and other adrenaline-driven misdeeds, someone had badly miscalculated the human pain threshold.

I flung myself on top of my double, using my weight to pin his flailing arms. Neither of us was up to snuff physically, but I still had my superior human musculature and knew how to use it. The regular shocks from my neck implant were now so strong that I was moaning in agony.

I kept on doing what I had to do.

His struggles weakened and finally stopped. I held the pillow down hard for another minute or so, then pulled it away. His lips were cyanotic, smeared with blood from his bitten tongue. The wide-open eyes had tiny points of red dotting the whites, and the pupils were wide and black. I felt for a pulse in his throat and found nothing. The monitor continued its shrill distress signal.

He was clinically dead, but they'd be able to revive him. Unless . . .

The pain from the neck shocks was becoming unbearable, and I knew I'd pass out unless I could do something about it. I staggered across the room toward the small kitchen, scratching impotently at my nape with Halukoid fingers lacking nails. Tore open drawer after drawer, finally found one with small cooking utensils. What to use? I couldn't find any knives, which figured.

That! If only it's sharp enough . . .

I grabbed it, thrust it awkwardly against the tiny lump, and gouged with all my strength.

One last bellow emptied my lungs. Then pain—but of a

new sort, related to torn flesh. I dropped the melon baller with its malignant contents on the floor, grabbed up a dish towel and pressed it against the streaming wound. My blood was very red, very human.

As his would be, no longer circulating. But the Haluk medics would be able to do something about that unless I made it impossible.

I dived back into the drawer of kitchen utensils and rummaged frantically, cursing the absence of sharply pointed implements until I realized that any damage I might inflict with them would be easily repairable. I had to *destroy* Fake Helly, and do it within minutes.

A thought.

The wet bar. Did it have what I needed?

Yes! My blue hand closed over the drink-mixing wand. I stumbled back to the motionless body. Eyes wide open in death, he didn't feel a thing as I positioned the implement and bore down with gruesome effect. To my surprise, the eyeball didn't rupture but simply slid aside. The thin wall of bone behind it crunched and I was through to the brain.

And activated the mixer's control to the highest setting: STIFF WHIP. Inadvertent morbid humor there. The efficient little machine didn't even make a mess.

Try to repair that in your dystasis tank, huckleberry balls!

I made the mistake of withdrawing the wand, only to drop the thing on the floor as my stomach gave a terrific heave and thin bile flooded my throat. Fortunately, my guts were almost empty because of the dystasis, but it still took me a few minutes to recover. After all, I'd just done a cerebral puree job on myself . . .

Enough. Think escape.

I was surprised that no Haluk had responded yet to the medical alarm or to the signal that had set off my neck-shocker. It was time for me to get moving. Steal a set of clothes, flee into the alien landscape of Artiuk, or whatever planet I was on.

Better check the weather outside. I'd been on Artiuk only once. The climate was torrid and subject to heavy rains.

I ran to the wall of draperies, hoping they covered windows, pulled aside the hanging fabric and uttered a disbelieving expletive.

Outside the glass was an immense city, viewed from a height. It was night. Soaring towers rose on either hand as far as I could see, their shining colored forms enmeshed in webs of skyways and high roads with streams of cars zipping along them. Aircraft moved in traffic-controlled pathways like regimented fireflies through a sky tinted bright gold. It had to be snowing hard outside the force-field umbrella.

That wasn't Artiuk out there, or any other Haluk colony. It was Earth. And the city was one I knew intimately: Toronto, capital of the Commonwealth of Human Worlds.

Still holding the blood-soaked towel to my neck, I began to laugh like a maniac. I only stopped when the outer door of the room crashed open and the two medical technicians rushed inside, followed by a pair of uniformed Haluk guards armed with Ivanov stun-pistols.

Chapter 2

Last April, when I still wore the outward appearance of a human being, I said goodbye to my legal staffers and got the hell out of town. While the judges considered their verdict, I intended to rest up at my family's Sky Ranch in Arizona and consider my future—especially in regards to the Barky Hunt.

For the first couple of days I did nothing but sleep. Then I worked out in the ranch's well-equipped gym, swam laps in the indoor pool—it still being a trifle brisk outdoors in the high country—read some vintage Louis L'Amour and John D. MacDonald, and finished off each evening riding out to watch the sun go down in a different part of the sprawling Frost family spread.

My favorite mount was a horse named Billy, a huge sweet-natured gelding of the type southwesterners call a flea-bitten gray. That's not to mean he's infested or broken down; the odd term describes a variety of pale horse speckled all over with tiny spots of blue and red hair. Billy was strong and smart, he obeyed orders, and he didn't spook when an unexpected quail or jackrabbit exploded out of the chaparral right under his nose. In Arizona you can't hardly ask more of a horse than that.

On the tenth day of my holiday, Billy and I plodded easily uphill in the lengthening shadows while thin clouds turned from white to pink beyond the Tonto Basin. Spring in the Sierra Ancha is unobtrusively lovely. Golden yuccas, buckbrush, and manzanitas were blooming, tiny little humming-birds with amethyst throats poked busily around the flowers for a final snack before nightfall, and the ethereal song of the hermit thrush echoed among the mesas and canyons.

It was a great place for unwinding, as different from the capital of the Commonwealth of Human Worlds as it could possibly be.

I'd left Toronto in a seriously fatigued state. Only my close-mouthed executive assistant, Jane Nelligan, knew where I was going, and she was under orders to reveal my whereabouts to no one. I told the ranch staff to ignore my presence, and they did—except for the horse wrangler who cared for Billy, and Rosalia the cook, who supplied me with three gourmet squares a day and kept the chitchat to a min-imum.

I'd earned some incommunicado time. After more than two years of cosmic-class courtroom warfare, Rampart Con-cern's civil suit against Galapharma was finally ready for adjudication. Now it was up to three justices of the Com-monwealth Tribunal to produce a verdict in what the media had deemed the corporate trial of the century, David vs. Goliath.

Little Rampart, youngest and smallest of the Hundred Concerns, was suing the pants off Galapharma, one of the oldest and largest. We alleged conspiracy to devalue for the purpose of hostile acquisition, sabotage, industrial espi-onage, theft and subsequent malicious use of data, suborna-tion of Rampart employees, and a lengthy laundry list of other major torts. Pursuant to Statute 129 of the Interstellar Commerce Code, Rampart demanded as redress the maxi-mum damages set by law—namely, all assets tangible and intangible of Galapharma Amalgamated Concern, including their 5,345 booming planetary colonies.

If we won, Gala belonged to us. If we lost, the best we could hope for was that Commonwealth prosecutors could make an assortment of criminal charges against the big Concern stick. The odds of that happening were slim. Important evidence had vanished, and crucial witnesses were dead or had disappeared. The one man who might have fingered Galapharma for its crimes was also the principal material witness in Rampart's civil suit; and Oliver Schneider had struck an immunity deal that precluded any obligation to give testimony under the criminal statutes.

If Gala won, its lawyers would waste no time slapping Rampart with a colossal civil countersuit, stunting the growth and profitability of its small rival for years to come—if not destroying it outright.

As Rampart's interim Chief Legal Officer, I had been in total charge of orchestrating our case, always working behind the scenes. Not that I'd asked for the job! I'd fought like a wildcat to avoid it. But my father, Simon Frost, and my big sister Eve—Rampart's Chairman of the Board and CEO, respectively—had leaned on me, inviting my scrutiny of certain inescapable facts.

My older brother, Daniel, the former Rampart corporate counsel and secretary, could hardly head up the litigation. An unindicted Galapharma coconspirator, Dan was kept doped to the eyeballs and under heavy guard in a fishing lodge up in the Ontario North Woods, where he stubbornly professed his complete innocence.

None of the subordinate officers in Rampart's legal department were deemed capable of directing a complex, unprecedented civil action such as this one. To bring in an outside team of litigators was not an option, either. There were aspects of the case that didn't bear close scrutiny: for instance, the strong probability that Dan had engineered our mother's death, acting under orders from Galapharma.

And there was also the secret Haluk connection, political dynamite now that the blue buggers were legitimate trading partners of the Commonwealth . . .

Simon and Eve maintained that only one candidate for Rampart legal battlemaster had it all—being a major stakeholder in the Concern, a trusted member of the family, and a highly trained lawyer (although nonpracticing) familiar with every aspect of the case.

Yours truly, Asahel Frost.

Trying to wriggle out of the fast-closing trap, I reminded them that I was not a member of the Commonwealth bar and could not be quickly qualified by any string-pulling finagle of theirs. Even though my citizenship had been restored through a technicality, the felonies I'd been framed for were still on my record. In the eyes of the law I was still a convict on probation. In the eyes of the media I was a misfit—a charismatic one, though!—the black sheep of a distinguished family, a notorious loudmouth with eccentric political leanings. There was no way I could represent Rampart before the Judicial Tribunal in person.

No problem, said Simon and Eve. What they needed was not Rumpole of the Bailey or Perry Mason, but rather my expertise in rousting corporate outlaws, gained during my aborted career as an enforcement officer with the Interstellar Commerce Secretariat. A staff of talented associates would handle the actual pleading before the court. If necessary, the underlings could be coached by me every step of the way through cerebral chips.

I shifted into whine mode. Hadn't I already risked my life half a dozen times to obtain crucial evidence supporting Rampart's case against Galapharma? Hadn't I rescued Eve from kidnappers that would have demicloned her and seized control of Rampart? Hadn't I saved Simon himself from a fate worse than death in the infamous prison known as Coventry Blue? Wasn't that fucking good enough? I didn't want to spend years on a convoluted legal case. I had other plans for my life.

"Like what?" my father had bellowed. "Stirring up a fresh hornet's nest with the damned Reversionist Party? Or maybe reverting to beach bum status on that boondock South Seas planet back in the Perseus Spur?"

I invited him to go to hell. He suggested that I perform a sexual act on myself. The discussion trended downhill from there.

Simon and I have a long history of horn-locking, beginning from the time fifteen years ago when I refused on principle to join the family starcorp. Now he castigated my selfishness and lack of filial loyalty. He dredged up my fancy-pants doctorate from Harvard Law School that I'd more or less tricked him into paying for.

Finally, in a fit of bogus cowhand vituperation, the old coot allowed as how if'n I let Rampart—i.e., him—down, I was nothing but a chicken-livered pecker-ass bastard with a yellow streak so wide it lapped plumb around to my brisket bone.

I was about to tell Simon to stuff his John Wayne act where the sun doesn't shine when my sister Eve ordered us both to shut up. Then she made a single point that stabbed me to the heart and put an abrupt end to my weaseling.

"Asa, have you forgotten that our mother's murder was instigated by Galapharma's chairman? Dan only acted as Alistair Drummond's cat's-paw. We probably couldn't prove Drummond's complicity in the crime even if we found he was still alive, but his Concern is still a legitimate target. Do you want some kind of justice for Mom, or don't you?"

Aw, shit . . . Damned right I did.

So I caved in.

And worked my tail off for two solid years. When the case went to the judges at long last, I figured we had an excellent chance of winning.

I guided my horse Billy along Bear Head Canyon trail, approaching the undistinguished peak we call Copper Mountain. At 2,071 meters, it's the tallest of a scrub-covered range near the southern boundary of the Sky Ranch.

When we were kids, my brother and sisters and I were forbidden to go up Copper because of a dangerous abandoned gold mine on its eastern slope. So of course we made that our favorite secret spot. It was our hideout when we played outlaw, and the den of xeno monsters when we pretended to be Zone Patrol troopers. Just inside the mine entrance, I'd once killed a blacktail rattlesnake that had menaced my little sister, Bethany. Another time, my brother, Dan, risked his neck exploring a tumbledown side tunnel and found a glittering chunk of mineral that he declared was real gold. Dan was always the lucky one—until he grew up and succumbed to the temptations of a lunatic Scotsman.

Who might or might not be buried deep inside that very gold mine.

Three years ago, in a last ditch effort to salvage his faltering conspiracy, Alistair Drummond had narrowly missed killing my family and the rest of the Rampart Board of Directors by blowing up the main house of the Sky Ranch. He tried to escape by driving up Copper Mountain in a Range Rover, and when I came after him, he almost managed to nail me before taking refuge in the abandoned mine. I used a Harvey blaster to bring down a landslide on top of him.

Trouble was, we'd never found Drummond's body in the rubble-filled mine shaft.

The horse carried me toward the gap that separates Copper Mountain from Bear Head Peak to the west. I reined in before the going got too rough, pulled a set of power oculars out of my saddlebag, and swept them over the brush-covered flanks of Copper. Of course I found nothing unusual; even the site of the great slide and the subsequent excavation were on the opposite side of the mountain.

"What do you think, Billy? Did the damned mine have another way out? Us kids never found one, and we explored the hell out of that old hole in the ground."

The horse kept his opinion to himself.

I sighed and put the ocs away. To hell with Alistair Drummond. To hell with everything connected to Galapharma and the trial. This was my time to kick back and drift. I turned the mount around so I could concentrate my attention on the sunset beyond Bear Head. The western sky was slashed with crimson and purple streaks of cirrus cloud. The color faded slowly as I sat in my saddle, deliberately emptying my mind. Billy did a different sort of emptying, then nipped at some fresh greenery. A bat chased a flying bug through the chaparral. The high country was very quiet.

After a while the horse left off browsing, nickered softly, and cocked his ears. He was listening to something upslope. I heard it, too—an irregular metallic *tink-tink tinkety-tink* that sounded almost like a spoon handle rattling faintly in a thick coffee mug: completely unnatural. A minute later a spherical black thing about the size of a golf ball came creeping down the steep rocky trail on thin jointed legs. Its two rateyes glowed in the dusk and its sensors swiveled busily.

A SPYder. It tippy-toed to within four meters of my fascinated horse and came to a halt.

"Good evening, Citizen Asahel Frost," it said. "I am not here to threaten or harm you. Please confirm this by drawing your own weapon."

The robot's voice was a human transmission. The controller had probably been tracking me by satellite from the moment I left the house. The Sky Ranch doesn't bother with ground-based optical dissimulator technology, although it has a full arsenal of intruder deterrents and multiphase alarm sensors.

"You're trespassing," I said, obediently pulling a Finnilä Bodyguard photon carbine from its gun boot on the saddle. The weapon switched itself on automatically and scanned the thing that confronted me.

Device is unarmed, my gun reported. I activated the targeter anyhow.

"I repeat!" said the SPYder. "I am not here to threaten or harm you."

"Goody. But you weren't invited, either. Give me one reason why I shouldn't fry your tiny Tootsie Roll."

"That would be illegal," the machine said smugly, "since you've passed nineteen meters beyond the boundary of the Sky Ranch into public lands."

"Maybe I have," I conceded, lowering the gun. The perimeter in this remote and rugged area was unfenced and unmarked, the scanner units that guarded it were hard to spot, and I'd deactivated the saddle alarm days ago so it wouldn't bug me when I strayed off the spread. "Who are you and why are you stalking me?"

"Jordan Sensenbrenner of the *Wall Street Journal* here! Would you care to comment on today's Rampart-Galapharma verdict by the Commonwealth Judiciary Tribunal?"

My jaw dropped. "A decision already? My God—it's only been ten days! How did the judges rule?"

"You mean you haven't heard about it?"

"I've been totally incommunicado. Getting some much-needed peace and quiet. You want to tell me what happened?"

The SPYder's voice went cagey. "Perhaps you don't know about Simon Frost's sensational announcement, either. The *Journal* would definitely like to hear your reaction to that."

"My saddle has a datalink and display. Why don't you pass along what you've got. When did the verdict come down?"

"Mmm . . . Maybe we should talk quid pro quo. You give me a decent statement for attribution, I'll have our comsat download the *Journal* articles we'll be posting later tonight on our site. They contain full details of the court decision given an hour ago, along with your father's announcement. Deal?"

Damn webcrawlers had more nerve than a sperm whale's wisdom tooth. This one was starting to annoy me, so I lifted the Finnilä and blasted a rock just a mite to the left of it.

The SPYder skittered sideways and instantly deployed a

miniature force-field. "You can't do that! I claim media privilege! I'm just trying to do my job!"

"I can do whatever I please—provided I don't give a damn about the consequences. You're trying to pressure me, Jordan Sensenbrenner. There are people who'd tell you that's not a very smart thing to do."

"I assure you I didn't mean—"

"That puny shield your bot is wearing can stop a laser bolt but not a gross physical assault. Suppose I kick your expensive little toy down a coyote hole and roll a rock on top? Or maybe stomp it till it's crippled and smother it in some of the horse apples Billy just dropped? Would that make your editor happy?"

The SPYder dropped its defensive shield. It was groveling time. "Citizen Frost, perhaps this interview got off on the wrong foot—"

"It's not an interview yet, only a close encounter of the Wild West kind . . . However, I admit I'm anxious to hear the big news before it hits the PlaNet. I suppose I could call the folks down at the ranch and ask them to patch me into Rampart Tower in Toronto, but it might take a few minutes to organize the relay. So I'd be much obliged if you'd just pass on the information out of the goodness of your heart, no strings attached. Don't you think your boss at the *Journal* would consider that a wise move?"

"Oh, very well," the SPYder grumped. It told me the satellite's access code.

I uncovered the unit on the saddle pommel, activated the antenna and expanded the viewscreen, entered the data and tapped SAT DOWNLOAD. A moment later I was reading the *Journal* copy quoting the judges' unanimous decision.

Galapharma AC was found guilty on all charges, with no appeal to be entertained by the Tribunal.

Compensatory and punitive damages owed by Gala to Rampart were still to be assessed, but the consensus among legal scholars was that the greatest pharmaceutical and genetic technology company in the galaxy was fucked to a finality. The Tribunal would probably order Galapharma to be turned over lock, stock, and barrel to Rampart, instantly lofting my family's firm into the exalted company of the Big Seven.

Some observers attributed Rampart's victory to the brilliant litigation strategy of its unofficial CLO, the dashing and unconventional Asahel Frost. He was also rumored to have personally apprehended the principal material witness for the prosecution, using highly unorthodox methods.

I finished reading and eyed the SPYder. "Very nice, Jordan. You may quote me as being personally gratified by the verdict, which affirms my faith in the CHW judiciary system. All corporate entities, most especially those of high status whose actions influence the very integrity of the Commonwealth, must conform scrupulously to the dictates of the law."

"Have you yourself always done so, Citizen Frost?" Sensenbrenner inquired blandly. "There's been speculation that the witness Oliver Schneider was—"

"Next question."

"Perhaps you ought to read your father's statement first."

I skipped through the sidebar articles and trial commentary, scanning for Simon's name. I found the piece, read the headline, and uttered a shocked expletive.

RAMPART CHAIRMAN, JUBILANT OVER GALAPHARMA VERDICT, DECLARES HE WILL STEP DOWN IN FAVOR OF MAVERICK SON

by Jordan Sensenbrenner

Toronto, Earth, 19 April 2236—In the wake of today's historic verdict favoring Rampart Concern, its Chairman of the Board, Simon Frost, 88, declared: "This is the happiest moment in my life." After congratulating his legal team on its success, he made a sensational announcement.

"During the past few years," Frost said, "Rampart has not only repulsed a criminal hostile takeover attempt but also managed to thrive and expand. We've risen from a closely held Interstellar Corporation to an Amalgamated Concern, thanks largely to the efforts of a brilliant group of top executives headed by my daughter Eve Frost, Rampart's CEO. I'm proud to have played a role in this expansion, just as I'm proud to be a cofounder of Rampart.

"Back in 2183, when my brother Ethan and our partner Dirk Vanderpost and I went out to the Perseus Spur to seek our fortunes, we never dreamed that a day like this would come. It was enough that our little Starcorp could meet its payroll and keep the Haluk and Qastt pirates from stealing our cargoes.

"Well, times change. Today both of those races are CHW trading partners. The Spur boasts 219 prosperous Rampart Worlds, with more being opened to human colonization and economic development every month. I'm tickled pink that I lived to see that happen.

"Now that Rampart has weathered its greatest crisis and come out on top, I've decided that it's time for me to step down from active corporate leadership and make way for younger blood. I intend to retire as Chairman of the Board. And I hereby nominate my son Asahel Frost to take my place. Without him, Rampart would have succumbed to Galapharma's hostile takeover ploy. Without him, we would never have won our civil judgment against Gala.

"I haven't consulted Asa yet, so this is going to be a bit of a surprise to him. But I'm confident that he'll accept the chairmanship, just as I'm confident that Rampart Concern will continue to prosper in the years to come."

Having delivered the antimatter warhead, the article continued with a summary of my roller-coaster career. Sensenbrenner glossed over my stint as a Divisional Chief

Inspector in the ICS, where I had been one of the valiant, overworked band charged with ferreting out wrongdoing among the Big Businesses that effectively control the Commonwealth of Human Worlds. In contrast, the details of my conviction, my dismissal from the enforcement arm of the Commerce Secretariat, and my disenfranchisement were presented in lip-smacking detail. He had even interviewed a few of my more vengeful acquaintances on the planet Kedge-Lockaby, who painted a revolting and accurate picture of me in my days as a drunken Throwaway.

My rescue of Eve from her kidnappers and my alleged apprehension of Oliver Schneider in an illicit raid on the Qastt planet Dagasatt were described more cautiously to skirt the libel laws. (I was a citizen again by then.) The article was silent on my role in the presumed demise of Alistair Drummond.

Katje Vanderpost's mind-boggling gift to me of her Rampart quarterstake had lifted me into the ranks of the political movers and shakers. The writer seemed to have no idea why I'd dedicated almost all of the obscenely large income from my mother's stake to projects of the underdog Reversionist Party. (I'd made a promise to carry on her own sponsorship, since party principles coincided with youthful ideals I had mothballed while serving in the ICS.) Jordan did concede that I'd made a notable splash for ten entertaining months, attacking the Commonwealth Assembly's craven symbiosis with Big Business, until the Galapharma trial forced me to put my political life on hold.

The article ended with speculation on what course I'd choose to follow next.

If they only knew . . .

"I can't answer that question yet," I told Sensenbrenner. "I'm going to have to think long and hard about it. But you can quote me on this: I will do nothing that will contravene the Reversionist Guiding Principles, nor do I intend to completely abandon politics." I couldn't resist adding, "Perhaps it's possible that under my leadership, Rampart Concern could modify its operations to reflect the philosophy of Reversionism."

Wow—heresy! The reporter couldn't keep the expectation of a major scoop out of his voice.

"But . . . most Reversionists favor drastically limiting the political influence of the Hundred Concerns—in effect, destroying the galactic economic structure!"

I laughed. "I admit that some party zealots might feel that way. My own views on the subject are not nearly so radical. Nevertheless, for nearly two centuries Big Business has exploited the stars with only minimal checks and balances by the Commonwealth. I want the Hundred Concerns made more accountable to the Assembly. To the elected representatives of humanity at large. I'd like to see laissez-faire interstellar economics reined in or even abolished, along with the laws that enable human business interests to do just about anything they please if it means increased profits for their stakeholders. I also favor just treatment of nonstargoing Indigenous Sapient races whose worlds are colonized and developed by humanity. And closer regulation of trade with interstellar alien civilizations that might not be fully committed to . . . interspecies goodwill."

"Are you speaking about the Kalleyni, the Joru, the Y'tata, and the Qastt, Citizen Frost? Or about the Haluk?"

"No further comment at this time."

"As chairman of Rampart, do you really believe you could implement your Reversionist ideals?"

"If I took the position, I could try. My late uncle, Ethan Frost, who headed Rampart in the beginning, was one of the first galactic entrepreneurs to give Insap workers human-equivalent wages and decent working conditions. I'm convinced his policy was the principal reason Rampart prospered in the Perseus Spur, while Galapharma and the other oppressive outfits who tried to make a go of it failed and had to withdraw."

"But the majority of economists and financial authorities don't believe that approach would be practical in the longer-settled Orion Arm worlds, much less in the Sagittarius Whorl—"

I flapped a dismissive hand at the SPYder. "Stop. I won't argue the point with you now. I told you that I don't know yet what I'm going to do with my life. Maybe I'll accept the Rampart chairmanship. Maybe I'll go back to being gadfly-in-chief for the Reversionists. Maybe I'll do something completely different. Right about now I feel like flying away to some quiet little planet where nobody knows my name. The Galapharma trial left me worn down to a nubbin. Simon's proposal couldn't have come at a worse time. I need to re-tune my perspective before I commit myself."

"How long before you—"

"That's enough," I said. "End of interview." I turned Billy away and started back down the trail. The high clouds had lost their color and the first stars were popping out in the east.

The SPYder came scuttling after me. "Citizen Frost! Just a few more words! When do you expect to return to Toronto? Would you grant the *Journal* an in-depth interview concerning your political ambitions? Or discuss the direction Rampart Concern might take under your—"

Casually, I shifted in the saddle, raised the carbine and fired from the hip, drilling the little machine through one of its glowing eyes. It exploded in a brief puff of smoke and plasma. Billy didn't even flinch.

Then I started back to the ranch house. I figured it wouldn't be long before my father showed up.

I half expected Eve to accompany Simon, the better to co-erce me. But when I arrived an hour or so later I found him alone in the big living room of the fully restored main house, staring into a blaze of piñon logs in the big fireplace and sipping his usual bourbon and branch water. A magslate, the

logo of the *Wall Street Journal* shining on its viewer, lay on
the polished petrified-wood coffee table behind him. The
late edition had been posted. I presumed that my interview
with Sensenbrenner was in it.

Looking glum, Simon nodded but didn't speak as I came
through the open French doors, still covered with trail dust.

I took off my stained old Stetson hat and Pendleton blanket jacket and went to the sideboard where the drinks were.
Passing by the Maker's Mark Limited Edition, Hirsch Pot
Still, and other upmarket tarantula juice that my father fan-
cied, I helped myself to my favorite blue-collar tipple: Jack
Daniel's, straight up. A single shot sufficed to demonstrate
that I hadn't reverted to the lush life. After tossing it down I
drew a tall draft beer from the keg of Dortmunder tucked in
a compartment of the sideboard, sat on one of the leather
couches in front of the hearth, and began to haul my boots
off.

Simon stood watching me out of hooded green eyes. His
hair was light brown with a prominent widow's peak, just
like mine. I'd inherited his thin-bridged nose, too, and the
wide mouth with downturned corners that was capable of
blooming in a megawatt smile. He'd taken full advantage
of modern medical science and genengineering to stave
off time's ravages, and usually gave an impression of indomitable physical vigor.

But not today.

He was dressed in one of his semiformal riverboat gambler suits rather than the tailored ranchman outfits he usually
sported, perhaps signaling the special character of the occasion. He seemed tired and wary, and the black broadcloth of
his suit emphasized his abnormally wan aspect. I recalled
being taken aback when the *Journal* article gave his age.
People—including me—tended to forget how old Simon
Frost really was.

"They were having a victory bash at Rampart Tower when
I left," he said to me at last. His voice was just a bit too loud.

"Everybody was toasting you—even the people who pissed and moaned the loudest when Evie and I appointed you acting legal chief and gave you free rein. The whole gang agreed we never would have won a nonappellate verdict without your leadership. I suppose congratulations are in order."

I thought: Well, thanks all to hell, Pop! But I said nothing.

He continued. "You were the best one for the job and you did it. 'Nuff said. And now there's another job needs doing . . ." He let the words trail off, as if daring me to turn him down flat.

Oh, no you don't, you old buzzard. This time we play by Helly's rules.

I finally got rid of the boots, put my feet up on the low table, took a deep swallow of beer, and slid forward on the cushions so my rump was almost level with my shoulders. "I'm surprised Evie didn't come with you."

"The quick verdict caught her by surprise. She's four days out, en route to the Spur, and didn't want to backtrack. There's some sort of conkbuster situation connected to the Cravat facility expansion. Zed couldn't seem to get a handle on it so she decided to take care of the matter personally. She'll return to Toronto as soon as the flap is resolved and help you and the other legal eagles work out the petitions for redress."

"Sam Yamamoto and Marcie Kirov are perfectly capable of supervising that—along with all the other post-trial stuff," I told him. "I got you your damned verdict. Don't expect me to shovel up after the circus parade."

A long silence, broken only by the faint cries of nighthawks. The doors were still open to the patio, and I could smell the perfume of the hundred-year-old wisteria growing on the *cenador* next to the barbecue pit. Miraculously, the explosion that destroyed the main house had spared the rustic dining shelter and the adjacent gardens, as well as most of the trees and ranch outbuildings.

I said, "How'd you know where I was?"

"A pushy *Wall Street Journal* reporter told me. He found you with a Big Eye satellite three days ago. Figured you might give him an interview on your trial strategy once the verdict was in. Seems you didn't try very hard to keep undercover once you got out here. Right after I issued my statement at the media conference, this *Journal* joker was all over me wanting an exclusive follow-up. Said he intended to contact you here at the Sky Ranch, too. I told him lotsa luck getting through the security umbrella. But I reckon he did."

"A SPYder robot tracked me down as I was riding outside the perimeter this evening. I gave a few quotable remarks before I zapped the bot to smithereens with my Finnilä. It was giving me attitude."

"Goddammit, Asa! What's the sense antagonizing the legitimate media? It's not like the webster was from a tabloid."

"The real question," I said, pushing myself upright and looking him dead in the eye, "is why the hell you chose to offer me the Rampart chairmanship via a media release instead of putting it to me privately, in person. Do you really think it's an offer I can't refuse?"

"More like a trial balloon," said the crafty old bastard, "to see how the Hundred Concerns might react to the idea. Especially Adam Stanislawski and his venture-credit hardheads at Macrodur. Rampart will need them more than ever after the Gala consolidation. I wanted to float the idea of you as my replacement while your reputation is still sky-high and shiny."

"As opposed to it taking a dive into the cesspool if I get involved in politics again? . . . And what about my standing felony convictions? Ollie Schneider's ready to make a deposition about the trumped-up charges, but it'll take forever for a reversal to work through the courts."

"That's a dead issue, boy. Even if it can't be proved that you were framed, anyone with half a brain figures Gala drygulched you so's you wouldn't be able to use your position in the ICS to stymie the takeover. As for your flaming lefty politics, if you just soft-pedal things a little—"

I uncoiled and climbed up from the couch, invading his private space until we were nearly nose-to-nose in front of the fireplace. "Let me tell you something, Simon," I said quietly. "My Reverse principles are still very much alive. I won't soft-pedal them, no matter what decision I make concerning Rampart. And I'm going to do something about the Haluk situation, too."

"Send out more hothead media releases denouncing the trade agreement?" He gave a snort of derisive laughter. "Fat lot of good that'll do. The deal's done, and Rampart's in the Haluk Consortium with both feet."

I said, "Those slippery Haluk bastards are making fools of us, pretending they've given up their aggressive expansion policy. They're already pressuring the Assembly to grant them more Rampart Mandate worlds immediately."

Simon shrugged and sipped his drink. "So long as the xenos pay a good price in ultraheavy elements, they'll likely get what they want."

I let loose a flare of temper. "And that's just dandy for you and for the other Concerns in the consortium, isn't it! Business as usual. Everybody wallows in profits, never looking beyond the bottom line. Meanwhile, nobody's quite sure just how much expanding the Haluk intend to do! How many of them are out there in that star-cluster, anyhow, champing at the bit to emigrate to the Milky Way? . . . We don't know! They don't allow visitors to their cluster and they vaporize trespassers. And your consortium doesn't give a rat's ass about the Haluk's long-range intentions so long as trade keeps booming."

"Zone Patrol and the SXA will keep an eye out for funny stuff. It's not the consortium's responsibility to monitor a sovereign alien race."

"No," I agreed. "So perhaps someone else will have to look into the matter."

A faint expression of alarm flitted behind his eyes. "Who'd be nutty enough to do that? Don't tell me you—"

"I can't believe you've forgotten what the Haluk did!" I yelled. Simon blinked and backed away from me. "Marooning me on that goddamn comet . . . collaborating with Drummond's goons . . . snatching Rampart World colonists and using them as slave labor and lab rats! And what about those two hundred human templates on Dagasatt that got blown to hell along with the Haluk demiclones? The Haluk were manufacturing fake humans to spy on us, and nobody seems to care why."

"Industrial espionage," he opined. "To infiltrate Rampart and Gala—why else? They were desperate to obtain our PD32:C2 genen vector. The demiclone spies were gonna help 'em get more of the stuff in some scheme or other. But now they can buy the vector from Rampart on the open market, so the demiclone thing is a dead issue."

"You think so, do you?"

"Yes, dammit, I do!" He did a double take at my skeptical sneer. "What? You think the blue-balls put demi moles into some human government agency? You still think they're cooking up a fuckin' war?"

"We've got lots of good stuff the Haluk want besides PD32:C2. Why should they buy it in dribs and drabs for a whopping high price over a long period of time if they can take it for free? And get unlimited lebensraum besides?"

"Horse puckey," Simon scoffed.

"They've hated and feared humanity ever since we came into the Perseus Spur and stopped their colonial expansion cold. They covet our superior technology and envy our ability to stay awake and active all year 'round. That kind of mind-set didn't evaporate when they signed a couple of treaties two years ago."

"Wouldn't be the first time in history that old enemies kissed and made up," Simon said reasonably. "Hey—look at you and me! The Haluk've tried to make amends for the past. Agreed to pay reparations to the families of the kidnapped engineers and template victims. Paid Rampart for deprivation of employee services and the damage done on Cravat, too."

"And that's supposed to wipe the slate clean? I suppose you don't give a damn that Haluk are flooding into the Perseus Spur by the millions. The fifteen new T-2 worlds they were granted by the Assembly last year are already bursting at the seams."

He finished off his drink. "They pay through the snoot for Rampart Mandate planets. So why not?"

"If their long-range expansion strategy includes forcible penetration of the Milky Way," I said in a low voice, "there are lots of reasons why not."

"Nobody believes they'd make war except you, son. And you don't have one smidgen of proof to back it up."

I enumerated what I considered to be valid evidence. "*Uno*: the ruthless way they went after PD32:C2 to erase their allomorphism. *Dos*: their refusal to allow unrestricted inspection of their home worlds or Spur colonies by humanity. *Tres*: the vastly overpopulated planets of their home starcluster. And if they continue to eradicate their allomorphic trait and no longer have half their people in hibernation at any given time, they'll need even more room! . . . Do you have any idea how many top-line transports the Haluk have purchased from Bodascon over the past couple of years? Nearly three hundred! And that doesn't count the starships they're building on their own, copying human high technology."

"That's not proof, that's unsupported inference—worthless as a bucket of mule piss."

"I'll find evidence that not even the ostriches in the Assembly can ignore. Don't think I haven't been working on it! And now that the Gala case is won, I intend to work even harder."

Simon turned his back on me and headed for the booze

table. He uncorked the bottle of rare old Hirsch bourbon and half filled his Waterford tumbler. No water to dilute it this time. He moved toward the open French doors. "Let's step outside. I need a breath of fresh air, and you could use cooling down yourself."

I padded reluctantly after him, bringing my beer. The patio flagstones were chilly, and a cutting breeze came from the west. Discreet gas-flame lanterns mounted on low posts had come on automatically at dusk, giving soft illumination to the expanse of irrigated lawn, the surrounding gardens, and the driveways that led to the other buildings. The main house stood on a rise and had a magnificent view of the mountains that completely surrounded the ranch. Now, with night having fallen and no moon, the sky was crowded with incredible numbers of stars and banded by the Milky Way. The Perseus Spur, at the galactic rim fourteen thousand light-years from Earth's solar system, was visible if you looked carefully to the north; but the small Haluk Cluster that lay seventeen thousand light-years farther out from the Spur's tip was hidden by intervening dustclouds. No one had known it existed until human explorers crossed the Black Gap.

My father gave a sigh that was just short of being theatrical. "Damn, that sky's a pretty sight. I never get tired of high-desert nights."

"I do," I said evenly, "when I'm standing on a cold stone pavement in my stocking feet."

He chuckled uneasily. Then came a very long silence while he lowered the level of his costly panther pee and I finished off my beer. His voice was somber when he finally said, "Do you really hate me so much, Asa? That you'd abandon Rampart when it needs you, just to get even with your old man?"

"I don't hate you, Simon. You and I just have different priorities. We always have. A long time ago you tried to bully me into accepting yours. When I rebelled, you washed your hands of me . . . until you were desperate for my help."

"That's true enough. And you came through like a champ, several times over. I'm damn grateful."

"Then let it go at that." I couldn't keep the bitterness out of my tone. "It's not true that Rampart needs me now. Eve has done a marvelous job as CEO during the past three years. She's restructured top management and gained the full confidence of the Macrodur financiers. There's no reason to believe that she and her team won't be able to handle the Gala consolidation just as competently, provided you continue as chairman and give her the benefit of your experience. There's nothing inherently rotten in Galapharma, you know. Its basic corporate infrastructure is sound. Alistair Drummond was a megalomaniac and a crook, but he was also a brilliant businessman. And he was right to believe that Rampart and Galapharma are ideal corporate harness mates. All Eve has to do is weed out the handful of bad apples who were direct participants in the conspiracy, and integrate Gala's management into Rampart's."

"You make it sound simple—but it's not. Your sister's an outstanding executive officer and she's come far in a very short time. But she's still just a beginner in the top Concern ranks, about to start swimming with some very large sharks. She wants you to be part of Rampart just as much as I do."

"I doubt it."

He looked at me with what seemed to be genuine puzzlement. "What's that supposed to mean?"

"You read my interview with the *Journal* reporter. Eve has, too, by now. Did you think I was just playing mind-games with the guy when I talked about the Reversionist Principles—and possibly applying them to Rampart if I accept the chairmanship?"

He didn't reply.

"Come on back inside," I said. "My feet are freezing—as you know damned well—and I haven't had my supper yet. Starry vistas don't make me choke up the way they used to."

He followed me and closed the French doors behind us. "I wouldn't mind a little snack myself. I'll talk to Rosalia."

"Chili con carne and a big salad for me. She knows what I like."

"I'll just have me some shrimp nachos with Navajo sheep cheese and salsa."

He contacted the cook through the old-fashioned intercom. Domestic robotics had been taboo in the original Sky Ranch main house because my late mother Katje believed that they deprived human beings of jobs and had the potential to invade privacy. When Simon rebuilt after the explosion, he restored the place exactly as it had been before.

I stood on the hearth and warmed my feet, declining his offer of another shot of whiskey and accepting more beer. Then we arranged ourselves on opposite sides of the petrified wood table and waited for the food.

"So you really did mean it," Simon said tentatively, "when you threatened to screw up Rampart's Insap policy if you became chairman."

"Not screw up. Modify humanely. Preindustrial natives should get more than a few jobs when their planet is exploited by humanity. They deserve a stake in the profits. Plus subsidized education options for those races that can take advantage of them. Anything short of that is unjust—and I'm not alone in believing that's true."

"Dammit, Asa, it's just not practical! Usually it takes years before a newly developed world starts showing a profit. What about our human stakeholders and the Macrodur finance people? You think they'll just lie down, roll over, and let you scratch their tummies when you spring this crackpot scheme on 'em? And what the hell will happen when Insaps on our new ex-Galapharma Orion Arm worlds decide they want the same deal as the Perseus planets?"

"We give it to them. In a prudent manner, over a reasonable period of time. Education first, then stakeholdership."

"It won't work! Way back when interstellar commerce first got going, a few limp-weenie outfits tried to organize human-alien cooperatives and suchlike shit. The Insaps got uppity ideas, wanted a bigger and bigger piece of the enchilada. First thing you know, the humans had full-blown worker insurrections to deal with. Preindustrial xenos can't be treated like human beings! Some of 'em are barely rational. Others are stuck at the tribal or feudal social level and only respect an iron fist. Some have goofy counterproductive customs that preclude any kind of discipline. Most don't understand free enterprise at all!"

"I didn't say I thought the modification would be easy. Perhaps the policy won't be feasible with marginally sapient peoples. But if I become Rampart chairman, the board members will have to accept the policy."

"Even if it throws the Concern into chaos?"

"I'll do my utmost to see that doesn't happen. But yes— I'm willing to take a huge risk in hopes that Rampart's example will spread to others of the Hundred Concerns. If you and Eve and the board of directors are afraid I'll fail, then forget about me. Keep your chairmanship. I'll do what I can to promote Reversionism in other ways."

I sat back then waiting for the bluster, the combination of wheedling and threats that he'd used to bulldoze me in the past. Either that or he'd withdraw the nomination forthwith.

All he said was, "Son, I can't retain the chairmanship. I'm no good for it anymore. I'm too old."

I couldn't help a snort of disbelieving laughter. "You're healthy as a horse! You could carry on for another twenty years."

A slight, rueful smile lifted his thin lips. "Nothing wrong with me physically. I'm old inside my skull. Tired. Running out of steam and moxie. It happens . . . But I'm smart enough to recognize that I'm past it, and that it's time for me to step down. Rampart'll get a new chairman one way or t'other. Eve doesn't want the job, and neither does Gunter Eckert or Caleb Millstone. They're happy where they are. You refuse, what might happen is we'd have to accept Ellington or some other Macrodur nominee because of the twenty percent stake they got from me in the venture credit scheme."

"Well, shit," I muttered, mainly because I couldn't think of anything else to say.

"Adam Stanislawski likes you," Simon said. "Ellington does, too. Most of the other Macrodur wheels were mighty impressed with your legal tactics against Gala." He scowled and looked away. "Of course, that was before you came out with that chuckleheaded interview in the *Journal*—all in living color, no less, posed against an Arizona sunset with a carbine in your armpit like Wyatt-fuckin'-Earp. God knows what the Macrodur directors think about you now."

"The reporter posted our live conversation?" I was aghast. According to stubborn tradition, conservative news media such as the *Journal* nearly always reported news in a read-only format. Sensational video clips were for the tabloids.

"Ee-yup," Simon drawled, nodding at the magslate on the coffee table. "Check it out if you like. You sure come off as one trigger-happy cowpoke, son."

"Rats!" I didn't bother to pick up the slate. Jordan Sensenbrenner had got the last laugh after all. "I guess I did shoot myself in the foot this time. Sorry. I'll take full blame for my idiocy, try to smooth things over with Macrodur if I can."

"Do it soon." The brief flash of amusement faded from Simon's face and he looked draggle-tail weary.

"I'll go to Toronto tomorrow," I said. "And I hereby swear off impromptu interviews—at least until I decide what to do about your proposal."

"You better make up your mind pretty damned quick."

"I won't be stampeded, Pop. You know me better than that." His eyes lit up as I made rare use of the paternal familiar. "When I gave that interview, I was pretty certain I'd reject your offer. Now . . ." I shook my head. "You'd still want me, knowing what I'd do with the chairmanship?"

"I figure you're bound and determined to give Reverse activism a try. But I don't think for a minute you'd run Rampart into the ground just to make some quixotic philosophical point. Shit—maybe you're right and the Hundred Concerns are wrong! Stranger things have happened."

"I need time to think," I insisted. "There are things I could accomplish in the political arena that might be difficult to pull off if I were a mere businessman."

"It'll be half a year at least before the Galapharma dismantling protocol is finalized and the Concerns merge," Simon pointed out. "I guess I can hold the fort that long. Nothing much can happen till then."

"I guess not."

Clairvoyance has never been my strong suit, nor Simon's, either.

"So take a nice long vacation," he urged me. "God knows you earned it."

"I might go out to Kedge-Lockaby for a couple of months. I'll be fairly safe from media harassment there. The locals in the Out Islands aren't fond of busybodies. I can drive my submarine and scuba-dive and weigh the options. If you need my input for something of cosmic importance, my next door neighbor on Eyebrow Cay has a subspace communicator. He'll know how to find me. You remember him: Mimo Bermudez."

A nod. "The old smuggler. Nearly as squirrelly as you."

"My best friend. Another man with quixotic principles."

We sat in silence for a time, watching the fire. Then, on impulse, I asked him, "Did you ever hear of another elderly smuggler named Barky Tregarth? He operated out in the Spur over forty years ago, peddling contraband weaponry and matériel to the Haluk and Qastt."

"Damn! I haven't thought about Barky for years. How'd you hear about him? From Bermudez?"

"Yes." And Karl Nazarian had known about the old crook, too.

Simon's brow wrinkled thoughtfully. "Hamilcar Barca Tregarth, teller of tall tales! Spun this crazy yarn about going to the Haluk Cluster on a bet, back when Galapharma owned the Spur. Said he ran rings around their patrols, then managed to sweet-talk the Haluk leadership into letting him land on one of their major worlds to refuel. Even claimed the aliens gave him the key to the city because he reminded 'em of some legendary Haluk hero. The poor bastard never did collect on the bet—and it was a sizable one. Seems nobody believed his story when he got back to the Spur. The souvenir he claimed he got from the Haluk could've come from anywhere."

"Did you meet Tregarth personally?"

"Once. Before his alleged trip. I had a drink with the guy in a saloon on Hadrach, maybe half a dozen years after Rampart got the Perseus Mandate. Jesus, he was a piece o' work! Sharp as a Buck knife and talk an arm and leg off you. My Lord, Barky'd be over a hundred twenty years old if he's still alive."

"Do you think his story about going to the Haluk Cluster might have been true?"

"Most folks thought he was lying in his teeth. Especially those in on the bet. But Barky sure as shit ran a lot of guns to the eleven Blueberry colonies in the Spur when Rampart was just getting started. Zone Patrol finally nabbed his ass—when?—maybe just after the turn of the century. Somebody broke him out of the Tyrins slammer before he came to trial. He was Thrown Away in absentia. Never operated in the Spur again." Simon eyed me dubiously. "What's your interest in Barky Tregarth, anyhow?"

I was saved from having to answer by a gentle knocking

at the inner door of the living room. It opened and the cook, Rosalia Alejo-Mertz, came in with a food-laden serving cart. "I hope you two are hungry," she said. "I brought some extra things I happened to have cluttering up the kitchen. Spit-roasted turkey slices, duck liver pâté, and wild strawberry shortcake."

In an instant Simon forgot about Barky Tregarth. "Rosie, you angel! Me'n Asa are hungry enough to eat a folded tarp and burp grommets!"

We began helping ourselves to huge portions of everything. Rosie smiled at us benignly and left us to our supper.

Time for further distraction away from the Barky Hunt.

I said, "Tomorrow I intend to have a little chat with Adam Stanislawski at Macrodur, see if I can do damage control for the *Journal* gaffe."

"Good idea," Simon said. "At least get his reaction to your nomination, so we know where we stand."

I spooned chili into my face and talked with my mouth full. "I've decided to make a surprise visit to Galapharma Tower, too."

Simon stopped short in the act of devouring his fifth shrimp nacho. "Why?" he asked suspiciously.

Oops. Maybe I shouldn't have mentioned that. A Freudian slip? My wise old pal Mimo Bermudez would have called it seeking Big Daddy's approval even as I spit in his eye.

"It's something I've been planning for some time, contingent on our winning the court case. There's an informal request I want to put to their top brass—preferably Lorne Buchanan, the CEO—while they're still reeling from the verdict. If Gala gives me what I want, I'm ready to promise that Rampart will mitigate bloodshed among Gala's management during the consolidation. Maybe try to stave off criminal prosecution, too."

My father's eyes narrowed. "Informal request? What the fuck *kind* of informal request?"

"I'd rather not say." Because it involved sharp practice at

best, and trade-treaty violations at worst. But it did have the potential for uncovering Haluk double-dealing, so I reckoned the risk was worth it.

Simon exploded. "Dammit, Asa! You're not the boss hand of this outfit yet. Tell me what you're up to!"

Well, I'd opened my big yap.

"I'm going to suggest that Gala immediately give me everything they have concerning the allomorph trait eradication and demiclone procedures that they developed for the Haluk. Most specifically, I want the genetic marker that Emily Konigsberg incorporated into the demicloning process. The thing that ID's the fake humans. The marker was Drummond's secret way of keeping tabs on the Haluk scheme. Emily told Eve that the alien leader, the Servant of Servants, knew nothing about the marker. I also want complete details about the clandestine demiclone labs that were in operation prior to the Dagasatt blowup. Karl Nazarian and his crew obtained some intelligence about them from the data-dump of *Chispa Dos,* that starship I stole from the Galapharma agent. But it needs verification from another source before we can present it as hard evidence."

Speechless with consternation, Simon gaped at me. I plowed on.

"I also want to know how many imitation human beings those demiclone labs produced. Someone at Galapharma knows! Its security people were in charge of most of the demi facilities, and its agents tracked every gram of PD32:C2 illegally sold to the aliens."

Simon relaxed in premature relief. "All those incriminating Gala files were sealed by the Secretariat for Xenoaffairs as part of the new Haluk nonaggression pact."

"I intend to unseal them—very carefully—and pass on selected excerpts to an influential friend of mine in the Commonwealth Assembly. Efrem Sontag is Chairman of the Xenoaffairs Oversight Committee. He'd go along with immunity for the Gala execs involved if I asked him to."

"What the fuckin' *hell* do you hope to accomplish?" Simon exclaimed furiously.

"You were wrong when you said I was the only one dubious about the Haluk. Sontag has already initiated a secret probe of demiclone shenanigans, based on intelligence supplied by me right after the Dagasatt affair. He also believes that SXA's cover-up deal with the aliens stank to high heaven, even if it did pave the way for the new trade treaty."

"But . . . Christ on a crutch! Something like this could swamp the consortium if the Haluk find out!"

"Nonsense. The aliens won't like it, but they'll hardly stop buying human products. You're going to have to trust me on this, Pop. *We need this information.* I know Gala was supposed to have surrendered all the incriminating data to Xenoaffairs, but you can bet your left nut that somebody in the Concern kept copies—just in case Gala won the civil case and it needed an ace in the hole sometime in the future. As an edge against other consortium members, maybe. Or even against the Haluk themselves. Alistair Drummond didn't trust our needy blue buddies either."

"Couldn't you hold off until—"

"No. Right now, I'm in a perfect position to exert pressure on Galapharma's top officers, while they're afraid of losing their precious jobs and stakeholdings. If I wait for the consolidation, it could be too late. Gala will wipe the computers clean rather than take a chance that Rampart would discover the data. They could be doing it right now."

"Maybe it's done."

"No—they'd wait until the trial verdict was in."

"You really got a wild blue hair up your ass, don't you, boy?"

"I'm convinced the Haluk are mortally dangerous, yes."

"God almighty!" My father shook his head. "All right. Put your goddamn request to Lorne Buchanan. Nobody else. He's got the most to lose in the consolidation, and he has the power to get what you want if anyone does."

"I promise to use the utmost discretion. I'll get Ef Sontag to promise the same. We won't go public unless we have proof of malicious intent by the Haluk."

Simon pushed his plate of food away, shaking his head, and got to his feet. "You just can't leave things be, can you? Always lookin' to stir up trouble."

"Where the Haluk are concerned, damn right I am. But I'll do it as quietly as possible now—for Rampart's sake. I'm not trying to dissolve the Haluk trade treaty, and I certainly don't intend to force them back into their overcrowded star-cluster. But I do aim to make sure they behave if they move into our neighborhood."

"Arrogant, self-righteous young prick!" Simon growled. "Who elected you Speaker of the Commonwealth Assembly?"

"Nobody," I said. "Frankly, I'd rather be a beach bum on Kedge-Lockaby. But if I decide to give Rampart's chairmanship a pass, I may just turn into the meanest goddamn Reversionist beach bum you and the Assembly and the Hundred Concerns and the Haluk ever met."

"I've lost my appetite," my father said unhappily, heading for the door. "I'm going to bed."

"You can always fire me," I called after him. "By law, I'd revert instantly to Throwaway status. I'd be out of the galactic poker game for keeps and out of your corporate hair."

"Nope," Simon Frost said. "Gonna let my bet on you ride. God help us all."

The door closed behind him.

I decided it was high time for some more of Jack Daniel's best. Maybe even a double.

Later, when it was a reasonable hour on Kedge-Lockaby's Eyebrow Cay, I called Mimo Bermudez on the ranch's subspace com. He'd seen the *Journal* posting and congratulated me on Rampart's legal triumph while being tactful about Simon's notion to promote me beyond my station.

Then we got around to the reason for my call: the Barky Hunt. Mimo had promised to make discreet inquiries about the ancient gunrunner among doddering members of the Spur underworld. My friend's courtly Mexican manners had thus far precluded his asking me for an explanation.

"I found several people who knew Tregarth in the old days," Mimo said, "even a few who had participated in the original wager that supposedly sent him off on his incredible journey. All but one of those that I spoke to branded Tregarth a bare-faced liar with an overly fertile imagination. The exception was a certain *vejarron* named Clifton Castle who once worked as a fence on Tyrins. After Tregarth escaped from the lockup there, he contacted Castle and sold him an extremely rare jewel to finance his flight back to the Orion Arm. It was a exotic fossil cabochon set in platinum—beyond a doubt Haluk in origin. Tregarth claimed it had been a gift from the official of a planet he visited in the Haluk Cluster."

"He might also have got it from one of their Spur colonies."

"That's always a possibility. Clifton Castle had another interesting piece of information. Tregarth made a condition that the fossil not be resold for one month, saying he hoped to buy it back—at a premium, of course—since it was his only souvenir of the great adventure."

"Pawning the thing. Did Barky redeem it?"

"Yes, three weeks later. Castle sent it by registered StelEx to the planet Famagusta in Sector 5. This happened in the year 2201."

"I don't suppose this Castle knows whether Barky is still alive."

"He had no idea. I could send out more feelers, but as you know, my principal sources are in the Perseus Spur, not the inner Orion Arm. You might have better luck consulting our mutual friend, Chief Superintendent Jake Silver. Tregarth might be in the CCID database."

"Maybe I'll talk to Jake. I'm heading for Toronto tomorrow."

My pal's dark eyes peered from thoughtful slits. "You've never told me why you're so anxious to find this geriatric *contrabandista*."

"Mimo, it's better you don't know."

He shook his frowsy head in chagrin. "Helly, Helly, Helly. It's rather obvious, isn't it? You still believe that the Haluk intend to wage war on humanity."

"I think they might—if their population pressure is exceptionally severe. This guy Tregarth might be dead or he might be a total shuck-and-jive artist, the biggest liar since Baron Munchausen. On the other hand, he might just know more about our mysterious blue buddies than any other human being. I want to talk to him."

"And then what?"

I smiled at the SS com screen. "I've got a sabbatical coming, while the Galapharma settlement is sorted out and I decide whether to accept the Rampart chairmanship. I told my father I'd spend the time loafing on K-L—but it might be more fun to take my modified Y770 starship on a grand tour."

"Caracoles!" The semiretired Smuggler King of the Perseus Spur immediately guessed what I had in mind and was appalled. "Please tell me you're joking!"

"Of course I am," I lied.

"I'm relieved to hear it. You realize that a private individual who traveled to the Haluk Cluster would violate both the nonaggression pact and the trade treaty with that race, laying himself open to sanctions from both the Xenoaffairs and Interstellar Commerce Secretariats. Every asset the individual possessed might be seized—and he himself would not only be disenfranchised, but probably also incarcerated without possibility of parole."

"Unless the illegal expedition was accomplished without the individual being caught. And the individual came back with significant intelligence data."

"Why you?" my old friend exclaimed in exasperation.

"Who else?" I retorted. "I've got the inclination and time to spare. I've also got the ship."

My personal blitzboat was named *Makebate*—an old word meaning "troublemaker." She was a Rampart executive perquisite, the only expensive toy I'd allowed myself during the two tedious years of brain-bending legal work associated with the Galapharma trial. I'd managed to take only rare brief jaunts in her to visit my friends on Kedge-Lockaby in the Spur. A chance remark of Mimo's at a luau on Eyebrow Cay three months ago had planted the seed for the Barky Hunt . . . and what might follow if it was successful and the old crook really did have important information about the Haluk Cluster worlds.

Returning to Toronto for the climactic part of the trial, I had arranged for Rampart Fleet Maintenance technicians to modify *Makebate* while I was grounded. Her fuel bunkers had been greatly enlarged and her weaponry significantly beefed up. She now carried state-of-the-art sublight drive dissimulators for stealthy near-planet maneuvering and or-bital concealment. I was having special bodycount gadgetry installed that would make clandestine fly-by census scans of hostile planets feasible, and I also intended to look for war-ships. The Commonwealth seemed content to believe that massive Haluk purchases of astrogational equipment were intended for use in colonial transports; I thought that notion was pure bovine excrement.

Mimo sighed. "Always the cowboy! I had hopes that your stint as Rampart's Chief Legal Officer would have mellowed you."

"Tourism can be amusing and educational," I said. "Wanna come along? I could use some human company. Talking to the ship's computer gets boring after a few days. And there's always the possibility of a good fight."

"And a quick death. Or worse, if you're captured."

I just grinned at him. "I'm going to count blue noses and

look for blue battleboats whether or not the Barky Hunt works out. Come on! It'll be a hoot."

"Unfortunately I have a previous engagement in the tank."

It took me a moment to realize what he was saying. "The—The tank?"

"I'd accompany you to the Haluk Cluster if I could, Helly, if only to keep you out of trouble. After all, I'm a much better shot with a photon cannon! I'm also curious how the Haluk manage to mine transactinides, given their technology lag. But this old body of mine is in need of serious repair. I must go into dystasis in Rampart Central's big hospital on Seriphos, since the doctors at the Big Beach don't have the resources to deal with my case."

I tried not to show my dismay. Mimo was a man in late middle age, but as far as I knew, he was healthy. "So. It's something serious?"

"It is," he said gently. "A flare-up of an old problem. However, the prognosis is good. All that's necessary is a grotesque amount of money to pay for the sixteen-week procedure. *No importa dos cojones.*" His standard disclaimer: It doesn't matter two balls' worth.

Of course money was no problem to Mimo. Decades of smuggling fine liquor, Cuban cigars, premium coffee, and other luxuries past Rampart excise collectors had made him one of the wealthiest private individuals in the Perseus Spur. But I felt a pang of guilt as I recalled the threadbare state of Kedge-Lockaby's modest little hospital. I should have done something about that a long time ago, now that I had the means. K-L had been good to me.

And so had Captain Guillermo Bermudez Obregon.

I said, "You have a nice long soak in the tank, Meem. Cure what ails you. With luck, I'll be there on Seriphos waiting for your rollout. I'll ferry you back to K-L and wait on you hand and foot while you convalesce. I owe you, *amigo.*"

"All you owe me is staying alive." He was no longer meeting my gaze. "For the sake of prudence, I've sent a small package to your office in Rampart Tower via StelEx. You should find it waiting when you arrive tomorrow. Please take good care of what's inside. Do what must be done if . . . circumstances warrant."

I felt a cold breath of irrational dread and pushed it aside, knowing that Mimo was going to be fine. The hospital at Rampart Central on Seriphos had the finest genetic engineering therapy department in Zone 23, and I'd pull strings to make certain that Mimo had Ultra Important Patient status.

The rest of our conversation was little more than gossip about our mutual friends on Eyebrow Cay. Eventually we told each other good-night and signed off.

I left the com center and shuffled through the darkened ranch house toward my bedroom, brooding about mortality and about two very different old men and the influences they'd had on my life.

It had been a busy day. Tomorrow would be even busier in Toronto. If Lorne Buchanan yielded to my pressure, I'd have to touch base with Efrem Sontag and arrange for him to take charge of the sensitive information.

And there was Jake Silver. Maybe he and I could have dinner, perhaps catch the acclaimed new production of *Macbeth* at the Winter Garden Theater, if he hadn't already seen it. Both of us were Shakespeare buffs. The Bard had a keen understanding of the criminal mind, and so did Jake and I.

As it happened, I never got to see the play. The damned criminal minds were already cooking up a different sort of melodrama.

Starring me.

Chapter 3

Chief Superintendent Jacob Silver of the Commonwealth Criminal Investigation Department was a man done wrong by fate, who managed to crawl out of life's manure pile with a rose in his teeth.

He reminded me a bit of myself.

Banished to the outermost Perseus Spur for daring to blow the whistle on a superior who'd taken a big bribe from the Carnelian Concern, the powerful producer of electronic weapons and devices, Jake Silver had been demoted to the tiny Public Safety Force of freesoil Kedge-Lockaby. He'd been stuck in this dead-end office on a minor resort world and Throwaway haven for nearly ten years before I arrived in 2229, newly disenfranchised and determined to pickle my brain in ethanol as a prelude to suicide.

Jake had no difficulty ferreting out the true identity of the derelict who called himself Helmut Icicle when I applied for K-L resident status. During my slow rehabilitation, he occasionally called upon my ICS expertise to outwit visiting corporate connivers—most notably a gang of Native American sharpies from Infinitum, the monster entertainment Concern, who tried to seize control of K-L's casino. A takeover would have deprived the little planet's schools of their principal source of revenue. I showed Jake how to legally spike the redskins' guns, and he and I became cautious friends.

He risked his professional neck to help me during Rampart's fight with Galapharma. So I made a promise—rashly improbable at the time—to do my damnedest to get him posted back to Earth. I was able to come through for Jake when Simon and Eve pressured me to head up the legal case against Gala. Rampart itself didn't have the political clout to bring the Super back to his family in Toronto, but its prestigious venture-credit stakeholder, Macrodur Concern, sure as hell did.

Macrodur is the proverbial 400-kilo gorilla, the largest and most connected of the Big Seven Concerns by reason of its monopoly on computer products. I made Jake Silver's reinstatement—with promotion—at CCID headquarters a condition of my acceptance of the interim CLO gig. Macrodur wanted me as chief architect of the case against Gala just as badly as Rampart did. The gorilla leaned. The fix went in.

The upshot was that Jake Silver returned to a cushy staff job in the capital cop shop. He and I had a celebratory dinner at Truffles, then for two years we mostly went our separate ways.

Using the ranch's secure landline, I called him before breakfast on the morning after the big verdict, announcing myself to his assistant as "Helmut Icicle, confidential informant."

The face that appeared on my vidphone display was leaner than it had been on K-L and more mastifflike. The jowls drooped and the shrewd, watchful eyes peered from deep pouches that were not disfiguring but seemed oddly appropriate to a watchdog lawman. Chief Superintendent Jacob Silver was now fifty-six years old, no longer the sweaty, sartorially challenged mess I'd known on K-L's Big Beach. He wore a black cashmere sweater vest over an expensive pink designer shirt, and his gray hair was carefully styled.

Jake's greeting, however, had all its old familiar charm.

"Mother-o'-pearl!" he groaned. "If it isn't Hell-Butt, the

conquering shyster and tsar of *tsuris*. I smell trouble . . .
Don't tell me! Payoff day is here. You want reciprocity for
engineering my transfer, and I have to put my decrepit cock
on the block for you again and risk losing my pension."

"I need a very small favor," I soothed him. "Nothing to
jeopardize your desk-riding posterior. How are Marie and
the kids and the grandkids?"

His forbidding features relaxed into a rare broad smile.
"They couldn't be better, thanks to you. Nice going, shooting down Galapharma." He chortled wickedly. "On the other
hand, that interview in the *Wall Street Journal* sure made you
look like a horse's patoot. You gonna hook up with Rampart
permanently now?"

"I'm thinking about it. I may postpone the decision indefinitely. Meanwhile, I'm doing some private investigating. I
need to find a guy."

Jake rolled his eyes. "Here it comes . . ."

"Hamilcar Barca Tregarth," I said. "Nicknamed Barky.
Disenfranchised for gunrunning and peddling embargoed
high tech to aliens around 2201. He used to operate in the
Spur but fled to the inner Orion Arm or maybe the Sag
Whorl after escaping custody on Tyrins. He might still be
alive."

"That's it?" Jake seemed disappointed.

"Locate Barky Tregarth for me, Super. I'll be grateful.
Buy you a steak tonight at Carman's. Also treat you to *Macbeth* if you're free. Got two good seats."

" 'By the pricking of my thumbs,' " Jake quoted the Scottish play, " 'something wicked this way comes!' I hope that's
not you, Hell-Butt."

"Absolutely not. I am a paragon of corporate probity. For
the moment, anyhow."

"Okay. I accept your offer to dine. Sorry about the Shakespeare, but Marie and I saw the production last week. Bring
one of your ladies and give her a treat. Micklewhite and

Dorsey are outstanding as Lord and Lady M. The set designers got the holo FX right without screwing up the traditional mise-en-scène."

"Always a good thing."

"You want to hold a minute, I'll check the roster of lowlifes for Tregarth. We might hit an instant jackpot. Why is his name familiar?"

He turned away from the phone to consult his computer.

I considered his suggestion about feminine companionship only momentarily. My sex life had been pretty arid during the trial, due to the long hours of grinding work. When I did take a rare break, it had invariably been a casual fling with one of the politically active sophisticates I'd met through the Reversionist Party. Their partisan intensity had been a welcome distraction from the legal fray.

But now, with the trial over and my imprudent blabbering a hot topic on the capital grapevine, the last thing I needed was the company of a political woman. I'd go to the play alone.

Jake Silver was emitting a ruminative humming sound as he searched for my quarry. Finally: "Last domicile of record for our chum is on Manala, Sector 4. It's one of those asteroidal fueling way stations located at the rim of the Sagittarius Whorl, almost out in Red Gap. Nasty shithole, as I recall, but handy to the trans-ack producers. Eleven years ago one H. B. Tregarth was nabbed and fined a whopper for violating the Y'tata high-tech weaponry trade interdiction. He left Manala and hasn't been arrested since, or compelled to submit a verifying DNA sample for any other reason. He's not in the rolls of the officially deceased, either—which may or may not prove anything. He might have died without a genetic assay. Most Throwaways do. As far as the Commonwealth of Human Worlds is concerned, your Barky doesn't exist."

"Rats. I was afraid this wouldn't be easy."

Jake glowered at me. "You really *really* need to find him?"

"Yes."

"May I ask why?"

All I said was, "Is there any unofficial way you can track him down?"

"There are always ways. They can take time, which I don't have, and cost money, of which I am chronically short. Why don't you hire one of the big tracer outfits? Or—" He broke off. You could almost see the legendary lightbulb clicking on above his head. "Wait a second, now. Tregarth last came to our attention peddling actinic-beam weaponry from a Carnelian subsidiary to the Y'tata. It occurs to me there's something quick and dirty I could try."

"Do it."

"Meet me in the lobby of CCID HQ about 1730 hours. Bring an open-ended blind EFT card. If my idea pans out, maybe you can use the card to buy something besides a night on the town."

He ended the call and I went to breakfast, whistling "Empty Saddles in the Old Corral."

Rosalia served me huevos rancheros and a honey-sweet Chilean watermelon the size of a grapefruit, remarking that my father had already left for Toronto in his private hopper. Not in a good mood.

"Too bad," I remarked. "I hope it wasn't something I said."

I'd already talked to Jane Nelligan at Rampart Tower, a couple of time zones ahead of Arizona, asking her to get a status report on the refit job on *Makebate* and make appointments with Adam Stanislawski and Lorne Buchanan. She called back as I was finishing my second cup of coffee, and I answered on my pocket phone.

"Chairman Stanislawski has a very crowded schedule today," she said briskly. "He can see you for fifteen minutes at noon in his office at Macrodur Tower if that'll suffice. Otherwise he's not available till Monday."

Jane is always brisk, as well as tactful and awesomely efficient. Since I am nothing of the sort, I value her as a pearl beyond price. She is married to the head vet at the Sunderland Racecourse, has twin sons in business school at Commonwealth UT, and copes like a steely eyed drill sergeant with the forty-six gung-ho lawyers who comprise Rampart's Toronto-based legal staff.

I told Jane that a noon touch-and-go at Macrodur was dandy. All I wanted to do was get Adam's reaction to my nomination. Unless I missed my guess, his opinion was going to coincide with my own and save me a lot of aggravation with Simon and Eve.

"Lorne Buchanan's gatekeepers were reluctant to accommodate you," Jane continued. "I took the liberty of taking your father's name in vain since you told me the meeting was urgent. That did the trick. Citizen Buchanan prefers to come to you. He won't be in his office today."

"I can't imagine why."

"I've made the appointment for 1430 hours in our penthouse conference room. Citizen Buchanan will stay as long as need be. His security people insist on sweeping the place for bugs before the meeting. They want to check you out personally, too. I couldn't get them to budge on the stipulation."

I laughed. "Perfectly acceptable. See that Rampart InSec returns the courtesy to El Queso Grande himself and his flunkies. Also, alert Karl Nazarian to expect one psychotronic interrogation subject following Buchanan's meeting with me."

"Himself?" Jane's eyes widened.

"Yep. And I want the results before the end of the afternoon."

"Right . . . The final fuel-bunker and radiation barrier modifications of your starship were completed last week. The survey instrumentation is installed, except for a Carnelian LRIR-1400J scanner that seems to be on permanent back order."

"Tell the mechanics to find one any which way and plug it in immediately. I don't care if they have to steal it off a Carney dock or buy it on the goddamn black market."

"Very well." She turned away from the phone video pickup, then returned holding a StelEx letterpak. "This arrived less than an hour ago, marked 'personal and confidential.' The sender is your friend, Captain Bermudez."

"Would you please open it?"

She did. "A small e-slate requiring your ID for activation. And this."

She held up a platinum neck chain holding two gold wedding rings.

I felt my breath catch. Mimo had been holding the rings for me ever since they were rescued from the stomach of a house-eating sea toad. They had belonged to me and my former wife, Joanna DeVet.

I told Jane, "Please put the rings and the slate in my office safe."

"Right. There have been more messages for you since we spoke earlier, most of them from the media. I gave them the standard referral to our public affairs department. Geraldo Gonzalez also called and said it was very important that you and he talk before you, um, quote, flit off to some godforsaken boonie planet, unquote."

Gerry chaired the Reversionist Nominating Committee, the group empowered to select the single Commonwealth Assembly delegate the party was newly entitled to, following the latest poll of CHW citizens. The committee had been deeply divided on my tentative candidacy, in spite of the fact that I was their principal financial resource and had also brought them the publicity that had finally gained the party its lone seat. However, certain Reverse stalwarts felt I wasn't anti-Big-Business enough to be their standard bearer. Others contended I was too flaky. Both points were valid.

After reading last night's *Journal*, Gerry and his crew were probably scared to death that I'd accept the Rampart chairmanship, mutate instantly into a capitalist swine, and cut off all their lovely money.

"I'll give Gonzalez half an hour. Make the appointment for 1300 in my office. Anything else?"

"Bethany Frost heard you were coming in. She wants to talk to you briefly about your brother, Dan."

"Rats." This I didn't need. "Maybe for a few minutes in my office, if there's time after I finish with Buchanan. But I'm off to meet Jake Silver around 1715. Two for dinner, just me for the show. Cancel the second Shakespeare ticket. Jake begged off."

"I'll take care of it. Is there anything else you need me to arrange before you arrive? A limo and security escort for the restaurant and theater?"

"Nope. I'll wear my Anonyme and take the Path just like an ordinary citizen. Media stalkers will never notice me in the capital crush. I'm in disguise." I held the phone at arm's length so she could check me out.

I'd seen no reason to conform to Rampart Concern's dress code during my stint as Chief Legal Officer, since I rarely left the tower. My customary work attire of ratty jeans, scuffed boots, and tired western-wear shirts had scandalized Jane Nelligan sadly, although she never said a disapproving word. Today, however, I'd donned a featherweight charcoal worsted business suit with a matching silk turtleneck, a muted aquamarine scarf, and a silver neck brooch inset with a small nugget of turquoise. The only vestige of maverickhood I'd allowed myself were a pair of well-polished, low-heel, pointy-toed, Tony Lama cowboy boots in black mokcrok, peeking out from beneath my elegantly creased trousers.

"Unbelievable," Jane murmured. "You'll certainly impress Stanislawski and Buchanan. If they recognize you at all."

"Oh, they will," I said dryly. "I can guarantee that."

I said goodbye and finished my coffee. Then I exited the

ranch house through the kitchen, kissing Rosalia the cook on her cheek as I passed by.

It was a beautiful Arizona morning, clear and cool, with the sun shining over Buzzard Roost Mesa and warblers singing their hearts out among the ponderosa pines. I heard the faint whinny of a horse from over by the stock barns. Maybe it was Billy, saying *hasta la vista*.

Empty saddles in the old corral.

Carrying a briefcase full of executive paraphernalia, I trudged down the manicured gravel path to the hopper pad, where my Garrison-Laguna hoppercraft waited. No pilot. I almost always do my own driving. It's a control thing.

Control.

I'd fallen asleep last night brooding about it, and when I woke my mind was firmly made up. It wasn't going to take me months to decide on my future—assuming I had any when my Haluk excursion was over. I knew for certain that I'd never again relinquish control of my life to any person or any institution. Not to Rampart Amalgamated Concern. Not to the Reversionist Party.

The head seat at Rampart's boardroom table had never been a viable career choice for me. It was true that I'd be in a powerful position to advance Reversionist ideals if I became Rampart's chairman. Setting the agenda and having a tie-breaking vote on the board could significantly affect company policy. But the personal independence that had always been so important to me would be lost if I took Simon's place. I'd be fenced in by constant decision-making, forced to weigh every action and utterance because it could influence the lives and fortunes of billions of people, poisoned by creeping expediency, morphing inevitably into the kind of corporate drone I professed to despise.

I couldn't do it. My skills were adversarial, not executive. I'd been a competent cop, a cunning legal strategist, and a damned fine vigilante. But I was no organization man. No way, no how.

Serious politics wasn't an option, either. It was one thing to play grandstanding left-wing firebrand as I'd done two years earlier, trumpeting radical ideas without taking responsibility for their implementation, happily twisting establishment tails while the tabloid media egged me on: Asahel Frost—another rich man with a big mouth and a bee in his bonnet, convinced he has the answers to the galaxy's ills!

I still thought my answers were good ones. However, serving as the sole Assembly Delegate of a fledgling splinter party was simply not a practical course of action. Why, I'd have to learn tact and diplomacy. Legislative horsetrading. The art of graceful compromise.

Me?

Who was I kidding? Even the best and brightest Liberal Party lawmakers, such as my friend Sontag, endured a perpetual uphill battle in an Assembly dominated by Conservative creatures of the Hundred Concerns. An amateur like me didn't have a prayer.

There was a more appropriate way for me to advance the Reversionist cause. I intended to discuss it with Gerry Gonzalez today.

Whistling "Happy Trails to You," I climbed into my flying machine, entered the destination in the navigator, and let myself be whisked off to Toronto.

You pronounce it "Trawna" unless you're a hopeless clodhopper or belong to an alien race, in which case you or your mechanical translator doggedly voice every vowel and consonent. While Torontonians snicker.

The city was born as a native "place of meetings" where two rivers flowing into Lake Ontario flanked a convenient marshy plain. Scattered tribes came there to swap furs and copper and shell beads. It became a small French trading post in 1720, and later it was briefly the capital of British Canada. Waves of immigration in the nineteenth and twentieth centuries brought steady economic growth and a uniquely cosmopolitan character that made Toronto a popular choice for the United Nations' permanent headquarters, then for the capital of the Commonwealth of Human Worlds as the commercialization of the stars began.

By the year 2236 the conurbation sprawled across 20,000 square kilometers above the northern shore of the lake. Its population was about seventeen million—most of them human. Viewed at night from space, Toronto proclaims itself with a triumphant blaze of light, beyond any doubt the largest and most prosperous city on the planet Earth.

The original mosquito-plagued trading ground between the Humber and Don Rivers remains the city center, augmented now by scores of artificial islands out in the lake. A semipermeable force-umbrella 40 kilometers in diameter fends off inconvenient weather phenomena. Toronto's heart bristles with hundreds of multihued crystal towers crammed with offices and apartments, interconnected by skyways and the computerized highroad network. Beneath the surface streets lie rapid-transit and service subways, along with the unique warren of underground pedestrian walks known as the Path.

Many of the modern buildings stand astride venerable Canadian structures that have been carefully preserved. Churches, grand hotels, theaters, and picturesque old shopping precincts and restaurants are hedged by clear piers and buttresses that support the soaring towers.

Sometimes the new hovers pleasingly over the old. The massive Commonwealth Assembly House rises on sturdy glassy stilts above the old Ontario Parliament buildings; historic BCE Place is comfortably embraced by Omnivore Concern's fanciful obelisk; Macrodur Tower benevolently engulfs St. James Cathedral. But in other cases the overall effect is more ominous. Carnelian's ugly needle of beef-bouillon-colored silica glass, entangled in a dozen skyways, overwhelms the stately old City Hall, while the 400-story ithyphallic monstrosity that houses Galapharma seems on the point of crushing the Queen's Quay Terminal.

Rampart Tower, only thirty-five years old and innocent of historic underpinnings, is a relatively modest blue-and-white skyscraper across the street from Grange Park. It is neither distinguished nor ugly, a mere hundred stories high, served by three vehicle skyways and having a hopper pad for aerial access. Before Rampart attained Concern status, it only occupied the top fifteen floors, leasing out the rest. The expanded firm now filled the entire building. God knew what would happen after the consolidation.

The conference room where I would meet Lorne Buchanan today was a circular chamber at Rampart Tower's summit. My offices and the rest of the Legal Department occupied the ninety-sixth floor. The place I called home while I resided in the capital was a small clutch of rooms on the lake side of the seventy-third floor, identical to the suites housing transient junior executives, except for a hologram mounted over the fake fireplace that depicted a yellow submarine named *Pernio II,* chugging wistfully along the surface of a sapphire alien lagoon.

I hated my Rampart Tower apartment. But I'd resisted Simon's urgings that I get myself a more suitable dwelling in The Beaches or one of the other upscale parts of town. No use bothering, I told him. I wasn't planning to stay.

He'd never believed me.

The sky was leaden and a combination of cold rain and sleet was falling when my aircraft arrived at the southern outskirts of Toronto Conurbation ATZ. I gave Traffic Control my destination, Macrodur Tower's upper landing shelf, and was promptly shunted into a holding formation over the dull green lake while computers sequenced my hopper—and about four dozen others—to touch down in the identical place.

It was already quarter to twelve. I'd been delayed by a

traffic-vector glitch in Chicago airspace. I got on the phone
to warn Stanislawski's secretary that I might not be able to
make the appointment unless I jumped the line.

"I'll arrange priority routing," she told me. "You'll be
landing in a restricted area. Please wait in your aircraft until
a transport capsule arrives."

Beneath the force-field, Toronto's central district was sheltered from the icy rain. But occasionally, vagaries of cold
air-flow and high humidity conspired to produce weird artificial clouds under the protective roof. It was happening
today. Although it was high noon, the fielded part of the city
was sunk in heavy twilight. Swags of mist hung spookily
around the illuminated towers and hid the tips of the loftier
ones.

The engineers at Macrodur's skyport dealt efficiently with
the nuisance, clearing the air with infrared beacons. My
hopper settled onto a sequestered pad, alphanumerics and
transponder ID discreetly masked by security electronics
from the moment I exited controlled airspace. Not a living
soul was in sight, in spite of the fact that scores of aircraft
were taking off and landing.

A VIP transport capsule with one-way windows came
gliding out to meet me and extruded a boarding tunnel that
docked with the door of my hopper. A robot voice requested
an iris scan to confirm my identity. I showed it my eyeball,
then climbed in as instructed.

The skyport, like the rest of the building's gold and white
exterior, was exquisitely designed. But once inside the tower
walls, the visitor was conveyed through corridors and antigrav transit tubes that were uniformly mushroom-colored,
blank, and claustrophobic, lacking any directional signs. All
I saw as I sped toward Stanislawski's offices were anonymous carts and capsules traveling on unfathomable errands.
The doors leading off the access platforms were unmarked,
giving no hint of what lay beyond them.

I had visited Macrodur Tower—but not the chairman's

lair—numbers of times over the past couple of years. Worrywart financial mavens concerned about Macrodur's investment in Rampart periodically commanded me to explain my more bizarre tactics during the Galapharma trial. Sometimes Adam Stanislawski attended the interrogations; more often he didn't. But he had always expressed complete confidence in me, and on one occasion had gone out of his way to reaffirm his personal decision to grant Rampart the venture credit it had so desperately needed. His action had paved the way for Rampart's upgrade to Concern status and finally forced the hand of Galapharma's lunatic CEO, Alistair Drummond, contributing to his downfall.

The Macrodur chairman's access platform was as featureless as all the others. There were no obvious security features guarding the great man, who admitted me to his private office himself. Three walls of the large room were covered with alternating strips of dark wood paneling and buff grasscloth. The fourth wall, behind a vast Victorian partners desk, was an enormous window. Heavy drapes of dark green monk's cloth framed the eerie scene outside. The pictures on the walls were nonholographic, romantic terrestrial landscapes with the exception of a woman's portrait in oils above the green marble fireplace. No modern data-processing or communication equipment was in evidence, but I suspected that most of the antique cabinets, presses, and escritoires furnishing the room had been gutted and stuffed with cyberware.

"Filthy day," said Adam Stanislawski. "Let's sit by the fire and have some coffee."

He was in his mid-sixties, of stocky build, and had abundant white hair and a grandfatherly mustache, in defiance of alpha male corporate chic. His hyacinth-blue eyes were small, alive with intelligence, humor, and fuck-not-with-me authority.

"Thank you for seeing me, sir," I said, taking a designated

chair. Adam is one of the few persons I know who naturally rates an honorific.

"My pleasure, Helly. I believe you take your coffee black these days." He handed me a plain stoneware cup of steaming brew.

For the sake of politeness I took a sip. "I won't waste your time with preliminaries. You're aware that my father has proposed me to succeed him as Rampart's chairman. I'd like to know what you think of the idea."

Adam Stanislawski snapped the ball back to me without hesitation. "It sucks. Like the Great Sagittarian Mother of All Black Holes."

I burst out laughing. "Would you care to elaborate?"

"The chairman of an Amalgamated Concern is responsible for the long-term direction of the firm. He or she must have a coherent vision of the firm's future. But having a vision isn't enough. A successful chairman needs the force of character to make that vision a reality."

Zing! A perfect gut-shot. I started to speak, but he held up a hand and forged on.

"You'd like to steer Rampart in a completely new direction, beginning immediately. That won't work. I'm not saying your dream of Insap small-stakeholdership is foolish or impossible. Only that it's premature and currently inappropriate. Marrying Rampart and Galapharma is going to be godawfully difficult. The new Concern will not merely be the sum of the parts of the previous two. The transition requires a generalissimo who can identify and encourage those executives who'll be the most effective leaders for the future. He'll have to scrutinize every major project and decide whether it should be retained, modified, or discarded. Rampart's new chairman will have to be a hard-nosed evaluator. Even a hatchetman. This is not a job for"—he smiled good-humoredly—"a spontaneous paladin."

"Or a rogue cowboy," I said, drinking more coffee.

"You're both of those things, Helly Frost. Someday in the far distant future you might make a good Rampart Chairman of the Board. But not now."

"Not ever," I said.

"Have you ever thought of becoming Rampart's syndic? I should think that job would suit your talents rather well."

The Corporate Syndic was a glorified lobbyist, the principal liaison between a Concern or Starcorp and the Commonwealth Assembly. At present, my cousin Zared Frost held the position, in addition to that of Chief Operating Officer. The latter job took most of his attention, and also required his residency on the planet Seriphos in the Perseus Spur. He was a competent syndic, but an unspectacular one.

"The idea's interesting," I told Stanislawski. "The position certainly has more appeal to me than the chairmanship. But perhaps Simon would be a better choice, given his long years of experience."

The Macrodur chairman shook his head. "Your father's day is done. When Rampart consolidates with Galapharma, your corporate syndic will have to be a vigorous person, able to stand up to the pressures of capital politics. Think about it seriously, Helly."

I smiled noncommittally. "I will. But right now I'd like to know who you think would make the best chairman for Rampart."

Without hesitation Adam Stanislawski said, "Gunter Eckert, your Chief Financial Officer. He's a founding stakeholder and one of the best intellects on the Rampart team. I know he doesn't want the job. But he'll take it and do it well. I'd like our director, John Ellington, to be vice chairman, a close adviser to Gunter without additional voting authority. The two of them, working with your older sister, will keep the reorganized Concern on track. If you like, I'll pass on my considered opinion to Simon and Eve."

The "opinion" of the 400-kilo gorilla.

"I'd appreciate it if you would, sir."

Adam Stanislawski rose from his chair. Taking the cue, I did, too, figuring that our short meeting was over. I felt relieved and vindicated. Better get one thing straight, however.

"I don't plan to give up my Rampart directorship," I said. "Or my notion to apply Reversionist principles to the Concern's relations with nonstargoing Insaps. Even if I don't become Corporate Syndic, I intend to exert continuous pressure on the other directors. Rampart is going to initiate experimental programs on suitable worlds where fuller Insap economic participation is most feasible."

"Good! I'll be watching with interest." He shot me an oblique look. We hadn't started for the door yet. "And I'll keep an eye on your other activities, too."

"My financial support of the Reversionist party will continue, but I'm no longer interested in becoming an Assembly Delegate."

"That's not the kind of activity I was referring to."

Uh-oh . . .

Adam Stanislawski went to the window. The view was stupendous, a forest of jewel-bright spires glittering with countless points of light, the arching high roads and their streaming traffic, controlled swarms of aircraft—the whole wrapped in glowing bands of mist.

"I have the reputation of being a straight-arrow," the Macrodur chairman said. "Galapharma's vicious raid on Rampart bugged the hell out of me. So when your sister Eve proposed her venture-credit arrangement, I was receptive. Helping a feisty little outfit poke a sharp stick in Alistair Drummond's greedy eye sounded like a great idea. But I'm a practical businessman, too. Macrodur never would have taken a stake in Rampart unless I'd been convinced that the investment was a good one. The deciding factor was the potentially huge Haluk market for your genen vector, PD32:C2."

"I realize that."

"I've heard that you have a private vendetta against the

Haluk. That you're looking for a way to discredit them and abrogate the new treaties. Is it true?"

"I believe that the Haluk can't be trusted, and that our treaties with them are severely flawed—especially since there's no provision for close human inspection of their planets. The Haluk almost certainly have a severe overpopulation problem in their star-cluster that's being made worse by eradication of their allomorphism. The severity of the problem deserves investigation."

"Ah." A restrained nod.

"The only recourse the aliens have is to move into the Milky Way," I went on. "To do that without destroying their economy, they need our advanced starship technology, as well as human expertise in other scientific areas. If the Haluk were content to migrate to our galaxy in a peaceful and civilized manner, there'd be no problem. My personal experience with them suggests they'd prefer a more drastic solution to their predicament."

"But you have no concrete proof of hostile intent."

"I have presumptive evidence. It's kept under conditions of the most stringent security by Assembly Delegate Efrem Sontag, an old friend of mine from Harvard Law School. I hope to obtain more proof, working very discreetly as a private citizen. I have a certain talent for clandestine operations. Since no one else seems interested in analyzing Haluk ways and means, I'm taking on the job by default."

"I see. Let me be frank, then. Macrodur and its affiliates will never do anything to impede your investigations—provided you keep me personally informed of verifiable dangers to the Commonwealth."

Well, who'da thunk it!

"You surprise me," I said evenly.

"If you knew me better, Helly, perhaps you wouldn't be surprised. But don't assume that other Concerns share my point of view. If you are seen to *openly* endanger the new trade treaty, you risk lethal retaliation. Most specifically, from agents of Carnelian and Sheltok, the Concerns that have the most to lose."

"I understand."

"I wonder if you do, entirely." Stanislawski was staring out the window with his hands clasped behind his back. "The ultraheavy transactinide elements vital to antimatter fuels and other high-energy applications are devilishly difficult to obtain. For the most part, they're found on R-class Sagittarian worlds—appalling planets in recurrent-nova systems where humans can't survive, even in full armor. Mining these elements robotically from orbit is becoming increasingly expensive, as the more accessible lodes are worked out. And now, suddenly, a new source of these crucial energy products has unexpectedly opened up. By some astrophysical fluke, the Haluk Cluster is also rich in the ultraheavies, perhaps because it's a tiny captive galaxy rather than a true satellite of the Milky Way. So, in a certain sense, the Haluk have us over a barrel."

"A nice metaphor," I remarked cynically, "that most people take care not to examine too closely."

"I won't belabor the point." Stanislawski took me gently by the elbow and steered me toward the door. "The Haluk trade treaty with humanity is mutually beneficial. Antimatter energy is vital to the continuing growth of interstellar commerce. Remember that."

"I'm not a loose cannon, Adam," I said softly. "Just an ex-cop who can't resist analyzing evidence when it's shoved into my face."

"I appreciate that. Which is why I won't stop you from gathering more of that evidence." His blue eyes twinkled benignly. "You do realize that if I wanted to stop you, I would. Decisively."

"Oh, yeah."

He opened the door for me. A transport capsule waited. "You know, Helly, thus far in our exploitation of the stars, we've been very lucky. We've never come up against an alien race with the inclination *and* the capability to successfully wage war on us. That good luck has made us complacent. Complacency is bad policy—for a business, and for a government." He shook my hand. "It was good to talk to you . . . Let me know what Barky Tregarth has to say, if you find him."

He stepped back and the featureless door slid shut, leaving me alone on the platform with my wild surmise.

Geraldo Gonzalez met with me in my office at Rampart Tower and went away doubly relieved when I told him I would continue my lavish funding of the Reversionist party and promotion of its ideals, while not demanding the Assembly seat in return. I wasn't surprised when he admitted that the Nominating Committee preferred him for the new post.

I strongly advised Gerry against squandering our lone vote in futile causes. He said I was a fine one to talk. We parted amiably, after agreeing that I deserved a long holiday, untroubled by political hassles.

When he was gone I opened my office's wall safe and took out the slim StelEx package from Mimo Bermudez that I had not yet had time to examine. I tipped out the encrypted slate and the two plain gold wedding bands on their chain. The larger ring fit exactly over the small one. The fact that I'd kept them had convinced both my big sister, Eve, and Matilde Gregoire, a woman I'd once asked to live with me, that I was still in love with my former wife.

I'd denied it. But it was I who had divorced Joanna DeVet following my frame-up and criminal conviction, even though she had been willing to share my exile in the Perseus Spur. Crushing humiliation and despair made it impossible for me to accept her sacrifice.

Joanna had never remarried. She was still a professor of political science, teaching at the central campus of Commonwealth University only a few blocks north of Rampart Tower. It might as well have been 14,000 light-years.

Eve, wed only to her job but a soppy sentimentalist all the same, had urged me again and again to call Joanna. But I could not bring myself to do it, any more than I could analyze the reason why.

Setting the rings aside, I opened Mimo's slate. The letter on the small screen was what I half expected. My friend had sent me a copy of his last will and testament. Since I was due to go to the meeting with Lorne Buchanan in just a few minutes, I only scanned the document briefly. The principal legatees were the schools and hospital of Kedge-Lockaby's Big Beach continent, which would receive his substantial fortune in semi-ill-gotten gains.

But Mimo had left his beautiful bungalow on Eyebrow Cay to me, along with the rest of the island.

Lorne Buchanan and I, our bodies certified to harbor no nano-eavesdropping devices, met alone in the equally bug-free premises of the spacious Rampart conference room. We quickly came to an agreement that was mutually gratifying.

He was a young man, only in his mid-forties. His build was athletic, his brow clear and wide, his jaw forthright and spade-shaped, and his manner confident. Only the smallest whiff of fear lurking in his deeply shadowed eyes acknowledged the fatal quagmire that now threatened to pull him under. He had been Gala's Chief Operating Officer before becoming CEO upon the death of Alistair Drummond. He was a doer, not a schemer, whose Concern responsibilities had principally involved overseeing commodity production on the thousands of Gala worlds in the Orion Arm.

Lorne Buchanan swore to me—offering to confirm the fact by submitting to the truth machines—that he had had no direct involvement either in Gala's illegal Haluk adventure or in the dirty tricks of the Rampart takeover conspiracy. He claimed to have advised Drummond against a Haluk alliance from the time the scheme was first broached. Buchanan stopped short of calling his former boss a stone nutcase, but the inference was there. Other members of the Galapharma board, he said, were furious and frightened at the mess Drummond had gotten them into. After Drummond's violent demise, the board had elected Buchanan in a vain hope of salvaging the situation.

When I dangled my deal, Lorne Buchanan swallowed it hook, line, and sinker. He readily agreed to affirm the agreement by undergoing psychotronic interrogation by my trusted associate, Karl Nazarian, before leaving Rampart Tower.

I wanted truthful answers from him to the following questions:

1. Are you a Haluk demiclone? Can you identify any demiclones now working in Galapharma AC?
2. Are you willing to obtain and hand over to Delegate Efrem Sontag all information pertaining to the allomorph trait eradication and demiclone procedures developed by Galapharma for the Haluk, including details and locations of all clandestine demiclone labs that were or are now in operation, plus the total number of human-Haluk demiclones produced there?
3. Are you willing to obtain and hand over to Delegate Sontag the secret genetic marker identifying a Haluk-human demiclone?
4. Are you willing to obtain and hand over to Delegate Sontag all information available on the supervision of Haluk demiclone labs by Galapharma Security personnel?
5. Are you willing to ensure that Delegate Sontag alone, and no other person, government agency, corporation, or media data retrieval system gains access to this information—preferably by destroying all traces of it personally?

Lorne Buchanan declared emphatically that he was not a Haluk ringer, nor did he know anyone else who was. As I had suspected, the "sealed" data concerning the Haluk still resided in Galapharma's computers under heavy encryption. He was certain he could obtain everything I requested, send it to Sontag, and obliterate all traces of it from the Gala database.

In return I agreed to give him a document carrying my personal iridographic seal, stating that Rampart would not cooperate in any criminal prosecution against him or designated close associates. Furthermore, we would hire him as Assistant Chief Operating Officer in the consolidated Concern, and continue his employment for a minimum period of ten years or until he chose to vacate the position.

Jane Nelligan brought the document to the conference room. Buchanan and I eyeballed it. The Gala CEO zapped a copy to his personal attorney and I sent others to the offices of Simon, Eve, and Efrem Sontag. Then I handed Jane the questions for Karl Nazarian and she courteously escorted the visitor away to the torture chamber.

Lorne Buchanan would fulfill his promises scrupulously. Sadly, he would not live long enough enjoy the perks of the trade-off. There was another question I should have added to that list of his:

6. To the best of your knowledge, is Alistair Drummond dead?

"Helly! Felicitations on winning the Galapharma verdict!"

"Thanks, Ef."

"I presume you want me to forego wisecracks about your loony-tune interview in the *Wall Street Journal*."

"I spoke from my heart of hearts," I retorted, "and shot from the hip. As the king said, *Honi soit qui merde y pense*."

"That's *mal y pense*."

"It's all shit to me, pal . . . For your information, I have declined the Rampart chairmanship. Neither will I seek a seat in the Assembly. Gerry Gonzalez will hoist high the banner of Reversionism among you and your colleagues. Be kind to him."

I had reached my friend Sontag in his hopper. He was flying home alone to his home on Lake Simcoe following the early Friday adjournment of the Assembly. After he had secured our call with Phase XII encryption, I filled him in on details of the deal I had struck with Lorne Buchanan.

Ef was cautiously enthusiastic. "If Buchanan comes through with everything he promised, we'll end up with enough solid data to finally make a presentation to my committee. Then the matter can be opened to debate on the Assembly floor. Perhaps I can even force a special review of the no-inspection clause of the nonaggression pact. The existence of sizable human-Haluk demiclone factories alone is prima facie evidence of some sort of questionable intent by the aliens. During the treaty talks, the Haluk Servant of Servants maintained that only a handful of human transforms had been created. As I recall, his explanation was ingenious but not very plausible from a human point of view.

"The fakes were supposedly going to serve as some sort of goodwill envoys on Haluk planets in their star-cluster, where we humans are viewed as big bad boogymen. The Haluk fed that ridiculous story to Galapharma to get the demiclone project going in the first place. I'm sure Alistair Drummond didn't believe a word of it. But it was expedient for him to accept it, just as it was expedient for Concern-connected bureaucrats in Xenoaffairs and Interstellar Commerce to do the same when they drew up the treaties."

We briefly discussed legal aspects of Buchanan's material—mostly ways our political enemies might attempt to discredit it. Then I told Ef my plan for pumping Barky Tregarth about life in the Haluk Cluster—provided I could locate the old Throwaway. I said nothing about going extragalactic myself, but Mama Sontag didn't raise any dummies.

"I like the idea of checking out Haluk demographics

through an informant," he said. "Even if he's disenfranchised, his deposition *sub duritia* would be admissible if it
pertains to the security of the Commonwealth. Ask Tregarth
about the Haluk military-industrial capability. Ask him for
details of their production of transactinides. But don't even
think about buzzing off to the Haluk Cluster yourself to verify Barky's story."

I started to deny I had any such notion, but he cut me off.

"Don't try to bullshit me, Helly. A snoop job like that
would violate the nonaggression pact. I wouldn't be able to
use any evidence you gathered."

"Not in a formal Assembly inquiry, perhaps. But it could
still be useful poop for you to leak to the media, sway public opinion, pressure the other Delegates—"

"I can't be seen to condone your breaking Commonwealth
law."

"Not even the asinine ones? I can tell the difference, you
know. I'm a Juris Doctor from Harvard, just like you."

He shook his head wearily. I was testing his patience with
my lame humor. "And *I'm* a politician with a certain reputation for probity, working in a government almost entirely
under the control of galactic Big Business. The public re-
spects my integrity, and so do the media. My square-shooter
image is the source of my power and I can't do anything to
endanger it. Why do you think I've been so cautious about
waiting for the appropriate time to present the evidence
you've already gathered? Two years ago you weren't a credible source. Today, by some miracle, you very nearly are . . .
unless you fuck yourself, pulling some idiotic stunt."

Ouch. "Can we at least agree that you'll hold off asking
your big question on the Assembly floor until I question
Barky Tregarth?"

"You don't know how long it will take to find him. And
what if the man's a washout?"

I just had to give it one last try. "Look. A quick survey of
selected Haluk Cluster worlds would take me ten weeks

maximum. I've got the ship and the equipment, and I can do the job. Ten weeks, Ef! I could release the information to the media anonymously. Sure, the Haluk and the consortium will suspect that I'm the secret source—but so what? They won't be able to prove anything."

"Helly, the Assembly is on the verge of approving the sale of fifty more Rampart Mandate T-2 worlds to the Haluk. It'll happen in June, just before summer recess. Less than eight weeks from now."

I voiced a heart-felt "Fuck!" No one at Rampart Tower had said a word to me about this.

"It gets worse. A new bill that would let the aliens buy three hundred *more* Rampart worlds will come out of committee and be put to a vote shortly after the new session begins in late August. All of the Conservatives and many of the incoming new Liberals will vote for it. There's been a tremendous push from Sheltok and Bodascon and the other consortium members to give these additional Haluk colonies the green light. The only chance I have of preventing the bill's passage is by preventing its introduction: killing it in committee. To do that we've got to ignite a firestorm of public opinion on the PlaNet that even the most venal Delegates can't ignore."

"Can you kill the fifty-planet giveaway?"

"Impossible. It would be terrible strategy to open the Haluk inquiry just before the summer recess. We have to concentrate all our efforts on scuppering the second bill. Ideally, the evidence should be placed before my Xeno Oversight Committee when the Assembly reconvenes. And you should be prepared to testify personally. We won't use psychotronic interrogation on witnesses before the committee—but it may be necessary when the inquiry moves to the Assembly floor."

"I understand."

Efrem Sontag and I stared at each other in silence. We were the same age but he looked ten years older. The image on my office communicator showed a slightly built unhandsome man with lank dark hair, oversized ears, and the scorching eyes of an indomitable fighter. In spite of his membership in the principal minority party, he was one of the most powerful Assembly Delegates, a true untouchable, the scourge of fellow legislators who dwelt cozily in the pockets of the Hundred Concerns.

The inquiry he was about to orchestrate would touch off one of the biggest political rows in the history of the Commonwealth. While the Concerns screamed bloody murder at the prospect of Haluk trade disruption, the tabloid media would joyfully fan the flames of controversy. We hoped that the Commonwealth citizenry would be sufficiently alarmed at the notion of Haluk doppelgänger spies that they would pressure their Delegates interactively over the PlaNet, overriding the influence of the Concerns and forcing a review of the dubious treaties.

And what would the Haluk do then, poor things? Cave in, confess all, permit full inspection of their worlds, and promise to behave in the future if we let them continue to colonize the Milky Way?

Maybe. If the heat was turned high enough.

I said, "It's in your hands now, Ef. I have a few reliable people who've worked with me that I'd like you to consider taking on board. People with reputations above reproach like Karl Nazarian, and Beatrice Mangan of the ICS Forensic Division."

"I'd welcome their help."

"I'll do my best to get Barky Tregarth's deposition for you quickly. Meanwhile, take very good care of yourself, old buddy."

Sontag uttered a brief laugh that had no humor in it. "The Concerns wouldn't dare send their thugs after me."

"I'm not worried about the Concerns. The problem could be Haluk demiclones operating right here in Toronto. Fake humans."

He gazed at me for a moment in shocked silence. "Are you serious?"

"Dead serious. I've met a few who were masquerading as Galapharma Security personnel. They were extremely convincing. The Haluk are at least as intelligent as we are. And they have a really steep learning curve."

His expression remained neutral, but I knew he was finding it hard to believe that a disguised alien entity could successfully pose as a human being over a significant period of time.

I said, "One of the most important pieces of data we're supposed to obtain from Lorne Buchanan is the gene market that identifies demiclones. Pass that information on to Bea Mangan as soon as possible. Then get her to secretly test all of your close associates for creeping Halukitis." I hesitated, hating to say what had to come next. "And test Liliane, too."

Sontag exclaimed, "Are you out of your mind, Helly?"

"All you need for a proper DNA assay is a snotty Kleenex or a hair with a live follicle. Neither your wife nor your staff people have to know they're being checked out. Dammit, Ef, the demiclone moles are out there! I'm sure of it. The Haluk ringers who penetrated Gala Security are probably long gone, but there have to be others holed up for the long haul."

"I'll get on it," he said grimly. "God—you really know how to spoil a man's day."

"Think how useful it would be to our case," I said, "if you found Haluk spies in sensitive government positions."

"Useful!" He made a face.

"I'll talk to you again as soon as I know anything useful."

"Have a safe Barky Hunt," he said.

"You keep safe, too, Ef. No joke."

"I know." He ended the call.

I sat quietly at my desk for some time after that, alone in my familiar messy office with suitcoat, vest, and neck scarf discarded. Running over the events of the afternoon. Feeling both drained and exhilarated at what I'd accomplished in a few brief hours.

It was almost as good as lying on a tropical beach on far Kedge-Lockaby.

My desk clock said 16:42. In less than an hour I'd be meeting Jake Silver. Should I put off my younger sister, Beth, or do my family duty?

Maybe she hadn't shown up.

I touched the intercom. "Jane, did Lorne Buchanan finish his psychotronic session with Karl Nazarian?"

"It went very well. All responses were positive and there was very little discomfort because of the cooperative mind-set of the subject. Citizen Buchanan left the tower about ten minutes ago with his entourage. He asked me to tell you that the requisite data will be transferred to Delegate Sontag's office immediately under conditions of strictest security."

"Outstanding. Um . . . do I have anyone waiting in reception?"

"Your sister Bethany has been here for over two hours," Jane said, with a hint of reproach. "I informed her that a meeting today might not be possible, but you would do your best to see her."

Rats.

"Send her in, please."

Rising from the desk, I opened the door to my seldom-used clothes closet to expose the full-length mirror and began reknotting my scarf.

Beth wafted in. "Good afternoon, Asa." Her voice was almost inaudible, a bad sign. The quieter she spoke, the more pissed off she was likely to be.

"Please sit down," I said. "Forgive me spiffying myself up. I have to rush out of here in a few minutes for an urgent appointment."

"It's quite all right." She refused my offer of coffee and sat silently for several minutes while I finished dressing.

Bethany Frost was wearing a smart walking suit of teal silk tweed with shimmering greenish highlights. Dark blue ankleboots, a matching handbag, and a choker of heavy gold links inset with a myriad of tiny diamonds completed the ensemble. As always, in spite of her high-fashion clothes, she managed to look ephemeral, like some delicate butterfly that the slightest breath of wind would crumple. Beth is not as petite as Eve, but like her, has the fine bone structure and fair coloring of our late mother, Katje Vanderpost.

I call Beth my little sister because she was born seven years after Eve and has always looked more youthful than her years. She is actually two years older than I. Her intellect is sharp as a scalpel, with a mathematical bent, but her emotional temperament is unstable. For nearly ten years she served Rampart as its Assistant Chief Financial Officer under Gunter Eckert, until our brother Daniel's fall from grace drove her to a nervous breakdown and she retired from the business world. She and her husband, a cybernetic researcher named Carter Berg, had two teenage children.

Beth and I were never particularly affectionate toward one another. When we were small children, she and I were rivals for the quasimaternal attentions of Big Sister Eve, who for some reason enjoyed the company of a brash baby buckaroo rather than Beth's tiresome coy brilliance. Beth retaliated by bestowing her sibling loyalty on Daniel, two years Eve's senior. In adulthood the brother and sister remained very close.

When I refused to join Rampart after finishing law school, Beth concluded that I was a traitor to the family. She had always believed me guilty of the trumped-up charges that destroyed my career in the Interstellar Commerce Secretariat. During Galapharma's rough wooing of Rampart, she had sided with those who favored a sellout.

Beth remained stubbornly convinced of Dan's innocence, in spite of all Eve and I had done to prove that our brother

was a secret collaborator in Alistair Drummond's conspiracy
and directly responsible for our mother's death.

I went back to my desk and we stared at each other without speaking. It was an old ploy of Beth's to put one on the
defensive. Her huge blue eyes were full of unshed tears, but
with the tyranny of the meek, she waited me out until I was
forced to break the silence.

"What can I do for you, sis?"

She whispered, "Let Dan go."

"That's not possible."

"It's killing him, Asa—penned up like a dog in that
damned wilderness lodge up in the Kenora! Snow on the
ground six months of the year, nothing but moose and mos-
quitoes and loons the rest of the time. And that filthy medication the InSec people use to keep him docile . . . Dan
can't hurt anyone. Let him go home to Norma and Jamie."

"Norma sees Dan every weekend. Jamie could visit his
father if he chose to." But he didn't. My nephew, a busy
young microsurgeon, was convinced of his father's guilt and
made only rare trips to isolated Kingfisher Lodge in the far
northern reaches of Ontario.

Norma Palmer, Dan's wife, a long-time Conservative
party Delegate in the Assembly, was a more enigmatic figure. She had always kept aloof from the rest of the family,
and now used her political influence to keep the media away
from her luckless husband. It was plain that Norma still
loved Dan, doubtful that she would have approved her sister-
in-law's desire to set him free.

"The trial's over," Beth persisted. "The tabloid hacks will
back off once consolidation of Rampart and Galapharma begins and find other fish to fry. Let Dan come back to Toronto
and have a normal human existence. He promises to live
very quietly, without rocking your precious Rampart boat."

"It's impossible."

"Why?" she whispered ominously. "Because you and Eve
say so?"

"Because of what Dan did. The way he colluded with Alistair Drummond's criminal tactics during the takeover fight. Our brother is a crook, Beth. He could sabotage the consolidation. By rights, he should be facing criminal prosecution."

"Alistair Drummond lied to Dan! The merger tactics were never supposed to involve illegal activity. It was to be strictly business, with only a little computer snooping to smooth the way. Dan knew nothing about the sabotage, Qiu's death, Eve's kidnapping, any of that. And he swears that he never did anything to harm our poor mother. I believe him."

"Then let him tell his story to the machines," I said coldly, "and see if they do."

"You know those horrible devices can cause brain damage! When you were on trial for malfeasance, your lawyer wouldn't let you submit to them. Why should Dan?"

"We've been over this before. The reason Dan won't undergo psychoprobing is because he's guilty. For the love of God, Beth—he confessed to Simon and me while he was flying us to Coventry Blue at gunpoint! He extorted our voting proxies from us by threatening to have us transmuted into alien sex slaves!"

"That's absurd," she said. "That story is so ridiculous not even a child would believe it. Dan convinced you two that there was nothing further to be gained by opposing the Galapharma merger. You and Simon gave him your proxies willingly, then you reneged and came storming down to the Sky Ranch because—"

"That's not true. Dan's lying, manipulating you."

"Asa, he's our *brother*. A good husband and father. A man who worked faithfully for Rampart for over twenty years, making it strong."

"Who sold out when Pop wouldn't appoint him CEO." I rose from my seat. "I'm sorry, Beth. I know you love Dan, but he's a dangerous man—perhaps as crazy as Drummond himself. The proof that he had our mother killed is overwhelming. But Dan shows absolutely no remorse, only de-

nial. We've done the best we can for him, under the circumstances."

"Is that your final decision?"

"Mine, Simon's, and Eve's. Now I'm afraid I have to
leave. And so do you."

I crossed to the closet and got my Anonyme anorak, a
garment esteemed by shy skulkers such as minor celebs, unfaithful spouses, and urban misanthropes. The thing is available in a several fashion colors. Its privacy-field visor is
guaranteed to be proof against any scanner. My anorak even
boasted a special feature, a comfy light armor lining—not
that I needed that kind of protection anymore. With Alistair
Drummond presumably gone where the goblins go, and the
Haluk still unaware of my plan to cramp their style, no one
had a motive to whack me. My greatest enemies nowadays
were media busybodies.

I slipped the anorak on, drew up the open hood, and
flicked the switch. Presto! No face. The tiny force-field is
unnoticeable to the wearer. You can even eat and drink
through it—although I didn't intend to insult Carman's
mouth-watering menu by doing so.

Beth remained in her chair, posed as rigidly as a statue.
Her voice was still low-pitched and calm, but tears coursed
down her cheeks, ruining her flawless makeup.

"All Dan wanted was the best for Rampart. He was deceived. He would have made a wonderful CEO, but our
father chose Eve instead. His precious pet! Simon is an arrogant, misguided fool. And you, Asa . . . you're—"

I opened the office door. Jane Nelligan was at her desk.

"Please see that my sister Beth gets safely home," I said.
"It would be best if you can contact Dr. Berg and advise him
that his wife is feeling upset and needs him. Failing that,
have one of the InSec officers take her home in a hopper." I
lowered my voice. "Make a note. Her visitation rights and
phone access to Daniel Frost are suspended until Eve or I
say otherwise. And now I'm outta here."

"Bastard!" Beth screamed. "You fucking heartless bastard!"

My sister's furious shouts continued as I hurried to the bank of ordinary inertialess elevators that serve Rampart Tower and descended to the underground thoroughfare called the Path.

Chapter 4

The force-umbrella sheltering the capital is proof against high wind and precipitation, but it doesn't modify the ambient air temperature or humidity. So millions of office workers, junior execs, bureaucrats, and other downtowners seeking to avoid chilly or overly hot weather walk from place to place along an extensive system of subterranean concourses that has been a Toronto fixture for over 250 years.

The Path connects rapid transit subway stations with every commercial and government tower in the central core. Its multiple levels comprise a virtual underground city of bright tunnels having sections of moving walkway, shopping malls, and jogging lanes. The Path's busier corridors are lined with fast-food eateries, amusement arcades, and service establishments. There are even miniature parks where flowers and trees grow under artificial light, fountains contribute beneficial neg-ions, and the city's famous black squirrels cadge handouts from people having lunch on patches of grass. Nothing with wheels or antigrav lifts—except city cops on bicycles and the personal powerscooters of the disabled—is allowed in the Path's pedestrian-friendly network. It invites those interested in a casual stroll as well as bustling, single-minded commuters.

The Path has its own folklore, too. Certain little-traveled parts of the system to the north are alleged to be haunted by the ghosts of Thrown Away panhandlers and unlicensed vendors, cleared out in a pitiless sweep thirty years ago. A mazelike area near the university subway station is fraught with urban legends of suicidal lovers, a berserk sweeper bot that attempts to suck up the unwary, and the Headless Professor—behind whose privacy visor lies *nothing*. The lowest levels, shut off behind locked access hatches, are a labyrinth of disused shopping corridors dating from the previous century, old service tunnels, ancient sewers, and modern storm drains. They supposedly form a Dark Path frequented by the lawless, the desperately poor, and uncountable hordes of giant rats.

During my recent term of legal servitude, I would sometimes take a break and hike long distances in Underground Toronto. I enjoyed the infectious vitality of the Path and the human diversity of its denizens. Some of them walked shrouded in anonymity, as I always did; but the majority went about their business with the boisterous self-confidence of a youthful elite fortunate to have good jobs in the most exciting city on Earth.

Fair numbers of aliens mingled with humanity on the Path. The city center had embassies for four of the five stargoing Insap races. (The grotesque Kalleyni, who found Earth gravity oppressive, kept a legation at Luna Landing—a fortunate thing for human dignity, since they were such appalling practical jokers.) A stroller on the Path might expect to encounter towering Joru in elegant black-and-white habits, irascible little Qastt, pale Y'tata under strict orders from their protocol people to take their charcoal pills and antiflatulence medication, and—most numerous of all—the Haluk. They had flocked to the human capital in droves after the signing of the treaties. Their blue-skinned trade attachés lobbied relentlessly in the halls of government, and their commercial reps infested the executive suites of half the Hundred Concerns, wheeling and dealing.

The Haluk were the only aliens who adopted human clothing during their Earth sojourn. I had never been able to get used to the sight of them, striding boldly through the underground thoroughfares, always in groups of three or more, dressed in expensive high-style outfits. Members of the Joru, Y'tata, and Qastt races lived in apartments scattered throughout the central city; but all of the Haluk resided in their embassy, which comprised the top two-thirds of the enormous Macpherson Tower on Edward Street, just across from the headquarters of Sheltok, the Big Seven energy Concern.

Like the restricted Haluk planets, their embassy was strictly off limits to humanity.

Thanks to my sister Beth, I was late for my meeting with Chief Superintendent Jake Silver.

I took the McCaul Street leg of the Path north to the edge of the university campus, then turned east beneath the teeming government area until I reached CCID Tower on College Street. An escalator brought me into the historic lobby, which is part of the original Toronto police headquarters. I found Jake fidgeting and glaring at his wrist chronometer. He was wearing a natty camel-colored overcoat and a black beret.

I sidled up to him and deactivated my visor. "Yikes! The fuzz!"

He gave me a dirty look. "It's about time. You know what happens to people who come late for a reservation at Carman's? Come on. We'll save time walking outside."

He strode through the front doors, with me trailing apologetically after. I turned my privacy visor back on. "Don't get all in a snit, Jake. They won't throw you out of the place if you're with me. I'm a star! Rich, too."

"Wiseass. When was the last time you had dinner at Carman's?"

"Recently," I prevaricated. But I actually hadn't been there for over two years, back when I was still a political wannabe, wining and dining Liberal party Delegates sympathetic to

Reverse notions, hoping they would allow me to address their open committee sessions and badmouth the Haluk.

"Did you get a line on Barky Tregarth?" I inquired.

"I'll answer that," Jake said, "when I have a tumbler of Clynelish scotch in my fist and my steak is smiling up at me. You better pray that the maître d' is in one of his good moods."

"Is Albert still there?"

"He is. And merciless to the tardy."

The restaurant was only a couple of blocks away, on Alexander Street. Damp cold struck through my anorak, making me wish the garment had environmental controls instead of armor. April can really be the cruelest month in middle North America. Down on the Path, daffodils and tulips were in exuberant bloom. Aboveground, it still felt like winter.

Jake and I charged along the crowded sidewalk without speaking until the traffic signal at Yonge Street caught us. VIP cars and taxis were in a state of gridlock, as usual, waiting to get onto the computerized high-road ramps. The City Council's latest proposal to ban private ground vehicles from central-core streets had once again been shot down by the Hundred Concerns.

"Have a hard day, Chief Superintendent?" I asked Jake neutrally.

"The usual. Squabbling with a Zone Patrol liaison, chewing out the idiot droids in Data Processing, accepting shit with a smile from the powers that be." He paused. "And renewing an old and very unsavory acquaintance, thanks to you. I got what you wanted, but you're probably not going to like it."

He didn't say another word until we reached the 275-year-old steak house. We were twenty minutes late, but Albert's austere face lost its scowl as I hove into view, shucking my anorak. An attendant took it and Jake's overcoat.

"Helly!" The maître d' beamed at me. According to Rampart's standard operating procedure, Jane Nelligan had booked the table in the Concern's name, not my own. "Welcome back! I was afraid you'd forgotten us."

"Never. I've just been working my butt to the bone, forced to live on junk food."

Albert nodded. "The trial of the century! Your name is on everyone's lips."

Everyone who reads the *Wall Street Journal,* anyhow. I gave a wry smile as I slipped him a fat gratuity. "How about a spot in a very, very quiet corner?"

"Certainly." He'd make certain that no newshounds or table hoppers annoyed us during dinner. It was all part of Carman's service.

More than one head turned as we were conducted through the crowded main room, where copper and pewter pans and utensils hung thickly from the ceiling like metallic bats. The air was filled with the smell of pricey broiled meat and garlic toast.

Our table was secluded, in one of the cellarlike annex rooms. We perused leather-bound menus while sipping aperitifs. I had a dry sherry while Jake knocked back a double of the fiery Highland single malt that was his favorite.

"Seems a pity to anesthetize your taste buds with that kiltie coffin varnish in a restaurant like this," I murmured. "What the hell proof is it, anyhow?"

"A hundred twenty-two cask strength, sonny-boy, and only an ignorant Arizona shitkicker would insult this nectar of the gods. All my years exiled on K-L, I only managed to get two bottles of Clynelish from the local bootleggers. Now I'm back on the Blue Marble, I'll make up for lost opportunities—especially since you're paying."

"I apologize. Have another wee dram."

"Damn right I will. And I expect a decent wine with the meal, too."

So I got us a noble Haut-Brion '21. Jake ordered a grilled T-bone, potatoes Lyonnaise, and sautéed morels garnished with Aeolian krill—which he insisted were kosher. I decided on a flash-seared Wagyu filet, a side of asparagus with mustard miso, and a salad of nittany ears. He had an appetizer of artichoke-stuffed ravioli. I chose tiny last-of-the-season Quilcene oysters, definitely not kosher.

"You want to tell me what you found out about Barky Tregarth?" I asked him after his second double scotch arrived.

"Give you a little back-story first. Long time ago, when I was young like you and full of the same sort of sappy ideals, I got the goods on a superior of mine named Ram Mahtani. A tipoff and a data-trail seemed to show that Ram had taken juice—probably from the Carnelian Concern—to quash an investigation into violations of the Y'tata high-tech weaponry embargo. Mahtani had always been a decent boss to me. And he was a devoted family man with a daughter who had lots of medical problems. So before I filed a report with Internal Affairs, I asked him if he had an explanation for the suspicious behavior."

I said, "Oops."

"Exactly. I used to be a hopeless softy. Anyhow, overnight the incriminating data disappeared in a convenient computer crash, and my tipster changed his story. Poof went the case against Mahtani. Three weeks later I was bounced from Criminal Investigation, transferred to Public Safety, and outward bound to a jerkwater world in the Perseus Spur. Ram Mahtani took early retirement from CCID the following year and became a highly paid security consultant for Carnelian."

"Sad." I nibbled on a garlicky breadstick.

"I remembered Ram when you asked me about Barky Tregarth. It's an open secret that Carnelian wholesalers in remote Sectors wink at contraband transactions. Their security people are alleged to keep a secret roster of trustworthy smugglers. I contacted Mahtani—anonymously, of course. He told me that Tregarth is very much alive. I said that my client had a business proposition for him and wasn't out to nail him. Mahtani might or might not have believed that. His price for Barky's current alias and address is two million in untraceable funds."

"Holy shit!"

"I told you you wouldn't like it."

"Like it? I haven't *got* it."

"Come on. You own a quarterstake in Rampart, for chrissake. Two mil isn't chump change, but it wouldn't even fuel that muscle starship of yours for a round-trip to the Spur."

"Rampart pays my fuel bills. I do get a sizable draw—a salary—as a corporate officer, but I've been treating it like Monopoly money, funneling almost all of it off to needy Reversionist causes as soon as it hits my account. I've done the same with the income from my Rampart quarterstake."

"Tell the party to give some of it back."

"It's probably spent. You know pols."

The succulent little oysters arrived. I gave them my full attention for the few minutes it took to wolf them down.

Jake said, "So you really can't hack the bribe? I thought all you Frosts were richer than God."

"I have some money of my own, but I was planning to use it to grease Tregarth." And for other upcoming expenses. "You think this Mahtani might haggle?"

"The man's no street-corner fink, Helly. Two megabux was his price. And you might want to think very seriously about why he set it so high."

I gave a gloomy nod. "To see how badly some anonymous party wants old Barky."

"Here." Jake took a tiny notepad from his inner breast pocket, tore out a page and handed it to me. "Mahtani's contact number."

The piece of paper had a phone code scrawled on it. "An ultrasecure routing server, I presume."

"Of course . . . And there's something else you should consider before you deal with this joker. He's a top-notch professional investigator and he has Carnelian resources to back him up. If you pay him, even with a blind EFT, he might be able to track you down and screw up your operation."

"Yeah. *Gran dinero* leaves big footprints."

All I needed was a Carnelian bloodsucker snatching Barky before I could milk him. Or interrogating him after the fact, which would be even worse—provided the guy did have crucial information about the Haluk. Adam Stanislawski's warning about lethal retaliation from threatened Haluk Consortium Concerns was still vivid in my memory. The question was, did Ram Mahtani know enough about Barky's past to make the Haluk connection?

Rats. Maybe I'd have to forget about the old gunrunner. Unless I could spike Mahtani's guns, get what I wanted while simultaneously warning him off . . .

The waiter appeared with our main course. We waited until he had finished arraying the planks with their sizzling chunks of meat and the various side dishes.

I said to Jake, "I just had a brilliant idea. I'm going to try a loanshark for that two mil. A very large shark that Mahtani might not want to mess with."

Jake shrugged. He tucked in with gusto while I entered a code into my pocket phone. It was one that I had never had occasion to use before, and I held my breath wondering whether the call would go through.

But a familiar face finally appeared on the small screen. We stared at each other for a moment and then I lifted the instrument to my ear, cutting off the video.

"What is it, Helly?"

"Sorry to disturb you at home, sir. I have an urgent need for a large sum of untraceable credit. Naturally I will personally repay the loan at a future date, along with whatever interest you deem appropriate."

"I see," Adam Stanislawski said. "How much?"

"Two million, right now."

"Very well."

"Can you load a blind EFT card so that the hidden source of the funds will be Macrodur, not A. E. Frost, Esquire?"

"Yes. Is this payment going directly to the person I mentioned at the end of our visit this afternoon?"

Crafty old Adam. "Unfortunately not. It's a bribe to a go-between, a highly placed informant in Carnelian who knows the whereabouts of this person. The informant might be able to do me damage—but probably wouldn't dare go up against you."

"The name."

"Ram Mahtani."

"I understand completely."

"Let me level with you: I can't afford this steep a bribe, even if I wasn't scared stiff of Mahtani."

Stanislawski laughed. "I can afford it. And I'm not afraid. Plug your card into the phone."

I complied. The instrument's data strip indicated a transfer of funds, triple the amount I'd requested.

"A contribution to the war chest," said the Macrodur chairman. "If Tregarth comes through, you'd better bring him back to Earth for safekeeping. Tell him I'll personally make it worth his while."

"Will do. Thanks for the vote of confidence, sir."

He nodded and broke off.

"So that's how the simple folk do business," Jake marveled.

"You ought to know," I said, very quietly.

He sat still, his fork poised halfway to his mouth. The faintest trace of guilt shadowed his eyes. Then he calmly resumed eating.

Gotcha, Jake. How else would Adam Stanislawski have known about the Barky Hunt?

I picked up the phone again, engaging maximum encryption, a voice disguiser, and a masked code of my own to accommodate the server-link to Mahtani.

A robot voice said, *Code entered. Please hold.*

I put the phone down and we ate and drank in silence for a few minutes. Jake didn't meet my gaze. The Bordeaux was splendid and my chunk of pampered Japanese cattle flesh so tender that it surrendered to the knife with hardly any pressure. I only managed to gobble a few subtly flavored quivering slices before my phone, sitting on the table beside the asparagus, began to blink.

I picked up and said, "Yes."

"Do you accept my terms?" a disguised voice inquired. The view screen remained blank.

"I have the EFT card ready."

"Transmit the agreed-upon honorarium."

I sent the *mordida* winging through the ether. Words popped up instantly on my instrument's readout strip.

BARNEY CORNWALL—PHLEGETHON, ZONE 3

"It has been my pleasure to assist you," said Mahtani, or whomever. "The information is accurate, as of today. Good evening."

And he was gone.

I showed the phone to Jake. "Where is this place? I've never heard of it."

He munched a 'shroom redolent of shallots, wine, and exotic crustacea before answering.

"It's a hollow asteroid in a Sheltok Sagittarian system. One of the way stations for Shel UH carriers traveling from assorted R-class hellmouths in Zone 1 to the Orion Arm. Over the years, it attracted small-time human operators who traded with the local Joru and Y'tata worlds. The place expanded internally—sort of like an old tree getting hollowed out by more and more termite galleries. Now Phlegethon is a entrepôt for all kinds of fences and sleazy little trading outfits. Some are even legitimate."

"Sounds like a perfect place for Barky."

"Let's see if his Barney Cornwall alias computes," Jake said.

He pulled out his own personal communicator, a police jobbie with more bells and whistles than mine, unfolded it, and summoned information from the CCID database. There was no trace of Barky Tregarth's revised moniker in any official listing.

"Can you get direct access to the Phlegethon resident census through Sheltok?" I asked.

"Officially, no. Unofficially . . ." He entered a confidentiality override code, but gave a muttered curse of disappointment. "No one using the Cornwall or Tregarth names is on the asteroid's roster. Mahtani could have jerked us around, but I don't think so. He has a certain reputation to maintain. I think old Barky is lying low. You'll just have to go to Phlegethon and start digging." He grinned at me. "I'd lay odds that he'll know somebody's looking for him, too."

"It figures," I said. "What else can you tell me about that part of the galaxy? How about checking the ZP crime stats for Zone 3?"

He did so. "Hmm . . . There's been a severe outbreak of piracy in those parts during the last couple of years. Twenty-one Sheltok megacarriers vanished without a trace, and others had close calls. I can get details from Zone Patrol."

"I'd be obliged."

His search indicated that the energy-ship attacks had been laid at the doorstep of Y'tata freebooters, denounced—but of course!—as outlaws by the righteous Y Federation. Jake popped me a data-dime with full particulars and I filed it for later study.

"There could have been other hijackings that Sheltok didn't report to ZP," Jake said. There was something elusive in his tone that I didn't pick up on immediately. "Just rumors."

I nodded. Sheltok might have good reasons of their own not to publicize the attacks, especially if they'd been skimping on fleet security. It was unusual for Y'tata crooks to be hijacking transactinides so aggressively. They were an ancient race of nearly humanoid albinos, with about a thousand planetary colonies on both sides of Red Gap. But their population was nearly stable, and they seemed content to piddle along with their relatively low-tech interstellar civilization, only occasionally resorting to piracy. Since they owned long-established ultraheavy element sources of their own in the Whorl, their marauders usually targeted freighters with more generalized cargoes . . .

For a while we ate in silence. I finished my main course and began on the salad. The nittany ears were crisp and tart, just the way I like them.

After a time Jake said casually, "You planning to head for the Sag?"

"In a few days, maybe. If Barky's inside that Sagittarian rock, I'll find him and wring him dry. Whether he has any useful information for me is another matter."

"He might run," Jake said. "Mahtani is sure to warn him that someone's very anxious to meet him."

"I'm betting he'll stay put, take precautions, and see what the deal is. I would, if I was in his position."

"Whole lotta money to pay, long way to go, on an off chance."

I gave him a cynical look. "Adam Stanislawski already knows why I'm interested in Barky Tregarth. No need to pump me, Jake."

He grinned sheepishly. "What can I say?"

Not much, I thought.

"You're wondering what *my* price was," Jake went on. "The answer is: zero, zilch, zippo. You know I owe the Big M even more than I owe you. For my posting home. The agreement was, if I ever came across anything that might affect Macrodur significantly, I was to pass it along. Your peculiarly urgent need to interview Tregarth, a guy who once engaged in illicit trade with the Haluk, tripped the alarm."

"You're a smart cop, Chief Superintendent."

"And you're a crazy hotdogger. When you get on some-body's case, *meshugeneh* things happen. I remember Helly's Comet. I remember Cravat and Dagasatt. So you won't tell me what you want with Barky. But I happen to know that the guy's only claim to fame is a drunken boast that he once went to the Haluk Cluster and got back to tell the tale."

"Bull's-eye." I refilled his empty wineglass.

He eyed me with what might have been real concern. "You're not planning to go after Tregarth alone, are you? It wouldn't be wise. The old kocker didn't pick a dump like Phlegethon as a retirement haven. He's still on the job."

There were people I might have asked to join me on the Barky Hunt: a smart young bodybuilder and an ex-ZP offi-cer who'd started as hired hands and later became my friends; a small group of retired Rampart security agents re-cruited by Karl Nazarian to assist my semilegal campaign against Galapharma; even several private investigators I'd worked with during my Reversionist period. But Ivor Jen-kins was far away in the Perseus Spur, operating his own gym on Seriphos, and Ildiko Szabo had taken over the wholesale flower business of her aging parents in Hungary. I'd lost touch with Karl's Over-the-Hill Gang during the long trial, and the PI's were experienced in ferreting out capital chicanery, not crewing deep-space rumbles.

Going after Barky Tregarth alone seemed a perfectly fea-sible option. Phlegethon would certainly cater to Joru traders as well as Y'tata, since both races lived in that sector of the galaxy. This fact had suggested to me a way I might visit the place under cover. I had no intention of telling Jake Silver about my scheme, however.

"Thanks for the warning, Chief Super. Actually, I'm plan-ning to muster my usual task force of space dreadnaughts and a brigade of commandos for the Barky bust. You can't afford to take chances with senile gunrunners."

"Not Tregarth, you putz. His friends. I'm serious."

"Y'tata pirates? Or are you talking about Carnelian's thugs? Or Sheltok's?"

"All of the above—and maybe a wild card as well." He paused for an uncomfortable beat. "There might be funny business going on out there involving the Haluk."

My jaw sagged. "Why didn't you say so before?" I demanded, none too politely. "You know you can set your own price."

Jake winced. "I suppose I deserve that . . . But what I know, you can have for free. God knows it's little enough. A single report, about eighteen months ago, kept ex-database by special order of Xenoaffairs to avoid distressing our new blue trading partners. A patrol cruiser responded to an emergency call—the attempted hijack of a Sheltok trans-ack carrier in the Zone 3 section of Red Gap. The patrol captain claimed that they scanned four bandits during the attack. Three were typical Y'tata pirates. The fourth ship was a hell of a lot faster, with a slightly different fuel signature. It hung back during the firefight, then broke off and ran with the others. ZP's conformation scan of number four was futzed by weaponry EMI during the encounter, but the bandit wasn't human. Or Joru or Kalleyni, either. The fuel signature might have been Haluk."

"In the Sagittarius Whorl? That's crazy! Too far from their Spur colonies, way beyond their lines of supply."

Jake sawed away at the remains of the T-bone. "I heard about it from a half-drunk ZP Assistant Deputy Commissioner at a fuckin' cocktail party. We were discussing the Haluk expansion in the Perseus Spur. Their starships are all over Zone 23 now, scoping out potential colonies, trading with the Rampart worlds. Blueberry scouts have even been seen in the outer Orion Arm—and there was this one anomalous spotting in the Sag, which might or might not have been Haluk."

"It makes no sense. Why would they go there? And why throw in with Y'tata trans-ack nabbers? The Haluk don't need to steal ultraheavy elements. They *sell* them, for chrissake. The notion's ridiculous on the face of it."

"Right. Whole lotta ridiculous shit going down these days. I'm glad I'm just a simple desk cop who doesn't have to worry about such things."

The waiter materialized. "Can I interest you gentlemen in our dessert menu?"

"What d'you think, Jake?" I inquired. "This might be our last meal together for quite a spell."

"Coffee and cognac," the Chief Super said. "I don't suppose you have any Ferrand Réserve Ancestrale?"

"Of course. An excellent choice."

"Two," I said.

The waiter nodded and went away.

"Figuring to get in one last lick before riding into the sunset?" I asked Jake sadly. The cognac was one of Earth's finest, and the price was cosmological.

"I guess that's up to you, Helly. Serve me right if you shit-canned our friendship."

"Problem with that, I haven't got very many. Friends, that is." And he hadn't really done me any harm by telling Macrodur about the Barky Hunt. Maybe just the opposite.

"How about I pay for the Ferrand?" he suggested. "Peace offering."

"Peace is good," I said.

When the waiter returned with the cognac and coffee, we drank to it.

I saw Jake off on the Yonge Street subway, which would whisk him to his home in German Mills in about fifteen minutes, then started down the Path to the Winter Garden Theater, a twenty-minute walk south of Carman's restaurant.

The commuter rush had slackened a little now that the day-shift workers from the towers had left and those on the evening watch were settled in, but there were still throngs of pedestrians heading for downtown attractions: shopping, nightlife, amusement, fine dining, and most especially the innumerable watering holes where congenial companionship of one sex or another awaited trolling lonelies.

I got onto a very crowded moving walkway. Many of its riders were striding along to enhance their groundspeed, but I stood still at the far right side, since I was in no particular hurry. I was jostled often and hard by impatient passers, but thought nothing of it until a particularly sharp jab insulted my left hip and made me grunt with pain. The guy who did it sped past without an apology. He was small and slightly built, wearing a bomber jacket and carrying a bulky portfolio of the type favored by commercial artists.

I stepped off the conveyor at a Jolie Jacqueline lingerie shop, cursing mildly. My assailant had left the moving walkway ahead of me and was skipping nimbly across the mainstream of pedestrian traffic on the opposite side of the concourse. He disappeared into a corridor leading to the Bodascon Tower escalators.

There was a small hole in the side of my anorak that looked almost like a stab from an icepick. The armored lining was visible and the edges of the hole seemed wet. What the hell had Bomber Jacket hit me with—a large pen or some other sharp artist's implement? Mellow with expensive alcohol and the heavy dinner, it never occurred to me that the poke hadn't been accidental. My survival instincts, which had been on red alert during the perils of the late Galapharma takeover, were rusty after nearly three years of disuse.

I looked up at the opulent window display of silk and lace in Jolie Jacqueline. A thought came to me, a way to repay Jake's favor while simultaneously playing a mild practical joke to point up his treachery. I stepped into the shop.

"May I be of assistance, m'sieu?" A saleswoman of a certain age, wearing a little black dress, approached me with an encouraging smile. Her name badge said ANNETTE. She did a very creditable French accent.

I flicked off my intimidating privacy visor in a gesture of

civility. "Would you please show me your very nicest night-gown and peignoir set? I'm not sure of the size, but I think I can eyeball it."

"Of course. Let me bring you several choices."

I followed Annette to a counter. The items she showed me were very pricey indeed. I selected an ensemble in cherry-red silk chiffon with lots of lace inserts, gave her my corporate EFT card, and consulted my phone dex for the home address of Chief Superintendent Jake Silver and his wife of twenty-eight years.

"I'd like the package gift-wrapped and sent to Marie War-rener, 163 Linden Crescent, German Mills, Markham."

"Certainly, m'sieu. Will there be an enclosure?"

I took one of the tiny cards she offered and wrote, *From your adoring Snuggle-Puppy, Jake.*

While Annette wrapped Marie's present, I wandered idly around the small shop, indulging a fantasy or two. There were no other customers in Jolie Jacqueline. The place had a boudoir decor with soft lights, gauzy hangings, discreetly semitransparent holograms of lovely ladies modeling sexy underthings, and a lot of gold-framed mirrors. In one of the angled ones I caught a close-up glimpse of my own back.

Right at rump level, the Anonyme's outer fabric had been perforated twice more. Around each small hole was a damp-ish corona.

I felt my throat tighten. Those earlier jostlings on the walkway had been less vigorous attempts to stab me. The wet spots suggested that Bomber Jacket had tried to inject me with an unknown substance, probably poison.

Damn! Think, Helly, think. Get your sozzled brain back in gear.

A random attack by a psycho? It had been known to happen, even in beautiful cosmopolitan Toronto.

Had Ram Mahtani traced me after all and taken out a contract on my life now that he had his money? Impossible. The time frame was too tight and the motive wasn't there.

Had Jake Silver sold out my ass to somebody other than Stanislawski? No way. It made sense that Jake would nark on me to Macrodur in a manner that did me no particular harm. That he'd be an accessory to my murder was inconceivable.

Think, Helly, think.

Bomber Jacket could have trailed me from the moment I left Rampart Tower. If he was a real pro, he could have ID'ed me easily through a body language analysis, in spite of the concealing Anonyme. Everybody has a distinctive walk, individual arm and head mannerisms. During my brief political fling the media had made countless holovids of me. My motion signature would be easily obtainable.

So who genuinely wanted me dead?

The minor villains in Galapharma had been neutralized long ago. If Gala's ex-CEO, Alistair Drummond, was still alive, he was certainly crazy enough to come after me out of revenge. But Bomber Jacket himself wasn't Drummond. My old nemesis was a tall Scotsman with a princely bearing, not a skittering runt. And why would Drummond have waited so long?

The only others who had any motive for killing me shouldn't have known yet that I was an immediate threat to their galactopolitical ambitions. But maybe the Haluk had other reasons for wanting me out of the picture. The article in the *Journal* would have reminded them that I was now at leisure and once again in a position to cause them serious trouble in the Commonwealth Assembly.

And if there were still Haluk demiclone agents in Galapharma's woodwork, they might have learned about Lorne Buchanan's transfer of incriminating data from the Concern's computer to that of Efrem Sontag.

I let out an involuntary snarl of disgust. My night at the theater was a scrub. I'd have to get back to the safety of Rampart Tower as quickly as possible, then lie low until I could take off for the Sagittarius Whorl—

"Is there another way I can be of assistance, m'sieu?"

Annette had snuck up on me. "No thanks. I was just checking a rip in my jacket."

I turned my visor back on and drifted to the door. Blank-faced, I carefully studied the crowd outside. There was no sign of Bomber Jacket. I exited the shop and walked a few meters away to put a solid wall at my back, then took out my phone and called Rampart Internal Security.

"InSec. Duty Officer Callahan."

"This is Asahel Frost, Sean. I need a squad to come and get me. I'm on the Path between Bodascon and Daimler Towers. Someone just tried to stab me. Three times. My jacket armor saved me."

Sean Callahan stifled an exclamation. "I understand. I'll have bike patrol cops get to you immediately. Just activate your personal emergency beacon. Meanwhile, my situation team will take a hopper to Bodascon skyport and—"

"No. I don't want Bodascon Security involved." The colossal aerospace Concern was a prominent member of the Haluk Consortium. "Or Toronto Public Safety, either. This has got to be kept quiet. Now listen carefully. Put three of your plainclothes people on the subway at Osgoode. Let them come up the loop from the south. I'll backtrack north on the Path and meet them at College Station."

"The *subway*?" Callahan was incredulous. "It would really be safer If you remained right where you are, under police guard, and we flew in. If you don't want a touch at Bodascon skyport we could come via Daimler."

"The hit man ran up into Bodascon. He could call for re-inforcements from—" I shut my mouth. I hadn't seen any Haluk pedestrians for a long time, but their embassy was only a couple of blocks away. However, I didn't want to share my suspicion of the aliens with a low-level employee like Callahan.

"Sir?"

I said, "I think the perp is long gone. I'm safer moving

with the crowd than standing still. The call is mine to make, Sean. Have your troops meet me at College Station. We can all take a nice slow taxi ride to Rampart Tower. Frost out."

I started back the way I'd come, not using the moving walkway and staying near a wall whenever possible. There were only two short blocks to go. The crowds were thicker, but the hustle and bustle seemed entirely normal. I made it to the subway intersection without incident and turned east. Access to the transit station above was via an escalator. I got on a rising step just behind a young woman in a red coat who carried a Bergdorf shopping bag.

We'd nearly reached the upper level when I felt a stinging sensation in my left calf. Almost instantly my body's voluntary muscles began to freeze. I felt myself toppling toward the woman. She made a dismayed noise.

"Whoa! Easy there, Fred. We gotcha, ol' buddy."

A man two steps below came up beside me and took hold of my arms to support me. Another guy joined him immediately. Stiff as a board from the injected paralytic, I felt small objects being shoved into each of my armpits. All of a sudden I wasn't falling anymore; I was floating.

The faces of my assailants were unremarkable. The first wore a black leather car coat and blue jeans. The other had a brown fleece jacket over a business suit and carried a sport duffelbag on a shoulder strap, which must have concealed the injector. The pair worked together, one at my side and the other on the step below, clamping my upper arms firmly to my body and keeping a tight grip on my elbows. The antigrav devices in my pits made manhandling me a snap.

Boozy fumes wafted from somewhere. I presumed one of the goons had spritzed it onto me to enhance the charade of drunkenness. The woman in the red coat stared over her shoulder with ill-concealed disgust, and so did a few rubberneckers on the adjacent descending escalator. Thanks to the Anonyme, no one could see the twisted expression of fury on my face.

"We'll take care of him," Black Leather told the woman glibly. "Not to worry. Sorry if he bumped into you."

"Poor old Fred," Brown Fleece added. "He had a really bad day, y'know? Lost a major client, then tried to kill the pain with too many vodka martinis."

The woman turned her back on us. Some of the other stair riders looked sympathetic.

"You just take it easy, mate," Black Leather told me in a jovial voice. "Try not to throw up on these nice people. We'll get you safe to a taxi and home to beddy-bye."

"What're drinking buddies for?" Brown Fleece chimed in. "You're gonna be okay, except for a helluva hangover tomorrow."

I tried to speak. Couldn't produce more than a breathy croak.

My cowboy-booted feet floated a centimeter off the ground as the escalator reached the subway station level. There were no Rampart Security personnel existing the standing train. Probably they'd be along on the next one, for all the good it would do me.

I wafted between the pair of abductors like a human balloon. They steered me onto another escalator going up to the street, continuing their solicitous patter. I was just another upper-class lush being helped along by friends.

Outside, we crossed Dundas Square. Pedestrians averted their eyes. A bike cop gave us the once-over, decided all was cool. We moved along the sidewalk, turned into a narrow lane amidst a row of small historic houses that huddled beneath a stubby business tower. The crowd thinned immediately and the streetlighting became less intense.

A Mercedes limousine was parked illegally at the exit of an underground parking lot. Its doors opened as one of my captors zapped it with a remote control. They removed the lifting devices under my arms and eased me into a forward-facing seat in the capacious passenger section. Black Leather got in beside me. Brown Fleece tossed his duffel in front and slipped behind the wheel, leaving the sliding privacy panel open. The car doors shut.

Fleece addressed the car navigator. "Enter Ottawa Highroad eastbound. Go to Express Lane Six. Go to Peterborough 122. Exit highroad northbound and revert to manual control."

En route, said the car.

We were off, circling around Ryerson Tower and hanging a right to the on-ramp of the highroad. A longish wait in line until it was our turn to accelerate—then up, up and away, thirty meters above the teeming city on an elevated twelve-lane ribbon, our limousine guided precisely into the far-left express lane where motorists in a hurry paid a premium toll to travel at speeds of 300 kph. Unfortunately, because of tonight's heavy volume of traffic, the express lane was limited to a mere 230 kph, while the five nonpremium eastbound lanes limped along at 170.

Any hope I might have entertained that my kidnappers were human melted away when Leather said something to Fleece in the Haluk language. Fleece laughed—not human-style, but in the throttled-puppy mirth idiom of the blue aliens.

Black Leather reached into the right sleeve of my Anonyme and flicked the switch. The visor blinked off and the security catch unlocked. He pushed off my hood and spoke to me in Standard English.

"If you make a very strong effort, you'll be able to blink your eyes. I suggest you do it as often as possible to avoid desiccated corneas. You should voluntarily swallow your saliva, too, unless you enjoy drooling. The drug has no other unpleasant side effects. The rest of your autonomic nervous system should remain safely operational until we give you the antidote later." He smiled. "Much later."

I managed a grunt, then blinked and swallowed.

It wasn't hard to do, it was rather easy. And my previously numb toes and fingers and tongue were starting to tingle.

Hello!

They'd shot me with a toxin that preserved consciousness, going for the leg after my armored anorak had foiled the body hits. A jab in the lower calf would have worked nicely on somebody wearing conventional executive footwear.

But I was a cowboy.

The injector had penetrated the tough leather of my boot with difficulty. It must have been slightly deflected and failed to deliver the entire dose. I'd taken in enough chemical to paralyze me, but the stuff might already be starting to wear off.

I sat absolutely still. We were traveling through the rainy night, out from under the force-umbrella now, soaring over Toronto's eastern suburbs. I speculated briefly upon the reason why my captors hadn't taken me to the Haluk embassy or even Oshawa Starport out in Lake Ontario rather than heading out of town toward Peterborough.

North of the interchange at kilometer 122 were roads leading into the Kawarthas, a picturesque region of lakes, rolling woodlands, and pretty little towns: Bridgenorth and scores of other dormitory exurbs, modest art colonies and resorts like Fenelon Falls where my friend Bea Mangan and her husband had a technocottage, enclaves of stunning affluence such as Mount Julian, where top Concern executives maintained pseudorustic pieds-à-terre on Stony Lake.

Come to think of it, when he wasn't hunkered down at Galapharma HQ in Glasgow, Alistair Drummond had lived up in the Kawarthas, too . . .

The demiclones talked freely to each other in the difficult Haluk language, confident that their paralyzed prisoner, like so many lazy translator-addicted Earthlings, was unable to understand them.

Mistake.

During my politically active phase, when I was eloquently disparaging the secretiveness of the Haluk before one of the commerce committees and it looked as though the Delegates were starting to take me seriously, the Servant of Servants of Luk made a diplomatic gesture intended to defuse a deteriorating public relations situation.

The Haluk leader proposed a guided tour of Artiuk, their principal colony in the Perseus Spur, to show that his race had nothing to hide. The invitation was extended to twelve influential members of the committee, three media representatives from *Newsweek, Cosmos Today,* and the *Times . . .* and me, badass motormouth celebrity. Because of delicate Haluk cultural inhibitions, no audiovisual recording devices would be allowed; but we visitors would be able to dictate copious notes into handheld computers.

The SSL's invitation was eagerly accepted.

Alone among my human colleagues, I chose to take a sleep-course in the Haluk language during the eight-day trip out to the Spur. It was something I'd been meaning to do for a long time: know thine enemy, and all that. The other members of the group opted for the greater convenience and efficiency of mechanical translators. I intended to wear one, too; but I'd hatched a vague plan to discard the thing conspicuously at some point during the tour, hoping to provoke our Haluk hosts into making imprudent comments in the belief that I wouldn't understand them.

As it happened, my subterfuge wasn't necessary. The translators worn by us humans malfunctioned almost from the first moment we set foot on Artiuk—perhaps because its solar system was in the throes of a sudden ionic storm, perhaps for another reason altogether. Whatever the source of the problem, the fritzed-out devices reduced Haluk speech to incomprehensible gibberish, and they could not be repaired with the tools available on the alien world.

This might have put a serious damper on our visit, had not the Servant of Servants graciously provided each one of us with an English-speaking Haluk escort. These high-ranking officials of his personal staff subsequently accompanied us everywhere and filtered all conversations between us and the Artiuk locals.

The Haluk facial structure is not conducive to emotional display. I was able to discern that the instant translations the guides provided us were often very creative.

As I'd expected, the "fact-finding tour" turned out to be little more than a puff job. It revealed only superficial aspects of Haluk life and absolutely nothing about their military-industrial capability. We were allowed close contact only with gracile-phase humanoid individuals.

"It would be depressing for you to meet the poor lepido-dermoids, much less view the dormant testudinals," our hosts said, gently reproving curious members of the delegation. "And besides, there are no longer very many nongracile Haluk residing on Artiuk, thanks to the miracle of your PD32:C2 genetic engineering vector, which has changed our lives so marvelously by eradicating the curse of allomorphism."

So we saw what the Haluk wanted us to see: performances of dissonant Haluk music, displays of beautiful Haluk artwork, timid Haluk children at crowded primary schools who presented us with bouquets of alien flowers, Haluk agronomists operating impressive hydroponic farms that grew produce mildly poisonous to the human digestive tract. It was all very edifying, and to sophisticated human galaxy trotters, duller than belly-button lint.

Unless one happened to understand what the non-English-speaking Haluk were actually saying about their distinguished visitors.

The adults hated our collective entrails because we had cruelly stalled Haluk emigration to the Milky Way and charged extortionate prices for PD32:C2 and other vital technology. The poor little Haluk kids were scared rigid of us because the adults had told them that humans were cannibals who ate misbehaving children.

I did my best to share eavesdropped intelligence with the

Assembly Delegates and the reporters, but my well-known anti-Haluk bias bent my credibility. In the end the relentless hospitality of the Servant of Servants and his minions won the hearts of our group.

When we returned to Earth, the media special reports were glowing. A month later the Haluk treaties were ratified by the Assembly.

From my alarmist point of view, the trip had been worse than useless. All I'd really gained was a superficial knowledge of an abstruse alien tongue, most of which faded from my mind almost immediately.

But not all of it.

Under computer control, the limousine roared along the storm-lashed elevated road. The rain was now mixed with ice pellets. Brown Fleece relaxed behind the wheel, lit a cigarette—the vice had spread like wildfire among the blue aliens resident on Earth—and spoke in the Haluk language to the leather-jacketed demiclone seated at my right.

"*Blah blah* will be up a copulatory orifice because we are so late. One fears the road *blah blah blah*. It is the last day of the normal human work *blah* and *blah blah blah*."

Black Leather said, "One might as well be fighting the *blah* back home on *[some Haluk planet]*. Great Almighty Luk help our *blah* posteriors if we *blah blah blah*."

Fleece: "One is carefully watching the *blah blah*. At present the sky road is *blah* all the way to Peterborough."

Leather: "Thank Almighty Luk . . ."

The demiclones were complaining about Friday night traffic. Welcome to the club.

Fleece said, "One presumes that our next *blah blah* will be to take the brother."

What!

Leather: "Ru Balakalak will decide. The angry human *blah* still strongly resists that idea. He *blah blah blah*. And he thinks the brother lacks *blah blah*."

I exerted all my willpower to avoid flinching in dismay. Were these turkeys referring to my disreputable brother ·Daniel?

Fleece: "This one believes the revised plan using the brother is superior. And the *blah* younger sister would *blah blah blah* his disappearance."

Leather: "Perhaps. The brother is surely more easily *blah* than the appalling human *blah*. But does he possess *blah blah* to accomplish *blah blah blah*?"

Fleece: "Maybe not, if one can trust *blah* of the angry human *blah*."

Leather: "Curse all humans! The plan itself is excellent but *blah blah* of it stinks like lepido nose wax. This one will continue to urge strongly that a Haluk *blah blah* be used, rather than any human *blah*."

Fleece: "Who will listen to one? Ru Balakalak leads. He is a stubborn *[epithet]* and favors the quickest *blah blah* in order to please the Servant of Servants. The danger *blah blah blah*."

Leather: "*[Epithet.]* One wishes we would *blah blah blah* and put an end to it."

Fleece: "We are not ready. One knows that. When we are ready, it will happen."

There followed an interval of portentous silence, during which I felt my guts twisting into a granny knot. Were they talking about an attack against humanity? And what kind of plan would they have that would involve me, my wretched brother, my sister Beth, and another human? I was trying to sort this out when my thoughts were suddenly interrupted by a resounding Haluk curse from Black Leather.

"Are we slowing down?" he called out to his compatriot. "We are!"

Up front, Brown Fleece was studying the navigation display, which was not visible from the passenger compartment. "Almighty Luk! The *blah* indicates a *blah blah*!" He broke into a tirade of alien vituperation.

Black Leather spoke impatiently to the car in Standard English. "Navigator, why is traffic decelerating?"

The robot voice said, *A vehicle on-board computer has malfunctioned catastrophically and caused a multiple-car accident with injuries at kilometer 100.4. All six eastbound lanes are blocked at that point.*

A sea of red brakelights glowed in the sleet storm outside as the marvelous automated speedway reverted to ox-road status. Pavement deicing equipment had kicked in, adding clouds of steam to the atmospheric mélange.

"Exit!" Leather commanded his associate. "Hurry, before we are *blah*!"

But we had just passed the ramp at Enniskillen. Fleece asked the navigator, "What is our next exit option?"

Exit 80, the Lindsay-Clarington freeway, fifteen kilometers ahead. Estimated time of arrival at this exit is now approximately 21:10 hours.

Black Leather spat more exotic obscenities and smacked his fist furiously against the refreshment console just in front of our seat. Our speed was now less than 40 kph and still dropping. We were going to be hung up for over an hour, creeping at a snail's pace toward the next exit together with hundreds of other luxury vehicles and their fuming occupants.

I wiggled my toes. The tingling had faded.

"Can we not summon an aircraft to *blah* us out of this *[expletive]*?" Black Leather asked his companion.

The limousine, of course, could be programmed to exit the highroad all by itself if we were evacuated via hopper. Perhaps other trapped bigwig motorists were also considering that extreme option, although private aircraft were forbidden to land on the highroad, and the storm made the prospect of being winched into the sky through the roof hatch an uninviting one.

Fleece said, "One doubts that would save significant time, since our *blah blah* aircraft are *blah* at Mount Julian."

Leather groaned. "*[Convoluted expletive.]* Then we are truly *blah*, my friend."

"One must *blah blah* our delay." Fleece began to speak in an undertone into the driver's communicator.

Muttering, the alien sitting on my right opened the refreshment console and took out a packet of cigarettes. The limo was rolling more and more slowly. At speeds of less than 10 kph it would be possible to unlock the doors manually from the inside.

I flexed the fingers of my left hand. They worked. So did the other muscles of that arm, which I tensed gingerly without making any suspicious motion. The paralyzing agent seemed to have almost worn off.

Right. Wait for the moment.

Slower. Slower.

Now.

Black Leather was holding a flameless electric lighter to his smoke. I slammed a roundhouse left hook into his face, singeing my knuckles on the glowing cigarette tip as I drove it and the red-hot lighter against his mouth.

He let out a hideous cry and clawed at me like a madman. I slammed his head down onto the console and flicked the lock switch. In the front seat, Brown Fleece whirled around, gabbling in Haluk. He was too far away to reach me. I tore open my door, dropped outside onto the road shoulder, picked myself up, and stumbled toward the inner guardrail.

Fleece was opening his own door as I vaulted over the barrier onto the median safety catwalk that separated the eastbound highroad lanes from the westbound. It was very cold. Traffic was now nearly at a standstill on our side, and vapor from melting pavement ice swirled amidst the driving sleet. Crouching low, I raced back the way we'd come, forgetting that I would be silhouetted against the headlights of oncoming cars. I still wore my Anonyme anorak. With the hood off I was half blinded by the torrent of stinging sleet pellets. They hissed against the vehicle surfaces like a nest of rattlesnakes, almost drowning out the roar of turbo engines powering the automobiles of more fortunate motorists in the open westbound lanes.

Solid ground lay thirty meters below the catwalk grating, hidden by mist and the purple glow of the powerful antigravity reticulum that buoyed up the ribbon of reinforced pavement. The AG field was generated by machinery housed in huge pylons situated every 500 meters along the highroad. The only emergency exits for pedestrians were inside those pylons. Under normal conditions, auto breakdown service and ambulance evacuation for accident victims were accomplished by Highroad Authority hoppercraft. The police used hoppers, too.

Over the noise of the westbound traffic and the storm I heard ominous sharp pinging sounds. A volley of stun-darts zipped around me, striking the ceramalloy stanchions and railings.

Running flat-out along the catwalk, I managed to pull up my armored anorak hood an instant before one of the darts struck the back of my skull and bounced off. The impact caused me to see stars momentarily and stagger with pain.

I recovered my senses, belatedly realized that the unimpeded stretch of catwalk was a perfect shooting gallery, and flung myself back over the railing onto the shoulder. Bobbing and swerving, I darted like a cockroach into the six lanes of crawling cars, now spaced precisely three meters apart by the traffic-control computer. A few startled drivers honked and flashed their headlights frantically. Most of them ignored me.

Brown Fleece was galloping along the shoulder, showing no inclination to follow me out among the moving cars. Darts loaded with sleepy-juice flew through the sleet-streaked headlight beams like supercharged fireflies, missed me, and ricocheted off the vehicles.

Nobody opened a car door and invited me inside to safety.

My bruised head hurt like hell. The sleet was changing to heavy flakes of wet snow and visibility was terrible.

Another dart hit me in the back of my armored jacket. I thanked God that my vulnerable legs were shielded by the surrounding cars. All I could do was continue to zigzag through the traffic jam, taking small comfort from the realization that Brown Fleece certainly had orders to take me alive. His weapon was probably an Ivanov stun-pistol that typically fired small missiles with a limited range. It would be virtually impossible for the Haluk demiclone to use the gun's none-too-reliable autotargeter system while taking snap shots in a storm.

I was moving faster than Fleece, but for a time he nearly kept pace with me, not having to lose ground by dodging. Two more darts hit my right arm and upper body, painful but not incapacitating. There was a lull in firing when he might have replaced the magazine, then the pops came faster and more furiously. All of the darts missed. I had pulled well ahead of him.

Less than a hundred meters away was one of the massive pylon structures, barely visible in the thickening snow. If I reached it I could escape down the emergency stairway that spiraled through its interior. Perhaps the alien wouldn't follow. Some of the motorists might have reported the running gun battle to the police by now, if only because of superficial damage done to their expensive vehicles by the fusillade of stun-darts.

I heard a distant shout in the Haluk language and understood only one word: *coming.*

I didn't dare look over my shoulder, but I had a bad feeling that Black Leather had pulled his scorched shit together and joined the chase. Slush was beginning to accumulate underfoot in spite of the deicing grid.

Run, Helly, run! It's not far now. Don't slow down . . .

But I was. Residual chemicals circulating in my bloodstream had diminished my stamina. My lungs were on fire,

my vision was going blurry and weird, and my leg muscles
were seizing up.

Rats.

The two Haluk behind me were shouting back and forth
to each other. No one in the soundproofed vehicles would
hear them, much less catch the alien intonation. Brown
Fleece had once again stopped shooting at me with the
Ivanov. Maybe he was out of ammo.

I quit jinking among the cars and did a straight sprint,
tearing along the line of glowing little eyes that divided lane
five from lane four, squinting into the misty headlight glare.
Snow pelted my face. My mind was empty of all thought except attaining the shelter of the massive pylon that arched
above the road ahead of me, floodlit and crowned with ruby
aircraft-warning lights.

I was only forty meters away when I skidded on a slippery
patch, lost my footing, and crashed to the slushy pavement
right in front of a slow-moving Volvo taxi. I rolled aside just
in time to avoid being crushed, then heard a sudden loud
noise followed by shrill female screaming.

My fall had apparently saved me. I hauled myself up and
saw that the safety-glass windshield of the Acura sedan next
in line had been holed and spiderwebbed by a missile. The
hysterical woman behind the wheel cowered away from the
empty front passenger seat, where a slim black object with a
distinctive shape was embedded in the headrest. It was a
magnum stun-fléchette from an Allenby SM-440 or some
other high-powered carbine. Black Leather had brought in
heavy artillery.

"Lady, get down!" I yelled. She dropped out of sight, still
wailing, as her car moved on. A second fléchette barely
missed my head and soared over the traffic into the darkness
beyond lane one.

I took a dive myself, scrambling along on hands and
knees, hugging the shelter of the slow-rolling automobiles.
Then Black Leather changed his tactics. Big darts began to

whiz beneath the vehicles, clanging occasionally against their undercarriages and wheels. The fléchettes were no danger to the cars' self-sealing tires or sturdy chassis, but I wasn't at all sure that the thin armor of my anorak would protect me from them.

Was Leather using a warm-body scope or a light magnifier to spot me? The capability of either one would have been stretched to the limit in a snowstorm, with the target skittering among closely packed moving cars whose engines radiated infrared, on a heated pavement swirling with vapor. Maybe he wasn't trying to hit me at all, but hoping to flush me out of the traffic so his buddy could shoot me on the side of the road.

I went into a crouch and duckwalked ludicrously between the lanes, splashing through icy slop, doing my best to shield my legs under the skirts of the anorak. God only knows what the passing motorists thought about the wacky spectacle. Not a one had attempted to intervene personally. In their place I'd have opted for noninvolvement, too.

The firing stopped. So did I, a few minutes later.

I'd made it—sort of.

I was beneath the gargantuan pylon structure at last, shuddering with cold, squatting between creeping streams of traffic in lane five and the express lane. All I had to do now was cross the exposed shoulder, pass through an opening in the inner guardrail, and climb three steps onto a small platform where there was a door in the pylon wall. The illuminated sign above it said:

EMERGENCY EXIT ONLY
USE PHONE TO SUMMON ASSISTANCE

If only! The phone was on the wall right beside the door. As I contemplated the useless instrument in bemusement, a single small Ivanov stun-dart smacked into it and rattled onto the platform.

Wonderful. Brown Fleece was back in the game, probably shooting from the median catwalk, daring me to make a run for it.

What an idiot. If he hadn't given himself away, I might have dashed right across his field of fire. I tried without success to spot him in the blowing snow and steam clouds outside the pylon archway, but I figured that the dumb xeno couldn't be very far away. And his pal—

A magnum flechétte hummed past my head like a wasp. Its trajectory indicated that Black Leather was firing from the same lane divider I was parked on. A sudden gust of wind tore the mist and I saw him, his body eerily illuminated by the lights of cars passing on either side. He was no more than twenty-five meters away, with his carbine stock against his cheek.

I was a sitting duck.

"The next dart will take you down, Frost!" he shouted. "Get up! On your feet! Now!"

Why didn't he just nail me where I was?

. . . Because he was afraid that I'd convulse as the magnum load of toxin hit me, fall under the wheels of a car and be injured or killed. The earlier wild firing had been a panic response. Leather definitely intended to herd me onto the road shoulder, where Brown Fleece would drop me safely with the Ivanov.

An idea.

I turned away from Black Leather, ignoring his shouts, and studied the oncoming traffic in the express lane. A Volkswagen Lady Bug trundled past, followed by one of those ass-dragger Maseratis—scant shelter for a cowering fugitive. Behind the Italian car came an enormous black Dodge Bighorn sport utility vehicle with chrome rollbars and noseguards and great deep-tread balloon tires. It was the kind of transport that intrepid wilderness travelers favor for jaunts to Hudson Bay or the Canadian tundra. Silly role-players used them for city commuting.

"Stand up, Frost!" Black Leather yelled. He sent another fléchette over my head, missing me by a whisker. "On your feet, dammit!"

Instead, I began to squirm and moan as though I'd been nicked, crumpling onto the wet pavement. The Maserati passed by. As the lumbering SUV drew even with me, I rolled sideways beneath it, caught hold of an ice-encrusted shock absorber inside the monstrous right front wheel, hooked one leg over a transmission bracket and hoisted myself off the ground.

Screamed my lungs out. Then shut up abruptly.

I could hear the two Haluk demiclones bellowing incomprehensibly at each other in their own language. Would the ruse work? Only if Fleece, over on the catwalk and hopefully closer to me than Leather, took the bait.

Someone came running, splashing through snow saturated with meltwater. Legs clad in sodden suit trousers trotted along the shoulder, close beside the slow-moving juggernaut. Brown Fleece shouted: "One does not see him! Perhaps he is beneath, being dragged by the *blah*!"

Oh, yeah! I let go and fell unharmed between the four great wheels. Lay still a moment, then rolled quickly onto the shoulder as the big black SUV moved on. It was no trick at all avoiding the Toyota estate wagon creeping along behind it. Brown Fleece hadn't seen me. He was still scuttling along, Ivanov in hand, trying to peer under the chassis of the Dodge behemoth.

Black Leather did spot me and yelled a sharp warning to his buddy.

Too late. I tackled Fleece. We both went down hard, less than half a meter from the stream of traffic. The stun-pistol flew from his hand and disappeared among the cars. We wrestled on the shoulder pavement for a few moment before he managed to slither out of my grasp. He bounced to his feet, leaving me sprawled in the slush, and fetched me a nasty kick in the head. When he tried to stomp my face I seized his foot in midair with both hands, twisted viciously, and felt a satisfying crackle of anklebones. He howled and fell.

Fleece rolled in the direction of the guardrail, trying to rise in spite of his injured ankle, roaring with pain and rage. I lay much closer to the express lane traffic. I was having trouble standing myself. I'd bashed both knees badly during the tackle, and the kick in the head had rattled my neurons.

Fleece made a flying leap, knocked me onto my back, straddled my body, pinned my right arm, and began to batter my face with both fists. Spiking him in the kidney with my left mid-knuckle didn't do him much harm; the fleece jacket was excellent padding. I bucked up my hips, throwing him unexpectedly forward and forcing him to brace himself against falling by extending his arms. Then I caught him in the crotch and squeezed his genitals with all my strength. He screamed and writhed sideways into the express lane, clutching himself, just as a big Daimler towncar cruised sedately by.

Both left wheels went over his neck. The towncar deviated not a millimeter from its computerized vector. Its cocooned occupants might not even have seen what had happened. They would have felt only a minimal double bump.

In the stormy sky to the southwest a small constellation of fuzzy blue lights was intermittently visible, flying at a low altitude.

Chapter 5

I was dazed, hurting, soaked, and half frozen. My face was one huge bruise, my hands were flayed, and the rest of me felt like it'd been stomped by Cape buffalo.

With difficulty, I pulled Brown Fleece back onto the shoulder and crouched beside him. Blood leaked from his mouth. His head was impossibly twisted to one side, the jaw dislocated and the windpipe crushed. The pupils of his eyes were totally dilated, and a growing stench indicated that his sphincters had relaxed. When I thought to check his mangled throat for a pulse, I couldn't find any. The alien spirit that had animated his humanoid flesh had fled.

. . . But the unknown man whose DNA had been stolen to disguise Fleece was probably still alive, floating comatose in a dystasis tank on an exotic world, forced to share his genes again and again in order to create more perfidious replicas of himself.

I felt no sense of triumph at Brown Fleece's demise. Instead, there was a flashback. To the last time I'd killed Haluk who masqueraded as human beings.

On the planet Dagasatt, I'd found hundreds of demiclone subjects in paired tanks in a secret laboratory. Many of the Haluk floaters were already transformed into perfect human replicas, while the pathetic human templates had partially morphed into Haluk form, a side effect of the genen procedure that precluded rejection of their DNA by the alien receptors.

I shot each demiclone in the head. It was not a part of my life I was proud of, but I had no regrets, either.

Before I could rescue the captive human templates on Dagasatt, alien gunships arrived and leveled the facility with heavy blasters. I escaped the holocaust; but I still walked through that damned laboratory in my nightmares, staring in disbelief at the paired tanks with their Halukoid humans and humanoid Haluk . . .

Enough. It was time to deal with the nightmare at hand.

For the first time, I realized that the alien I had nicknamed Black Leather was no longer shooting at me. The reason why was sporadically visible up in the snowy air. The blue pulsing lights were mounted on a squadron of cop-hoppers coming out from the Highroad Authority barracks in Pickering. My surviving assailant now had other things on his mind besides the capture of Asahel Frost. He was probably hotfooting it back along the median catwalk to his limousine. If he had any brains at all, he'd already disposed of his Allenby stun-carbine through one of the drainage openings in the road shoulder.

The eastbound lanes of cars were finally beginning to accelerate slightly. Their dark-tinted side windows hid the occupants from my sight. Were the riders gaping at the scene beside the road as they glided by? Or had they done the sensible thing and activated their windows' projection option, substituting images of some pleasant landscape for the tedious reality of a creeping mass of vehicles bogged down on a stormy night?

The fuzzy blue lights in the sky came closer.

The cops were going to nab me.

Black Leather would reach his limo safely, escape the traffic jam, and vanish into the unmonitored maze of coun-
' lanes around the Kawartha Lakes. Meanwhile, the High-
' uthority would haul me off to the nearest Justice
media circus would strike up the band as I at-
'lain my abduction, my great escape, and my

subsequent lethal brawl with a well-dressed individual—undoubtedly possessed of impeccable credentials—whose true nature and motivation I didn't dare reveal.

Perhaps the police would believe I had acted in self-defense. Or they might just charge me with manslaughter.

I waited numbly for spotlights to stab down from the hoppers. Nothing happened. Four aircraft sailed over the pylon and continued moving in the direction of the distant accident scene.

I couldn't believe my luck. If the woman with the shattered windshield or any of the other motorists had reported shooting on the highroad, the news apparently had not yet been passed on by dispatchers to the cops in the air.

Time to hit the trail, buckaroo.

Adrenaline generated during the fight still kept me warm, but every bone in my body seemed to be aching, particularly my skull. I got up and started for the pylon platform, only to stop short as I realized what I was leaving behind: the only existing tangible evidence of a Haluk masquerading as a human being, evidence that had eluded me and my investigators for over three years. If I abandoned the demiclone corpse, it would almost certainly be taken to the closest county morgue. Brown Fleece's alien confederates would retrieve his remains with laughable ease.

That wasn't going to happen if I could prevent it.

I unzipped my anorak and fumbled for my pocket phone. Punched up the code that would connect me to the computer of my private hopper. I could program it to come and get me once I got down off the highroad. Even a few hundred meters away from the pylon the airspace would be unrestricted.

The phone said, *We are sorry. The code you have entered is temporarily ex-operational.*

Rats! The damned Haluk must have sabotaged it, perhaps to make sure I didn't use the aircraft to escape their dragnet. My car was probably ex-op, too.

Right. So I entered the personal code of my friend and associate Karl Nazarian.

Karl was a charter Rampart Starcorp stakeholder and
its first security chief at the operating HQ on the planet
Seriphos in the Perseus Spur. My father made the huge mistake of putting him out to pasture after long years of service,
installing a hotshot named Oliver Schneider in his place.
Schneider sold out to Galapharma and became their main
mole inside Rampart.

I came along and drafted Karl Nazarian to assist in the
search for my missing sister Eve. The veteran security man
helped make that operation a success, and continued the
good work in subsequent covert actions that culminated in
the capture of the material witness Schneider and the indict-
ment of Galapharma. Since then Karl had shared my private
investigations of the Haluk.

When Rampart became an Amalgamated Concern and I
agreed to become Acting Chief Legal Officer, I saw to it that
Karl was appointed Vice President for Special—i.e.,
spooky—Projects, a post that Simon had originally dra-
gooned me into accepting. Karl reported only to me. During
the pretrial phase of the Galapharma case, he supervised
"discoveries" for my cadre of legal eagles, helping to organize—and edit—ultrasensitive pieces of evidence. When that
work was done, he and his small staff of trustworthy cronies
occupied themselves gathering information about the shady
machinations of the big businesses that called themselves
the Haluk Consortium. Not that I was in a position to do
anything with the intelligence during the trial, other than
pass on the juicier bits to Ef Sontag.

Karl was the only person I would have trusted to do the
delicate psychotronic interrogation of Lorne Buchanan. I'd
˙˙ded my early hopes for the Barky Hunt to him, too. And
˙˙˙erately needed his help again.

˙˙˙˙re." The gnarled face, like a topographic map

of Armenia divided by a rocky cleaver of a nose, gazed at me from the phone screen. "Good God, Helly, you look like a drowned rat. A thoroughly buggered-up drowned rat."

"I feel even worse. I'm sitting on the shoulder of the Ottawa Highroad in a snowstorm, next to the corpse of a Haluk demiclone."

"That's fantastic! You're certain it's a Haluk?"

"Absolutely. The demi's mine if I can sneak him out of here before the county mounties spot us. It could happen any minute. Can you come and do an evac in your hopper? Mine's ex-op."

A shocked silence, then: "I'm not in Toronto Conurb. I'm nearly 1,200 kilometers away, out in the Kenora at Kingfisher Lodge."

I knew what that had to mean. "Oh, shit—not Dan!"

"I'm afraid so. Your brother flew the coop a couple of hours ago. He had help. Four of the six guards are dead. The survivors can't tell us much. The lodge just wasn't secured for a massive armed assault. An EMP blast took out the sensors and the rest of the electronics. A single large hopper carrying a dozen bandits did the job in less than ten minutes."

"Karl, there's a good chance that Dan didn't escape. He might have been kidnapped by Haluk."

"Christ!"

"My sister Beth could also be in danger. The aliens might try to nab her, too. She'll need round-the-clock security."

"I'll get InSec over to her place immediately. What kind of a cluster-fuck have we got going here?"

"The situation is even worse than you might think. Earlier this evening two Haluk demiclones snatched *me.* Bold as brass. The bastards took me right off the Underground Path in the midst of the Friday night crush. They talked to each other about some plan involving Dan and maybe Beth. I couldn't make any sense of it. My knowledge of the Haluk language is too rusty. I managed to get out of their limousine when the Ottawa Highroad shut down with a multicar accident. One of the alien goons is with me here, stone cold dead on the tarmac. The other one skipped out."

"Oh, boy. More demiclone operatives! Just what we were afraid those blue bastards would do—"

"Listen, Karl. You know how vital it is for us to hang on to this corpse and get it to Bea Mangan for a genetic assay. But I can't use regular Rampart Security for transport. There's no way I could explain this situation to them. And if we're caught with the stiff, Rampart itself could face criminal charges. I killed the Haluk accidentally, in self-defense, but body-snatching is a felony, and interfering with the scene of a fatality could lead to a charge of obstruction of justice, at the very least. You got any thoughts?"

"You say you want to take the body to Mangan right away?"

"I'll check with her first, but I know she won't have any scruples about cooperating. This is the break we've been waiting for. The smoking gun that proves the Haluk are infiltrating humanity."

"Then call Bea herself for a lift," Karl advised. "Her place in Fenelon Falls is—what?—only fifty klicks or so north of the highroad. She's sure to have a hopper at her disposal. Or her husband Charlie will."

"Damn. I should have thought of that. The Haluk punched out my lights and I'm kinda nebular at the moment."

"Is there anything else I can do to help?"

I tried to think. It wasn't easy. "Cover me with Sean Callahan at Rampart Tower InSec. Just before the Haluk grabbed me down on the Path I phoned Sean and asked for help. He sent a situation team, but too late to do any good. Tell him I'm with you—that my emergency turned out to be a false alarm. He'll be suspicious, but there's nothing we can do about that."

"Listen, Helly, if you can't reach Bea Mangan, call me again. I'll get to you, but it could take a while."

"Let's hope it doesn't come to that. I think you should return to Toronto as soon as possible. We'd better meet at Bea's place. I don't want to go back to my apartment just yet. Haluk might have the place staked out. *Hasta luego.*" I ended the call.

The cold was beginning to get to me. My hood had come off again and melting snow ran from my hair into my two blackened eyes. I wiped them, cringing at the pain, pulled the hood up, and summoned Mangan's personal code from the dex. The phone buzzed.

"Pick it up," I prayed. "Please, Bea." I stared at the small blank screen, shivering hard now, and waited. After five buzzes a robot voice asked me if I wished to continue my attempt to reach Beatrice Mangan directly, or if I wished to go to voice mail and leave a message. I told it, "Try again." The robot hadn't said she was unavailable; for some reason she just wasn't choosing to answer. Busy people did that all the time.

The buzzes resumed, and every five seconds the artificial voice cut in again. I kept saying, "Try again," and watched the display that said STAND BY FOR CONNECTION. Snowflakes fell on me and the demiclone corpse, coating us with tiny points of light that sparkled in the sweeping car headlights.

Beatrice Mangan, who held the rank of Chief Superintendent in the ICS Forensic Division, was a respected expert in molecular biology and the criminal aspects of genetic engineering. She was also an old friend from my days in the enforcement arm of the Interstellar Commerce Secretariat, one of the few people who had not believed the trumped-up charges that led to my disgrace and dismissal.

I had drawn her into the Galapharma conspiracy almost from the beginning of my own involvement. She helped me to nail Bronson Elgar, Galapharma assassin and master of dirty tricks—who unfortunately proved to be completely human. Later, she'd continued to lend her expertise to my quest for evidence that Haluk demiclones were wearing Earthling bodies with nefarious intent.

Bea had shared my frustration when every likely lead dug up by Karl and his associates petered away into failure or uncertainty. The efficient robotic cleaners so ubiquitous in modern society made it almost impossible to find castoff bits of incriminating DNA in starships or buildings that we knew had harbored faux humans. The biosamples Karl's people did manage to glean had been too badly damaged by mechanical housekeepers to be conclusive.

But now I had a whole demiclone corpse for Bea to analyze—if she'd just answer her goddamn phone!

All she had to do to prove conclusively that Fleece was a Haluk in disguise was take cellular material from him, run it through a fine-spectrum genome analyzer, and compare its DNA profile to the genetic marker data that Lorne Buchanan had just turned over to Efrem Sontag. By consulting the population database, she could also ascertain the identity of the human template who had been used to engineer Fleece's transformation. Along with our other evidence, the demiclone corpse would tangibly demonstrate to the Commonwealth Assembly that Haluk were infiltrating humanity.

What Fleece's body wouldn't necessarily prove was malicious intent, although we could show that the Haluk leader had lied when he claimed that all of the living demiclones had gone to the Haluk Cluster to serve as goodwill ambassadors. Getting more concrete evidence of alien evil-doing might take a long time, unless—

The interminable buzzing stopped.

"Bea? Thank God! I'd about given up."

"Helly?" a nonrobotic voice said. "That is you, isn't it? Your code is security-blanked and the video pickup on your phone isn't working very well." Bea Mangan's gentle round face, framed with a loosely wound turban of white toweling, smiled at me. She'd been taking a bath.

"It's probably melted snow blurring the sensor. I'm sitting on the side of the Ottawa Highroad in a blizzard, and I have a wonderful present for you. The only catch is, you have to come and collect it—and me, too. Do you have a hopper available? I'm not far from the Clarington interchange."

"Charlie and I can be there in fifteen minutes."

"No. It would be best if your husband knew nothing about this—at least for the time being. It's a matter that relates to our . . . alien extracurricular activities."

She stared in silence for a moment. "Tell me your exact location."

I gave it to her, trying to keep my voice from quavering. "Bea? Bring along a thermos of hot coffee and an electric blanket, will you? Maybe some painkillers and antibiotic goop, too."

"Oh, my. What *have* you been up to?"

"We'll also need a body bag." I punched out using a frigid finger, the color of which closely approximated Haluk blue.

I made one last phone call, to the voice-mail option of Efrem Sontag's ultrasecure private code, and left a request for him to allow Bea Mangan unlimited access to the computer files obtained from Lorne Buchanan. I told him I had finally obtained a valid biosample from a Haluk demiclone for Bea to analyze, but gave no other details. I asked him not to call me; I would call him.

Then, groaning with the effort, I grasped Brown Fleece by the wrists. It took nearly all my dwindling strength to drag him to the pylon platform and get him through the emergency exit door onto the upper landing of the open spiral staircase. There was no way I could carry him down, but I'm not squeamish and Fleece was beyond caring, so I folded him over the stairwell railing and let him fall thirty meters to the bottom of the shaft. Then I lugged him off into the snow.

We hid together in a nearby thicket, me shivering convulsively and he taking it easy, until Bea Mangan's hopper arrived. She was flying very low, without navigation lights, to avoid being seen from the highroad. Snow was falling thickly. I staggered out to greet her, arms wide, using my last erg of energy, and fell flat on my face. By then I was so deeply hypothermic that I suspect my internal temperature nearly matched Fleece's. Her scanner found me anyhow.

She used an antigrav tote to hoist me into the aircraft's passenger compartment, stripped off most of my icy clothes, wrapped me in the electric blanket, and clamped my chilled fingers around a cup of steaming coffee. I made pitiful noises as the thawing process began.

"You belong in a hospital, Helly. I'll call Charlie and he can have an ambulance—"

"N-N-N-Noo!" I groaned, through chattering teeth. Her husband, Charles White, was a family practitioner in the small resort community of Fenelon Falls. He was aware that Bea had given me unofficial help gathering evidence of the Galapharma conspiracy, but he knew nothing about the Haluk demiclones.

"I'm going to have Charlie look at you, whether you like it or not," she insisted stubbornly. "You need a full-body scan."

Which would turn up the needle puncture in my calf and suspicious drug residuals in my blood. Perhaps Dr. White would have to be let in on the secret after all.

"Go get your present, Bea." I jerked my head in the direction of the thicket. "Over under the little trees. Sorry if he's a trifle stinky."

"First, you get dosed with analgesic. It may make you drowsy."

She held a device tipped with a glass knob to my jugular. *Ooh. Fly me to the moon.* Then she smeared my damaged face and hands with antibiotic and pressed prickly bruise-diffuse pads gently around my eyes. A not quite painful tingling ensued. I could feel the swelling begin to subside.

"Feel better?"

"Much. Got the body bag?"

She nodded resignedly. "Who's the deceased?"

"Don't know his name. But he's a genuine twenty-four karat totally authentic Haluk demiclone. I killed him . . . didn't mean to. Mighty convenient for a comprehensive DNA assay, though."

"Jesus, Mary, and Joseph!" she said.

"I don't think he's part of their congregation. Check with Great Almighty Luk."

Bea was dressed in an orange snowmobiler's suit with a fur ruff around the hood. She slipped a pair of protective plastic mitts over her gloves and went to get the corpse.

Pain free at last, I sipped caffeine-laden elixir and felt warmth and life seep back into my anatomy. In a few minutes Bea returned with the loaded tote floating behind her and stowed the sealed body bag in the hopper's cargo compartment. Then we lofted into the sky. She kept the running lights off and flew low until we were safely away from the highroad.

I finished the coffee, drew the blanket close about me, and allowed myself a nasty smile, thinking about Black Leather. He'd have a hell of a lot of explaining to do once he reached Mount Julian. Not only had he lost me, but he'd also let his fellow demiclone fall into the hands of the one person in a position to do serious dirt to the alien cause.

My eyes were drifting shut, but I resisted sleep. Something important about the town of Mount Julian . . . *What?*

Other thoughts swirled in my punchy mind: I'd have to leave Earth as soon as possible . . . stay out of reach of Haluk kidnappers and consortium thugs . . . at Phlegethon, go in without giving away my identity . . . disguised . . . mustn't let Barky know I'm the guy who paid off Ram Mahtani . . . need some gimmick to get me close to him . . . trade goods . . . meanwhile, Karl works with Bea and Ef Sontag . . . coordinates the search for my brother.

Poor old Dan! Once, I was the prodigal son, he was the golden boy with high hopes of someday heading up Rampart. Now the Haluk had taken him—

Suddenly, I thought I knew where.

"Bea?" I mumbled.

"Yes, Helly."

"Do something very important for me. My phone . . . inside pocket. Find Karl Nazarian's personal code in the dex. Call him as soon as you get to your house. Tell him you have me and the dead demiclone safe. Tell him . . . urgent he takes an armed security team to Alistair Drummond's former country home in Mount Julian. Place might be a hive of Haluk . . . maybe they're taking my kidnapped brother Dan there . . . old bastard *himself* might still be alive . . . crazy as a bedbug, working with the blueberries. Tell Karl."

"I'll tell him everything you said," Bea Mangan said, "even though it doesn't make much sense. Rest now, Helly. It's the best thing for you."

So I did.

I woke up in a quaintsy-poo guest room, tucked in a four-poster bed beneath a flowery comforter. I was wearing an honest-to-God flannel nightshirt, and there were small adhesive medical sensors stuck to my forehead, sternum, and inner left wrist, which I peeled off and dropped into the wastebasket. The old-style bedside alarm clock with external bells read 7:13. The turquoise pin from my neck scarf, my pocket phone, wallet, and wrist chronometer were there on a bedstand. I ascertained from the latter that it was Saturday evening. I'd just about slept the clock around.

Rolling off the bed, I lurched over to the chintz-curtained windows and opened the blinds. Gray twilight. A soft rain was falling and the snow had all melted away. The cottage garden had patches of pink daffodils, purple and white crocuses with their petals clenched, and yellow forsythia bushes. Green-painted wrought-iron furniture stood on a patch of winter-sere lawn faintly tinged with new growth. Beyond a screen of balsams and budding maple trees, Sturgeon Lake was a silver glimmer beneath a cloudy sky.

The bedroom door opened behind me. I turned around and there was Dr. Charles White, looking benign and reassuring in an open-necked shirt, khaki pants, and a tattered brown cardigan. He was a tall man, skinny as a rail, with skin the color of polished teak and eyes that were a startling sea-green. His tightly curled dark hair was worn in a sculptured style, with long sideburns like the cheekpieces on a Roman helmet.

"Ah, Helly. So you're finally up and about." He pronounced it *a-boot* in the good old Canadian way. "The med monitors showed you perking along in fine fettle before you eighty-sixed the poor little things. How do you feel?"

The mirror above the dresser showed me a sandy-stubbled face, slightly purplish-green around the eyes, but unlikely to frighten timid toddlers.

"Good enough. Thanks for the repair job, Charlie. I presume I'm pretty much okay?"

"You're normal except for scabs on your knuckles and healing contusions. There'll be no lingering side effects from the paralyzing agent. The needle only grazed your calf, gave you a minimal dose."

"Lucky me." I checked my bare shank. A faint red line was the only souvenir of my narrow escape.

He tactfully didn't ask what kind of fine mess I'd gotten myself into this time. "Fresh clothes for you in the closet. Your business suit was ruined but the handmade cowboy boots survived with a little attention from the valet machine. The syringe puncture in the left boot is repaired. I've got supper downstairs, pizza and spinach-tomato salad. Karl and I have already eaten, but we'll keep you company with coffee and homemade German chocolate cake."

"Pizza and salad would be marvelous, and you know I'm a sucker for Bea's cake. Is she here?"

He shook his head. "She went to her lab in Commerce Tower to do some work. Don't worry about your deceased friend. I'm Deputy Coroner for Victoria County. The body is tucked away in our little hospital morgue with a John Doe tag on its toe, and none of the staff saw Bea and me bring it in. It'll be secure for as long as need be."

I hesitated. "What did Bea tell you about the guy?"

"That he drugged and kidnapped you. That he's important. That overzealous parties in the Secretariat for Xenoaffairs might try to take his body away, and we have to prevent that."

"I didn't mean for you to get involved in this, Charlie. It could be a massive crock of shit."

He shrugged and smiled and headed for the door. "Well, I'm involved. So don't worry about it."

"Give me a few minutes to dress," I said. "I'll be right down."

I shucked the nightshirt, emptied my bladder, slapped depilatory gel on my face, and had a quick shower. The clothes my host had provided were just my style: Levi's, a black rollneck tee, and a red wool buffalo-plaid overshirt.

Before I left the guest bedroom I entered Bea's personal code in my phone. She didn't answer. Then I called a guy named Cosmo Riendeau, the night supervisor at Rampart Fleet Maintenance at Oshawa Starport. For special consideration, he and his crew had been expediting the off-ticket refit of the good ship *Makebate*.

"She's ready to rumble when you are, Helly," Riendeau told me cheerfully. "We tracked down an LRIR-1400J scanner for you in Chicago, scheduled to be installed in an Astrophysical Survey vessel. Bribery triumphed and it'll be here tomorrow. I tested the new dissimulator and weaponry systems myself. That buggy of yours is now one righteous bandit-killer."

I resolved to send the perennially funds-strapped survey a replacement scanner, plus a corporate donation, as soon as possible. "The ship's gig all refitted, too?"

"Absolutely. Extra shielding and new cannons. The provisions and the personal gear you ordered are stowed, and the fuel bunkers are topped. *Makebate*'s new range is forty-kay lights at a conservative fifty ross cruising pseudo-vee—twenty-eight thou if you put the pedal to the metal and exceed eighty. Of course, from now on you'll have to eat and sleep on the flight deck. The only accommodations we didn't rip out for the jumbo fuel-cell installation were the captain's head and a little snack bar. It's gonna be pretty claustrophobic."

Cosmo Riendeau and his team had no notion why I'd had the starship modified so radically. There had been no alternative when I conceived my aborted exploration of the Haluk Cluster, 17,200 light-years from the closest Rampart refueling depot in the Perseus Spur; but now the ship's extreme range gave me a tactical advantage in tracking Barky Tregarth to Zone 3. Normally, a Y-770 speedster like *Makebate* would have been obliged to make three pit stops to cover the 9,600 lights to Phlegethon at top ross. Rampart owned no planets along the route to the inner galactic arm where I might have refueled with a reasonable expectation of confidentiality, and unfriendly folks would have been able to follow my progress easily if I'd used commercial facilities. But now I could approach Barky's world from a totally unexpected direction if I wanted to, with fuel to spare for the trip back to Earth.

I said, "Nice going, Cosmo. There'll be a juicy bonus for you and the gang, subject to keeping zipped lips about the refit details per our original agreement."

"Goes without saying," Riendeau said. "That's a joke."

I gave an obligatory chuckle. "One final thing: Have you or your people noticed any outsiders poking around the shop during the past couple of days, maybe asking questions about when my ship would be ready?"

"Nobody came during the night shift. I can check the day and swing crews. Call you back."

"Do that. And get hold of Monte Gill at Fleet Security and tell him to post armed guards at *Makebate*'s bay until I fly her out of there."

"You got 'em."

I thanked Riendeau and ended the call, then went downstairs to the cottage kitchen. Through the window, a Rampart hopper was visible on the pad beyond the rainswept garden: Karl Nazarian's ride. He was sitting at the table with Charlie White, drinking coffee. A delicious-looking cake, only minimally dissected, sat on a platter covered with a glass dome.

"You look pretty decent, considering," Karl said.

"There's nothing wrong with me that food won't fix."

"Drink lots of water, too," Charlie ordered. He had already laid out the salad and a pitcher of icewater, and he now took a plate holding three huge wedges of steaming pepperoni pizza out of the microwave and gave it to me.

"Yes, Doctor. Thank you, Doctor." I picked up a dripping slice, corraled the cheese strings, and started chomping. Even warmed over, it was very good. I was both famished and thirsty.

Karl said, "A few things happened while you were sleeping."

Charlie gave us a tactful look. "Why don't I let you two discuss your business in private."

"Don't go," I said. "You're part of the Baker Street Irregulars now by virtue of the body-snatching. Accessory to a felony. You might as well know the rest of the story. Just let me get an update on current events from Karl first."

The doctor nodded and sat down again. He uncovered the cake, cut three generous pieces, and passed them around.

Karl said to me, "Your sister Beth is safe. She hasn't left her house. I personally told her that Dan had escaped with the help of unknown confederates, and she seemed genuinely surprised. Pleased, at first, but the fact that four of Dan's InSec guards were killed cooled her jets a little. She's promised not to go to the media or otherwise impede our investigation. I suspect she might be rethinking Big Brother's protestations of innocence."

I doubted it. "We'll have to keep Beth well guarded or even get her offworld. The two Haluk thugs who bagged me last night had some sort of plans for her . . . What about Dan himself? Did you check out Alistair Drummond's old place in Mount Julian?"

Karl's expression turned grim. "I had a Rampart incident team hop over there as soon as Bea called me last night. They were there within an hour. By then the firefighters had pretty much gotten things under control."

I yelped around a mouthful of pizza. "A fire—"

"The big old wood-frame main house was totally destroyed, right down to the foundations. The battalion chief said the place went up like a bomb. It must have happened just about the time you first contacted me from the highroad. There were no human remains found. Or Haluk. A sophisticated accelerant that generated a very high-temperature burn was used to torch the house. All that's left is white ash and slag."

"Damn! The demi who got away must have sounded the alarm. A fire would have ensured that there were no bits and pieces of incriminating DNA left behind."

"I went out to the scene myself this morning and interviewed the arson investigation people. Talked to the neighbors—such as there are in an upscale area like that. The property has extensive grounds, a wooded perimeter with a security fence, beam-guarded frontage on Stony Lake. It's not easy for unauthorized persons to get close to it. The adjacent homes are owned by wealthy types or corporations that use them mostly in summer. No one saw anything unusual immediately preceding the fire. Of course, there was a minor blizzard raging at the time. A caretaker woman who lives in a place half a kilometer down the shore says the house was inhabited for at least the past two months. She thought she might have seen a hoppercraft landing on the property yesterday afternoon, when the weather was better."

"Who's the owner of record?" I asked.

"Livonia Holdings SC, a Carnelian subsidiary, bought it from Galapharma after Alistair Drummond's death. About a year ago Livonia leased the place to S'yoma tib Katatosi—a Y'tata trading company—after installing a heavy-duty ventilation system. The Y's wanted it for an executive vacation retreat. An entity that I reached at the Y'tata embassy claims that the Katatosi outfit is only sporadically in residence on Earth. Conveniently absent at present. The entity was of the opinion that Katatosi *might* have sublet the house to some human business clients. The place was automatically supplied with food and the like by RoboGrocer and kept clean by Livonia-programmed domestic bots. There was no live-in human help."

"Uh-huh. What about the security system?"

"That fed to a Y outfit in Toronto that alerted the local fire crew. The Y'tata security entities refused to give me any specifics."

"This suggestion of a Y'tata-Haluk connection could be significant, Karl. When I talked to Jake Silver about the Barky Hunt Friday night, he told me about a suppressed ZP report about collaborating pirates of the same two races operating in Zone 3, hijacking transactinide carriers."

"Zone 3?" Karl's expression was incredulous. "Haluk in the Sagittarius Whorl? That doesn't sound likely."

"I didn't think so, either. But Jake's source said that the Haluk presence was deliberately hushed up by Xenoaffairs. Maybe the blueballs are encouraging Y'tata freebooters to steal ultraheavy elements so that there'll be a shortage."

"To increase the profitability of their own trans-ack trade with us?"

"Maybe. Barky Tregarth is supposed to be hanging out in

Zone 3, too. Jake got me a solid lead on him that I intend to check out as soon as possible. If the Haluk are operating in the Sag, I'll bet Barky knows about it."

"There's more bad news," Karl said, "maybe unconnected to this business. Lorne Buchanan is dead. Apparently a suicide."

"My God! The secret Galapharma file data—"

"Relax. Everything pertaining to the Haluk was transferred to Efrem Sontag on Friday evening, just as Buchanan had agreed. His body was found Saturday morning in his Rosedale house. There was no note. He had apparently shot himself in the head with an antique Glock handgun."

"The poor bastard didn't kill himself," I declared. "You know that as well as I do, Karl! The Haluk found out what he'd done and murdered him. Maybe to discourage other Galapharma executives from coming forward with evidence against them."

"We'll never prove it."

"Probably one of those security people Buchanan brought to Rampart Tower—" I started to say.

"Any demis in the bunch will be long gone by the time we're able to check their DNA. It's a dead end, Helly. Now that they know we can spot them with the genetic marker, they'll be ultracautious."

"Shit. I hoped we'd be able to keep the Haluk in the dark about that—at least for a little while longer."

The good doctor had been looking more and more dismayed as the mystifying two-way conversation proceeded. I said, "Charlie, it's about time we put you into the picture."

He said, "Did I understand you to say that *Haluk* were responsible for your abduction yesterday? And for Buchanan's murder?"

"Yep. They probably kidnapped my brother Daniel, too."

"That's appalling! Why haven't you notified the Secretariat for Xenoaffairs?"

"Because SXA is hand in glove with the consortium and the other members of the Hundred Concerns who have a vested interest in keeping the Haluk happy. SXA knows very well that I have a hard-on for our devious blue brethren. As we lawyers would say, I am not a credible accusant."

"Then inform CCID—"

"There's something else, Charlie. Bea's probably working to prove it even as we speak. The Haluk who tried to nab me were demiclones. They had been illegally engineered into perfect human replicas."

"What! And the dead man in my morgue—"

"Is almost certainly an alien. Bea will know for certain when she finishes her genetic assay. The Haluk have been using demiclones as secret agents against humanity for several years now—predating their treaties with us."

"I can't believe that no one in authority knows about this!"

"People in Xenoaffairs and Interstellar Commerce almost certainly have proof of demiclone activity on Earth and on other human worlds that they've concealed from the public and the Commonwealth Assembly. But no one in SXA or ICS will blow the whistle because high officials in both secretariats are creatures of Big Business. Mustn't endanger the profits of the Haluk Consortium."

I'd finished the pizza and salad, and now I started on the slab of German chocolate cake. "Let me tell you the story, Charlie. It's a real seven-ply gasser."

The scheme was hatched from a miscegenation of deluded idealism and corporate greed. It started with a crackpot idea conceived by a naive woman who hoped to foment peace and love between the Haluk and humanity by means of genetic engineering.

Emily Blake Konigsberg was a brilliant and very attractive scientist who worked for Galapharma in the years before its unscrupulous CEO decided to take over the Rampart

worlds. Emily and Alistair Drummond became lovers. In the
course of their pillow talk she told him about her great
dream.

Emily was keenly interested in the Haluk and deplored the
fact that our two races were enemies. As you know, the
Haluk bitterly resented the fact that we halted their aggressive expansion into the Perseus Spur, forced them to accept
a humiliating armistice, and declined to share our advanced
technology with them. It was Emily's belief that the refusal
of the Haluk to even consider detente was largely rooted in
their envy of our stable physiology. She was probably right.

Humanity was spawned on a relatively benign planet.
Aside from some relatively minor seasonal glitches, we're
physically and mentally operational all year round. But the
Haluk evolved on a world with a highly eccentric orbit that
annually carried it into a region of intense solar radiation.
The result was allomorphy, an adaptation that originally enabled the race to survive.

For about two hundred days each year, while the home
planet was sufficiently distant from its sun, the ancestral
Haluk existed as smart, active, sexual, somewhat humanoid
individuals called gracilomorphs. But then, as the orbiting
world approached the zone of strong solar radiation, Haluk
bodies underwent protective changes. For about sixty days,
during their lepidodermoid phase, they became increasingly
thick-skinned and sluggish. They lost their sexuality. Their
brains began to power down, leaving them incapable of high
mental function. Finally, in a climactic Big Change, the lepidos morphed into a coffinlike testudinal phase. They slept
inside radiation-resistant golden chrysalids for 140 days.
When the home planet once again swung away from its fe-
rocious sun, gracile Haluk awakened from estivation and
emerged from their protective shells to carry on their interrupted lives.

Eventually the Haluk achieved interstellar travel. On
new planets, allomorphy was no longer a survival trait but

instead a tremendous inconvenience that slowed racial progress. Millennia passed. As the Haluk expanded throughout their star-cluster, the allomorphic cycles of individuals lost their ancestral synchrony. This lessened the annual nuisance somewhat. At least they weren't all asleep at the same time. But their civilization—and most particularly their science—suffered a great disadvantage compared to that of other stargoing sapients.

Especially humans.

The Haluk entered the Milky Way Galaxy at the tip of the Perseus Spur and established eleven colonial planets. At the time, the only local race having starships were the Qastt, and they were easily subjugated. But when humanity extended its powerful hegemony to the Spur, Haluk expansion was stopped cold by our superior technology.

So they hated and feared us and refused to trade or enter into normal diplomatic relations.

Emily Konigsberg told her lover, Drummond, that she was convinced Haluk hostility could be mitigated and the race's great potential realized if their allomorphy were to be eradicated. It was her opinion that the job could be done easily through advanced techniques of genetic engineering. She sincerely believed that Commonwealth policy denying this technology to the Haluk was immoral. If Galapharma Concern could see its way clear to bypass CHW strictures—that is, work with her to set up genen therapy programs among the blue aliens—a great wrong would be righted.

Alistair Drummond didn't have an altruistic bone in his body, but he liked Konigsberg's idea all the same. The Haluk Cluster was rumored to possess abundant supplies of valuable transactinide elements, which the aliens had heretofore adamantly refused to trade. Galapharma stood to make enormous profits in the therapy venture, doing well by doing good.

So Alistair entered into secret negotiations with the Haluk

leader, the Servant of Servants of Luk, and the deal was done. Emily set up a genetic engineering lab on the principal Haluk Spur colony, Artiuk, staffed entirely by Galapharma personnel. The project achieved success by inserting human genes into the Haluk. Modified alien individuals remained in the active, brainy, gracile phase permanently. And because the therapy also modified Haluk germ cells—so did their offspring.

The great achievement was doubly illegal under Commonwealth law, which forbade meddling with the genetic heritage of a sovereign race, to say nothing of sharing human DNA with aliens. This didn't bother Alistair Drummond. Galapharma was one of the almighty Big Seven Concerns. He figured that if they were caught, they could pressure the Commonwealth Assembly to legalize the scheme retroactively since it was good for business.

Eventually, that's just what happened.

It was a minor embarrassment to Emily Konigsberg that the only viral vector suitable for allomorph eradication therapy was not one under patent to Galapharma Amalgamated Concern. PD32:C2 was an exclusive product of Gala's small rival, Rampart Starcorp, which had obtained the CHW mandate to the Perseus Spur after Galapharma withdrew in 2176. The vector could not be grown under laboratory conditions or synthesized; its sole source was the planet Cravat, owned by Rampart.

PD32:C2 could be purchased on the open market, of course—cautiously, so Rampart would not know that the stuff was being resold at an enormous markup—or it could be stolen. Gala agents and Haluk pirates pursued both courses of action, while Alistair Drummond tried to engineer a hostile takeover of Rampart in order to regain control of the Spur planets—especially Cravat—that Galapharma had so imprudently let slip out of its hands.

At the same time, the wily CEO encouraged other large

Concerns—Sheltok, Carnelian, Bodascon, and Homerun—to join the illicit Haluk trading partnership. There was safety in numbers, and plenty of profits to go around. The Haluk were hungry for all kinds of advanced human technology and willing to pay through the nose.

Emily and Alistair were no longer romantically involved. Her idealistic pursuit of a "greater good" allowed her to turn a blind eye to the commercial shenanigans orchestrated by her ex-lover while she expanded the therapy program, training Haluk scientists to build and operate dynamic stasis units. The aliens were very quick learners.

Too damn quick—but none of the human conspirators had any inkling of the awful truth.

One day the Servant of Servants of Luk proposed a new genetic enterprise to Emily. He had conceived a plan that would open a great new era in Haluk-human relations. Its fulfillment required "a small number" of demiclones. These Haluk in human guise were to become special cultural envoys to the populous planets of the Haluk Cluster, supposedly soothing the intense xenophobia that had poisoned any hope of rapprochement between the two races from the time of their first encounter over a hundred years earlier.

Emily Konigsberg was dubious about this bizarre notion. Demicloning, like other extreme forms of genetic engineering, had long been outlawed in the Commonwealth of Human Worlds. But eventually she gave in to the Servant's pressure and even contributed her own DNA to the project.

When Alistair Drummond found out about the demiclones, he was furious. He believed the Servant actually intended to use fake humans to spy on the Concerns and gain trade advantages. Drummond's first inclination was to shut down the demiclone project, but he relented after the Servant hinted that serious consequences would ensue. By then, illegal trade with the Haluk had generated immense profits that Galapharma and its Concern collaborators were reluctant to forfeit.

Drummond hatched a ploy to minimize the danger of industrial espionage. He ordered Konigsberg to incorporate a genetic marker into the demiclone procedure without Haluk knowledge. In addition, the sole genen facility producing the clones was placed under strict human supervision, on a remote human world. Galapharma itself undertook to supply the luckless donors of human DNA.

Alistair Drummond's precautions worked well enough . . . until the aliens learned how to perform the complex demiclone procedure without the help of human scientists, built secret labs of their own, and discovered how easy it was to defeat the sporadic DNA testing of employees that was supposed to prevent Haluk ringers from infiltrating the human race.

As I reached this point in my narrative, my pocket phone trilled. It was Cosmo Riendeau. I excused myself from the table and went to answer the call in the cottage's living room, urging Karl to continue the story while I was gone.

Cosmo's report was disturbing. "Only one outsider took an interest in your starship, Helly—a very pretty young woman from the accounting department in Rampart Tower. She showed up here in Oshawa yesterday, around noon, and apparently had the proper pass and personal ID. This cutie told Ole Wiren, the day-shift supervisor, that she was at the port to reconfigure a billing procedure for our number crunchers. She said she was on lunch break and ever so curious about the big starships, and she begged Ole for a quick tour. He admits he came down with instant beaver fever and showed her around."

"She saw *Makebate*."

"I'm afraid so. Your boat was obviously something special—not just another freighter or ExSec cruiser. Ole told her your starship was almost ready to leave the barn—even let slip that we'd done a fuel-cell augmentation. Sorry, Helly. The whole team knew your refit was supposed to be

hush-hush, but that chick played poor Ole like a Stradivar-
ius."

"Probably no harm done," I lied. "Did the woman give her
name?"

"Dolores da Gama. I pulled her image and voice-signature
off the shop entry security monitor for you. Hold on while I
feed a dime."

He inserted a data disklet into his phone and a talking
image popped onto my screen. Da Gama was stacked like a
brick shithouse and had wide-set dark eyes, pouty lips, and
long black hair with a white blaze at the left temple. She
talked her way past the laxly guarded entrance to Rampart
Fleet Maintenance using a voice as sweet and seductive as
fireweed honey. If Dolores was a demiclone, her original
must have been a real hottie.

I cut off the replay. "Thanks for the information, Cosmo.
I'll look into this, but I'm sure everything's okay."

"Anything else I can do for you, Helly?"

"I'd like to lift off sometime early next week. Think you'd
have time to rig simple arm and leg restraints on the copilot's
chair—plus an exterior lock on the john door?"

"Prisoner transport, eh?"

"Something like that."

"I'll attend to it personally."

I thanked him and hit the End pad, then used the phone to
access Rampart's roster of accounting personnel.

There was no Dolores da Gama. Why wasn't I surprised?

I sent a copy of her mug shot to Sean Callahan at InSec
and told him to pass it along to his supervisor. I doubted that
the lovely lady would press her luck and try another incur-
sion, but Rampart Tower's doorkeepers had to be put on
alert.

And I had to get out of town before a fresh set of demiclone thugs came sniffing after me.

However, there was still unfinished business to be taken
care of with Simon, Ef Sontag, and a few other people. I also

needed to assemble certain items crucial to a successful Barky Hunt that probably wouldn't be available off-Earth.

I sat for a few minutes, thinking, then made two brief calls. The first was to Tony Becker, Rampart's brilliant but testy Vice President for Biotechnology, who grumped and bitched and asked questions that I didn't intend to answer. He only agreed to put together what I needed when I used both a carrot and a stick: the promise of a hefty bribe, plus a half-joking threat to have him fired if he didn't come through.

The second call went to Halimeda Opper, a venerable and trustworthy Reversionist party stalwart who was a media production designer by profession. She heard me out, then referred me to a theatrical supply house in Mississauga that would have exactly what I required.

I returned to the kitchen and helped myself to a second piece of German chocolate cake. Next to snickerdoodle cookies and rozkoz flan, it's my favorite confection. Karl was regaling Charlie with accounts of our more recent adventures with the Haluk—demiclone and au naturel—on Dagasatt and on the journey back to Earth following my capture of Oliver Schneider. I lowered my eyes modestly during the heroic parts, which seemed a lot more fun in retrospect than they'd been at the time.

When Karl wound down, Charlie said, "I'm still not clear on the aliens' motivation. Trade between humanity and the Haluk is regularized. On the face of it, we're friends. So why the continuing demiclone espionage?"

"Why indeed," I murmured. "Perhaps the Haluk have a hidden agenda that involves more than taking care of business. Perhaps they've had that agenda from the inception of the demiclone scheme! What if their moles have dug deep into the inner operations of the Hundred Concerns? What if they're rooting around inside our scientific establishment, our law enforcement agencies, and our government?"

"To what end?" He asked the question, but an intelligent man like Charlie White had to know the answer already. I spelled it out anyhow.

"Maybe the Haluk aren't willing to wait patiently while the Commonwealth Assembly doles out small numbers of new Milky Way worlds for them to colonize. I have this theory that population pressure back in the Haluk Cluster is dire—otherwise, why would they have made the desperate and difficult step of jumping to our galaxy in the first place? The only Spur colony of theirs I ever visited seemed conspicuously lacking in elbow room. The school I toured was jam-packed with youngsters. Now that allomorphy can be eradicated *in the germ line,* parents no longer pass on the allomorph trait to their offspring. Pretty soon everybody'll be wide awake back there in the Haluk Cluster, as well as in their Spur colonies. If they already have an overpopulation problem, doing away with allomorphy will make that problem worse."

"You believe the Haluk intend to seize planets in our galaxy by force?" Charlie said.

"I think it's a strong possibility. So do Karl and Bea and a few other voices crying in the wilderness."

"The difficulty," Karl interposed, "has been proving Haluk hostile intent beyond a shadow of a doubt. Placing concrete evidence before the Commonwealth Assembly so the matter must be openly debated—not swept under the rug, the way the Hundred Concerns and corrupt elements in SXA and ICS would prefer. Up until now, we've never even been able to prove conclusively that demiclones exist."

Charlie said, "The body in my morgue—"

"Is a corpus delicti," I said. "The legal meaning of that term has nothing to do with a cadaver. It means 'the body of the crime'—the substantial proof that an illegal act has been committed."

Charlie nodded slowly. His lucent green eyes had a de-

tached thousand-meter stare, looking into a future almost
too alarming to contemplate. "If only the Haluk weren't so
intelligent! It's said that they haven't simply purchased our
high technology—they've improved on it."

"That's a fact." Karl looked bleak as he cut himself another hunk of cake. It was almost gone. "Some of their starships are equal to the best we have. Most are inferior. But the
technology gap will close as they obtain advanced production machinery from us. There's still an embargo against
selling weapons to the Haluk, but you know how effective
that will be. Gunrunning to the Insaps is a fine old human institution, tremendously profitable."

"They'll wage war on us," I said, "unless we expose their
hostile intent. Force them to allow human inspection of their
worlds on pain of full trade interdiction."

"Force them?" Charlie White exclaimed. "In heaven's
name, how?"

"I'm working on it," I said.

"Do the Haluk know that?"

"Probably," I admitted.

"Maybe that's why they tried to kidnap you," Charlie said.

I'd pretty much come to the same conclusion. "Yeah. But
I'm damned if I can figure why they didn't just kill me outright. Why take me alive? I don't have possession of the crucial evidence against them. Efrem Sontag does, and he'll
back up the data and secure it so immaculately that not even
I can touch it. It's still too early in the game for us to have finalized our anti-Haluk strategy, so I can't spill any great se-
crets under psychotronic interrogation. And why would they
need to snatch my brother Dan and sister Beth along with
me?"

Charlie just shook his head.

Outside, the shades of night had fallen. Patio lights
gleamed in the rain and reflected on the smooth sides of
Karl's big hoppercraft. I ate the last piece of chocolate cake.

Charlie made fresh coffee and we sat around drinking it and waiting, not saying much.

Finally, about 2100 hours, Bea Mangan's hopper wafted down and parked beside Karl's. She came in through the back door, looking tired but pleased with herself, and dropped a magslate on the table in front of me. "Here's the report, Helly. I've already sent a copy of it to Delegate Sontag."

Charlie helped his wife off with her coat, heated water, and put a couple of peppermint teabags into a big china cup labeled $C_{10}H_{19}OH$. I pulled out a chair for Bea and apologized for the fact that we'd scoffed up all the cake. She said she'd eaten supper at the cafeteria in Commerce Tower. After she had relaxed for a few minutes and sipped some of the calming brew, I asked the pertinent question.

"What did your genetic assay show? Speak freely. Charlie knows the score now."

Bea gave me a reproachful look. "Helly, I thought we—"

I said, "Your husband is in this thing up to his neck, just like the rest of us. He deserves to know what's really going on."

"It's for the best," Charlie said to her. "At least now I know the importance of that bod stashed in my morgue under false pretenses."

"So—is he a demiclone?" I asked Bea.

"He is," she said, "provided the data Lorne Buchanan sent to Sontag are correct. The so-called marker incorporated by Emily Konigsberg is actually a unique suite of introns—multiple noncoding sequences of DNA—occurring on four different chromosomes, plus a single mutant exon from the complex controlling telomeric proteins. The genetic profile of the individual you nicknamed Brown Fleece contains both the intron suite and the mutant exon typical of demiclones."

"What are telomeric proteins?" I asked.

Dr. Charlie said, "Telomeres are ribbonlike appendages

on the ends of chromosomes. Each time a cell divides—and those in the normal human body split about seventy times before kicking the bucket—the telomeres diminish a little. Youthful cells have long telos. Old worn-out cells have shorter ones. Tinkering with the genes that influence telo proteins is one of the important ways that dystasis therapy brings about cell rejuvenation and healing. There's an enormous scientific literature on the subject."

Bea said, "Brown Fleece's telomeres seem to be of an appropriate length for a human male of his apparent age. It's quite possible that the exon mutation's effect is negligible."

I frowned. "Then why would Konigsberg bother to include it in the demiclone marker group at all? Wouldn't the intron suite adequately label fake humans?"

"It would," she said. "Emily was *forced* to include the exon—for a very odd reason that I'm going to tell you about."

"What does this mutant thing do?" Karl asked.

"Apparently nothing," Bea said, "if we're to judge by Brown Fleece. In the biosample I briefly studied, the telomeric proteins seem completely normal."

"Isn't there any way to check it out more intensively?" I asked.

"One would have to do some rather time-consuming research," she said, "in vitro tissue culture of cells from different parts of the demiclone body—artificial acceleration of cell division to determine whether the overall aging process or specific bodily functions were being significantly affected. Perhaps the exon is a protogene—one that's effectively dormant until it's switched on by some external factor. In that case, a researcher might not uncover the mutation's effect unless she found the relevant trigger. Perhaps Haluk scientists have already noticed this rogue exon and researched it. However, given their relative backwardness in molecular biology, I'd be inclined to doubt it."

"Me, too," I said. All this was more genetics than I really

wanted to hear about right now, even though I suspected it might be important.

Bea took a long drink of the mint tea and sighed. "Let's move on to the other interesting—and very puzzling—thing I discovered. Do you remember the Haluk cadaver that was sent to Tokyo University by Rampart? This happened several years ago, just before Eve was abducted."

Karl and I nodded. I explained to Charlie: "The body was a gracile. It looked like a normal allomorph, but it wasn't. It had human DNA mixed with the Haluk. During the long period of hostility, human researchers had very little opportunity to study the Haluk genome. So when Rampart captured a Qastt pirate vessel that had a Haluk suicide aboard, it sold the body to Tokyo University for a nice price. That particular corpse unexpectedly provided the first proof that Haluk allomorphism was being erased by unauthorized genen therapy. Bea had it briefly but was unable to do much research."

"That's right," she said. "The body was returned to the Haluk as a provision of the new trade treaty, supposedly for religious interment. The Secretariat for Xenoaffairs confiscated and sealed the Japanese researchers' data and mine for policy reasons that weren't made clear to the scientific community . . . Perhaps you *don't* know that officially the Haluk genome remains pegged at its pre-allomorph-trait eradication status. Fresh research by human scientists into Haluk biology is now allowed only with SXA permission. And no permits have been issued."

I gave a cynical smile. "Right. The Haluk—and our goddamn government—don't want to publicize the fact that human genes were used illegally to wipe out allomorphism. That's why the Tokyo study was never published. My father obtained a précis of it by twisting academic arms, but the full report was quashed."

"Nevertheless," Bea said demurely, "I managed to obtain a copy of it two years ago, as did a number of other people in my line of work. Today, when I finished assaying Brown Fleece, I compared his genetic profile to that of the Tokyo Haluk. I did this for technical reasons, to see how much of the redundant human DNA in the Tokyo body might have survived in a demiclone. Of course, the Toyko Haluk didn't contain the intron marker suite typical of demiclones . . . but the body *did* have the mutant telomere exon."

"What the hell does that mean?" I demanded. I was beginning to feel very confused. All this science was giving me a headache—or perhaps it was too much German chocolate cake.

Bea said, "I think we can presume that every nonallomorphic Haluk possesses this small exon mutation. Older studies of Haluk genetics confirm that the altered gene is not present in Haluk possessing the allomorph trait. Nor has the mutation ever been noted in human beings. I have to conclude that the exon is an artifact. Emily Konigsberg created it."

Karl's bushy brows rose quizzically. "She added a little something extra to *both* the trait eradication and the demiclone genen procedures?"

"Apparently so," Bea said, "but there's no documentation for it in her research materials. I haven't been able to read everything in the secret Galapharma files yet, of course. But there was an extensive section dealing with allo-trait eradication that I did study carefully. I found no reference to insertion of the mutant exon. Konigsberg must have concealed it within another gene-resequencing procedure, keeping it secret from both Haluk authorities and the Galapharma technicians. Later, when the demiclone project was established, she was forced to describe the mutant exon in the marker group. It would be detectable, you see, when Gala checked its employees' DNA to be sure they weren't Haluk spies."

And a mighty sloppy job they did of that, too . . .

"So Emily's magic exon occurs in nonallos and demiclones both," I said, "and we have no notion why. Aren't most mutations harmful?"

"Not necessarily," Bea said. "Given the highly idealistic temperament of Konigsberg, it doesn't seem likely that the exon would be deleterious. She wouldn't want to harm her Haluk friends. The mutation is probably neutral—or even beneficial."

"For who?" I murmured. "Humans or Haluk?"

A silence.

Finally, I said, "This new information bugs the hell out of me. What if that damned woman figured out a way to increase the Haluk lifespan, or make them super-healing, or something?"

"That's extremely unlikely," Bea said mildly. "But I could discreetly consult my forensic colleagues. Perhaps some of them would agree to quietly undertake some tissue-culture experiments, using biosamples from Brown Fleece. They wouldn't have to know the subject was a Haluk demiclone in order to investigate the effects of the mutation."

"Go ahead," I said. "But for God's sake stress the need for secrecy."

"I don't think we have to worry about their discretion." She paused. "However, there's another kind of secrecy we should be very concerned about. Have you considered that there might be demiclone spies in Efrem Sontag's office? His association with you and his skeptical attitude toward the Haluk Consortium are well-known."

"Sontag and his staff and even his family will have to be vetted," I said. "He's already agreed to it. We'll obtain DNA samples without the other subjects' knowledge and you can do the assays." I glanced apologetically at Karl and Charlie. "You'll have to test us, too, Bea."

"Oh, I've already done that, Helly." She smiled into her cup of peppermint tea. "I took biosamples from you to the lab and compared them with the Vital Stat database. You three are absolutely authentic. But I'm afraid you'll have to take *me* on faith—at least for the time being."

"We'll risk it," I said.

Not long afterward, Karl and I boarded his hopper and took off into the rainy night sky. For no reason other than an old security chief's love of arcane gadgetry, he had installed a sophisticated intruder-defense system in his small home in Port Perry, south of Fenelon Falls. It was the kind of setup that would hold off even the most determined Haluk kidnappers, far superior to that in my Rampart Tower apartment. I asked Karl if I could stay with him, and he readily agreed. He was a widower and lived alone except for a ten-kilo purebred, bluepoint Ragdoll cat named Max. The cat even liked me.

"It'll just be for three days," I said, "while we work out a long-range game plan with Sontag based on all this new evidence. After that, I'm off to a Sagittarian asteroid named Phlegethon. Barky Tregarth is supposed to be holed up there—literally. The friggin' place is an orbiting rabbit warren. Hollow."

Karl turned in the pilot's seat and regarded me with amazement. "But you can't go now—not after what's happened!"

"Sure I can." I was scrolling through the hopper's music library. Mostly classical, dammit, and heavy on Khachaturian. Finally, I found a Cal Tjader collection and called up "Running Out." Apropos, no?

"You're needed here!" Karl protested.

"No, I'm not: You need Cassius Potter, Hector Motlaletsie, and Lotte Dietrich." They were the retired Rampart security agents who had worked closely with us in the Perseus Spur during the Galapharma takeover attempt. The three were among the few people fully cognizant of the Haluk demiclone threat.

"My Over-the-Hill Gang?"

"Sign 'em on again," I told him. "They'll come running if you explain the situation. We're going to need Lotte's computer expertise to analyze the archival material we got from Lorne Buchanan. She'll know how to validate its authenticity for Sontag, in case SXA tries to discredit the chain of evidence later. Cassius and Hector will have an even more sensitive mission: collecting biosamples from every Delegate in the Commonwealth Assembly. They should all be tested. So should as many of the Delegates' aides as we can grab DNA from. If any demiclones are found, we leave them in place—then let Sontag blow 'em sky-high when he starts his committee hearings."

"You should be here for those. You've *got* to be here! You're a principal witness."

"My Barky Hunt won't take long. Maybe not even two weeks. Five days to reach Phlegethon, maybe a few more to track the old gunrunner down and hook him up to the truth machines I'm packing on *Makebate.* If he comes up aces, I'll transmit the results of his interrogation to you immediately via encrypted subspace com, then hightail it back to Earth with Barky lashed to the copilot's chair."

"And what if something goes wrong? Nothing that superannuated crook is likely to tell you is worth risking your life for."

"That's not true." I told him about the upcoming Assembly vote that would permit the sale of fifty T-2 Rampart Mandate planets to the Haluk, as well as the bill that would be introduced in the next session opening an additional three hundred worlds to the aliens. "Sontag thinks it would be bad strategy to attack the fifty-planet bill by introducing the demiclone evidence during the final eight weeks of this Assembly session. I don't agree. Maybe Barky Tregarth can help me change Ef's mind."

Karl was quietly appalled at the political news. "I never dreamed that the pro-Haluk faction was pushing ahead so fast! T-2 worlds . . . not as desirable as T-1's, but bad enough. Isn't there anything you could do as a Rampart director to stall the sale?"

"Me?" I let loose a cynical cackle. "Not a prayer. The Rampart board would vote me down in a landslide if I tried to block either deal. A huge credit infusion right now is just what the doctor ordered to grease the wheels of the Galapharma consolidation. The only way to force an open-door treaty on the Haluk and slow their influx is by discrediting them in the Assembly."

"We already have the evidence to do that, using Brown Fleece and the new Galapharma material. Dammit, Helly! Galloping off after a long shot like Barky Tregarth is reckless and irresponsible. To say nothing of bloody dangerous!"

"My life's in danger if I stay on Earth," I pointed out. "So I might as well go. At least there won't be any Haluk demiclones gunning for my butt around Sagittarius."

"Jesus Christ," he muttered darkly. "Why not just admit you're hot to trot on a new offworld adventure after two years of boring legal shit?"

"There's that," I admitted, grinning.

He turned away and stared out the side window of the hopper. Cal Tjader was playing his great Latin take on "'Round Midnight."

"So follow your damned cowboy instincts," Karl said softly. "If you end up dead, the rest of us will carry on the crusade somehow."

"I know," I said quietly. "I'm counting on it."

"The bad hats will be expecting you at Phlegethon, you know."

"That's why I'm going there in fancy dress. I'll disguise myself as a Joru trader. A very *short* Joru trader. And I'll have trade goods that no Haluk-oriented smuggler can resist. I twisted Tony Becker's arm and he's putting the stuff together for me." I told Karl what merchandise I planned to offer and he laughed. "If I give a decent performance, none of the local wiseguys will connect my Joru persona with the guy in Toronto who paid big money to learn the whereabouts of one Hamilcar Barca Tregarth."

Karl thought about it. "Hmm. This goofy idea could actually work."

I flashed a confident grin. "Of course it will. And you know what? Masquerading as an alien might even be fun!"

What an idiot I was.

Chapter 6

Tony Becker, Rampart Vice President for Biotechnology, was an ultraefficient executive and a fine scientist who didn't suffer fools—or cowboys—gladly. He was scrupulously upright, loyal, hardworking, and couldn't stand the sight of a certain flamboyant black-sheep lawyer who used his family name and fortune to make political waves.

Tony was also the only one I would have trusted to put together my Barky bait.

When I coerced him into cooperating with me, I made it clear that I needed the crucial materials no later than 0400 hours on Wednesday morning, the day I intended to leave Earth from Oshawa Starport. Tony grudgingly promised to meet the deadline but said he'd probably have to bring the trade goods to the Rampart pilot's lounge at the last minute.

The starport serving the Human Commonwealth capital had such heavy traffic that landings and departures were firmed up two days ahead of time. To keep Haluk agents off balance, I planned to usurp the liftoff slot of another Rampart ship scheduled to depart at 0440. It was a fairly common ploy of impatient VIP executives. The bumped vessel would be banished to the end of the line and endure a forty-eight-hour delay. Taking its place, *Makebate* would be entered into the starport computer record only at the last minute.

Promptly at four in the morning I sat alone in Rampart's pilot lounge in the central module of the lake-island platform, waiting for Tony. Through the observation window I could see the cloudy sky brightening in the east. Every few minutes a massive starship lofted silently off one of the thirty-six floating cradles that encircled the tower structure, then vanished into the overcast under sublight drive.

Makebate was on the conveyor already, moving along the underwater tunnel from our shoreside maintenance facility to her designated cradle. At 0430 I'd have to be on her flight deck, going through the final checklist of procedures for liftoff, or else forfeit my slot.

The wall chronometer showed 0410 hours, and still no Tony Becker. I couldn't believe the prickly bastard would screw me, but it wouldn't be any surprise if he shaved the time to the bone just to make me squirm.

Phone him? Nope. I just cursed and waited.

At 0415 the pork sausage patties, scrambled eggs, and fried tomatoes Karl had given me for breakfast did a fandango in my gut. For some reason, the notion of postponing the Phlegethon trip for two days was unthinkable. If the Biotech vice president didn't show, I'd leave without the trade goods and think up a new way to entice my quarry into range. As for Tony Becker . . . would I really have him fired if he failed me, as I'd threatened? Would I dismiss a valued Rampart executive, a tireless charity fund-raiser, a devout churchgoer, a staunch family man, merely because he'd refused to be an accomplice in my cockamamie scheme?

You're damned right I would.

But he strolled into the pilot lounge at 0419, blasé as you please. I climbed to my feet and said, "Hey, Tony. Almost missed you."

Becker was a round-faced blond man in his late thirties who wore a white track suit that was not only immaculately clean, but *pressed.* He looked at me as though I were something that needed scraping off his pristine athletic shoes, then thrust a padded fabric lunch pak into my hands. It was the kind of thing small children took to school, imprinted with images of the cartoon character Daffy Duck.

"Here," he said snippily. "One of my kids contributed the deceptive packaging. Do you have *any* idea how tough it was to get this material put together? You'd better be damned sure nobody ever traces this unethical stunt of yours back to me."

The Daffy pack contained only two items. One was a semiobsolete Macrodur magslate with a chipped case and a dirty screen. The other item was an important-looking little technical container about the size of a sandwich box that had built-in refrigeration and self-destruct units and biohazard symbols stuck on all sides. I tipped it carefully out of the pack onto a coffee table.

"Here's the key." Tony handed me a dime.

Inside the box were six smaller self-refrigerating biocontainers nested in contour padding. I opened one and found a sealed, unlabeled vial nearly full of viscous purplish liquid.

Tony Becker said, "The viral vector is the real thing, with an admixture of harmless contaminants and stain in the culture to make it look exotic. It'll pass any test. The slate contains a complicated production protocol that I faked up, using data from our own Spur factories, and translated into Joru. It'll serve your purposes. However, I should warn you that a really competent biotechnician will probably suspect that the alien manufacturing procedures are bogus. They're too efficient."

"That's okay," I said, "so long as the vector itself passes muster."

"I told you it would, didn't I?" Tony snapped.

I handed him a plastic card. It represented five hundred shares of Rampart Preferred, signed over from my personal stakeholding. "A tangible token of my appreciation, as I promised. But perhaps your tender conscience won't allow you to accept a bribe."

I swear that he hissed at me. Then he snatched the card, shoved it into his belt wallet and stomped off, leaving me grinning. I took a last look at the small vial before putting it

away with the others. What looked like runny grape jelly
was actually the genetic engineering vector PD32:C2. Barky
Tregarth would be led to believe the vials were samples—
from a brand new source of the invaluable virus located on
a Joru planet.

I locked up the container, slung the Daffy pack over my
shoulder, and dashed to the transporter. I arrived at *Makebate*'s cradle with two whole minutes to spare.

The early part of my voyage to Phlegethon was spent in
dress rehearsal for my upcoming role as a Joru. I strode mas-
terfully about the cramped flight deck practicing xeno ges-
tures, dressed in flowing black-and-white brocaded robes
reminiscent of those worn by medieval Dominican friars,
doing my best to convey the impression that I was a third of
a meter taller and weighed an additional 45 kilos. (A few
shrimpy Joru were my height, 193 cm.) My stage presence
had to reflect the almighty chutzpah of a person who believed, as every supremely self-confident male Joru did, that
the sun, moon, and stars shone out of his cloaca.

The costume I had purchased at the Mississauga theatrical supply establishment recommended by Halimeda Opper
was elaborate and expensive, intended for human actors impersonating Joru in close-up holo performances. The fabric
and accessories seemed authentic at close inspection. My
body, beneath the voluminous robes, was modified by a
padded suit that gave it additional bulk in the right places. I
also wore soft-armor longjohns and had additional armor in
the hood of the costume. My hands were enclosed in six-
fingered gloves—the prosthetic extra digits were even capable of movement—that simulated hairy orange paws
adorned with heavy golden rings. I slipped small armor pads
into the gloves to guard the backs of my hands.

Disguising my head and face was trickier, requiring the
use of recontouring makeup appliances, bulging faux eyes

with vertical pupils, skin texturizer, and a bald cap sporting a knobby crest and tufts of apricot fur.

Alien oxygen-concentrating equipment hid the lower part of my face—and made the entire impersonation feasible, since Joru had peculiar narrow jaws that were impossible to simulate on a normal human skull. The mask wasn't operational, of course. Instead it was fitted with a special internal translator device that modified my whispered utterances into the alien language and broadcast them through an annunciator at normal volume.

I also wore an earpiece that would decipher Joru in case any member of that race tried to speak to me in the mother tongue. A second pendant-model translator, clipped to my collar in the usual fashion, could be activated to *retranslate* my Joru words back into appropriately florid Standard English; I wasn't a good enough actor to reproduce the mechanical idiom on my own.

After getting my moves down pat and polishing my conversational candences, I used the ship's computer library to brush up my knowledge of Joru culture. I also created a personal legend that was loosely based on a Joru criminal I'd known in the old days.

My new identity was that of Gulowjadipallu Gulow, a native of the planet Didiwa in Sector 7 in the inner Orion Arm. I had three wives, fourteen offspring, and a pet *wulip* back home. I was a professional middleman, an information broker, as were so many other members of my urbane and discreet race. I was semiretired, but still kept a paw in when a truly unique opportunity presented itself. Because I was rich and my time was so valuable, I traveled in a late model starship of human manufacture. No one at Phlegethon would scan it closely because I'd leave it in orbit, hidden in its impenetrable dissimulator field, and dock at the asteroid in my ordinary-looking ship's gig.

With luck, minions of Ram Mahtani or other unfriendlies

would never see through my elaborate camouflage; and Barky Tregarth, even forewarned and wary, wouldn't suspect my true identity until it was too late.

Four days out of Earth, as I was traversing Red Gap, between the Orion Arm and Sagittarius, I picked up a distress call on the generalized subspace communication channel. At the time, *Makebate* was outside the normal shipping vectors, streaking through faintly glowing drifts of interstellar gases slightly below the galactic plane. There wasn't a star within 350 light-years, and no solid matter larger than a mouse turd within 100.

The automated beacon-style subspace signal was so faint it almost missed me. But *Makebate*'s gonzo receiving equipment managed to pull one of the flashes into dimensional focus, enabling us to lock on. I only hesitated for a moment before transmitting a beamed response.

"Vessel in distress," I said, "do you copy on Channel 6113?"

". . . We copy on Channel 6113. Thank you for responding."

The voice was human with a heavy ethnic accent, indicating that its owner was Earth-born and probably used his ancestral tongue at home in preference to Standard English. Lots of people were like that, defying the language police.

My instrumentation showed that the com beam was very weak. The starship sending the SOS traveled anonymously, as was common in regions frequented by pirates. I, of course, was anonymous, too. My rangefinder placed the other ship 154 light-years away in the direction of the Sag, well out of scanner range.

"State the nature of your emergency, vessel in distress," I said.

"Responding starship, please identify yourself."

The hell I would. With a focused SS com linkage established, the other ship could now calculate my hyperspatial pseudovector with precision. If it was an innocent, I'd do my best to help. If it was a trolling buccaneer playing games, attempting to entice me within striking distance, I'd teach it a painful lesson.

I repeated, "Please state the nature of your emergency. My name is Hugo. I'm a human trader who prefers to remain incognito at this time." This was a coy admission that I was a smuggler. A few of them, like my pal Mimo Bermudez, were not entirely devoid of humane impulses. "I will attempt to contact Zone Patrol on your behalf if you wish."

Abruptly, the vessel in distress deactivated its ID blank-out. The data display on my console showed its registration and ICS-approved itinerary. SBC-11942 was a Sheltok bulk trans-ack carrier en route from Shamiya in the Sag to the big fuel-plant complex on Lethe in Zone 8 of the Orion Arm.

"Citizen Hugo, this is Ulrich Schmidt, master of the *Sheltok Eblis*. We are under attack by a fleet of sixteen bandits. Our ULD engines are disabled and we are operating under minimum subluminal drive—effectively dead in the void. Our AM torpedoes are exhausted. We have diverted nearly all remaining power to our defensive shields. Uh . . . I estimate that we can hold out for two more hours, then we will have to surrender."

"I understand. What can I do to help?"

"The initial attack severely damaged our communication system. Our SS com input is too weak to reach Sheltok Fleet Security on Lethe or any of our Sagittarian units. We have also been unsuccessful in attempts to contact Zone Patrol. Please notify the patrol of our situation if you can."

"I copy that and will comply, Captain Schmidt," I said. Then I added mendaciously: "My long-range scanner picked up a ZP heavy cruiser in my slice of hyperspace less than half an hour ago. It might be able to reach you in time to drive off the bandits. Do you have a racial ID on them?"

"It's the *verfluchte* Haluk again! No doubt about it. I hoped to outwit them by vectoring below the galactic plane on this trip, but they found us anyhow. Twenty of the pig-dogs! I popped four with AM torpedos before they needled my engines."

"Haluk? Are you sure of that identification, Cap'n?" I tried to keep the excitement out of my voice. The Barky Hunt had paid off already.

"Of course I'm sure, *du Scheisskopf*! Do you think I'm the first carrier to be ambushed by these *doppelgurken'* fuckers? They're bleeding Sheltok dry in Zones 3 and 4."

"Well, that's a rotten shame, but it sure as hell ain't my fault."

Schmidt was instantly contrite. "I'm sorry I lost my temper, Hugo. Please—if you aren't able to contact Zone Patrol within . . . a viable time frame, then I request that you tell Lethe what happened to us, as soon as you are able to do so."

"You just hang tough, pardner. I'll do my best to set the patrol onto those fuckin' blue scrotes. Good luck! Hugo out."

"Thank you, Hugo. *Sheltok Eblis* is out."

I'd lied to Schmidt just in case his emergency was a hoax. I hadn't scanned a ZP starship for over thirty hours, and that one had been back in Zone 8 of the Orion Arm, nearly 2,200 light-years away. The patrol has precious few high-ross vessels, and they use them to guard heavily traveled regular shipping lanes, not the godforsaken underbelly of Red Gap.

But not to worry, Cap'n! *Makebate* could substitute nicely for a ZP heavy cruiser. And I was bored and ready for some Lone Ranger action.

Roaring down the hype at max pseudovee, I arrived at the ambush scene well within Schmidt's estimated two-hour limit. Still, it was a near thing. The shields of the great eight-kilometer-long carrier were flickering crimson by then, and they wouldn't have held up much longer.

The bandits were so intent on savaging *Eblis* that it took them forever to spot me coming at them from down under, among the dust clouds. When one of them finally scanned *Makebate*, the whole bunch broke off their bombardment, engaged ULD, and sheered away in sixteen different directions. They were driving speedy small starships that looked something like Bodascon Y600 knockoffs, ornamented with those odd cobalt-blue running lights the Haluk are fond of. They had plenty of horsepower to fly rings around a slow-moving leviathan like *Eblis*, but were hardly a match for my souped-up sled and its extravagant weapon systems.

I played reasonably fair—aside from misrepresenting myself as Zone Patrol—sending warning shots from my actinic cannons at the Haluk ships and calling for them to throw in the towel or sincerely regret it. They kept running, most of them too panicked by my scary conformation and superior speed even to fire on me. I made a recording of each pirate ship's image and fuel signature before wasting it. It took me almost two hours to chase down the last of the sixteen, by which time I'd lost my appetite for one-sided combat—not that I had any alternative to slaughtering them. If I gave them a pass, they'd just find fresh prey.

There was no way to tell if the doomed Haluk had sent subspace alarms to their base. I was already having uneasy second thoughts about the wisdom of my knight-errancy, but I put my worries aside, figuring I hadn't really compromised the Phleg operation. If the Haluk high command recognized *Makebate* from a pirate's description—so what? They already knew I was prowling the galaxy; the lovely Dolores da Gama had seen to that. But they didn't know my destination or my mission, and they certainly had no idea I'd be doing a turn in Joru disguise.

Look on the bright side, Helly! I told myself. You did your good deed for the day.

And now I had proof of Haluk freebootery in the inner galactic whorl to add to the pile of accumulating evidence against them, plus some interesting questions that needed answers:

Were Haluk trans-ack pirates operating out of an independent base in the Sag, or were they using Y'tata facilities? Was it possible that the Haluk had formed a secret alliance with the frolicksome albino farters? Were the hijackings intended to create an artificial shortage of ultraheavy elements, or did the Haluk have other motives for grabbing the stuff?

Perhaps Barky Tregarth would know.

If he didn't, I might just be forced to nab me a Y pirate out of some low Phlegethon dive and hook him to the truth machine. It would be a nasty interrogation for both of us. Sometimes aliens didn't survive psychotronic questioning. (Occasionally humans didn't, either.) And unless I corked the victim securely, the stress of the procedure would generate a stomach-churning stench. Maybe I could grill the Y while wearing a space suit . . .

I returned to the immediate vicinity of the derelict trans-ack carrier and dropped out of hyperspace. The region was still boiling with ionic crud from the earlier bombardment, futzing the big ship's scanners, but to be on the safe side I erected *Makebate*'s dissimulator before hailing Captain Schmidt on short-range RF. I didn't want him or his crew to get a close look at me.

"*Sheltok Eblis*, this is your old pal Hugo. Do you copy? The bandits are gone and won't be back. You can relax now."

A Germanic expletive came out of my com speaker, and then the viewer showed an agitated middle-aged man in the ugly marigold-colored Sheltok uniform. He had brush-cut hair and a thick neck.

"You destroyed the Haluk pirates! All sixteen! Who are you? *What* are you?"

I had the recorder going again. I ignored the skipper's demand that I turn on my flightdeck video. "Captain Schmidt, congratulations on your survival. Do you have any casualties?"

"No, *Gott sei Dank!* But it was a close call for the engineers when our ULD powerplant was disabled. We—We are very grateful for your assistance, Hugo."

"Are you aware," I said formally, "that Sheltok management has suppressed information about Haluk pirate attacks against ultraheavy element carriers? The media and the general public know nothing about them."

The captain's hooded blue eyes looked away. "*Ach*, it's a political thing, you know? Anyone who speaks of it . . ." He trailed off, shaking his head.

"How long have Haluk bandits been attacking Sheltok ships?"

But he was too shrewd to fall into my clumsy trap. "I know what you're trying to do," he growled. "You think you'll sell my admission to the web-tabloid muckrakers. Wouldn't they pay a pretty penny for a sensational story like this! Well, you won't get any more out of me, whoever the hell you are. What good is it to be rescued from killer pirates if one ends up Thrown Away for corporate disloyalty, eh? Answer me that!"

"If criminal behavior by the Haluk is brought into the open, they can be pressured to cease and desist. You could avenge the other victims and prevent—"

He interrupted me with a scornful laugh. "I thought before that you were a fool, Hugo. Now I know it for a fact. Sheltok will stamp out these Haluk vermin and their renegade Y'tata confederates without having its affairs smeared across the filthy media. Meanwhile, the situation must be kept under wraps so as not to undermine public confidence in the Concern. Do you understand?"

"I only want to help."

He suddenly sounded very tired. "Then call Lethe on your subspace communicator and ask them to send a tug for us. Send it soon, Hugo. *Eblis* out."

The viewer went dark. And that was that.

I did as Schmidt asked, in a roundabout fashion. As I resumed my interrupted voyage, I contacted Karl Nazarian on the SS com and fed him the recorded information I'd gathered on the pirate attack.

"Sixteen Haluk bandits attacking one bulk carrier?" he marveled. "Good grief. It almost sounds as though your war has already started."

"Pass this fresh intelligence along to Ef Sontag. Then find a way to anonymously relay *Eblis*'s request for a tug to Sheltok Tower. Their external security people will take it seriously if they're given the coordinates of the derelict."

"What about informing Zone Patrol?"

"Don't bother. The report would only be suppressed. The carrier captain let slip that Haluk attacks are common out here. Sheltok's just keeping it quiet so as not to rock the consortium applecart . . . Do you have any good news for me?"

"Well, there are no demiclones on Sontag's staff or in his family. Hector and Cassius are skulking around the Assembly dining rooms, pinching used water glasses and half-eaten croissants. So far, no Delegates test positive. Lotte has analyzed and recollated all of the Gala secret files. She's working with Sontag's people to mesh the new data with the old. Bea Mangan found six scientists willing to do tissue-culture research with the mystery gene."

"That's great."

"Other news: Simon nominated Gunter Eckert to be the new Rampart chairman and John Ellington to be VC. The board will vote when Eve returns from the Spur next week. Not a trace of your brother Dan. However, one of the injured guards recovered enough to help InSec make up computer-model images of three of Dan's abductors. Let me show them to you. I think you'll find them interesting."

Three male faces, side by side, flashed onto the com display. Two of the men were totally nondescript; but there was something disturbingly familiar about the third, and I felt a sudden dry sensation in my throat.

"Karl, is it my imagination, or does the guy in the middle look a little like Alistair Drummond? Remove the mustache,

add more flesh to the cheeks, and lose the eye bags, give him
a designer haircut . . ."

"The resemblance isn't very close, but I spotted it, too."

"Drummond and the *Haluk*? The aliens washed their
hands of him—all but betrayed him to us!"

"Yes," said Karl. "The resemblance is probably coinci-
dental. But I wanted to show it to you anyhow. Give you
some food for thought."

"Thanks all to hell," I grumbled. "Anything else?"

"The weather in Toronto is sensational—twenty-three de-
grees celsius, bright sunshine, balmy spring breezes. The
Conurb Council turned off the force-field umbrella for the
first time this year."

"Wish I was there."

"No, you don't," said Karl Nazarian.

He bid me goodbye and I resumed my interrupted journey
to Phlegethon. A day or so later I arrived at the asteroid
without further incident.

From space the little world looked like nothing much—
perhaps a pitted and decaying pumpkin, dull orange-black in
color, with a handful of tiny orbiting craft floating around it
like fruit flies. Here and there amber lights shone out of
craters in the surface. What seemed to be scores of deformed
silver minnows nibbling the pumpkin rind—together with
numbers of smaller noshmates—were actually huge transactinide carriers and lesser starships, either taking on fuel or
docked nose-to-ground while their crews rested and recre-
ated inside the not so heavenly body.

I have been told that the original Phlegethon of Greek
mythology was a fiery river in Hades. Sheltok Concern
owned a dozen or so similar way stations with brimstony
names—Gehenna, Styx, Sheol, Tophet, Avernus, Niflheim,
and the like—that served vessels bound to or from the terrible R-class worlds where ultraheavy elements are mined.
Compared to the genuine inferno of the Sagittarian arm

of the Milky Way—nearly lifeless, seething with deadly gamma and x-radiation blasted out from the galactic hub, clogged by colossal interstellar dust clouds and minefields of cosmic debris, and infested with malignant little black holes and the weird oscillating novae that generate stable transactinide elements—dreary Phlegethon was a Garden of Eden.

My computer told me that the asteroid was only 163 kilometers in diameter. It followed a distant orbit about a melancholy blood-orange sun near the outer margin of the Whorl. The other planets in its solar system were tired gas giants and waterless desert worlds. What made Phlegethon appealing to starfarers was the fact that it was not composed of solid rock or sterile meteoric metal, as are most asteroids. Phleg was a carbonaceous chondrite.

CC's are as common as comets in our galaxy. Most of them are smaller than a bread box, a mixture of iron and magnesium silicates, other minerals, and generous amounts of dihydrogen oxide, plus lots of simple organic compounds—including amino acids, the building blocks of life. Little CC's, falling as meteorites, can seed the oceans of newborn worlds and cook up primordial soup. Large CC's, judiciously carved and riddled, are the best possible interstellar way stations.

Warm one of these lumps up with an internal powerplant to melt the embedded ice, provide light and enough artificial gravity inside so denizens and visitors can walk about in reasonable comfort, crack some of the organic compounds to release nitrogen, oxygen, and carbon dioxide for a breathable atmosphere in the tunnels, and you have an instant space station. Add fertilizing trace elements to the pulverized asteroidal substance and you can build yourself a garden in space, for an asteroidal carbonaceous chondrite is nothing but a big ball of rocky dirt. Carbon-based foodstuffs will grow like mad in an enhanced CC. So will marijuana, magic mushrooms, coca shrubs, dilly beans, pseudopoon, rakka, hebenon, and a host of other recreational narcotic plants. Phlegeton grew those, but it was also noted for its succulent salad veggies, suzyberries, sweet melons, and barley.

Yep, barley. For beer. The place had five microbreweries.

Even though Phlegethon was Sheltok property, it operated as a freesoil world. There were none of the usual arrival formalities when my gig docked at one of the small-craft mooring facilities. I came through the airlock carrying only a locked titanium case hanging at my hip on a baldric. It contained the contents of the Daffy pack and a Hogan H-18 miniaturized low-power psychotronic interrogation device that would enable me to learn whether Barky knew anything at all useful. If he did, I'd take him back to *Makebate* and attach him to really efficient truth machines for more serious discussion.

I'd be returning regularly to my starship to sleep and get a decent meal. My costume's mask had ports for drinking through a straw and the insertion of small edibles, and Joru readily consumed many kinds of human alcoholic beverages and snack foods; but I wasn't going to give up my favorite rib-stickin' ranch-type vittles for the duration. My other personal needs would be take care of in the asteroid's public conveniences, omniracial cubicles of the type that are blast-sterilized after every use.

Hidden under my robes was a collection of special equipment that included both a stun-gun and a Kagi blue-ray blaster, restraint cuffs in several sizes, antigravity supporters similar to the ones Black Leather and Brown Fleece had used on me during my abduction, and a projector capable of generating a movable small force-field hemisphere. My flexible body armor would protect me from stun-darts and most types of photon pistols, but I really hoped I wouldn't get into a gunfight. The damned six-digit paws didn't enhance trigger dexterity.

The arrival-departure lobby of Phlegethon was a rough-hewn cavern, very well lit, swarming with people of four races. Humans were the most numerous, but there were plenty of Y'tata and Joru. A few groups of ponderous Kalleyni slouched about, giggling and gaping at the goofy-looking humanoid entities.

Gravity in this part of the asteroid was about seven-eighths terrestrial, enough to put a good bounce in your step. The air was chilly, humid, and smelled faintly of formalde-hyde, one of the simple organic compounds abundant in the asteroidal substance. A thin mist hung about the light fixtures. I could hear the dull roar of powerful ventilation equipment.

The floor appeared to be wet tarmac, cambered for drainage and punctuated by openings covered by ceramalloy grates. The walls and ceiling, so heavily pocked and cratered that they resembled gritty dark Swiss cheese, were covered by a transparent sealant that had cracked in numerous areas, allowing meltwater and gases to seep through. You could see embedded chunks of dirty ice everywhere. A rat's nest of ex-posed cables, pipes, and utility ducts decorated the ceiling.

At regular intervals around the chamber perimeter were large tunnels topped with directional signs. They served as pedestrian thoroughfares, or gave access to elevators and the small network of transport capsules. Other openings in the lobby wall, stoppered by glass doors with heavy gaskets, led to Sheltok offices, the better human-style hotels, and the quarters of legitimate trading establishments.

I wasn't interested in the latter.

As I stood in a small alcove studying a holographic map of the place, a young Y'tata sidled up to me. His wrinkled albino skin was an unhealthy gray and the beady red eyes were crusted with matter. He was dressed in light green pants, a long-sleeve green shirt, and a copper-scaled kilt and vest. The garments were typical of a Y starship crew mem-ber, but they were shabby and tarnished.

"Hey, Mr. Joru, welcome to Phleg! You maybe need a

guide? I'm your main man. Whataya say?" He spoke in
Standard English, as aliens are obliged to do on human
worlds—at least when humans are likely to be listening.
Y'tata translation devices have a snappy command of semiobsolete English slang.

"Go away," I said shortly. I figured him for a maroony, one
of those unfortunate wretches who can be found on almost
any galactic way station, dumped off for some infraction of
ship's discipline and trying to earn enough credit through
odd jobs to get back to their home world. Human and Y ma-
roonies were the most common, although Qastt castaways
were coming on strong in the Perseus Spur now that they'd
signed a trade treaty with the CHW.

"I'm Sh'muz. Good name for a fast talker, hey? Or
doesn't that translate? Ha-ha! I can help you find abso-
fuckin'-lutely *anything* you need. How's about a comfy
high-oxygen hotel with nice hard beds? A restaurant with
juwulimopsh like your dear old mothers used to cook? Hey,
you into sex for hire? Primo dope? Honest Injun gambling?"

I stared haughtily at the entity in the condescending manner of my kind. Joru and Y'tata shared roughly the same region of the inner galaxy, where for over twenty thousand
terrestrial years they were the only stargoing Insaps. Their
relationship had been one of contemptuous toleration until
the advent of the appalling Commonwealth of Human
Worlds, with its superior technology and policy of relentless
racial aggrandizement. A sense of mutual humiliation had
drawn the Joru and Y'tata closer together.

But not too close.

For Y'tata digestive processes generate peculiarly mal-
odorous gases that once served as a useful deterrent to predators on their planet of origin. The effluvia are a rank offense
to the sensibilities of the fastidious Joru, whose breathing
equipment concentrates oxygen from the ambient atmosphere of exotic worlds and tends to amplify smells as well.
On Earth and the larger human colonies, there are laws re-

quiring Y'tata visitors to avert the danger of backfiring by taking special medication; but minor settlements like Phlegethon that make a special effort to attract alien customers tend to be more easygoing. With a little extra effort, your average Y-on-the-street can control himself in most interracial social situations.

Sh'muz was doing his best not to offend, but not really succeeding. I was much taller and probably scary-looking, making the creature nervous.

Maybe it was the olfactory assault that overcame my common sense. At any rate, I committed what eventually proved to be a major blunder. Stepping back a few paces from the worst of the fug, I muttered, "There is only one way in which you might assist me, disgusting noisome entity. Do you know where I might find a human trader named Barney Cornwall?"

Sh'muz blinked his red eyes rapidly, a mannerism indicating both disappointment and despair. "Never heard of the bugger." He perked up. "But I know a Bernie Cohen! Any kinda contraband you wanna buy or sell, Bernie's the guy. I can take you to his burrow in the Bazaar right now."

"Thank you, no." I began to move away.

"Look—I'll ask around, see if anybody ever heard of this Barney Cornwall. Get right back to you. You got a phone code? How about the name of your hotel?"

"No! Begone, obnoxious person!"

Sh'muz had no intention of letting go of a live one. "I'll find the guy for you, trust me. I got contacts! How's about we meet in about ten hours, see what shakes? There's this bar, La Cucaracha Loca, a human joint but all kinda entities welcome. On Level 4, near the heavy-craft refueling bays. Midnight. Whataya say?"

The answer to that one was: *Oh, shit.* I'd carefully worked out stratagems for introducing Barky Tregarth's alias into conversations with Phlegethon locals, in hopes of luring him to my bait. None of my tactical scenarios included a clown like Sh'muz trumpeting Barney Cornwell's name about the asteroid like some flatulent town crier.

"Please do not exert yourself on my account," I said firmly. "I am not really interested in meeting Trader Cornwall after all. Is that clear? Forget him and forget me!"

"Aww . . ." Utter dejection. The pathetic Y'tata maroony was probably counting on the tip for eating money.

I opened a pouch in my baldric, extracted a human hundred-dollar bill, and handed it over. "Please leave me alone. Here is a little something to tide you over until you find another client to guide."

The Y'tata's eyes blazed like the taillights of a BMW as he registered appreciation.

"Hey—thanks a bunch, Mr. Joru! You're a prince. Or prime minister. Or whatever! I'll find Cornwall if I hafta tear this orbiting garbage heap apart. Don't forget! Cucaracha Loca. Twenty-five hundred hours. Be there!"

He dashed away into the crowd, leaving me cursing in a miasma.

I got on an elevator and headed down.

The uppermost levels of Phlegethon were devoted to fuel storage areas, starship repair shops, Sheltok offices, and traveler amenities. Below were situated enormous ultrasecure warehouse caverns, many with access tunnels opening to the surface, labeled only with anonymous alphanumerics. Some of the merchandise locked inside might have been legitimate trade goods; a larger percentage was undocumented contraband. Sheltok's port officials didn't care what went into and out of the storerooms; they simply charged extortionate rent and collected stiff entrance and exit fees on every transshipment.

Beneath the storage levels the elevator passed farm galleries lit by dazzling vapor lights, alternating with blocks of environmental utilities. In the denser core of the asteroid, where embedded ice and volatile organic chemicals were at

a minimum, were apartment warrens for the permanent inhabitants and the catacombs where shady traders congre-
gated.

The more prosperous of these hucksters conducted business in an area called the Bazaar, on Level 32. Here hundreds of chambers had been carved out of the asteroid's
interior substance. Some were no-frill holes in the wall that
bordered on the squalid, wide open to passersby, crude ex-
cavations fitted out with desks, computers, com equipment,
and a few stools. Others, with sample merchandise on display, were fully enclosed and as elaborately tarted up as the
small retail stores in Toronto's Underground Path. Both
kinds of outfits were swarming with customers.

A directory, divided into categories, was posted next to
the elevator. I consulted it and made a list of arms traders.
There were over a dozen of them, peddling everything from
Kalleynian ceremonial tail-sabres to antimatter torpedoes.
Since guns and matériel had been Barky Tregarth's area of
expertise in the Perseus Spur, I hoped he was still in the
same game here in the Sag. It would certainly fit neatly with
his interest in the Haluk.

I visited each merchant of death in turn, beginning with
the humans. Most of them brushed me off almost immediately when they discovered the esoteric nature of my trade
goods. To those who showed an interest, I delivered my
spiel, which went something like this:

MERCHANT OF DEATH: What you want? I'm a busy man, Joru,
    so make it quick. None of your damned time-wasting
    yackety-yak.
HELLY AS JORU: I have some extremely valuable merchandise
    on offer, of a most unusual nature. It does not readily fit
    into any category listed in the Bazaar directory; but since
    the material has a certain strategic value, I wish to sound
    out your interest.
MOD: Extremely valuable? . . .

HAJ: *[Taking a single small biocontainer out of his baldric case while simultaneously allowing his sleeve to fall back, revealing an arm holster containing a Kagi pistol with a glowing ready-light]* Allow me to open this refrigerated cylinder. Ah—there! The contents are a genetic engineering viral vector known as PD32:C2.

MOD: Never heard of it. And I don't deal in biological warfare items. Get lost.

HAJ: This viral vector is of special interest to the Haluk race. They pay the human corporation Rampart Concern enormous sums for it.

MOD: *[Slight lessening of hostility]* Oh. That stuff.

HAJ: Precisely. In the Perseus Spur a similar small vial of this precious substance would bring 250,000 on the black market—twice as much if sold directly to the blue-skinned ones.

MOD: *[In disbelief]* Half a million bucks for one of those little ampules? You shittin' me, high pockets?

HAJ: That is still twenty percent less than Rampart retail. But here is an interesting thing: this PD32:C2 was not manufactured by Rampart! It comes from an entirely new viral source on a certain Joru world. The simpletons there do not realize that the vector they are producing for the genetic modification of livestock is identical to the substance so desperately coveted by the Haluk. This vial I have shown you is only a sample. I have access to unlimited quantities—and my price is a mere 120,000 per vial.

MOD: *[Shaking head]* You should be peddling this stuff in the Perseus Spur, fella. Around these parts . . . it could be really hard to move. Nobody's gonna give a guy like you anything like the kind of deal you quoted. Maybe not even a tenth the price.

HAJ: *[Seeming not to understand the implied invitation to dicker]* One hears rumors. Very persistent rumors of a clandestine Haluk presence in this Sagittarian zone, in association with individuals of the putrid Y'tata race. And so, rather than travel from my home base on Didiwa to the forbiddingly remote Perseus Spur, where Haluk trade operations are spied upon by arrogant agents of Rampart Concern and the Human Commonweal, and I or my agents might be imperiled, I traversed Red Gap to this place of . . . peculiar reputation, where I had never before done business. Even though Phlegethon is a possession of Sheltok Concern—may diseased *maslaw* defecate upon their corporate earnings report!—I understand that it is possible here to engage in confidential undertakings without personal hazard. I confess that I hoped to find knowledgeable and enterprising persons in this asteroid who might have access to the far-ranging Haluk.

MOD: *[Uncomfortably]* I've heard the rumors about Haluk pirates going after Sheltok carriers in the Sag. Far as I know, they're just rumors. No blueberry bandits ever drop in here to fuel up or hit the casinos.

HAJ: I must speak frankly now. The name of a certain human who has been known to trade with the Haluk was suggested to me by a colleague on Didiwa. I confess that I originally came to Phlegethon hoping to make contact with this trader—but no human I have spoken to thus far seems to know him. Or if they do, they will not reveal his whereabouts to a Joru. I would pay an extremely generous finder's fee to the person who steered me to him.

MOD: What's this joker's name?

HAJ: He is called Barney Cornwall.

MOD: *[Elaborately casual]* Mmm. The name's sort of familiar. I seem to remember that he's a hard guy to get a hold of. Comes and goes, you know?

HAJ: You do have his acquaintance, then?

MOD: I didn't say that.

HAJ: *[Taking a dilapidated magslate out of the baldric case]* This device contains the complete manufacturing sequence for the Joru vector production facility. Of course, the verbal portions are in the Joru language, but that should not prove too much of an obstacle. In order to prove the authenticity of my merchandise, I am willing to allow a cooperative person to copy this manufacturing data and pass it on to the man Cornwall.

MOD: How about handing over one of those sample vials? For all I know, you could be peddling grape jelly.

HAJ: *[Insulted]* It is the true PD32:C2, only from a new source! I vow it upon my honor as a Joru! The virus will pass any test. If you wish, we can take it to a bioassay establishment immediately. I note that there is one listed in the Bazaar's directory.

MOD: Well . . . maybe that won't be necessary.

At this moment of truth I would tell the arms peddler that he could buy the sample for fifty kay and resell it to Cornwall for whatever the traffic would bear. He would laugh scornfully and accuse me of playing a confidence game. I would become furiously indignant at the insult, grab up my things, and storm out of the place.

Four dealers called me back before I got out the door, calmed my wounded feelings, and eventually persuaded me to let them have a freebie along with a dime copy of the magslate contents, citing their excellent reputation among the local entrepreneurs and their strong hope of being able to track down Barney Cornwall. I promised to phone the next day.

After making my pitch to the last trader, I returned to *Makebate*, stripped off my disguise, and had a long hot shower. Then I reconstituted some barbecued baby back ribs, a baked potato, some Blue Lake green beans, and a handful of snickerdoodle cookies, and ate them seated in my command chair while listening to quiet jazz selections by Bill Evans and Marian McPartland.

By and large I was well satisfied with the day's masquerade. Surely one of the four traders who had taken a sample would pass it on to Barky Tregarth—or at least contact him with news of the sensational find. Then my only challenge would be figuring out a safe way to snatch him and do the preliminary interrogation. I hoped the old man wouldn't be too frail to withstand the rigors of interrogation. Maybe he'd spill his guts for a payoff, as Adam Stanislawski had suggested. Then all I'd have to verify was the general truth of his statements.

I put on another recording—surf breaking on a barrier reef, rustling mint-palms, crooning elvis-birds—reclined in the chair and fell asleep. I dreamed of my tropical island on Kedge-Lockaby, 23,600 light-years away, and my new yellow submarine, which I'd hardly had a chance to break in.

In the "morning" I ate a big breakfast, since I'd get almost nothing to eat while in costume. It took nearly an hour and a half to restore my Joru makeup. Then I climbed into the gig and returned to the asteroid. On the way in I phoned the four arms dealers.

Two of them said they'd had no luck finding Barney Cornwall. They offered to return my vector samples. The other two, shiftier than the first pair, told me they were still looking. I should call again tomorrow. Or maybe the next day.

Rats.

I'd have to try my shtick on the other contraband merchants. There were nearly a hundred of them in the Bazaar, trading in everything from scandium fuel catalyst to Kalleyni pornography, and lots more were doing business in bars of public corridors. Even if I confined myself to humans and Y'tata, those races were far and away the most numerous among the dealers. I was in for a long and unpleasant haul.

Y'tata offensiveness went without saying. And if yesterday's experience held true, the human traders would be spectacularly rude. Interspecies harmony wore thin in the galactic boondocks, especially between humanity's lower orders and the snotty Joru, who had a rep for pennypinching. It wasn't much fun being an alien after all . . .

I left the docked gig and reentered the asteroid's big lobby,

thinking depressed thoughts, for the first time facing the
possibility that my clever scheme was a piece of shit. Maybe
Ram Mahtani had suckered me out of Stanislawski's big
bribe after all. Maybe Barky Tregarth had been dead for
years. Or if he was alive, maybe Ram had warned the old
geezer to run for his life. Maybe I was a self-deluding asshole off on a futile snipe-hunt, and I should have listened to
Karl and stayed home on Earth making use of the evidence
we already had—

"Hey, Mr. Joru! Missed you last night at Cucaracha
Loca."

I whirled about and found Sh'muz. His garb was cleaner
and his complexion had lost some of its terminal lividity. A
little money, a little hope of cashing in further on a good
thing, can do that.

"I told you that I do not require your services," I har-
rumphed.

"Sure you do," he retorted breezily. "I found somebody
you might really wanna meet."

"What! Are you saying you found Barney Cornwall?"

"An entity who knows him." He paused, then rubbed his
digits together in a gesture nearly universal among sapient
beings.

"Of course I'll pay you for the information." I named a
sum that would buy a ticket to any Y'tata planet within
Zone 3. "You say 'entity.' Does this mean that your source is
not a human?"

"Y'tata starship captain. Independent operator." Sh'muz
meant pirate. "He'll want to be paid, too. Lots more than
me."

"That part of the transaction need not concern you. When
and where may I meet this person?"

He twirled his eyes in the Y gesture equivalent to a wry
human shrug. "You coulda done it last night if you'd met me
in La Cuca. Come tonight. Same time, midnight. I'll do the
introduction, you pay me, I skedaddle."

"You are *absolutely* certain that this person can put me in contact with Barney Cornwall?"

"Hey—is the Pope Catholic?"

I huffed disdainfully through my mask. "That Standard English slang phrase does not translate into Joru, but I presume it is affirmative. Very well. Expect me at the drinking establishment at 2500 hours."

Sh'muz gave a jaunty farewell bounce—fortunately without losing control—and skipped away into the throng. I stood there for a while, thinking. It seemed a good idea to retrieve the two samples of PD32:C2—after all, they were Rampart property—so I did so, giving modest tips to the honest gun merchants. Then I scoped out La Cucaracha Loca and its immediate environs, with a view to abduction.

The bar was close to Phlegethon's busy fueling bays, a handy little oasis for transient starfarers and the contraband traders who wheeled and dealed with them. Loud Latin jazz played over an uproar of voices. The place served only human beverages and snacks, and was packed with human, T'tata, and Joru drinkers. Even a few grotesque Kalleyni squatted in a corner where the gravity was turned low, slurping beakers of corrosive White Lightning and shrieking mirthfully at their own jokes.

I ordered a martini. I hate martinis, but that's what Joru drink in human dives; martinis with extra olives because that's the best part of the drink. The aliens poke the gin-soaked fruit through the eating ports of their masks and chew rapturously. I wasn't ready to suffer that much for my art.

The bartender said, "Something wrong with the olives?" He was a tough-looking human with a pencil-thin mustache and sallow skin.

"They are exquisite," I assured him, "but I am feeling a trifle indisposed. Please direct me to the relief facility."

He looked at me funny, as though this were a question I should know the answer to. "In the rear, in the alley. Pay for your drink before you go."

The dimly lit alley-passage backed on numbers of other grogshops, cheap cabarets, and modest eateries in the immediate vicinity. It contained two refuse-recycling units, a triplex latrine with an exterior puke-basin, haphazard stacks of empty crates, and a stock-delivery elevator. The latter was in use.

Leaning against the toilet cubicle near the basin, I fumbled with my mask and moaned, pretending to be unwell, and watched a human worker bring barrels of beer out of the lift and tote them into one of the other pubs. When he was gone I summoned the elevator myself and surveyed the interior. The control pads were labeled with the names of several beverage and food supply outfits located on lower levels. The only Up button wore a little sign that said DOCK G-6.

Well, well.

I pressed it and made a short ascent. When the door slid open I found myself in an area where medium-sized freighters and the lighters that served larger starships were discharging cargo and taking it aboard. Roboporters loaded with container pods were zipping all over the place. A human stevedore maneuvered a train of small cars carrying crates of familiar terrestrial booze into a kind of cage next to my elevator and began off-loading them. Unfortunately, he spotted me in the open elevator car.

"Hey, Joru! Whatcha doing in there?"

When caught flatfooted in suspicious circumstances, act blotto. "Aargh. I—I fear I am confused by strong drink. I am seeking my vessel, the *Julog-Wul*. It appears I have come to the wrong dock."

"Yeah, well, you get the hell back downstairs and find the right fuckin' lift. This is a human dock. Joru ships tie up at D-3 and D-4."

I apologized and returned to where I had started. Back in La Cucaracha Loca, I treated myself to a shot of Jack Daniel's. The bartender looked at me askance, since Joru don't drink whiskey, but I didn't give a damn. It was celebration time.

I'd found a way to remove Barky Tregarth unobtrusively from Phlegethon. All I had to do was lure him to La Cuca, slip him a mickey, take him into the alley, lose my Joru disguise, and get us both up to Dock G-6. *Makebate*'s gig would come for us on autopilot if I summoned it with my phone-link. The dock was so busy that I doubted if anyone in authority would notice another small orbiter craft nosing in among the lighters and picking up two human crew members.

Yes. It was going to work . . . provided that Sh'muz and his pirate pal weren't scamming me.

I went back to my starship to get things ready.

I arrived half an hour early for the rendezvous, just because it seemed like a good thing to do, and sat unobtrusively at the end of the bar nearest the front door. The Latin music was less raucous than it had been during my earlier visit. Sh'muz and a formidable-looking entity who was clearly his informant were sitting together at one of the little tables, drinking beer. Y'tata love beer. The maroony had a longneck bottle of Bud, and the large ugly Y in the shiny skipper's uniform had just picked up his freshly arrived stein of draft and started to drink it down.

But the brew didn't suit the alien starship captain's taste. He puckered up his pasty face in revulsion, slammed the mug down on the table, splashing poor Sh'muz, and roared, "Waitress! This overpriced belly-wash is flat!"

"That's our top-line house microbrew," the overworked human server said over her shoulder. "You want more carbonation, blow bubbles in it. Just be sure you sue your north end—or I'll have our bouncer cork you so tight you'll never whistle 'Dixie' again."

This provoked general merriment among the non-Y'tata patrons. A human starship crewman called out, "That's telling him, Gigi! Fuckin' Y bum-tootler."

Actually, members of the intestinally challenged race frequenting La Cucaracha Loca that night seemed mostly to be on their good behavior. No alien flatus defiled the atmosphere, which smelled of tobacco smoke, grass, hops, popcorn, bacon sandwiches, and the odd but not unpleasant aroma of Kalleyni slime. But storm clouds, so to speak, were on the horizon.

"Insolent human shitwit!" yelled the Y'tata skipper to the starman, surging to his feet and flipping up the back of his copper-studded vest in challenge. "Step outside and I'll toot you right off the friggin' asteroid!"

A barroom brawl wouldn't serve my purposes. I rapidly pushed my way to the scene of the confrontation and placed myself between insulter and insultee. Even though I'm a Joru midget, I was considerably larger than either the Y skipper or the human starship crewman with the big mouth.

"If you please, dispenser of beverages!" I thundered to the barkeep, waving a large-denomination bill. "Serve both of these worthy entities some Pilsner Urquell. Include a thirty percent gratuity for yourself and the female server, and let tranquility and good fellowship be restored."

Gigi the waitress brought open bottles of the pricey premium brew with crystal glasses upended over the mouths. She handed one to the appreciative human spacer, who said, "Wow! I always wanted to try this stuff."

I appropriated the second Urquell and sat down at the table of the two Y'tata. "Allow me to do the honors, Captain," I said suavely, easing the golden liquid into the tilted glass and creating a moderate head of creamy foam. "I pray you will enjoy this most excellent variety of beer with my heartfelt compliments. It is brewed only in a single city on Earth."

The skipper glared at me suspiciously as he reassumed his seat. It took the Pilsner glass from my hand, upended it, and downed the beer in a single heroic chug. "Good bubbles. I'll have another one, Joru."

I signaled Gigi, who nodded and went off.

"This is Captain B'lit," said Sh'muz. He'd turned a whiter shade of pale during the face-off and his voice still quavered slightly.

"I am Gulow," I said. "I hope to do business with you tonight, Captain."

"How much is it worth to you?" the skipper inquired insolently.

I lowered my voice almost to the point of inaudibility. The other bar patrons were ignoring us now that the danger of a pong assault had abated. "If you are truly an acquaintance of the human trader Barney Cornwall," I said, "and are able to introduce me to him promptly, so that I may offer him certain rare merchandise, I will vouchsafe an appropriate emolument." I named a sum that made Sh'muz gasp.

"Double it," sneered B'lit, "and you got a deal."

"The aforesaid generous price is firm," I said stonily. "Vulgar haggling is beneath the dignity of the Joru."

"Cheapskate," muttered B'lit. His second Urquell arrived and he took his time pouring and sipping it. Finally: "How do you figure to pay?"

"By means of preloaded blind EFT cards issued by a human financial institution. Once activated, the cards are negotiable on any human world and many alien ones, with no questions asked."

"Hmm. This rare merchandise you want to sell to Cornwall . . ." The skipper was elaborately casual. "You got it in there?" A pink claw pointed at the locked metal case hanging on my baldric.

"Certainly not," I said. "The most valuable thing I have to sell, Captain B'lit, is information. And it is most securely guarded. As is my own person." I let him see the arm holsters up my sleeves. "Do not take me for a fool. Furthermore, I will require proof of Barney Cornwall's identity before I pay you."

"Ask him yourself, you Joru prick," the Y skipper said.

"He's sitting over there in the corner. He owns the goddamn joint! C'mon—I'll introduce you."

The two Y'tata and I moved through the closely packed patrons. The man in the corner had an unusual area of empty space around his table. He sat with his back to the wall, nursing a stein of microbrew, and watched our approach with an ironic smile.

It was a setup. But what kind? I decided I'd have to carry on according to plan.

The man who might have been Hamilcar Barca Tregarth didn't look at all like the doddering centenarian I'd envisioned. In fact, he might have been fifty years old or even younger, with shoulder-length brown hair and unlined, rather handsome features. If he really was the man I was looking for, he'd been very extensively—and expensively—rejuvenated. He wasn't tall but his build was solidly muscular, shown to advantage by a tailored jumpsuit of dark blue leather, zipped open to the waist to reveal a trendy fishnet T-shirt. Around his neck hung a heavy platinum chain with a large pendant. When we were closer, I was able to identify the stone in the pendant as an exotic fossil the size of a plum. I'd seen its like before, in the Perseus Spur . . .

"Hey, Barney," said the Y skipper.

"Hey, B'lit. Been a long time."

The Y'tata winked one piggy red eye. "This is the guy."

I did my Joru thing. "Do I have the pleasure of addressing Barney Cornwall?"

"Pleasure?" The man in the blue jumpsuit gave a hard laugh. "We'll have to see about that."

"Before we go any further," I said firmly, "I must tell you that a certain associate on my home world recommended Trader Cornwall as the person most likely to know the true value of . . . certain extremely specialized goods I am offering for sale. You must forgive me if I verify your identity."

"What!" B'lit exclaimed. "You want a DNA profile? It's

Barney Cornwall in the flesh, you Joru dipstick! Every big-time freebooter in the Sag knows him. Now pay me!"

"Me, too," Sh'muz whispered. "Please?"

I took a pair of EFT cards out of my baldric and programmed them with the agreed amounts, flapped a wait-a-bit paw at the two Y'tata, and addressed the man at the table. "There is a simple way to prove you are Barney Cornwall. Please tell me your other nickname."

His dark eyes turned to slits and I felt a brief touch of uneasiness. But after a prolonged pause, he smiled again and said softly, "Some people call me Barky."

"The very answer I had hoped for! Thank you for enduring my necessary gaucherie in a civilized manner." I handed EFT cards to each of the Y'tata. "And now I must insist that you two entities depart forthwith." Sh'muz scuttled off, but B'lit continued to stand there, smirking insolently. "Go!" I roared. Grabbing the copper epaulets of his uniform vest, I spun him about and gave him a propelling knee in the backside.

Bad move. He laughed, then retaliated as only a Y'tata can, strolling out of the place in a fusillade of farts as patrons rushed to get out of his way, groaning and cursing. But an instant later some sort of powerful exhaust fan kicked in and quickly sucked up the reek. I suppose there was a special sensor for social errors in this sort of place. The bartender cried, "Drinks on the house!" and any potential exodus was nipped in the bud.

Barky Tregarth was unperturbed. He indicated the seat opposite him and said, "Sit down." When I did, he stared at me in silence for several minutes, finishing his stein of beer. Then he gave a little nod, as though satisfied by his inspection, and placed a small object on the table between us.

It was one of the biocontainers of doctored PD32:C2 I'd handed out to the arms dealers the day before.

"*Terrific* bait!" he said. "The real thing. I had it checked out. And that's a damned good xeno disguise, too."

My innards turned to ice. I sat without moving. He'd made me as a human and a fraud, probably knew I was Ram Mahtani's mystery client. But did he know who I really was? And was there still a chance I could pull off the abduction?

He continued, "I knew you were looking for me as soon as your Y'tata bud contacted Captain B'lit yesterday. I had to check you out, after a warning that I got from a friend on Earth, so I had one of my people zap your paw with a diagnosticon in the seventh gun shop you visited yesterday. A medical body scanner, you know? You never noticed the gadget sitting on the counter. It said the skin of your hand wasn't alive. Imagine that! So you're not a Joru, and there's no new source of PD32:C2, and I'm kinda pissed off 'cause I was really hoping somebody had the fuckin' key to El Dorado for sale."

"There's still a lot of money to be made," I said, and started to open my baldric pouch.

"Hold still," Barky hissed. "You wouldn't be dumb enough to reach for a gun, would you? An associate of mine at the table behind you has you targeted. And I know about the Kagi and the Ivanov stashed up your sleeves."

But do you also know about my body armor? And my force-field generator?

"I'm reaching for another EFT card," I explained. "A very friendly sort of weapon. May I?"

He inclined his head and I pulled the little slip of plastic out and passed it across the table. It was Adam Stanislawski's last minute contribution to the war chest. Barky Tregarth's eyebrows rose as he checked the load readout. "A nice sum. Not El Dorado, but . . . nice. What do you want?"

"Information only. Confirmed psychotronically."

He laughed. "I'm just a gunrunner and innkeeper. Moderately prosperous in my old age. What do I know worth that kind of money?"

I leaned forward and pointed to the pendant hanging around his neck. "Where did your jewelry come from?"

He sat stock still, then said, "So that's it."

"I've seen that kind of fossil before, on the planet Artiuk, a Haluk colony in the Spur. Some of the local officials and other dignitaries I met on a visit there wore the pendants as badges of honor. But you didn't get yours in a Haluk Spur colony, did you, Barky?"

"No," he said calmly.

"It was given to you in the Haluk Cluster, wasn't it? That's why you were so anxious to redeem it from Clifton Castle, the fence who lent you the money you needed to escape from Tyrins, thirty-five years ago."

"You seem to know a lot about me."

"I have no animus against you. I'm not at all interested in your shady business career. But I do want to know what you saw when you visited the Haluk Cluster. I want any information you have on their population density, the total number of inhabited planets, the demographic pressures that drove them to emigrate to the Perseus Spur. I want to know how big a supply of transactinide elements they have out there in their cluster, and how they mine ultraheavies, given their inferior technology. And I'd like to know what they're doing *here*, in the Sag."

"Who are you?" Barky Tregarth asked.

"My name isn't important, but I do have some important friends. One of them is responsible for the stake on that EFT card. I believe that the Haluk are still hostile to humanity and plan to invade our galaxy. Part of their strategy involves attacks on our starships. That's going on right here and now, in the Sagittarius Whorl. Haluk bandits are hijacking transack carriers, and Sheltok Concern is doing a big cover-up, pressured by other members of the Haluk Consortium who do business with the aliens. The Haluk scheme for domination also involves infiltration—a conquest from within. My friends and I have proof that Haluk masquerading as human beings have wormed their way into the Hundred Concerns. They may even have spies in our government. We need more evidence to support our contention that the Haluk represent a serious threat to human security. When we get it, we'll put it before the Commonwealth Assembly. Public opinion will force the Delegates to reexamine the Haluk nonaggression pact and their trade treaty."

Barky was still holding the nonactive EFT card, doing the old gambler's trick of "walking" it from one finger to another. "Politics!" He gave a bleat of derisive laughter. "Fuck that. I'm a Throwaway—a noncitizen. The Commonwealth says I don't exist. Why should I give a hoot in hell if blueberry raiders heist trans-ack carriers? In the Sag, Sheltok charges stargoing aliens and independent human operators twice as much for fuel as it charges Concern ships. So the Haluk even the score, with a little help from the Y'tata. Big deal."

"I think they're planning to wage war, Barky. Interrupting our supply of vital fuel elements is only part of their strategy."

"That's a crock of shit. The Haluk want to trade, not fight."

"Are they buying weapons from you?"

"Sure! It's no big thing. So do the real Joru, and the Kalleyni, and the Y. I'm the biggest gun-peddler on Phleg. And you know where I get my merchandise? From Carnelian, and from over a dozen other Concerns who wink at contraband trafficking. What do those corporate ass-wipes in Toronto care where the stuff goes, as long as the price is right? As for your war idea, I think it's crapola. There aren't enough Haluk fighting ships in the Sag to wage war on the Kalleyni fruit fleet—much less the Human Commonwealth."

"Do you know how many Haluk ships are operating here?"

He held up the EFT card between two fingers. "Will the blueberries know I sold 'em out if I talk to you?"

"No," I lied. "Whatever I learn from you will only be used

back on Earth. For political purposes, as you said. My friends and I have no interest whatsoever in shutting down your Phlegethon operation or halting your trade with the Haluk. Even if we did, how could we? The asteroid is Sheltok property. CCID and the Secretariat enforcers have no authority here unless Sheltok grants it. That won't happen."

"I can't compromise my Haluk tie-in."

"You don't have to. Any questions I ask that you don't want to answer—don't. We can still do business."

"Maybe." He was twiddling the card again, apparently weighing the pros and cons. As he'd observed, it was a nice amount of money.

I said, "If you talk to me, you'll be just another confidential source. CHW can't touch you. As you pointed out, you're an important man here on Phlegethon."

"Damn straight," said Barky Tregarth, grinning. "You try anything cute, you're one dead Joru fucker."

I nodded submissively. "I have a Hogan miniature psychotronic interrogation device in my case—useless for prying the truth out of reluctant subjects, but it will indicate whether a cooperative person is telling the truth. You can sit right here and tell me about your adventure in the Haluk Cluster—that's the thing I'm most interested in—then add whatever else you wish to tell me about Haluk activity in the Sag. I can check your veracity with a single question: 'Is everything you've said the truth?' If the machine confirms your reply, I'll activate the plastic. You'll be richer by four million. What do you say?"

"What the hey! Why not? You know, it's kinda gratifying to finally find somebody who believes that I made the Big Trip."

A waitress came up behind me and asked if we wanted another round of drinks.

Barky gave her a big smile. "Another stein of Peg-Leg for me, Lola. And my friend . . ."

"Jack Daniel's," I said. "Straight up."

"I thought Joru didn't like whiskey," the waitress said.

"It is an acquired taste," I replied over my shoulder, "and I've just acquired it."

It was not so much the great distance to the Haluk Cluster that had deterred exploration by the Commonwealth of Human Worlds so much as the uselessness of the enterprise. The implacably hostile aliens wanted nothing to do with humanity, and in the early days of human galactic exploration the Haluk backed up their antipathy with enough firepower to deter CHW survey ships and curious adventurers.

Later, after Galapharma AC began to exploit the Perseus Spur and faced attacks from Haluk colonies there, the big Concern and Zone Patrol got tough. Humans and Haluk fought a brief interstellar battle near the human colony of Nogawa-Krupp, and the aliens were soundly defeated. Facing the potential annihilation of their eleven colonial planets, the Haluk signed an armistice. One of its terms halted their Milky Way expansion; another precluded human exploration of the Haluk Cluster.

Barky Tregarth figured he had a chance of making the trip and coming back alive because he was a smuggler, not a representative of a Concern or CHW. The Haluk desperately needed the superior technical equipment made by humanity, and the only way to get it was through contraband dealers like Barky. Most human outlaw traders dealt with the Haluk in deep space; but a handful of the most favored made brief visits to Haluk Spur colonies.

One of the favored ones was Barky.

Without telling his wagering pals, he prevailed upon a Haluk business acquaintance on Artiuk to provide him with a letter of introduction. Then he returned to his base on the freesoil planet Yakima-Two, a notorious smuggler hangout, and made his wager. It was a very large one.

He fitted his starship, which was over twice the size of *Makebate*, with oversized fuel cells as I had done, and still had enough room left in the hold for a cargo that he thought would ensure him a warm welcome once he arrived. He loaded his ship with high-end computers, force-field generators, portable antimatter powerplants, programmable virtual-reality ticklesuits, a single Bodascon ULD engine of the latest type, and 1,500 Japanese silk kimonos in subtle colors, size *okii*, highly coveted by Haluk males as wedding garments.

Then he set off where no human had gone before.

Even thirty-five years ago the scanner technology on Barky's ship was hugely superior to that of the Haluk. He managed to elude all of their patrols, he found the solar system where the cousin of his Artiuk acquaintance resided, and after some very fast talking he was allowed to come landside in his gig.

The cousin, whose name was Ratumiak, was on the personal staff of the planetary governor and a person of considerable influence. He advised Barky to forget any notion of selling his valuable cargo. Instead, the smuggler presented everything to the governor as a gift. On Ratumiak's advice, Barky told the Haluk official the barebones truth: that he had made the trip on a bet.

The governor thought that was hilarious.

He compared Barky's lunatic exploit to a similar jaunt by a legendary Haluk hero and declared that the bold human voyager would be treated as an honored guest. Barky got a grand tour of the Haluk world and asked a lot of questions about the alien civilization. His roguish sense of humor, snarky jabs at Commonwealth policies, and shocking tales of Concern corruption made a great hit with his hosts, who showered him with gifts—some of great intrinsic value, including a diamond ear-stud from Ratumiak and the fossil set in platinum given to him by the governor.

Barky had a marvelous time during his eighteen-day stay and didn't mind that most Haluk looked on him as an entertaining freak. Amazingly, a few Haluk females found him sexually appealing, and taught him several astonishing things he would later find useful in his love-life. When it was time to depart, he was bid a cordial farewell and warned never to return to the Haluk Cluster under pain of death.

He set off for the Milky Way and had nearly made it back safely to his base on Yakima-Two when he was attacked by a human pirate ship. Its scanners were even better than Barky's, and its ship faster and better armed. The bandits forced Barky to surrender, boarded, and stole all of the Haluk gifts except the fossil, which Barky managed to detach from its chain and conceal in a bodily orifice. Then the pirates stole his ship, too.

He was set adrift in a lifeboat and eventually rescued by a Rampart freighter, which dropped him off on Hadrach, from which he made his way home to Yakima-Two and the heart-breaking discovery that he wasn't going to collect on the big bet.

"That was really an unfortunate happenstance," I said as he finished his tale. "Losing your ship on top of everything."

"Oh, I got that back a year or so later with a little help from my friends," he said. "I knew who'd taken it, you see. But the alien jewelry and stuff were long since disposed of." He shrugged. "Then I got busted by the patrol and jugged on Tyrins. I think you know the rest of the story." The ironic smile again. "I escaped, knocked around the galaxy, ended up here, got lucky. Just imagine my surprise when the Haluk showed up in the Sag. They hadn't forgotten me, either. We do good business. I intend to keep on doing good business." The smile turned cold, and once again I felt the frisson of uneasiness.

The waitress came up behind me again and asked if we'd like another round.

"A Peg-Leg for me, Lola," Barky said. He seemed relaxed and amiable. "And some of my private-stock whiskey for my friend, here. The Wild Turkey Single-Barrel." She left us, and he said to me, "You'll really get a kick out of it. Best I ever tasted."

"I've heard of it, never tried it."

He held out the EFT card. "You ready to validate this now?"

"Just a few more questions. Did the Haluk planet you visited seem heavily populated?"

"You better believe it. High-rise buildings packed to the rafters in the cities, affluent folks in the suburbs living in little cottages on handkerchief-sized plots. Ratumiak told me his planet had a population of nearly twelve thousand million. Other worlds were even worse."

"How many inhabited worlds were there in the cluster?"

"Around thirty thousand, Ratty said. Ideally, Haluk need T-2 worlds. They'd already colonized all of those, plus all of the T-1's and a few T-3's that weren't too hopeless. But they'd really run out of suitable land. That's why they made the big jump to our galaxy, even though it was a terrible drain on the economy."

I had already done the horrifying calculation in my head. Twelve billion times thirty thousand equals . . . *360 trillion Haluk?* It was forty times the population of galactic humanity!

"Uh—do you know how they manage to mine transactinides without sophisticated robotics?"

His expression turned grim. "The lepidos do it. You know, the thick-skinned intermediate racial morph. Even in heavy armor, the poor bastards don't live long on R-class planets. They're convicts. Gracile-phase cons work in the orbiting collection stations until they go lep. Then it's down to the mines. A lepido miner turns up its toes, the supers retrieve the armor, send somebody else down."

"Appalling."

He shrugged. "Different strokes for different folks. It's gotta be a dandy crime deterrent."

"Do the Haluk have a large supply of ultraheavy elements?"

"Don't have a clue."

"Would you say they're highly industrialized?"

"You bet. Not up to human standards when I was in the cluster, but I understand that's changed. Haluk are quick on the uptake. They're good at copying our technology. Even make improvements on the original."

Well, we had proof of that already. One of my friends had compared Haluk ingenuity to that of the preindustrial Japanese.

"Drinks, gents." Lola the waitress set them down.

I thanked her over my shoulder. "One last question, Barky." Then I'd hook him to the little machine and—*zotz!* I'd modified my earlier plan slightly. Instead of slipping him a mickey, I'd modified the interrogation device to deliver a taser bolt. If I acted fast, I could have both of us behind a hemispherical force-field shield within seconds. Then out the back door and into the elevator . . .

"Try the Wild Turkey," he urged. "Let me know what you think."

I sipped the exquisite bourbon through my mask's integral straw—not the best way to savor one of Earth's premium spirits, but the bouquet came through with a vengeance. "Superb," I said. "One of the best I've ever tasted."

"I think so, too. What's your last question?"

"What are the Haluk doing here in the Sagittarius Whorl?"

"Grabbing transactinides. They figure if we start experiencing a shortage, they can jack up their prices."

"It seems logical," I said. "Are you ready to undergo the truth test?" I took out the little machine and set it on the table right next to the EFT card. Barky had put it down when his fresh schooner of beer arrived.

"I don't think I'd better," he said, pushing the card toward me. "Our deal is off, Citizen Frost. But it was fun talking to you." He raised his voice. "Lola!"

Oh, shit. The force-field projector was in a pocket behind my robe's front scapular drape. I tried to reach for it, but my arm suddenly wasn't working. Neither were my leg muscles when I tried to jump to my feet. Earlier, when I'd been forced to visualize the failure of my grand scheme, Ram Mahtani had played the villain's part. But Ram wasn't the one who had worked with Barky Tregarth to play me for a sucker.

The waitress named Lola came around the table and for the first time I got a good look at her. She was drop-dead gorgeous, with glossy black hair that had a white blaze at the left temple.

"Dolores da Gama?" I managed to whisper. "You slipped me a mickey?"

"It seemed the simplest course," the demiclone said complacently, "with all the body armor you're wearing. The drug is a harmless and effective way to bring you down."

Barky was standing beside her. "My bouncers will take him to your starship gig. It was great doing business with you, Lola. You make a pretty good waitress. Sure you don't want a job?"

Dolores da Gama laughed richly and gave him a playful smack on his taut, leather-covered buns. I felt strong hands grip me, hoist me upright, move me toward the rear door. Dolores was utilizing my own abduction scheme.

"Why . . ." I gasped. "Why . . . want me alive?"

"We'll think of something wonderful, sweetie." Her smile was megawatt bright in my fading vision.

"How . . . find me here?"

"Your gunfight with our corsairs. One of the pilots transmitted your starship conformation and fuel-trace signature to our base on Amenti before you blasted her out of the sky. Your ship is unique. We sent out other corsairs to track you to Phlegethon."

We were in the elevator, going up. I was seeing the world

through a shrinking tunnel embedded in fog. "But how did . . . *you* get here so quick?"

"I left Earth the day after you escaped from us. So did other Haluk agents. The massive fuel-bunker refit on your ship showed your intent to undertake a long, stealthy voyage. It was a toss-up which way you'd go—either the Spur, for a penetration of our cluster, or the Whorl. We believed you might have found out about our campaign against Sheltok. Other Haluk were waiting for you near Seriphos and Tyrins, in case you topped off your tanks at either planet before leaving the galaxy. I drew the Sag assignment and went to Amenti with my assistants. And suddenly, there you were. Potting our people in cold blood. You're a ruthless man, Asahel Frost."

"What happen . . . *real* Dolores? You show her . . . any bloody compassion?"

We were out of the elevator, heading for a gig. I had no doubt that a fast Haluk starship was waiting in orbit, hidden with a dissimulator field a little less efficient than *Makebate*'s.

My head in its Joru makeup wobbled helplessly. In another minute I'd pass out, and she seemed to know it. "You're about to experience what Dolores did. It won't be unpleasant. But before you sleep, here's a little extra information to give you pleasant dreams. We have another reason for stealing transactinides: our ships will need extra fuel for the invasion."

"I knew that," I said, and faded to black.

Chapter 7

I expected they would take me to their secret base on Amenti—an asteroid station abandoned nearly eighty years ago by Sheltok—or even to a Haluk colony in the Perseus Spur. Instead, as I discovered much later, they brought me back to Toronto, to the commercial and residential tower where they had established their embassy and secure living quarters.

There I was demicloned. Twice. The complicated process took about seven months. When I was finally released from the dystasis tank it was mid-November, although I didn't learn the date right away.

I had the superficial appearance of a Haluk, a side effect of the preliminary phase of the demiclone process. The disorienting discovery didn't prevent me from executing the Helly Frost replica who shared my recovery room—the demiclone who had lived most of his life as a Haluk. But another perfect duplicate of me was already at large, committing God knows what sort of crimes in my name. The first impostor was a renegade human being, collaborating with the aliens.

I hadn't had much time to speculate on the identity of Fake Helly I. When the medical device monitoring Fake Helly II flat-lined, it triggered an alarm. Rather slow on the uptake, four blue-skinned xenos took their own sweet time coming to the recovery room to see what had happened. None wore translators. Two of the Haluk were meditechs, the same ones who had attended me and Fake Helly II while we recuperated from dystasis. The other pair were uniformed embassy guards armed with Ivanov stun-pistols.

The aliens stood in a close group, about ten feet away from me. They had me backed up against the tall windows. I'd opened the drapes earlier to determine my whereabouts, and outside was a nightscape of downtown Toronto, a glittering forest of colored glass towers.

The taller guard barked at me in his own language. "Human! Do not move!"

I understood. With two laser targeting dots shining on my sternum, it was easy. I stood still.

The female medic, Avilik, darted to the bed where the dead demiclone lay and checked out the corpse with a diagnosticon. She uttered a horrified expletive, then came away from the bed and spoke to me in the Haluk tongue. "Wah! What have you done? Ru Balakalak is not only dead, he is *blah blah*!"

"Yeah. He sure as hell is," I replied in English. My tongue felt funny and my teeth seemed to be too far apart. The larynx was mine, but it was laboring under some exotic handicap. My voice was gravelly and deeply resonant, almost Louis Armstrongesque. I continued in execrable Halukese. "This one did it! Ru Balakalak will not live again by dystasis. This one thinks that is very, very good!" I switched back to English. "And fuck you all very much."

The four of them exclaimed, "Wah!"

Then Avilik began to jabber rapidly with her male colleague, whose name was Miruviak. I only understood one word in ten of the agitated conversation, but the general tenor seemed to be that some maximal manure would impact the rotor when the Servant of Servants found out about the catastrophe. Damage control was the order of the day.

I was stark naked. My general bodily contour was still sturdily human, not nearly so willowy as that of normal Haluk males. I had a narrow waist and four-fingered hands without nails. My skin was sky-blue, except for the parts of me smeared with my own blood. My chest, arms, and upper legs were patterned with intricate ridges almost like glossy scars, some of them nicely marked with gold. I had seen my face briefly in a mirror before the aliens found me. By human standards I was hideous. I had short silvery hair. My normally green eyes were now a brilliant sapphire, with huge irises and no visible whites. My eye sockets were slightly smaller than those of a true Haluk, but any ordinary human observer would take me for a genuine blueberry.

Hey, all Haluk look alike.

I held a bloody towel to the streaming wound at the back of my neck. It marked the place where I'd hacked out a small shocker device, implanted in the skin at the base of my skull for the purpose of controlling me. It hadn't.

Avilik and Miruviak finished talking and stared at me balefully. The big guard rapped out a question to them in unintelligible Halukese. Probably: "Should I stun this fucker's ass now?"

"Don't shoot!" said Avilik. "Don't hurt him!"

Her male partner asked a question that I only understood part of. "*Blah blah* him now with *blah blah*?"

Avilik said, "Yes. Be careful and slow. He *blah blah* but we must *blah* and make a new demiclone."

Miruviak carried a small case, which he snapped open, revealing a shiny little instrument with a pistol grip, a cylindrical metal body, and a short barrel tipped with a glass knob. Bea Mangan had used one of those on me, the night she'd picked me up in the snowstorm. The thing was a hypodermic injector, the kind without a needle that squirts powerful little jets of liquid right through unbroken skin and clothing. It was probably full of a gentler sort of knockout juice.

"Human?" Miruviak said to me gently. "One will not hurt you. Only *blah blah* sleep."

He started toward me. In order to inject the drug he had to

touch me with the glass knob. The guards still had me targeted. They held their Ivanovs two-handed, in the approved
human combat style. I suppose Haluk demiclones had
bought the stun-guns on the thriving Toronto black market.
No aliens were permitted to carry arms on Earth.

Miruviak was coming at me from the right. Haluk faces
are hard to read because of the ridged patterns, but it seemed
to me that he was distinctly nervous at the prospect of putting down a brute my size.

The big guard must have thought so, too. "*Blah* Vumilak
and this one *blah* put our guns to his head *blah blah*. He is
too large and strong *blah blah blah*."

"Be silent," Avilik told Big Guy. She acted like the boss of
the outfit. "The human is frightened and *blah*. He is also feeble from *blah blah* in dystasis and *blah blah*. You shoot *blah
blah blah*."

Yeah. Only as a last resort. Okay, let's boogie . . .

I touched my bloody nape, let out a groan, and did a little
stagger dance that took me back against the windowsill.
Cringed away and whimpered in broken Halukese, "No! Do
not do it. No dystasis!"

Clutched the sopping scarlet towel tightly at one end.

Miruviak was closing in, making soothing sounds. I
turned toward him and whip-snapped the towel sharply in
his face, then flung the gory thing at the guards.

Eeeuw! They couldn't help flinching. By the time they'd
recovered, I'd grabbed the startled medic by both skinny
wrists and pulled him against me as a shield. The guards
fired their stun-guns. Miruviak took two bolts in the back
and sagged, dropping the injector.

I picked up his slight form and threw it at the guards.
Avilik was screaming unheeded orders. The unconscious
medic's body hit both Haluk and sent them sprawling.
Scooping up the injector, I took a headlong dive and skidded
across the slick parquet floor toward the floundering pile of
aliens. Found a uniformed leg. Pressed the injector ball

against a thigh and shot the high-velocity jet right through the cloth. The smaller guard let out a squawk and dropped his Ivanov. I grabbed it.

Big Guy was on his back, still entangled in the cold-cocked medic, waving his weapon and cursing. He fired a dart at the ceiling and another at the wall. A third barely missed my head. Then I shot him in the ribs and he subsided.

Avilik gave a wail and ran for the door. Firing from the floor, I popped her in the shoulder. She folded into a crumpled heap.

Intense! I stayed down for a while, drained of the raging hormones that had let me override my tank-induced debility. Avilik had been correct when she opined I was feeble from dystasis and scared stiff. I'd also suffered considerable blood loss. But I was a husky human male, not a Haluk, and under certain dire circumstances we can do great and wondrous deeds. I breathed deeply, psyched myself up, and got to my feet. Washed-up Supercop pulls his fraying shit together once again, spurred by the realization that time's a-wasting.

Get out of this goddamn place, Helly. And do it pronto.

I made my rubber-leggedy way to the door and tried it. It was locked. Somebody had to have a key-card. I knelt beside Avilik. If she was the boss . . . yes! An encoded red-striped plastic slip was in an outer pocket of her smock. I turned off all the room lights from the switch plate beside the door, unlocked it, and cracked it open the merest nanoskosh. Then I did my patented reconnoiter from knee height. Nobody ever expects to see a person peeking from down there.

The recovery room door was one of three opening into a small foyer at the end of a long corridor. The other two doors nearby bore Haluk ideographs that I couldn't decipher. There were more doors down the hall, all closed, and an alcove midway along that I hoped might contain an elevator. No one was in sight.

I closed the door again and locked it, turned the lights back on. Then I started undressing Big Guy. He had a nice

Breitling wrist chronometer that I strapped on. His spiffy gray uniform with black accents would be a tad snug for my human physique, but at least my wrists wouldn't stick out of the tunic arms like a scarecrow's, and the boots looked like they'd fit my funny feet. He wore grubby alien underwear, which I eschewed.

Big Guy's family jewels made a modest bulge in his drawers and seemed more meager than my own newly acquired exotic equipment. Maybe that explained Avilik's appreciative remarks earlier . . .

Before I put the clothes on I took a fast shower. My damned neck gouge was still leaking—I found out later that dystasis puts anticoagulants into the blood that take a few hours to wear off—so I ripped a pillow cover into narrow strips and bound up the wound as well as I could. *You* try tying a pressure bandage around your neck . . .

All dressed up, wearing Big Guy's holstered Ivanov and with the second stun-gun tucked inside my tunic, I looked like one dangerous Haluk. I felt on the verge of keeling over, but that was not an option. Searching the other three bodies, I found an assortment of colored key-cards and tucked one of each kind into my gun-belt pouch. All of the aliens carried phones, and for a few moments I thought I'd hit the jackpot. But when I tried to call Karl Nazarian's personal code—one of the few I could remember offhand—I reached a Halukese-speaker and hastily hit End. A check of the instrument's dex showed that only a list of preprogrammed codes were accessible—and they all had to be Haluk. I might have known there'd be no easy access to the general telecom net.

Rats. Without a pocket phone, and the personalized dex and datalink facilities that went with it, you were almost nonexistent on twenty-third-century Earth.

Well, if I couldn't call for help, I'd have to walk out. Or ride.

Unfortunately, the aliens weren't carrying human money

or credit cards, which might have been useful. The only other items I appropriated were the sedative injector—returned to its case; a flashlight, wrist restraints, and magazine pouch that were clipped to Big Guy's belt; an alien switchblade knife I was surprised to find on Miruviak; and a steel flask from Small Guy's inside tunic pocket that contained a facsimile of high-proof vodka.

Science tells us that alcohol is not a stimulant. I beg to differ. A quick snort perked me up considerably.

After momentary hesitation I also stole Big Guy's platinum ring inset with a fire-opal cabochon, slipping it on my own elongated alien finger. If I didn't have money or credit, maybe I could barter.

Before I left the room I returned to the window and tried to orient myself. The Haluk embassy occupied the top 210 floors of a huge structure called Macpherson Tower, on Edward Street near Yonge, right across from Sheltok's headquarters. My window looked south, toward Sheltok Tower, and by comparing the two buildings I figured I was on the 180th floor, or thereabouts. Most towers in this vicinity had automobile access ramps to the downtown skyways on the fiftieth, 100th, and 200th floors. Maybe I could commandeer a car at one of the upper ramp portals.

That would be my preferred plan of action. If it didn't work I'd try to descend to the Path—provided I could pass through the security system that sequestered the Haluk section of the tower from the human-occupied suites below. The only other way out I could think of was via the hopper skyport at the tower's summit, which was used exclusively by the alien tenants. But high-floor suites inevitably belong to high-ranking persons. Security up there and at the skyport was probably extra-tight. The 100th-floor auto ramp was my best hope.

I left the recovery room, found the elevators, drew the Ivanov from my tunic, and pressed the Down pad. The wait seemed endless.

Except for a few signs and door designations in Halukese and a nice piece of alien sculpture by the window at the end of the lift alcove, everything I'd seen in the corridor looked undistinguished and completely human—the carpeting, the light fixtures, card locks on the doors, even the occasional potted terrestrial plant. But it was a human-owned building, of course. The Macpherson management would not have allowed major xenoforming.

The elevator arrival chime sounded and I felt my muscles tense. I had tucked my right hand into the front of my tunic, Napoleon style, gripping the unholstered Ivanov. If the door opened on a squad of armed Haluk coming to reinforce the two I'd chopped—worst-case scenario—I was ready to fill the car with stun-bolts. But disposing of the snoozers would be risky, maybe impossible.

If I got lucky and the car held unarmed Haluk or demi-clones, I'd play it by ear. Act the aloof cop and keep my mouth shut if anyone spoke to me. I could only guess which pad designated the 100th floor unless the Haluk had left the original numbering intact. However, most commercial tower elevators had a hopper or auto icon next to the pads for the appropriate floors.

The door slid open. Only one person was inside, a tall, thin human male.

My older brother Daniel.

For a moment I was sandbagged with shock. But his glazed eyes slid over me, hardly seeing me. I was just another alien.

I stepped into the elevator beside him and glanced briefly at the panel. There were no icons designating the skyway portals, and the floors were designated only with alien symbols. I touched the pad for the lowest floor. A red light immediately began blinking beside a card slot that bore a little Halukese sign. The car door remained open and the chime pinged annoyingly.

Oops. I wasn't ready to try out my card collection just yet. I hastily hit a button a couple of floors above the interdicted one. The elevator door slid shut and we descended. My brother didn't even notice that I'd goofed. He seemed dazed.

Dan wasn't going nearly so far as the lower floor I'd randomly chosen. The car stopped, and when he got off I was right behind him. He slouched along like a sleepwalker. He was dressed in black slacks, an argyle sweater-vest, and a yellow shirt. He'd lost a lot of weight and there were dark circles under his eyes. I wondered if he was still drugged.

We were in a residential part of the building. A few other people passed us in the maze of corridors, evidently coming from other banks of elevators. They looked human and probably weren't. Some carried attaché cases and wore expensive outerwear. They appeared to be homeward bound executives and I wondered which Concerns they'd infiltrated. Domestic robots trundled along, carrying clean towels and other supplies. A servitron unit popped out of a little door in the wall, bringing room-service dinner to someone. Humanized Haluk have to eat human food. Their exotic edibles are slightly poisonous to the human metabolism. I caught a whiff of some savory entrée that made my empty stomach clench like a fist.

My brother Dan still didn't realize he was being followed. He slipped a key-card into his lock and opened the door to his apartment. I spoke in an imitation of mechanically translated Haluk speech. "Daniel Frost! One wishes to speak with you."

He whirled around, threw me a look compounded of fright and fury, then quick as a jackrabbit whipped inside and slammed the door in my face.

Well, shit.

I sorted through the access cards. The red one didn't work. Neither did blue, green, or gold. I tried an important-looking jobbie with silvery stripes: bingo.

When I came in and closed the door behind me, Dan was

standing there vibrating with rage. "Ah, for chrissake! I just finished a six-hour session with the damned tutors. Not even a fuckin' potty break! Can't you xeno bastards give me a minute's peace?"

"One must question you," I repeated.

"I'm taking a leak before you start," he said. "You don't like it, stun me." He disappeared into the bathroom.

I did a quick prowl of the apartment. There were no obvious surveillance devices, but that didn't mean the place wasn't bugged. Most likely the aliens had only installed antisuicide sensors that monitored the occupant's breathing.

The comfortably furnished living room had an infomedia center and a well-stocked library of slates and e-books. Tranquil pictures on the walls, nice gas-log fireplace, even a musical keyboard. Dan liked to noodle on the piano and faked jazz tunes rather well. The bedroom/office contained a queen-sized bed—made with military precision—and a computer desk. I sat down at the unit and tried to call up a general telecom link. No luck, but no surprise, either.

The closet held a fair selection of clothes and shoes, arranged meticulously. Good old anal-retentive Dan. There were a couple of track suits that might fit me. I took the roomiest one, which was navy-blue, and found athletic shoes and a gym bag to go with it. A dresser yielded socks, underwear, and even a baseball cap with a Toronto Blue Jays logo. I stuffed everything into the bag.

Dan came out of the john and did a disbelieving double take. "What the fuck! You're stealing my *clothes*?"

I said, "Give me your phone. Now." The instrument was no doubt as useless to me as the ones carried by the Haluk; but I couldn't trust Dan not to call on the aliens for help.

He dug in his pocket and handed the phone over. Trained to instant obedience. Good. If I kept a close eye on him, he wouldn't be able to raise the alarm.

I checked the phone dex and found only the same kind of preprogrammed codes the Haluk phones had contained.

When I asked the instrument if it had any extensions, it replied in the negative.

"You got anything to eat, Dan?" I'd dropped the Haluk diction, having decided how I was going to handle him, but he seemed not to notice.

"In the kitchen," he said sullenly. "But it's all human chow. We can order in if you like."

"No need," I said.

I herded him ahead of me and made him open the refrigerator. Saw sliced ham, Jarlsberg cheese, tomatoes, Grey Poupon mustard. *Perfecto!* I ordered him to build me two sandwiches and nuke them in the microwave.

"You're joking!" he exclaimed. His eyes were red and swollen and his pupils tiny. He was on something, but if he'd been working with Haluk tutors, his intellect was probably operational.

The little dining table was maple, with matching captain's chairs. I sat down, drew the Ivanov from inside my tunic, and put it on the table in front of me. "I'll also have some strong coffee with sugar. A big glass of water, too."

He moved about following orders and finally set my repast before me. I told him to sit down and wait, then fell on the food and drink like a famished coyote. The last time I'd been in dystasis, in K-L's little hospital, they'd fed me baby slop when I came out. Maybe solid food in my empty stomach would sicken me. I didn't care.

Dan watched, frowning and biting his lower lip, which was already raw. I'd almost finished eating when his eyes narrowed and he figured it out. He gave a terrified gurgle and bounded to his feet, nearly knocking over his chair.

"You!" he gasped. "Asa . . . my God, it's *you*, isn't it!" Sweat had burst out on his forehead and his eyes were bulging. He looked like he was about to have a coronary.

"Sit down." I picked up the stun-pistol and waved it casually. "Yes, it's me. Take it easy, Dan. It's all right. We have to talk. They'll be looking for me soon, but I figure I've got a little time yet."

"How did you get away? Jesus! We were supposed to begin the tutoring sessions for your second demiclone to-morrow. That's what—"

"Be quiet. I need answers to some questions. Tell me: Which floor is the skyway portal on?"

He paused for only a moment before answering. "The two hundredth is the only one the Haluk use. The one at the hun-dredth floor is closed for security reasons. It's at the bound-ary between Haluk and human occupancy. But you'll never escape through the two hundredth. It's used by Haluk top brass. There are at least three checkpoints, and the guards up there carry Kagi blasters."

"What kind of security do they have at the lowest Haluk level? The hundredth floor?"

"Double card-locks, gold and blue, guards armed with stunners. It's the main egress. Haluk are going in and out twenty-four hours a day."

Okay. So would I.

"Dan, I'm busting out of here. D'you want to come with me?"

"Yes," he said dully. "But I can't. And you probably can't get away, either. They've put control implants into us."

"In the neck. Right. I cut mine out and I can do the same for you."

He gave a hollow laugh and tapped his breastbone. "There's another one, Asa. In the thoracic cavity. You cross a blue checkpoint without your attendant entering the proper code, a tiny charge detonates and vaporizes your heart and lungs."

Rats! . . . But had the meditechs gotten around to in-stalling the lethal gizmo in me? Didn't I recall one of them saying they'd wait on it? Or was I mistaken? Had they put it in before I regained consciousness?

I said, "I'll get you out of this place. Trust me. If you give me truthful answers to some questions, I swear I'll come back and help you. And when you're out, and this Haluk mess is resolved, I'll let you live with your family again . . . if they want you."

Another dismal laugh. "I'm fucked, Asa. And so are you."

"Dan, I'm getting out, and I'm going to raise such a media stink that the Haluk will be begging us to rewrite their treaties and let us send inspection teams to their colonies."

"In your dreams."

"Who is the first demiclone?" I asked.

He stared at me stupidly. "I don't—"

"Fake Asahel Frost, Mark One," I prompted him. "Who's the human male the Haluk transformed the first time around? The one out there pretending to be me, right this very minute? The aliens didn't trust this mutt, but they had to use him until their own boy came out of the tank. I had half a notion the Haluk might have used you to impersonate me, but that didn't make sense. So it's somebody else. Who?"

Dan had gone white. He was shaking his head. "No. They'll kill me, Asa. I can't tell—"

I stood up, grabbed his shirt, and hauled him halfway across the table for a nose-to-nose. "*I'll* kill you, asshole, with my bare hands! But you won't go quick. You'll scream until your goddamn voice-box is in shreds. Tell me his name! Tell me! Tell me!" I shook him till his eyes rolled, then pushed him backward. He crashed into his chair. Spilled coffee spread over the table and dripped onto the floor. My brother crouched there, numb with fear. Then he began to weep.

First the Bad Cop, then the Good Cop.

I sat down again. "Danny, Danny. I know what happened. They took you from the Kenora fishing lodge and brought you here. Told you that you could go on living if you cooperated. They needed background material on me to make their demiclone masquerade work. Intensely detailed stuff. So their clone could fool Eve and Delegate Sontag as well as my associates."

"They had me hooked to the machines for nearly three weeks," he whispered, scrubbing at his face with the back of one hand. "I thought I was a goner. The pain, Asa! Like every nerve in my body was on fire. Like being wrapped in a burning net! They squeezed me dry. Then they fixed me up, let me rest and recover. I helped fine-tune the act of the first demiclone. They wanted me to do the same for the second one. And you would have helped with the coaching, too. Whether you wanted to or not."

He was shuddering as fresh tears ran down his ravaged face. I leaned forward, stretching my blue lips in a non-Haluk smile, and laid an alien hand on his shoulder. "Danny, you know what they intend to do. Colonize our galaxy by force. Destroy humanity if that's what it takes. How does my clone fit into their scheme? Are they using him politically, in the Assembly? Or did they wangle the fake back into Rampart upper management?"

"Both. You're—*he's* Rampart's president and syndic. Eve and the others were so relieved when you reappeared after being presumed lost in the Sagittarius Whorl that they didn't question your strange change of heart. Cousin Zed's still Chief Operating Officer, but he's permanently based on Seriphos now. You—I mean, the demiclone—and Eve are effectively calling the shots from Toronto, with Gunter Eckert and that Macrodur stooge Ellington and the rest of the board sitting back applauding."

"Eve has no idea she's dealing with a fake?"

"He's very well prepared. A natural actor with compelling presence." He flashed a twisted grin. "A lot like you, kid. It helps that you were always such a headstrong loner, not socializing with the rest of the family. And of course he knows the business inside out. The Rampart-Galapharma consolidation went through like gangbusters under his direction,

and he's got the Haluk Consortium following his lead like
Mary's little lamb. The fifty new Haluk colonies in the Spur
are up and running, with settlers flooding in by the millions."

"Did the Assembly approve the three hundred additional
colonies?" I asked grimly.

"Not yet. The vote is expected very soon. Last I heard,
maybe two weeks from now. Your demiclone has been guiding the strategy of the other Concern lobbyists, showing
them where to exert pressure and how best to counter Delegate Sontag's opposition. He and his Xenoaffairs Oversight
Committee threw open their meetings to the media. Released a shitload of evidence detrimental to the Haluk and
started a slam-bang row. The accusations of demiclone spying caused a furor."

Atta boy, Ef! "That's great. Are citizens pressuring the Assembly to revise the Haluk treaties?"

"Sure. But Concern lobbyists are fighting it hammer and
tongs. Bringing in their own experts to demonstrate that Sontag's 'proof' of a vast demiclone infiltration is nothing of the
sort. Only Macrodur and some of the smaller Concerns are
DNA-testing their top executives. The other big outfits are
stalling. No demiclone spies have been uncovered yet." Dan
gave me a sour look. "It doesn't help Sontag's case that his
chief witness has recanted his original testimony and now
claims that false depositions were entered under his name."

"Chief witness—"

"You." Dan managed a weak chuckle.

"Who is he?" I asked in a low, encouraging voice. "Who's
the first Fake Helly demiclone?"

He shook his head. His eyes were darting wildly.

"I've got to know. To stop him."

"They'll kill me."

"You'll tell me in the end, Dan. I'll hurt you if I have to.
Save yourself pain—"

He screamed at me: *"What do you know about pain? My
whole life is pain!"*

Julian May

Return of Bad Cop.

I hit him a sharp backhanded blow to the face. "Bullshit! Bull! Fucking! Shit! The worst pain you've experienced is hurt pride and failed ambition. You're an arrogant, self-centered fuckwad, Dan. A driven, calculating monster! You wanted Pop to make you head of Rampart. When he didn't, you lost it completely. You hooked up with a madman who promised to give you what you wanted. You did everything you could to ensure that Alistair Drummond would take control of Rampart. It was *your* twisted idea to demiclone Eve. *You* dreamed up the scheme to sell Simon and me to that freakazoid pimp in Coventry Blue . . . And you poisoned our mother, Dan, because Alistair Drummond threatened to kill you if she didn't turn over her Rampart quarterstake."

"I didn't," he mumbled, fingering his bashed nose. It was bleeding a little.

"You did," I said sadly. "And that's your worst pain of all."

I waited while he cursed and sobbed, denying it. Then I said, "It's Alistair Drummond, isn't it? He's alive, and he's wearing my face."

Dan gave a violent start and stared at me open-mouthed. "No! It's not him!"

But it was all the confirmation I needed. I'd never been able to believe Drummond was dead, and there was the tenuous bit of evidence that he'd been present at Dan's abduction from the fishing lodge. When I was in the tank, the Haluk leaders had discussed an unstable human rogue with a scheme that fit the Grand Design. The Haluk had suspected that the man might be insane. I knew for a fact that Alistair Drummond was a charming, plausible, brilliant sociopath.

And now he was *me*.

I climbed to my feet, picked up the Ivanov, went around the table to where my brother cringed in his seat. "I can't waste any more time on you. When the Haluk hook you up to the truth machines later, be sure you tell 'em I intend to fuck their shit. I'm going to rip my skin off Drummond and chop the rest of him into red-flannel hash."

"Asa, they'll torture me to death with the damned machine!"

"Maybe. But before you turn up your toes, be sure to tell the Servant of Servants I know about his invasion plan. Tell him he better give it up, cut his losses, and start begging the Assembly for mercy. If he doesn't, humanity is going to chase his baby-blue ass back to the Haluk Cluster and make damned sure that he and his people rot there till the Big Crunch."

"Asa, for the love of God—"

I shot Dan with two stun-darts. He'd be unconscious for at least half a day. I took off my uniform's weapon belt, since I'd never get out of the building wearing it, divested it of its useful equipment, and put the stuff in the gym bag with the change of clothes.

Then I headed back to the elevator. Maybe my vitals would explode when I tried to pass the checkpoint at the 100th floor, and maybe they wouldn't. There was only one way to find out.

Going down, I found that the gold-striped key-card did indeed give me a green light to the lowest Haluk floor. I was on my way to freedom.

Aliens joined me in the elevator car at lower stops, but there were no humanoid demiclones among them. I decided they must have private elevators. It would hardly be prudent for them to be seen entering or leaving those set aside for the building's Haluk tenants.

Some xeno passengers wore native garments, others were dressed like humans, perhaps off for a night on the town. No one paid any attention to me. I kept a position near the doors in case of an emergency.

And an emergency happened.

The door opened to admit another passenger, a Haluk male who wore a dull yellow smock and carried a technical magslate. When he saw me his pupils widened in the racial equivalent of surprise. He kept staring as we made other stops and the car became crowded. Then he was pushed to the rear, out of my sight.

But I knew him. Mustard Smock! He was the one called Archiator Something, who had shown me to the Servant of Servants and the VIP female Haluk when I was still in the tank. Then he'd acted like the demiclone project director or some other technical bigwig.

Was he alert enough to spot my anatomical anomalies?

Yep.

I felt someone grip my arm and speak in low Halukese. "Guard. Tell me your *blah blah*." Mustard Smock was asking for my ID.

The door opened again to admit three more passengers to the nearly full car, meditechs in pale green human-style hospital garb with diagnostic devices hanging on cords around their necks. In his own language I told Mustard, "Sorry. No time." Then I pulled away from him and slipped out just as the doors were sliding shut. He tried to squirm after me and didn't make it.

My heart was pounding as I dashed out of the elevator alcove and flattened myself against the wall just out of sight, expecting to hear the chime as the door reopened. It didn't happen. Perhaps Mustard couldn't get to the control panel in time to stop the car. Perhaps he'd decided to brush off his suspicions and get on with his business.

Perhaps he'd alert security at the checkpoint.

There were no sculptures or pretty decorations on this floor, and no windows, either. The area had subdued lighting and there was a chill in the air. I rejected my first instinct, which was to catch the next elevator down to the checkpoint and try to escape before the flap and foofaraw started.

Easy does it, Helly, I told myself. Haluk guards *do* tend to look alike. I needed to change my clothes. Maybe find another elevator bank.

There was no one in the corridor. I went down a few doors before using my master key, slipped into a dark room, and locked myself in. Then I turned on the light and spit out an astonished expletive.

The place was full of golden mummy-cases, standing upright in narrow open-fronted booths. They lined the walls and were set up in close rows like library shelves, with space to walk between them. A medical monitoring device was attached to each elegant coffinlike chrysalis. I knew very well what they contained—Haluk testudomorphs, the dormant phase of the allomorphic alien race.

But Haluk who had undergone allomorph eradication therapy with PD32:C2 didn't hibernate. And it was common knowledge that the Haluk did not send allomorphic members of their race to Earth. It wasn't cost-efficient for their embassy staff and trade attachés to sleep for half a year, and the Haluk were ordinarily very cost-efficient.

So what were the testudos doing here?

I went back to the door, doused the light, and did a low-boy scan of the corridor. Empty. I opened the door opposite and found more ranks of testudos. Racing to another chamber several doors down, I found still more. This time I shut myself in the room and rapidly began to change into Dan's athletic gear.

My mind was spinning and my overloaded stomach felt queasy. There seemed only one explanation: treated Haluk were somehow reverting to their original allomorphic state.

Had Emily Konigsberg done it deliberately with her mutant exon? Or was the odd bit of DNA some sort of necessary genetic stopgap that actually staved off a reversion process that was inevitable?

When these testudos completed their dormant cycle and hatched into graciles, could they be treated again? If so, what did the Haluk think about being obligated to human-ity—and especially Rampart Concern—indefinitely?

Rampart . . . the pieces of the puzzle were coming to-gether.

I fastened my shoes, put on the baseball cap, and pulled it low over my eyes. Took all of the hardware out of the gym bag except the spare Ivanov and sedative injector and stowed the stuff in the ample kangaroo pocket below my jacket's half-mast zipper. Put the key-cards in my pants pocket. Con-sidered leaving the guard's uniform and boots behind, along with the bag, injector, and extra gun, then remembered it was damn near winter outside of Macherson Tower. So I stuffed the uniform into the gym bag in case I needed it for warmth, and kept the other things, too. I was still wearing the fire-opal ring.

When I opened the door I discovered I was not alone in the corridor. Fortunately, the Haluk lepidodermoid pushing the gurney that held a gold chrysalis was going the other way. In their asexual intermediate phase, the aliens are thick-skinned, ponderous, slow-witted, fit only for simple tasks. The lepido pushing the gurney stopped at a door beyond the lift alcove, used a key-card, and rolled its burden inside.

I dashed for the elevator and caught one going down al-most immediately. It was only moderately crowded. But when we reached the bottom Haluk floor, the doors failed to open and the chime sounded its alarm. I felt my overloaded stomach contract with fear and almost disgraced myself.

One of the passengers said, "*Blah blah [expletive]* forgot to *blah* the gold key?"

The red light beside the card-slot was blinking. A sensor inside the car had counted us and counted the card inser-tions. One short.

There were disgusted mutters from the others, who glared at each other trying to spot the careless twit causing the delay.

I mumbled, "Sorry!" forced out a strangled-puppy Haluk

laugh, and plugged my card. The light went green, the doors opened and we all emerged into a crowded lobby.

There were eight lines at the outbound checkpoint gates. Everyone held a blue key-card at the ready and quickly passed through. I fumbled in my pants pocket and sorted out my own. When I inserted it, would my heart explode? Would that hurt? How long would it take me to die?

Guards stood beside a second group of elevator banks, those leading down to freedom. Were they watching for a bold impostor? If I got through the gate without popping my pump, would they seize me and escort me back upstairs to the tank?

Inhaling and squaring my shoulders, I pushed in the card.

The gate's indicator light glowed green.

My heart kept on beating and I went through. Keeping my head low, I shoehorned myself into a crowded elevator car. A few moments later the doors opened into the Path.

My first need was to get as far away from the vicinity of Macpherson Tower as possible. My second was to find a reasonably secluded public phone. Using it would be dangerous. Without money, and unable to eyeball my way into the iridoscopic ID system with my exotic irises, I would have to recite either my personal code or the Rampart general code, plus their authorization tags, to make a credit call. I didn't doubt that the Haluk had access to both codes. If they'd penetrated the telecom databank as well, they'd not only know where I'd called from, but also whom I'd called.

It required some serious thinking. If I attempted to contact my relatives, friends, or close associates, I might immediately endanger their lives.

And even if I did reach someone, would the person believe the Halukoid geek with the rumbly voice was me? Not bloody likely. All public vidphones transmitted the image of the caller unless you physically blocked the video pickup, a move justly regarded as suspicious by those answering the phone. People in the upper echelons of society—and that included Eve, Simon, Karl, Ef Sontag, and Bea Mangan—screened their electronic communications carefully. They probably wouldn't even accept a public phone call from someone who refused to show his face.

But I thought I knew someone who would.

Almost instinctively, I took the Path westward beneath Dundas Street, in the direction of the old Rampart Tower. (I'd only realize later that Rampart would have transferred its Toronto headquarters to the ithyphallic monolith on the waterfront that had once housed Galapharma.) At University Avenue, I rode the escalator to the upper level and found a suitable phone in a com bank at the St. Patrick subway station.

Using the Rampart code and ID tag, I called CCID Headquarters: Cop Central. I covered the vid pickup with my hand. When the duty officer responded, I asked for Chief Superintendent Jacob Silver. He wouldn't be working the night shift, but I was pretty sure they'd patch me through to his home if I stated a family emergency and gave my name and personal code. And the police link would be secure from Haluk snoops.

"I'm sorry," said the deskman. "Chief Superintendent Silver is deceased. May I route your call elsewhere?"

"No—"

Stunned, I cut him off. Stood there paralyzed.

Jake. Jake was dead. Because of me? Because Alistair Drummond had slipped up imperceptibly during his public playacting, and only Jake, the wise old cop, had spotted it? And not-so-wisely confronted my demiclone?

Jake.

Rats . . .

I don't know how long I stood there. My precariously stoked vitality was swiftly draining away. Several trains entered the station, discharged and took on passengers, glided off quietly, defying gravity. The crowds were moderate. A clock said it was 2002 hours.

I knew I had to get away from the public phones, so I moved to the nearest newsstand and pretended to watch the big-screen PNN posting of *News on the Hour.* Top Story: a tsunami on Hokusai causes heavy damage to a big Homerun Concern manufacturing facility. Oh, yeah—and five thousand people died.

I felt lightheaded and stupid. My belly was beginning to cramp. I could feel a hot throbbing beneath the improvised bandage at the back of my neck. Maybe the wound was infected with alien germs.

One thing was certain: my weakened body had been flogged enough. It now demanded to be horizontal. If I didn't go down soon of my own free will, I was going to collapse.

Where the hell could a Haluk in a track suit catch some z's?

I couldn't rest on one of the inviting Path benches. The searchers would find me. I had no money to patronize a spa or theater.

The subway station sign caught my eye. ST. PATRICK STATION. A church? . . . Many of them were open in the evening. Humans dozed in them all the time, but a sleeping alien would alert a suspicious sexton. A public database? . . . Lots of people rested their eyes in the library, but the nearest one was over a mile away, on Yonge Street. There was another in the university campus, closer but still at least twelve blocks away. I'd never—

Oh, shit. They were here! The first Haluk hunters.

I spotted them from the corner of my eye—I now had great peripheral vision—exiting from a northbound train. Two uniformed blue alien males and a female in casual attire. They found a vantage point near the escalator and stood slightly apart, carefully scanning the throng. One spoke into a handheld com device, no doubt reporting that I was no longer near the public phones. I pulled my cap even lower and hunched my shoulders, trying to look less conspicuous.

Right, Helly, you moron. Why not just hunker down on the floor and put your fat blue head between your knees and kiss your ass goodbye?

I straightened up and readjusted the hat. Tried to look confident and ordinary. Began to drift toward the subway turnstile, figuring to hop over it when the next train was about to pull away, slip aboard through the closing door and take my chances. Wondered if I had enough energy left to make the leap.

Stopped wondering when the female Haluk searcher spotted me and pointed me out to her companions.

The trio walked purposefully in my direction.

I panicked.

There was only one way open to me where they didn't dare follow. I dropped my gym bag, flung myself bodily over the turnstile barrier, and landed with a bone-jarring crash. A few people yipped and shouted. The three Haluk broke into a canter. I rolled to the platform edge and went over. This time the impact with the ceramalloy antigravity reflector grid did more than shake me up. Something in my left shoulder snapped and a white bolt of agony lanced through my brain. Broken collarbone. I'd suffered one before on Kedge-Lockaby when I fell off my sub's flybridge, drunk as a skunk.

Don't pass out! One last push, Helly. Come on, you gutsy blue fucker. Get up up up!

I struggled back onto my feet and scrambled into the subway tunnel. It was straight as a die, dimly lit with small yellow bulbs mounted along the ceiling every dozen meters or so. No sign of an approaching train.

Unzipping my jacket halfway, I thrust my injured left arm into it in an improvised sling. Better. I jogged clumsily along the grid side, where there was very little clearance between the reflector area and the wall. An uproar of voices echoed behind me. I dared a look over my shoulder. The three Haluk weren't following.

Pain pain pain. My shoulder. My laboring lungs. My heart thudding like a punching bag going full tilt: *whop-a whop-a whop-a*. Another goddamned chase scene, starring me. Monotonous.

My head ached like a sonuvabitch and I was starting to see double. My brain was losing contact with my legs and I tripped over a structural member and nearly took a header. Caught at the wall with my good hand and kept going.

There had to be an emergency escape hatch along here somewhere. I'd seen them myself, looking through the windows of speeding trains, inconspicuous niches with doors in them.

A soft breeze had begun to blow in my face and I heard a peculiar rushing sound, not very loud. Far, far away I could see twin starry pinpricks: train headlights. Shit. Not that ancient cliché! I tried to move along faster and failed. Picked up my heavy feet and laid them down. Felt giddy, sick, hopeless.

The dancing headlights were brighter, closing in. Soon the sensors in the lead car would take note of an unauthorized object on the grid ahead. They would bring the train to a halt, leaving me jacklighted in front of it like a trapped deer, waiting for the arrival of the Transit Authority Police.

I was staggering with pain and vertigo, ready to pack it in, when I finally came to the niche. Almost passed it by, not recognizing my salvation. Managed to pull open the narrow metal hatch, fell through onto my broken shoulder, screaming, and kicked the hatch shut.

A surreal interlude followed. The place inside was spinning, or I was, engulfing me in a cataract of deafening sound and colored kaleidoscopic shapes. After what seemed like a long time—but was probably only minutes—the chaotic noise diminished into a nearly subsonic drone and the psychedelic light show coalesced into solid retinal images, blurry but bona fide.

I sat up, hurting like hell, no longer suffering from incapacitating dizziness. My refuge was a lighted utility room less than ten feet square and about as high. The deep humming sound, which I presumed came from hidden antigravity generators, had just enough volume to set my teeth on edge.

The walls of the place were crowded with pipes, conduits, and impressive junction boxes with high-voltage warnings on them. Through bleary eyes I saw a prehistoric nonvideo telephone on the wall beside the exit to the tunnel, along with a cabinet labeled EMERGENCY EQUIPMENT. An iron ladder was mounted on the opposite wall. It went up to a dark shaft in the ceiling and down through an equally dark hole in the floor.

I opened the cabinet and saw a large canister of foam spark-suppressant, a pair of heavy insulated gloves, two ceram pry bars of differing lengths, a cutting torch, several oddly shaped wrenches, and a small first-aid kit. I took that, tucking it into my ever-handy kangaroo pocket, and turned my attention to the ladder.

I decided to go down, no contest. I lacked the strength to climb.

Slip, trip, get a grip. Here's Supercop, descending into a spooky abyss with one useless arm, wincing in agony every time he jolts his busted bone, pursued by Haluk fiends!

I found that I was grinning—even energized, in some weird way.

Go figure.

I must have slithered twenty meters down the narrow shaft before I came to a less constricted space, and then a solid floor. I pulled out the guard's flashlight and turned it on, discovering that I was in another small chamber almost identical to the utility room above. It had a similar equipment cabinet but fewer conduits and pipes lining the walls. The light had burned out and the place had a disused look to it. The exit door featured a substantial latch, a key-card slot, and a sign that said:

NO UNAUTHORIZED EXIT
IF DOOR IS OPENED WITHOUT KEY, ALARM WILL SOUND

I figured it had to open out into the University Avenue segment of the Path—useless as an escape route, even if I had been willing to risk setting off the alarm. The hunt was on, and soon there'd be Haluk strolling everywhere in the underground concourses. I knew what they'd tell the cops: "Officer, have you seen our poor deranged kinsman who wandered away from his sickroom? No, he's not dangerous at all. Only extremely ill, suffering from delusions. We appreciate your assistance in our urgent search."

Thus far I'd heard no signs of pursuit from above. It would come, though.

Andale! Going down, one more time . . .

The ladder didn't end at this level. Its uprights passed through two slots in a solid semicircular manhole cover set into the floor against the back wall. The cover looked old. There was a central inset ring to lift the thing, and I gave it a puny tug. The cover didn't budge. I didn't have the moxie to move the heavy thing.

Emergency equipment cabinet. The longer of the two pry bars, used as a lever. Squat. Heave very slowly, using my good right arm and my flabby leg muscles. With a rusty screech the manhole cover tilted up a few precious centimeters and promptly fell back into place. It probably weighed about twenty-five kilos.

Okay. Rest, then repeat the maneuver. This time, when the lid lifted, I kicked the tip of the smaller pry bar into the aperture. Then I collapsed. A smell compounded of mold and dampness wafted up through the crack.

In a few minutes, when I'd recovered a bit, I used both pry bars to move the metal cover aside. It had another inset ring underneath. A long piece of rope was knotted through it.

I felt a prickling along my spine. The rope was new.

Below, it was absolute blackness and a continuation of the ladder. I switched on the flashlight. The lower shaft was twice as wide as the one I'd previously negotiated and gleamed with moisture. Some sort of revolting crud was growing around the ladder brackets. The powerful little beam reflected from water that might have been another dozen meters below. The ladder continued into it.

Above the level of the water were two sizable circular openings. One was beside the ladder on the west wall of the shaft, and the other was directly opposite.

I didn't hesitate. I replaced the short pry bar in the cabinet and closed it. Then I positioned myself on the ladder a few rungs down and painfully maneuvered the cover back into position, alternately levering with the long bar and pulling on the rope. Finally, I twisted the rope around the bar and used my body weight to help seat the cover, millimeter by millimeter. It was very dark. I'd been afraid to prop the flashlight on one of the ladder treads for fear my exertions would dislodge it, and it was too thick to hold in my mouth; so it had stayed safely in my kangaroo pouch.

Finally, the lid dropped. So did I, nearly, as my foot slipped. But I clung to the rope and bar with my single hand, swung back to the ladder and wrapped my ankle around one of the uprights, sobbing with relief and renewed pain.

When I recovered a little, I jammed the bar through the manhole cover's ring so its ends extended evenly on either side of the semicircular opening and bound it in place with the rope. Now it was impossible for anyone to lift the cover from above. Then I crept slowly downward, dazed and exultant. The lit flashlight poking out of my pocket gave adequate illumination. A half meter or so above the water level,

I stepped into the round opening beside the ladder. It was a huge pipe, completely dry, made of old-fashioned cast concrete. Perhaps one of the old storm drains.

A short distance in from the shaft lay an empty Marlboro cigarette pack, a Starbucks coffee cup, and the bag from a McDonald's Happy Meal. They weren't dusty and old. They might have been dropped there yesterday.

Oh, Christ . . .

No. I wasn't ready to think about the implication of my new find. Not until I rested and did something about the pain.

I sat down and opened the first-aid kit. It had bandages, antibiotic ointment, and—best of all—some powerful analgesic self-dosers. I positioned one of the tiny pillow-shaped things on my left carotid artery—where I hoped it was, anyhow—and jabbed sharply with my thumb. The drug injected explosively. In a few seconds the pain from my broken collarbone vanished. So did my other miseries.

I swabbed the gouge at the back of my neck with antiseptic, applied antibiotic goo, and rebandaged it as well as I could using one hand. Then I improvised a more efficient sling. To celebrate my repair, I had a belt of alien vodka from the steel flask. Then I started to walk. Correction: shuffle.

I followed the storm drain for less than half a kilometer before finding a handmade ladder placed against a dry spillway. At the slope's top was a flimsy grate with light faintly shining through. Using my last bit of strength, I crept up the ladder, unhooked the grate, and emerged at last into the Dark Path.

I saw a ghostly subterranean concourse, eerily reminiscent of the familiar Path I knew so well, except it was in a state of abject ruin. The light came from portable camping glolamps someone had set out every ten meters or so along one cracked wall. My hole opened beneath a derelict escalator that had once led up into a long-vanished office building. Now it dead-ended in a ceiling slab of rough plascrete, swagged with dusty spiderwebs. A titanic structural pier made of modern material punched through the slab. Around its base heaps of rubble cut off the corridor on the far side of the broken stairs. On the other side stretched a line of decayed shops, some with familiar names. Their windows were gone and their interiors had been looted long decades earlier. Oddly, the corridor floor in front of them was fairly clean and dry. A couple of overhead ducts purred, drawing out stale air.

At first my fuddled brain didn't comprehend that the Dark Path was inhabited. Low walls of unmortared concrete block formed about a dozen open-fronted cubicles along the blank wall opposite the old shops. Each space held a few pieces of furniture and stacked small container pods. A dim night-light sat on one cinder-block wall.

I drew my Ivanov and shambled out of my hiding place beneath the escalator like a zombie. Saw a community kitchen in front of a ruined Taco Bell fast-food joint, a "reading room" alcove with shelves of slates and e-books, a billiard table and a collection of video game machines, laundry pegged to a line outside an old public rest room. Heard snoring . . .

Then a woman's quiet voice said, "You won't need the pistol, honey." She was sitting up in her simple bed inside the cubicle with the night-light, watching me, not yet recognizing what kind of a creature had invaded her secret world.

Tottering, I let my gun hand fall and must have groaned, because she said, "I'm Mama Fanchon. It's all right, sweetie-babe. Have you just arrived?"

Instinctively, I knew what she meant. "The—The police are after me. And the Haluk. I'm walking wounded, my collarbone and my neck. I can't—can't—"

I stood there swaying, seeing colored flashes again and hearing the cataract work up to a roar.

Mama Fanchon was putting on a robe and slippers. A moment later she turned up her glolamp and gave a sharp cry of dismay, seeing me clearly. "Santa! Mohammed! Leah! Sweet Lord, it's an alien!"

Muffled curses and squeals from the cubicles. A big old white-bearded guy whom I later learned to call Santa Claus demonstrated how he'd got his name by bounding out of his space and covering me with a Claus-Gewitter photon blaster. "Hoist 'em high or die, blueberry!"

Two adolescents advanced on me, armed with pry bars. The female shrilled, "You heard the man! Hands up, xeno!"

"I'm not!" I cried, consumed by despair. "Not an alien. They did this to me. I'm human. Human, for God's sake!"

"Bite me!" jeered the male adolescent.

"Does anyone have a phone?" I asked politely.

Then I crashed.

Mama Fanchon believed me.

She knew anatomy, being the tribal healer, and my thick neck alone was enough to show her that I was no true Haluk. She also regularly watched newscasts on her tiny portable TV and was aware of the accusations of illegal demiclonery being lodged against the Haluk by certain Delegates of the Commonwealth Assembly.

Others of the Grange Place Tribe were less willing to accept her kindly assessment; but Mama overruled their objections, put me to bed in her "hospital," and tended me during the three days of my recovery.

For part of that time I was delirious. I'm certain that I told her my name, also fairly sure that she recognized it and drew certain conclusions.

At one point, when I was only partially lucid, I pleaded again for a telephone. "Please, Mama! Have to call my sister Eve, CEO of Rampart Concern. To warn her! He's not me. The syndic. She has to fire him. Denounce him. Tell the Assembly he lied. The impostor. Get me a phone! Call Eve, get her down here. Convince her. A phone. Oh, God, Mama, please get me a phone—"

"No, honey-lamb. You're not calling anyone, the condition you're in. If that big-shot woman is really your sister, she won't talk to a poor sick Haluk. Or a well one, either. You better think of somebody else to call later on, when you feel better. Sleep now and think on it, Helly." I slipped back into unconsciousness.

Later, when I was back on the road to rationality, she told me her own story. Nine years earlier, Fanchon had been a hospital nurse. She accidentally gave the wrong medication to the son of a Bodascon Concern executive, and the child nearly died. Thrown Away, her every asset confiscated to settle the massive civil judgment against her, she had no relatives or friends willing to support her or pay for a ticket to a remote planet where she might have made a new life.

So she descended into the Dark and began another sort of career as a member of the Grange Place Tribe. There were twelve of them—eight disenfranchised adults, three runaway children who had fled abusive families, and one man wanted for the murder of his unfaithful wife. They lived together, defending themselves against human predators and the violent insane who stalked parts of the underworld. Their food and supplies were gleaned by "shopping"—the tribal euphemism for scavenging and clandestine requisition—in the Bright Path, which they visited during quiet hours. They'd left the rope on the manhole cover that I'd found. They'd also disconnected the door alarm and broken the light in the utility room, which was only one of many exits into the other world.

Fanchon's nursing skills came to be valued by other Dark Path dwellers because she was willing to help others without asking for payment. Many patients gave her gifts anyway. She always shared them with her tribe.

When I woke up at last with a mind that was fully clear, Mama Fanchon was the first person I saw, a woman in a red turtleneck sweater and padded goosedown vest, sitting in a folding chair just outside the hospital cubicle, smoking a briar pipe, knitting, and watching a soundless Maple Leafs hockey game on her small television.

Behind her, in the communal kitchen, Santa Claus was grilling some sort of spicy meat and toasting buns. The aroma was inviting. He was dressed in a wool shirt and dirty Carhartt insulated overalls, with a striped canvas apron tied over them. Next to the two-burner Gaz stove stood a table spread with clean newsprint. It was set with mismatched plates and cups and also held a restaurant-sized jar of kosher pickles, a bunch of spotty bananas, and a box of Krispy Kreme doughnuts.

"How are you feeling, Helly?" Mama Fanchon inquired. She put her knitting away and came to stand over me, hands on her ample hips. "Is the bone-brace treatment working? The medicine was a bit past its expiration date, but no one's been shopping in a clinic for nearly a month. Not since Johnny Guitar fell into the cistern under Spadina Chinatown and broke both legs."

"I feel much better, Mama Fanchon," I said. Unzipping the sleeping bag, I sat up. I was naked as a jaybird. Same color, too. "Need to use the facilities. I can walk. May I have my clothes?"

"I think someone had better go along with you, in case you need help." She called out: "Mohammed!"

A skinny teenage boy with sunken eyes and four missing front teeth came into the cubicle. Like the others, he wore winter clothing. The Dark Path was cold. My Ivanov stun-pistol was stuck in his belt.

The kid glowered at me. "So the Haluk's awake. About time." I recalled that he'd helped with my care while I was flat on my back, passing in and out of consciousness. He was a lot stronger than he looked. Young Mohammed adored Mama Fanchon and didn't trust me one micron's worth.

She was rummaging in one of the storage pods and said to the boy, "Supper will be ready soon, angel. Please get

Helly a nice warm jacket from the hope chest, and take him to the rest room after I check him out. Eeyore finally found a new power cell for my diagnosticon. Isn't that wonderful?"

She waved the device expertly around my bod while Mohammed went off. "Very, very good! Your collarbone is just fine now. It'll be tender for a week or so, but it's stronger than ever. Put your clothes on, honey-bunch. You can eat at the table with us tonight." She left the cubicle.

"Polish sausages almost ready!" Santa Claus called out. My mouth began to water. Three or four other members of the tribe drifted toward the kitchen.

Mohammed stood by while I pulled on my track suit and stuffed my feet into sneakers without bothering with socks. He handed me an Eddie Bauer car-coat with the price code still attached. The "hope chest" had nice merchandise.

Trailed by the armed boy, I trudged off to what had once been a public lavatory. Now most of the white tiles were cracked and stained black with mildew, and the mirrors were so cloudy that they were almost opaque; but someone had reconnected the water with jury-rigged plastic piping, and the old-timey tank toilets and sinks worked.

Mohammed scowled as I relieved myself. "You can't be human. Not with *those*."

I shrugged. "I told you, it's what happens when Haluk genetic engineers build a demiclone from your DNA. First they inoculate you with some Haluk genes. You end up looking like an alien on the outside."

"I'd kill myself!" the boy declared.

"When I get my life sorted out, I'll go back into the vat and get fixed. Look just like my old self again." I finished my business, had a fast wash, and slipped off the coat. "How's the wound on my neck looking?"

"Got a dry scab. The scab's purple. You're healthy, man . . . I mean, Mr. Haluk! Time for you to hit the road." He touched the pistol and his face was like polished golden marble.

"You're not hanging out here anymore. No matter what Mama Fanchon says."

"No," I agreed. "I'm very grateful for your help, Mohammed. And for Mama's, and all the rest of the tribe's. But I won't try to stay with you. There's something I have to do, a place I have to go. I'll need help to find it, though, traveling the Dark Path."

"Where?" he asked suspiciously.

I gave him an address in ultrafashionable Cabbagetown, just east of the city's central core, where once upon a time poor Irish immigrants grew their favorite veggies right in their front gardens.

"It's a long way," he said, looking dubious. "Can't get there direct. The DP's broken at Yonge. You'd have to detour south to the Inner Harbor, come back north through the Parliament Street drains."

"Will you take me?"

He laughed.

"I'll make it worth your while. When I'm a man again."

"Horseshit," Mohammed scoffed.

"My name is Asahel Frost. Once I was a convicted criminal and a Throwaway, just like Mama and the others. Then I became the Chief Legal Officer of Rampart Concern. I was rich and important. That's why the Haluk stole my identity. Do you watch the news on Mama's TV? Did you ever see the man who uses my name? Saying what terrific people the Haluk really are?"

"Never watch those talking-head dudes. Boring." But the boy's gaze had momentarily shifted. He'd seen Alistair Drummond, all right.

"The fake Asahel Frost is a traitor," I said. "Crazy as an outhouse rat, and just as vicious. He wouldn't give a damn if Earth and all the human planets became alien property. I'm going to cut his nuts off and stuff them down his lying throat."

A spark flickered in his bruised-looking young eyes. "Who lives in Cabbagetown?" he asked me abruptly.

I told him.

His mouth dropped open, showing the pathetic gaps in his teeth. Replacing them had been beyond Mama's skill. I wondered what else had been done to Mohammed in the world Upstairs. Who'd been responsible. Wondered whether I might do something about it someday, just as I intended to do something for Mama and the others if I ever became a man again.

"You're shinin' me on." His skepticism was weakening.

"Nope. God's own truth. I've got nowhere else to turn, Mohammed."

He was silent, then: "The Haluk *really* did . . . that to you?"

"They had help from some stupid and evil human beings. But, yeah. Haluk did it as part of their Grand Design to take over the damn galaxy. Some nerve, huh?"

"Motherfuckers," he said, shaking his head. "It's for real? This alien plot?"

"It's a nightmare, and it's for real."

"Jeez."

"I gave Mama Fanchon the opal ring," I said. "When we get to the place in Cabbagetown, I'll see that you get some money."

"Okay," he said softly. "I'll take you where you want to go. You *ruin* those blueberry fools, hear me?"

"That's my plan," I told him. "Now let's eat."

Together, we went back to the dim corridor where the others were already sitting at the kitchen table.

The next day, after Mama Fanchon checked me out again with the diagnosticon and gave her reluctant approval, we were ready to leave. Santa Claus had supplied us with a pack of food and bottles of water. He'd even refilled my flask with some of his own brandy. I wore my dark track suit over heavy polypro underwear from the hope chest, the new carcoat, the Blue Jays baseball cap, and gloves. Mohammed was all in black. He still had my Ivanov and the magazine pouch of stun-bolts. I was armed with the exotic switchblade and the sedative injector. (Mama didn't want that for her hospital. She preferred to use minidosers, which were much more common and easier to steal than high-pressure drug cartridges.)

The whole Grange Place Tribe decided to accompany Mohammed and me as far as the old Spadina Street utility tunnel, which was to be our principal route south. Santa Claus led the way with his blaster. The girl runaway named Leah was at his side, lighting the way with a brilliant argon lantern. Most of the others had glolamps. Mama placidly smoked her pipe, walking with the Thrown Away Omnivore executive called Johnny Guitar, who strummed his instrument in solemn march tempo: *brrrump, brrrump, brump-brump-brump.* Before long we were all whistling "Colonel Bogey."

Weirdly, other troglodytic figures carrying lights of their own emerged from shadowy side tunnels to join us as we moved through the debris-strewn Dundas West concourse. When we reached the utility tunnel, a crowd of almost fifty people gathered around me, smiling and shyly wishing me good luck. I was astonished and deeply touched.

"The word got around," Santa Claus explained. "Mohammed never could keep his mouth shut. These other folks . . . they heard you were a Throwaway, heard what the Haluk did to you. Most of them know how it feels to have a good life, then wake up one day to find the universe turned upside down."

So I made a little speech of my own, thanking them, making some wild promises that were greeted with disbelieving hoots and spatters of applause. Then the Dark Path people began to wander away.

Mama Fanchon kissed me on the cheek and slipped some-thing into my hand. "Here's what you wanted, Helly. My pocket phone. Take it with you. Not too many of these down here. Most of us haven't much need of them, but sometimes other tribes call me when a person's really sick or hurt bad."

"I can't take this," I protested. "Let me make my call now, right here."

"I don't think that would be wise. Wait till you're in Cab-bagetown, after you've checked the place for a stakeout. You'll want to be sure your friend is at home—and I'd also suggest that you give fair warning about your big surprise." She turned to Mohammed and spoke sternly. "And *you* won't take any money from Helly! Not a single dollar."

He shrugged. "I'll bring back your phone."

The journey was long, tedious, dirty, cold, and frequently dangerous. Our convoluted route covered over eight kilome-ters and took seventeen hours. I was strongly reminded of my trek through the caves of Cravat, several years earlier. But there had been no human crazies in that little planet's underworld; Bronson Elgar and his homicidal crew had been extremely sane, and the Haluk hiding in the Cravat caverns were unexpectedly lacking in malice.

On Toronto's Dark Path, there were malicious denizens galore. I never would have gotten to Cabbagetown without Mohammed.

He knew exactly how to calm nervous tribes ready to kill any stranger—especially one that looked like an alien—who entered their territory. Mention of Mama Fanchon's name turned them from enemies to cautious allies. The roving gangs of well-armed robbers and sex criminals infesting un-defended no-man's-land regions would have been more of a challenge; luckily, we didn't encounter large groups of out-laws during the southbound leg of our trip.

Small groups and loners, yes.

A pair of knife-wielding muggers sprang at us out of the

dark when we were halfway down the Spadina tunnel, just above King Street. Mohammed stunned them neatly, and after fettering them with the plastic wrist restraints I'd taken from the Haluk guards, he called the nearest tribe on Mama Fanchon's phone and coolly asked for "garbage disposal."

I didn't ask what that meant.

We continued on. A few minutes later a third robber dropped on me from a ceiling beam in the ruined King Street subway station. We grappled while my young companion danced around waving the pistol, afraid to shoot for fear of hitting me. The thug was a raving crankhead, the drug giving him almost superhuman strength. I finally thumbed his eyes and he turned me loose, giving Mohammed his chance. He plugged my frenzied attacker with three darts.

"That's usually fatal, you know," I told him when I managed to catch my breath. "Not that I'm complaining."

"Then I guess we don't have to bother the disposal folks. The rats'll take care of him." Mohammed helped himself to the late *bandido*'s money and wristwatch before resuming his interrupted guide duties.

Our narrowest escape happened hours later, down near the Inner Harbor, almost directly beneath what had once been Galapharma Tower. I presumed the structure now contained Rampart's Toronto headquarters, or would very shortly. In either case, the place offered me no refuge. *Au contraire . . .*

After a strenuous crawl through an abandoned sewer, we had come to a very old masonry culvert, part of some antiquated stream-diversion system buried deep under the old quay. The tall arched tunnel was half full of fast-moving black water. By that time I was exhausted, since we'd been on the go with hardly a letup for nearly eight hours.

I rested on a wide ledge with a lantern perched beside me, while Mohammed searched with his flashlight for the improvised bridge over the stream that existed in Dark Path folklore—and also, we hoped, in reality.

Suddenly, a pack of hideously diseased scavengers came

rushing out of the darkness, screaming like wildcats, intent on separating us from our possessions. I think they were human, but the few glimpses I caught of them in the lamplight were inconclusive. We fought. I threw four of the smelly varmints into the rushing water, where they either drowned or ended up dog-paddling in Lake Ontario. Mohammed used the last of his Ivanov darts subduing the other five.

We finally found the makeshift bridge, crossed over, and entered the Queen's Quay Dark Path. It was an abandoned goods-delivery system that once served waterfront buildings, now inhabited only by rats. They minded their own business and so did we, traveling eastward for three miserable kilometers through passages partially flooded with icy water. We nearly perished from hypothermia before finding a friendly tribe of genuine Indians, Throwaways from Infinitum, the gambling and entertainment colossus, near the Parliament Street junction. They let us dry out in front of their space heaters and gave us hot food and coffee. My Halukoid appearance didn't seem to bother them in the least.

The last part of the trip was anticlimactic, 1,500 meters of dry storm drains—we were still beneath the force-field umbrella—cramped utility conduits with snarls of ancient fiber-optic and electrical cable, and the walled-off subbasements of vanished public housing units.

We arrived in Cabbagetown shortly before midnight, emerging through a drain grate into a small park.

"The town house you want is in the next block," Mohammed informed me. "Make your phone call."

I sat in deep shadows with my back against a tree trunk. The little park was forlorn and deserted, its shrubs leafless, the flowerbeds empty, and the fountain turned off for the winter.

Mohammed crouched beside me. "Go ahead," he urged. "What are you waiting for? I want to get home tonight."

I hesitated because I was afraid. The long, perilous journey hadn't terrified me, but the prospect of making this phone call did. I stalled. "How do you expect to get back to Grange Place tonight? It's too far. Too dangerous."

"Damn right it is, man. But only if you take the Dark Path. I'm going to walk crosstown on the *surface,* right down Dundas Street for three klicks, till I get to Spadina and our regular bolt-hole. It'll be a breeze, now that I don't have a fuckin' Haluk fugitive in tow. Make the phone call!"

Dex Assistance gave me the code. I tapped it in, keeping the viewer inactive. Got an answer and a face.

"Yes? Who is this, please?"

"It's Helly," I whispered. "I need to see you immediately."

"Helly?"

"Please listen. I'm in trouble. Serious trouble. You know what—what's going on in the Assembly. The free-for-all about the three hundred new Haluk planets. My own close involvement as Rampart syndic."

"Yes. But I don't see—"

"The demiclone spy accusations. They're true. The—The person using my name, giving statements to the media, is an impostor. A clone. I've been kept prisoner by the Haluk for seven months while this other man has used my identity to discredit Efrem Sontag's investigation."

A protracted silence. "This isn't . . . some sick practical joke?"

"No. It's true. I only escaped from the Haluk tower a few days ago. I've been hiding in the Dark Path. Under the city."

"Good God. And you want—"

"Your help. Please. There's no one else I can turn to. No one who would believe me."

"Your voice—"

"I know. I've been through hell. It's not the only thing about me that's changed. But I can prove who I am. Here's a secret password: Kashagawigamog."

"The lake where you almost drowned when you were five years old."

"Where Eve saved my life, then beat the shit out of me for disobeying orders and going out in the canoe alone, without a life vest. I told you about it when we visited that art gallery in Haliburton."

Another interminable pause, then: "All right. I'll listen to what you have to say. Come to my town house. Do you know where it is?"

"Yes. I'm only a block away. I'll use the back door. You wouldn't want your neighbors to see me coming in."

"Why not?"

"Trust me."

"Very well. I'll leave the rear garden gate unlocked. Come through the alley."

"There's something I have to warn you about. My appearance. I don't want to frighten you, but—"

"I don't frighten easily. You of all people ought to know that."

"Yes. I'm sorry. But I'd better show you what was done to me by the Haluk. I'm not the man you remember." I activated my viewer pickup.

"Jesus Christ," Joanna whispered.

"They demicloned a Haluk, gave him my DNA. This—This change is a side effect of the genen process."

Her eyes were full of sudden tears. "Oh, Helly!"

My name. She used my name. "It *is* me, Joanna. I need you so very much."

"Come," my former wife said.

So I did.

Chapter 8

I jogged wearily toward Joanna's place with my baseball cap pulled low, praying I wouldn't meet another night-runner who'd notice my filthy athletic clothes and outlandish features. I figured the chance of Haluk agents physically watching her place was vanishingly remote. More subtle varieties of spying were possible—even satellite eyes. But I'd had no relationship with Joanna for years, and I was fairly certain that the aliens would have discounted her as someone I'd call on for help. They'd be concentrating their surveillance efforts on Karl Nazarian and my other associates, on my family, and on Efrem Sontag.

That night, the pleasant streets of Cabbagetown seemed almost deserted. Paving-stone sidewalks, lamp posts that simulated gaslights, big old trees. A two-meter-high ornamental iron fence surrounded each row of town houses. The locked gates in front of each unit had security boxes with viewscreens. Following inner-city guidelines, there was no private hopper pad anywhere nearby. You didn't fly into affluent enclaves like Cabbagetown; you drove or cycled or walked, and you didn't leave your vehicle parked overnight in front of the house, either.

There were six large town houses in Joanna's row, built in the gracious style of the previous century—gray clapboard facades, heavy white window frames, overhanging eaves, attic dormers on the third floor, multiple chimneys, little sheltering porticos with hanging lanterns above each front door. The houses shared a two-story mews in the rear that had garage space for twelve cars below, exercise and hobby rooms upstairs.

I jogged around onto a side street and entered the alley. The mews building sported brass carriage lamps. A single gate beside it gave admittance to the communal garden. The telltale on its card-lock box glowed green, and when I tried the gate, it swung open silently.

Her back porch light hadn't been turned on and the lower part of her house was dark. Blinds were drawn in two illuminated rooms on the second floor.

I crept up the steps. Before I could touch the bell pad, the door opened and I saw a tall, slender woman silhouetted against indirect light from an inner hall. She wore a tightly belted crimson velvet robe over a high-necked white nightgown. Her blond hair was still long, as I had remembered it. Freed from its chignon, a single glossy braid fell over her right breast.

She stared at me, austere features shadowed, eyes wide and touched with twin sparks from the carriage lights, lips parted in a soundless cry of trepidation. My grotesque face seen on a small phone viewer lacked the impact of solid, atrocious reality.

"It's me, Joanna," I said gently. "It really is me."

"Yes. Come in." Her voice was steady. She stepped aside as I entered and then locked the door. For a few seconds we stood still, studying each other in the half-light like cornball characters from an old grade-B science-fiction movie: the attractive woman in her nightclothes and the monstrous alien intruder.

Then she said, "Phew! Why didn't you tell me you'd been hiding in a sewer?" Before I could reply, she strode off briskly. "Come with me. Before we do anything else, you've got to have a long, hot shower."

I followed meekly through the kitchen and up the back staircase to a sumptuous bathroom on the second floor. "Put

those nasty clothes of yours into the valet and use the DISIN-
FECT setting. You'd better program a serious germkiller
bodyscrub, too. The shower has an enormous spritz selection—although I can't say I've ever had to use the industrial-
strength option myself. There are guest toiletries in the large
cabinet. Toothbrushes and the like." She paused and gave me
a quizzical look. "Umm . . . you *do* still have teeth?"

I burst out laughing and bared them in an un-Haluk grin.
They felt like my originals, even though the spaces between
them appeared to have expanded. Then I playfully stuck my
tongue out at her as well, and instantly regretted it. Earlier,
I'd vaguely felt that the organ was a tad abnormal. Now the
mirrors in the bright bathroom revealed that it had become
obscenely long and agile. I could easily touch the underside
of my chin with it. And it was colored a rich plum-purple.

"Holy shit!" said Joanna DeVet, Morehouse Professor of
Political Science. She backed away from me into the hall.
When I made a piteous noise she forced herself to smile.
"It's not such a bad tongue. Rather handsome, as those
things go. Can you unfurl it like a chameleon and catch
flies?"

"I'll have to give that a try one of these days," I said
wretchedly.

"I'm sorry, Helly. I shouldn't joke about it. It's just so . . ."

"Alien," I said softly.

"Yes," she agreed. "Are you hungry? Can you eat human
food?"

"My last meal was rat stew, dished out by feral Native
Americans living in waterfront catacombs. I'm famished."

"I have half a tandoori chicken with spicy yogurt sauce,
nan bread, and rozkoz-poppyseed coffee cake from Gra-
nowska's." Joanna hated to cook, but she knew the best take-
out and home-delivery places in the city.

I said, "The chicken sounds just great."

"Is there anything else you need, dear?"

She said it so sweetly, with such natural, heartfelt concern, that I felt my throat tighten and my eyes begin to fog.

Oh, Joanna. Why had I been such a self-centered fool?

But there was no time now for sentimentality. In spite of her composed demeanor, my former wife was undoubtedly in a state of profound emotional turmoil. I had to keep her calm if she was going to be of any use to me.

Use.

That was the only reason I'd come to her, right? Not for asylum and solace, but for help in resuming my quixotic crusade against the Haluk. So I'd better get on with it . . .

"Does your phone have Phase XII encryption capability?" I asked.

"Yes. I've never used *that*, either." She sighed. "I suppose we're about to go into serious cloak-and-dagger mode."

"Call the Interstellar Commerce Secretariat Forensic Division. Ask for the emergency voice mail of Chief Superintendent Beatrice Mangan. She's the head of the ICS molecular biology department and an old colleague of mine who knows all about the Haluk demiclone threat."

"Yes, I know who she is. She was one of the most impressive witnesses during Delegate Sontag's open committee sessions, testifying about the demiclone corpse."

I went on. "Show your face and transmit your iris ID, then leave a message asking Bea to call you at home as soon as possible, max encrypt."

"Do I mention your name?"

"Absolutely not. You're going to have to be my mouthpiece for a while until I gain credibility. Somehow, without telling Bea anything about me or my situation, get her to come to your house early tomorrow. It's imperative that she not be followed, and I don't want her to risk coming at night. The Haluk are certain to have her under surveillance. Ask her to bring a portable genetic assay kit with her, and a phone with a datalink to ICS."

"I see where you're going. Your DNA will identify you positively."

"Even better. Bea can confirm that the Haluk embellishments in my genome are the result of an illegal demicloning procedure."

"What will you do then—go to the media?"

"Eventually. There are more urgent matters to take care of. I've been in a dystasis tank for seven months, and I need to get back up to speed on current events before I make any drastic moves. For that I could use your help, Joanna. If you're willing."

"Of course. I have a large library of reference materials here. I can provide you with whatever information you need."

"As soon as Bea Mangan is ready to vouch for me, I intend to show myself to Delegate Efrem Sontag and my close associate Karl Nazarian—perhaps to Eve and my father as well. We'll work together to decide the best way of blitzing the blueberries. Don't worry, we won't use your house as our command post. I won't endanger you, any more than I have already by simply coming here."

"I'm willing to take risks, Helly," she said simply. "If it will help you."

Her unexpected loyalty struck me mute, shamed me.

"Joanna. Thank you. But I've got to get out of Toronto. The capital's a hotbed of Haluk. Everyone knows that their embassy staff and trade delegation number in the thousands. And I'd bet the ranch that a sizable percentage of them are out beating the bushes for me right now."

"What about the Haluk impostor using your identity? He's been very plausible, you know. I certainly would never have doubted him."

"The active Fake Helly demiclone isn't an alien. He's a transmuted human. The Haluk made two copies of me."

"Don't you want to expose him at once?"

"I'll need help blowing the whistle on this guy. He's more

than a Haluk apologist and secret agent—he's dangerously insane."

"You know that for a fact?"

"Oh, yes. And I'm not the only one who thinks so."

"Who in the world is this monster of depravity?"

"Alistair Drummond, the former Gala CEO. He didn't die in Arizona."

"Good heavens!" She thought about it for a moment. "How . . . absolutely perfect."

"I'm sure the Haluk thought so, too, when Drummond presented his ingenious little scheme to their leadership. They also realized that the man is a ticking timebomb, and planned to replace him with a more trustworthy Fake Helly as soon as possible. A Haluk demiclone. That won't happen now. My second clone is very, very dead." I couldn't help the grim satisfaction in my voice.

Joanna gave me a look. Political scientists aren't slow to grasp unpleasant tactical realities. "So the Haluk are stuck with Drummond, who no doubt has an agenda of his own."

"Damned right he does. When he tricked Eve and the Rampart board into making him president of the Concern, he put himself in a position to do immense damage. With the Galapharma consolidation, there are now nearly six thousand planets under Rampart control. Drummond has access to databases for all of them. He can control their starship fleets, their internal and external defenses, even their management rosters. For all we know, he might have put Haluk demiclone moles into top executive positions in Rampart Tower and on significant numbers of Rampart worlds in both the Perseus Spur and the Orion Arm. He's had plenty of time. Personnel reshuffling during the consolidation would have made his actions seem logical. I'm sure he's also used his position as Corporate Syndic to promote the Haluk cause effectively among the Assembly Delegates."

She nodded. "He's been very ardent in his defense of the aliens, personally appealing, utterly convincing. Certainly no one would ever suspect him of being—" She touched the side of her head.

"A flaming nutcase? Hardly. When he organized the Rampart takeover conspiracy, he was motived by hubris and overweening ambition. Now, I suspect he's out for revenge—against me, against Rampart, perhaps even against the entire human race. We can't simply discredit Drummond and expect him to quietly surrender. He'll find ways to fight back the minute he realizes he and his Haluk allies are being seriously threatened. There may be only one practical way to deal with him."

"I see." And she did, too. "You and your friends are going to be facing some tricky realpolitik decisions. The Assembly vote on the new Haluk planets is expected very soon. Perhaps within two weeks."

"We've got to shoot that bill down, Joanna." I spoke with desperate urgency. "The aliens can't be allowed to bring vast numbers of colonists into the Spur. With Drummond's help, they'd find a way to seize all of Zone 23. And that's not even the worst of it. The Haluk have a secret base in a Sagittarian asteroid. Last April their pirates were using it to hijack Sheltok transactinide carriers. By now the damn place might have been expanded into a staging point for an all-out attack against our starship fuel supply."

"Helly, this is appalling! You'll have to go to the media at once. Concentrating your efforts on the Assembly members themselves might not be effective. The Hundred Concerns want the Haluk colony bill to pass. A majority of the Delegates will bow to their pressure unless the constituency absolutely forces them to do otherwise."

"Through media exposure."

"Yes. The Commonwealth constitution has provisions for a citizen referendum under certain circumstances. But the Assembly itself must—"

I interrupted her, suddenly overcome by a crushing fatigue that was both physical and mental. "Later, Joanna.

Please. I know Sontag and the others will welcome your expert advice. We'll talk about all that tomorrow. But for now, just convince Bea Mangan to come over here in the morning. Before I can do anything else, I have to prove that I exist."

"I'll call her at once." Impulsively, she extended her hand. I took it very carefully in my inhuman blue one, bowed my head over it in an archaic gesture of courtesy that seemed instinctive, and released it.

Joanna blinked, then let her gaze fall. "I'll bring the food to my little sitting room at the end of the hall." She turned away and went down the back stairs.

I closed the bathroom door and stripped, inserting my grimy clothes and footgear into the valet machine as she'd instructed me. Then I stepped into the shower and did my best to wash everything away.

It didn't work, of course.

She was waiting when I padded into the sitting room in my stocking feet. The soaked and battered Adidas hadn't survived the valet's attentions and the car-coat was beyond salvage; but the other clothing I'd appropriated from Dan was fresh and clean again.

A thought of my wayward brother had flitted briefly through my mind as I dressed. I'd wondered if the Haluk had interrogated him yet. There was nothing he could say that would help the aliens find me, but they might persist in the questioning anyhow. Too bad for Dan . . .

"You smell much better," Joanna remarked. "Don't tell me you used the lavender bath oil."

"I needed some soothing aromatherapy," I said, trying to sound casual. "You know I always liked lavender. It makes me feel relaxed." And horny, worse luck.

Three couches were grouped in a U shape before a tall holoscreen. She'd programmed an underwater scene, blue-black tropical water with a school of gleaming opal moon-jellies rising and falling languidly amid ghostly spires of coral. The music was strange, soft blooming chords that might have been Olivier Messaien.

"I like the holo," I said. "It almost reminds me of home. Kedge-Lockaby, that is. The freesoil Perseus world where I lived. Except the planet's sea never evolved jellyfish."

"Is it a very beautiful place?" Joanna asked me.

"Oh, yes."

"And you were happy there."

"Not at first. Later, when I got my head back together, I was very happy."

The food waited in a covered hotdish on a low table in front of the couches. I sat across from her, noted the unfolded vidphone sitting beside a carafe of coffee and a bottle of Jameson whiskey.

"Bea Mangan hasn't returned your call yet?" I inquired.

"Yes, she did. She'll be here tomorrow morning at seven, with the genetic assay equipment. She said she'd take a taxi from ICS Tower."

"That should be safe enough in daylight if she takes precautions."

"Helly . . . I'm afraid she guessed the truth. I'm sorry if it upsets your plans. I never hinted—"

"It's all right. I might have known Bea would figure it out. After all, she's a cop."

"She wants to talk to you right away. She said it was extremely urgent."

"Rats." It had to be bad news. I knocked my fist against my ridged forehead, trying vainly to jump-start my brain. Switched the phone's viewer option off and went through the encrypt rigmarole. Bea picked up on the first buzz.

"Beatrice Mangan here."

"It's Helly. The weird voice goes with the rest of my Halukoid ensemble."

"So the aliens subjected you to the preliminary genen procedure—"

"Yes. And I escaped. Pardon me for not doing a vis-à-vis, but I'm really tired of being blue and hearing about it."

Her warm, maternal face was full of sympathy. "How awful for you. I'll do whatever I can to help. You know that."

"Thanks, Bea. Just verify my DNA tomorrow. After that I'll be getting in touch with Ef Sontag and some others to work out a plan of action. I haven't decided yet whether to go to the media right away or wait a couple of weeks to make my big revelation just before the Assembly vote on the Haluk colonies. In either case, I'd like you to redo my genetic profile in public, as part of the big show."

"Helly, that's why I wanted to speak to you immediately. Joanna mentioned the Assembly vote, too. But you won't have two weeks to prepare for it. Ef Sontag called me earlier this evening and told me that the Conservatives suddenly forced cloture on the Haluk colony debate. They passed a resolution calling for a vote on Wednesday, the day after tomorrow."

"No!" I whispered. "No no no."

There goes the ball game: Haluk—300, Humans—0.

Bea said, "On Tuesday, tomorrow, Ef and his group will be allowed to present a summary of their opposition. He asked me to appear as an expert witness reiterating the Brown Fleece cadaver evidence. The pro-Haluk committee will then do their own final summation. The Speaker will call for the vote promptly at 1000 hours on Wednesday morning."

"I know why the debate was squelched," I said dully. "The Haluk leadership hit the panic button after I escaped. They were afraid they wouldn't recapture me before I blew the lid off."

"I'm sure you're right about that. The Servant of Servants and the entire Haluk Council of Nine are here in Toronto. I've seen them myself in the Assembly Chamber VIP observation gallery."

"The Servant would be in a position to add threats to the

usual Haluk lobbying efforts with the Hundred Concerns. The corporate Syndics squeezed the pocket Delegates to force the early vote. Shit! This probably means that a majority of the Assembly will approve the colonies, too."

"Ef thought so. But I think you should talk to him, Helly. He's spending the night in Government House with his staff, working on last ditch tactics. Perhaps—"

"Sorry. That's a no-go. I'm totally exhausted. Too strung out to think straight."

The metaphoric black pit yawned in front of me, and oblivion had never looked so appealing. I'd go into hiding, fight the impossible fight some other day . . .

But Bea was saying, "Why don't I go to Ef early tomorrow, break the news about your return, and ask him to come along to Professor DeVet's house with me?"

"If his office has a demi mole—" I objected.

"All of Ef's people give DNA samples every week, and he has stringent security monitoring. There's no mole. If the Haluk do have his offices under surveillance, it can only be the crudest kind of corridor peeping. I can get him out of there cleanly, Helly. Trust me."

"I do . . . But damn it all to hell, Bea! What can we hope to accomplish in one day? Ef can present me to the Assembly as Exhibit A and I can give a nice little speech. But would it really make any difference in the voting?"

Joanna suddenly said, "Pocket Delegates, Helly. Rampart's own."

Stupid stupid. I didn't get it. "What?"

On the phone, Bea echoed, "What?"

I activated the speaker option and Joanna spoke louder.

"There are a substantial number of Delegates beholden to Rampart now, following the Galapharma consolidation. Those votes can be swayed if you undercut Drummond's influence immediately, by removing him from the syndic post and replacing him with an ally. Can't you think of some sneaky lawyerish way of doing it so you wouldn't have to confront the impostor himself?"

I finally understood what she was saying. The logjam in my cerebrum exploded in a flash of fresh hope. "Christ! If it could only work!"

I'd persisted in thinking of Rampart as it used to be, a beleaguered little outfit without political influence. Before the consolidation, the Rampart worlds of Zone 23 had rated a meager four Commonwealth Assembly votes under the complex allocation formula that took into consideration both population and corporate worth. With Galapharma's pocket Delegates added in, the total would now be eighty or ninety. It might be enough—

Bea Mangan's incredulous voice interrupted my train of thought. "Did I hear Professor DeVet mention Alistair Drummond?"

"He's me," I said tersely. "Fake Helly the First. There was also a Haluk copy of me. It died. If you want the complete scoop on Asahel in Demicloneland, I'll tell you tomorrow."

Joanna brought us back to the point. "How does a Concern oust its syndic?"

"According to Rampart's bylaws," I said, "he's customarily appointed or dismissed by the president. A simple majority vote of the Board of Directors can also do it. Drummond is president as well as syndic and he won't fire himself, so that leaves the board. Gunter Eckert, the chairman, can call an emergency meeting. But I'll tell you ladies right now that a hardheaded old businessman like Eckert won't accept me as the real Helly unless he sees a DNA assay done right before his eyes and then has me interrogated with a psychotronic probe."

"Then do it," Joanna said.

I had to laugh at her naiveté. "I don't even know Gunter's goddamned personal code! He's certainly ex-database. But that's moot. We'll never get him to call a meeting or watch the assay because he'll never believe that the Asahel Frost who's President of Rampart is an impostor. He won't *want* to believe it. Neither will Eve, or my father, or any of the other directors. Because if it's true, and the Haluk get their shit blown out of the water, Rampart stands to lose more than any of the other Hundred Concerns. There's no one on the board who—"

I shut my mouth, overcome with the abrupt realization that I was wrong. There *was* someone.

"Helly?" Bea Mangan said anxiously.

"I just had a thought. I'll have to follow through on it. The odds are long, but the Rampart situation might not be completely hopeless after all. Listen, Bea. You come here tomorrow with Ef Sontag and your genetic profiling equipment. And I'd also like you to bring a Hogan H-18 miniaturized low-power psychotronic interrogation device."

"Of course. I can borrow one from Enforcement. Is there anything else?"

"Pray," I said, and told her goodbye.

Joanna regarded me with a puzzled expression. I said, "Give me a minute." Then I sat still, closed my eyes, and tried to remember a phone code, unlisted, that I'd used only once before, months ago. A code that might mean the difference between galactic war or peace.

Got it, you crafty blue bastard, you!

I tapped the pads. This time I left the viewer turned on. There was no need for extra encryption. The man I was calling had the best personal security in the universe.

He answered his phone, stared at me, and said, "Good God in heaven!"

"No, sir," I corrected him. "Helly Frost, back from a *very* bad trip. Captured by the enemy in the Sagittarius Whorl. Demicloned and horribly transmogrified by Haluk villains. But my Barky Hunt wasn't a fiasco. I got the answers we were looking for. Do you want to hear about it?"

"Yes," said Adam Stanislawski evenly. "If you can prove you are who you say you are." No hesitation, no emotional dithering. He weighed Drummond's Helly persona against my unlikely claim and was willing to keep an open mind! What a guy . . .

"Have you ever heard of Joanna DeVet, Morehouse Professor of Poli Sci at Commonwealth University?"

"The former wife of Asahel Frost. I've read several of her books. Thought they were brilliant."

"I'm at her house in Cabbagetown. If you come here tomorrow morning at about 0700 hours, I'll prove who I am with a DNA test and a truth machine. After that I'd like you to get hold of your man John Ellington, Vice Chairman of Rampart. Have him force Gunter Eckert to call an immediate emergency meeting of Rampart's Board of Directors—without the participation of the individual presently masquerading as Asahel Frost."

Stanislawski frowned thoughtfully, then a broad smile broke over his shrewd, guarded features. "I see. Turning the pocket Delegates, eh?"

"There ain't no flies on you, sir. You guessed it. It was Joanna's idea."

"Is Professor DeVet there? Let me talk to her."

I pushed the phone in front of her. She said, "Good evening, Citizen Stanislawski. Thank you for your kind words about my books. I'm rather surprised, since they condemn the coercive role of business in galactic politics. I'm even more surprised that my former husband should have contacted you under these extreme circumstances."

"Is it *really* Helly?"

"Absolutely. Escaped from Haluk durance vile. They cloned him."

"I'll be damned. Tell me how to get to your house."

She did. "Until seven tomorrow, then, citizen."

"I'm really looking forward to it, Professor."

She ended the call, folded the phone, and uncovered the dish of chicken.

"Eat your food now, while it's hot. Would you like an Irish coffee? I'm going to have one. Maybe several. It's decaf, so it won't prevent you from sleeping." She picked up the carafe and began filling a glass mug.

Sleep! With my brain fumbling to process the stunning developments of the past half hour, there was small hope of that. But I said, "Sounds good to me, babe."

She partially filled both mugs from the carafe, stirred in a little sugar, added generous measures of whiskey, inverted a spoon and used it to carefully float a layer of heavy cream on top. We lifted the mugs and tapped them together, simultaneously murmuring, "Cheers." Sipped, avoiding each other's eyes.

I began picking dutifully at the food. The baked chicken was meltingly tender and delicious, but I had no appetite. I should have made small talk, asked about her work at Commonwealth University, her life during the years we'd been apart.

I couldn't. The nearness of her, the very real possibility that I'd be killed tomorrow by alien agents or the hirelings of Alistair Drummond—even the lingering scent of the goddamned lavender bath oil—had cranked up my blood pressure to the point where I didn't even trust myself to speak to the woman seated across the table from me.

I wanted her so much.

Goofy old human nature has a paradoxical instinct that sometimes asserts itself under circumstances of impending peril: before the male Neanderthal goes out to hunt the mammoth, before the knight sallies forth against the invincible foe, before the Sioux warrior meets the Seventh Cavalry, before battered Blue Supercop charges blindly into the lair of the corporate bad guys.

But this time around my body's urgent need to reaffirm

life was doomed to frustration. If it *was* only a need, and not a symptom of something deeper . . .

Seeing my alien hands clumsily manipulating the knife and fork, painfully conscious of the awful face that had stared back at me from the bathroom mirror, I was prey to a burning sense of self-loathing and despair that was only partially associated with my horrifying appearance. I had rejected my wife out of stupid pride, denied my feelings for her because I had been afraid, come back to her only as a last resort.

Persons I'd respected had told me that I had never stopped loving Joanna: Mimo Bermudez, Matilde Gregoire, my sister Eve. I'd denied it with all my strength, even as I kept the two wedding rings on their platinum chain. I was still trying to deny it, now that we were together again and the situation was hopeless.

I was no longer a man, and yet I was.

Joanna sat in apparent ease, bare feet crossed at the ankles, red velvet robe falling away from her white gown, watching the drifting moon-jellies when it became evident that I was incapable of conversation. Finally I couldn't eat any more. She cleared the table and put the dirty dishes into a dumbwaiter.

"Would you like another Irish coffee, Helly?" So polite and compassionate toward the poor freak.

"Yes, please. No cream this time."

She handed the cup to me but didn't resume her seat, walking instead to the windows overlooking the street and briefly parting the drapes. "This is a very safe part of the city, regularly patrolled and well-equipped with security devices. I'm sure you'll be all right staying with me."

"Just show me the guest room," I said. "Or I can lie down here on one of the couches."

"You're welcome to stay as long as you like," she insisted. "If we're careful, there's no reason why any of your enemies should suspect you're here. I'd also be happy to help with your . . . appointments at Rampart Tower and the Assembly tomorrow."

"I couldn't possibly jeopardize your safety or impose on you any more than I already have."

"But where will you go?" She seemed genuinely concerned. "Helly, there'll be a media frenzy! And you'll be in danger from Drummond and the Haluk, no matter how the vote goes."

"I have a hiding place in mind," I said brusquely. "Don't worry about me." After I'd done what I could in Toronto, I'd go to the place I'd thought of earlier. My first idea had been to retreat to Karl Nazarian's fortified cottage; but I'd rejected that idea instantly. It would be one of the first places my enemies would look.

And Karl might have already gone the way of Jake Silver . . .

I drank down the last of the coffee, gabbling about how grateful I was to Joanna for her kindness. If she wanted to do more, she could provide me with a file of news magazines and holovid newscasts. I'd spend the night skimming them, since I doubted I'd be able to sleep.

"Poor Helly," she said, smiling. "I'll gladly do that for you if you wish. But there are better ways to relax." She untied her robe, slipped it off, and tossed it onto a chair. Then she began to undo the long golden braid of her hair.

The coffee cup almost fell out of my hand. I said, "Joanna."

She said, "My dear. I've missed you so very much."

"No," I moaned. Alien flesh, human hormones. Oh, God. I was coming alive again. They were.

"Let me see you." She had turned off the room lamps with a snap of her fingers and was undoing the front buttons of her demure white nightdress one by one. It was made of some delicate opaque fabric, with soft lace at the wrists and collar. The only illumination came from the opalescent sea creatures that seemed to float in the virtual water behind her. I could see the thrust of her nipples, her shining eyes.

"I'm hideous," I said hoarsely. "Changed. You don't understand."

She shook her head, the smile widening. "You're intriguing. A fantasy come alive. Don't tell me you've never thought about such things. All human beings have."

The gown fell to the floor. Her wonderful body was the same as always, pale and glowing, with an ash-blond ecu that matched her long hair. She lowered the zipper of my track suit, removed the jacket, slipped her cool hands under my T-shirt and lifted it.

"Oh!" Not revolted, interested. Caressing my chest's bizarre cobalt trapunto ridges, the twin rows of vestigial mammaries like ornate golden buttons on a hussar's coat. "What in the world are these?"

"Fuckin' extras," I muttered. "The damned Haluk have litters." She pulled the T-shirt off. "And that's not the worst of it. Please don't—"

She was fitting her hands around my stupid wasp waist. "That's amazing! How in the world does it accommodate your diaphragm and digestive tract?"

"I don't know! Joanna, for the love of God—"

She took my face in both hands, drew it down and kissed me, long and slow, savoring the alien juices of my mouth, accepting the responding thrusts of my awful tongue, crushing her body eagerly against mine, feeling my erection but still not aware of the ultimate indignity.

"Now," she said at last, drawing me to the large central couch. Her eyes were like stars. "My love. My dearest alien love."

Despairing, desperate, on the brink, I said, "Look!"

Tore off the rest of my clothing and let her see me naked.

"Two?" she whispered in disbelief. "But how—"

"I don't know!" I roared, feeling tears of frustrated lust start from my eyes. "I don't *know*!"

"Then we'll have to experiment," she said. Her face was radiant and her touch gentle. "The entire ensemble is more streamlined. Elegant. Very different, of course, but actually quite beautiful."

"Beautiful. . . .?"

"Hush now," she said, and began the experimentation.

I crept out of her bed shortly after 0500 hours, leaving her deep in sleep, and had a quick shower. After collecting my clothes from the sitting room and putting them on, I took the phone down to the kitchen to make my call to Karl Nazarian.

Once again I cut out the video option. Before entering his personal code, I programmed an emergency voice-mail override and activated his ringer. Then I held my breath as the buzzing began.

Be there, old friend. Don't be dead because of me.

His face appeared, puffy from slumber and mad as a hornet. "Who's there? Do you know what friggin' time it is?"

I said, "It's five twenty-two on a dark November morning."

"Show your face, you inconsiderate bastard!" he raged. "Hector, if this is you calling from that goddamned deer-camp of yours, I'm going to wring your bloody black neck."

"It's not Hector." I tried to make my voice sound as normal as possible. "Engage Phase XII encryption, Karl. Do it now. Someone might be listening."

I heard cursing, some of it in a language that might have been Armenian, then the signals indicating that the call was secure.

"Well?" Karl snarled. "If you know me, you know that nobody ever, *ever* taps my phone. Who the hell is this?"

"It's Helly Frost. The real one, not the demiclone fake who's been masquerading as me for the past half year."

"The real—"

"Asahel Ethan Frost, alias Helmut Icicle, alias Cap'n

Helly, the fish-flickin' fool of Eyebrow Cay, freesoil planet
Kedge-Lockaby, Zone 23, Perseus Spur."

"Oh, my God!"

"The Haluk bagged me out in Sagittarius and made a
Helly demiclone. I finally escaped from the xenos a few days
ago—and I'm ringy, riled, and swoll up with mad like a
chuckwalla lizard trapped in a fuckin' hobnail boot!"

"It's you, all right," Karl conceded after a brief, incredulous silence. "Now that I think about it, your double never
did quite come across as a proper cowboy."

"I'll bet. The fictitious gent in question is none other than
our old chum, Alistair Drummond."

"Christ on a crutch! They turned Drummond into a demi
of *you*?"

"Yeah. I'm going to have a devil of a job taking him down,
too. But I'll do it or die trying."

"That sneaking bastard! He did an incredible job. Played
you to the hilt. I don't mind telling you it nearly broke my
heart when it seemed you were repudiating all the evidence
against the Haluk that we sweated blood for. I had to figure
you'd sold out to protect Rampart's bottom line. You want to
tell me the whole story?"

"Later. I need your help, Karl. Right now, if you can manage it."

"Where you calling from?"

"I'm at my ex-wife's place in Toronto." I gave him the address, told him about the lack of adjacent hopper pads,
pleaded with him to come as soon as possible, as clandes-
tinely as possible, in a ground vehicle.

"No problem at all. My girlfriend has a catering business.
I'll borrow one of her vans."

"Girlfriend?" Karl had been a solitary widower for as
long as I'd known him.

"Lots of things happened while you were floating. Some
good, some not so good. What do you need? Weapons?"

"An Ivanov Squire will suffice. I also need a phone

primed with a new personal code—use the name Helmut Icicle. Get into Rampart's database, retrieve all my old dex listings and links, and install them in the new phone."

"Uh-huh. Anything else?"

"A set of full soft body armor, size XLT; a regular Anonyme anorak in XL; a pair of lightweight mittens; a sturdy pair of boots, size twelve medium. Oh, yes. Another set of Joru robes. No makeup or fright-wig necessary this time."

I told him briefly what I hoped to accomplish that day at Rampart Tower and at the Commonwealth Assembly. He uttered a disappointed expletive when I told him how tight the time frame was for scrubbing the new Haluk colonies, and wanted to know how the interactive citizen vote could be invoked.

"I don't know that much about it. You can ask Joanna to explain the thing when you get here. Watch your back en route. The Haluk probably have had you under surveillance for several days, ever since I broke out of their embassy in Macpherson Tower."

"The day I can't slip a tail is the day I get fitted for my halo and start taking harp lessons. Is there anything else I can bring you?"

"No, but there are a couple of other things you can do. Do you remember the report I sent you on the Sheltok carrier pirate attack?"

"The Haluk corsairs operating in the Sag? Sure. I certified it."

"Can you access it quickly and send a copy to Ef Sontag's office?"

He didn't reply immediately. Then: "Yes, I can do that. What else?"

"After today's action, I'm going to hide out for a little while until things cool off. I'll need a fast, well-armed hopper. I'd like you to requisition one of Rampart's big Garrisons—"

"Sorry," Karl said. "Can't do that. Your alter ego cost me my job. A couple of weeks before you supposedly returned from the death-traps of Sagittarius and turned into a raving capitalist, I came down with a mysterious virus that the Rampart medics couldn't cure. I was bounced from my vice-presidency with a nice pension that I never thought I'd live to spend. Big surprise! When I went to an independent physician for treatment, the deadly bug turned up its toes. How do you like that shit? Fake Helly and his friends were clearing the decks."

That explained his hesitation about the Sheltok report. He'd have to hack it out of the Rampart database, along with my phone files. I had no doubt that he'd do the job immaculately.

"I suppose Lotte, Cassius, and Hector were deep-sixed along with you," I said.

"Correct. They're all living in the area, retired and bored stiff. You got something in mind?"

"I'll need the entire staff of your old Department of Special Projects immediately—provided I can pull off a certain ploy over at Rampart this morning. Put your folks on alert, but warn them it's gonna be balls-to-the-walls this time. I suspect Rampart may be infested with other demiclones besides Fake Helly. You and your gang may have to extract them, and the job just might begin this afternoon."

"Christ. Okay, I'll get on it. Anything else?"

"Can you get hold of any kind of hopper at all?"

"Cassius has a Tupo he keeps at Toronto Island Airport. Kind of slow and not armed. I'm sure he'd—"

Joanna had come into the kitchen and was listening shamelessly.

I said, "Get it if you can, but I really need that other stuff. Come as soon as possible. We'll sort everything out when you get here."

"Okay. It'll be damned good to see you again, Helly."

"Oh, no it won't," I said, and hit the End pad of my phone.

Joanna was wearing jeans, a metallic gold turtleneck, and a loosely knit white sweater with a shawl collar.

"You didn't show yourself to your friend?"

"Not everyone thinks the Haluk form is beautiful."

"All of you isn't," she said, smiling slyly. "Only the essentials."

"Well, Karl Nazarian is a tough old buzzard, but I still want to reintroduce myself to him tactfully. That goes for our other guests as well. I may need your assistance."

"Oh, my. Then you'd better strengthen my resolve by plying me with a pot of strong hot coffee. You do remember how to make it? If not, I'm open to other inducements."

"Are you, indeed," I murmured. "Let's induce."

A taxi carrying Beatrice Mangan and Efrem Sontag arrived shortly after seven. As we had arranged it, I lurked in the upstairs sitting room while Joanna gave Bea and the Delegate coffee, peppermint tea, and muffins with Bonne Maman black cherry preserves. After about ten minutes Joanna brought Bea up with her equipment to do the DNA test. The astonishment of my former ICS colleague was brief and her interest in my exotic body entirely clinical.

Joanna stood by during the blood-drawing and cursory physical exam. I absolutely refused to strip down.

"Damn," said Bea Mangan. Then she smiled at Joanna.

I swear Bea *knew.* How do women do that . . .?

Working with her impressive machine on the table in front of the blank holoscreen, Bea quickly developed a genetic profile from my biosample, then compared it with the one in her ICS files, studying screen after screen of esoteric data.

"Fascinating! It's you all right, Helly, but overlaid with suppressing sequences from your late Haluk demiclone. You're a genetic palimpsest, my man. A human parchment with the original writing not quite erased, written over with something terribly new."

Joanna laughed appreciatively. "What a cogent metaphor."

"I hate scholarly jokes," I growled, "particularly when I'm the butt. Can a layman make sense of this analysis? Will we be able to use it to prove my identity to people like Ef Sontag and Adam Stanislawski, who don't know anything about advanced biology?"

"Stanislawski?" Bea said. "You *have* been busy."

"He'll be here any minute, and so will Karl."

"Oh, dear," Joanna said. "I hope they're not hungry. Bea and Ef ate the last of the muffins, and there's not much else in the house."

"Hospitality," I muttered, "is the least of our worries."

Bea did something with the machine. "Look here, then. We start over. Enter Original Helly's DNA, *comme ça.* Now enter Halukoid Helly's DNA, *comme ça.* Tap the correlation pad, then hit précis, *et voilà!* Go ahead, do it yourself."

She walked me through it. At the end the readout said: POSITIVE MATCH PLUS 1623 ANOMALOUS CODING SEQUENCES SUBSTITUTED FOR PORTIONS OF NORMALLY NONCODING GENETIC MATERIAL. DO YOU WISH CODON-BY-CODON BREAKDOWN OF ANOMALIES? Y/N.

I told it N.

"Looks good, Bea. Thank you. Can I keep the machine with me today while I confer with some people?"

"You aren't getting rid of me that easily," she said. "If you hope to use that data to convince others of your identity, you'll need a live expert witness to vouch for it. Otherwise you might as well be demonstrating a video game. I volunteer my unimpeachable authority for as long as you need me. I'll operate the psychotronic device, too, if you like."

"Bea . . . there's no way I can say how grateful I am."

"Then don't," Bea said. "Are we ready for Sontag's show-and-tell?"

"I'd rather wait until Stanislawski shows up. It'll save time, maybe even reinforce plausibility. We won't wait for Karl Nazarian. He has some necessary items to assemble and it might take him a while. You and Joanna go down and

keep Ef company. Show him the test results. I want to sit
here and pull some ideas together."

"Of course," Bea said.

They left me alone. I'd already been briefed by Joanna on
events of the past half year as we ate our small breakfast, following the inducements. Seeing holovids of "myself" had
been bad enough. But I was even more shocked at how
quickly the Haluk had moved to insinuate themselves into
the Commonwealth economy, dismayed at how readily their
reassurances of goodwill had been accepted, in spite of
Ef Sontag's efforts to sound the alarm. Not even Brown
Fleece's demiclone corpse had significantly swayed public
opinion against the Haluk. The Concerns had produced experts of their own who contradicted Bea's evidence.

Ef and his committee had done their best. Unfortunately,
the fact remained that the blue aliens were very good for
business, and the Hundred Concerns were fearful of rocking
the prosperity boat. Their pocket Delegates would vote on
the Haluk colonies as they were told to, unless I could un-
leash a groundswell of citizen opposition in time to make a
difference.

I began to dictate to a small e-book. Doing my best to remember incriminating remarks made by the two Haluk leaders as they stood in front of my dystasis tank. Trying to
recall details of Barky Tregarth's story, Dolores da Gama's
spiteful boasts, and the Sheltok skipper's damning admis-
sions of Haluk piracy being swept under the rug by nervous
Concern management.

The front doorbell rang.

I looked out the window, saw a little red Honda Civic
parked in front of the town house, and assumed that Karl had
changed his mind and acquired another set of wheels. About
ten minutes later Joanna came up to the sitting room.

"Adam Stanislawski, the richest man in the galaxy, has arrived. Both he and Ef Sontag have accepted the proof of
your identity. You won't have to submit to the truth machine

on their behalf. On stage, Blue Boy. The dress rehearsal audience is waiting."

With her leading, I went down to the kitchen. Ef and Adam and Bea were sitting at the table, where cups of coffee and tea shared space with forensic apparatus.

Gasps at my entrance. The two men sat still as statues.

"Good morning, all," I said mildly. "Thanks for coming and thanks for believing. I'm sure you're curious about the circumstances that resulted in my physical change. In just a few minutes I'll satisfy your curiosity and tell the whole story. But first: I hope no one is in need of a defibrillator."

Strained chuckles.

"No? Excellent. There are two principal objectives I hope to accomplish today, with your help. The first is the removal of a demiclone agent, loyal to the Haluk, who has been taking my place as President of Rampart Concern and Corporate Syndic. Adam Stanislawski has pledged to help me accomplish this. When this impostor is deposed by the Board of Directors, I hope to have Vice-Chairman John Ellington, the Macrodur stakeholding representative, elected syndic in his place. He has the stature—and the motivation—necessary to pressure Rampart's so-called pocket Delegates into a one-eighty-degree switch."

Ef Sontag said, "Are you certain this new syndic will obey orders?"

Adam Stanislawski laughed. "John will do as I say."

"And you're certain," Joanna said, "that John *is* the man you think he is."

"All of my employees have been required to take DNA tests every week," Stanislawski said. "Delegate Sontag's open committee sessions describing demiclone infiltration scared the liver out of me. I instituted the policy at the beginning of September." The Macrodur chairman's blue eyes did their friendly twinkle thing. "And before you ask—I have not excluded myself from the testing. Even though I haven't heard Helly's story about his latest exploits, I've decided to accept his thesis that a vast Haluk conspiracy exists, and that it poses an immediate threat to humanity. All of Macrodur's, er, political influence will be exerted to defeat the Haluk colonial bill. I'll do my best to see that Rampart does the same. You have my word on it."

The 400-kilo gorilla had spoken. Ef Sontag nodded, showing admirable legislative sangfroid.

I said, "Let's move along. The second objective I hope to accomplish is the one Chairman Stanislawski just iterated. To this end I volunteer to appear today as a witness in Ef's opposition summation in the Assembly. Prior to my appearance, I'll undergo DNA testing and a brief psychotronic interrogation before a conference of the news media. I will then invite the man masquerading as Asahel Frost to step forward and do the same thing. He won't, of course. By the way, the impostor is a human, not a Haluk. He's a traitor to his race whose behavior can perhaps be explained by the fact that he's a dangerous sociopath. His name is Alistair Drummond."

"Sonuvabitch," said Adam Stanislawski.

"I have my reasons for unveiling myself to the media prior to my appearance before the Assembly," I continued. "It's good psychology to give the Delegates prior warning of a bombshell."

"I agree with the tactic," said Ef Sontag. "We don't want them so shocked by the revelation that they don't pay attention to what you're saying."

"There's another factor favoring media revelation," I continued. "It will warn the general population that something dramatic will happen during the Assembly session, and ensure that the session receives maximum viewer exposure. Professor Joanna DeVet suggested the possibility of an interactive citizen referendum on the colony measure. I believe there's constitutional provision for that."

Sontag didn't look encouraging. "In this situation, I doubt that a majority of the Assembly Delegates would yield their voting power to the people. The provision was designed to apply to grave emergencies, in situations where Delegate factions appear to be hopelessly deadlocked. A vote on new Haluk colonies might not qualify as a grave emergency—especially in the minds of my Conservative colleagues." He considered for a moment. "However, if the vote goes against us tomorrow, as it very well may, there's constitutional provision for an interactive *veto* if enough citizens express immediate disapproval. Am I right, Professor?"

Joanna nodded. "Delegate Sontag could call for citizen participation from the Assembly floor after the Delegate vote is tallied. Unlike the referendum, a citizen veto poll doesn't require Assembly approval. It can be okayed by the Speaker herself."

"She might be amenable," Ef said, "provided sufficient numbers of citizens had expressed opposition to the measure following the summations. I'll be sure to mention that during our media show."

"Say it again at the end of your summation," I urged.

Joanna said, "You realize that a final veto tally would probably take a couple of days, while PlaNet hits from remote worlds are collated and verified." She looked bemused. "You know, there hasn't been a citizen veto for sixty years. Not since legislation on the death penalty for all Throwaways was shot down."

And if the citizens hadn't gotten off their apathetic duffs and killed that draconian measure, Yours Truly would not be alive today, and in a position to make trouble . . .

"Are there any other questions or comments concerning upcoming events at the Assembly this afternoon?" I inquired.

"Do you really think it's wise to expose Alistair Drummond during a media conference?" Bea Mangan queried the room at large. "I'm a medical doctor as well as a geneticist and I did study psychiatry—although I admit mine is very rusty by now. But it seems to me that there's a danger of provoking this man to some very rash actions. He might even try to disrupt the media conference. Perhaps Assembly Security ought to be warned of that possibility."

I said, "Good point. But I think it's necessary that Drummond's credibility be destroyed immediately. I believe he's inserted demiclone agents into other Concerns besides Rampart."

"I agree," said Stanislawski, "but with one stipulation. Expose the fraudulent Helly, but don't name Drummond." He frowned. "There's bound to be confusion about why Helly looks like a Haluk, when his demiclone is a human being. I know *I'm* confused."

"I hope I can let that slide for today," I said. "There were two duplicates made of me. The first was Drummond and the second was a Haluk. I killed the Haluk demiclone in cold blood, while he was unconscious. It was necessary, but I don't intend to defend my action in a quickie media conference."

Everybody stared at me in silence for a long beat.

Then Ef Sontag cleared his throat tactfully. "The regular media room in Commonwealth Assembly House is probably too small for this affair. When we announce the purpose of the conference, every person in the capital with media credentials will want to attend. We might have a mob scene on our hands, even without interference from Drummond. I'm not sure that my staff will be able to cope."

"Suppose I have my own media-relations people liaise with them," said the Macrodur chairman. "You and I can discuss the matter after Helly tells us about his recent activities." He turned to me. "I'm very interested to know how you ended up blue. Lamentable as the condition is for you, personally, I'm inclined to believe it might be extremely advantageous to our cause. A humanoid Haluk corpse wasn't dramatic enough to shock people. A live Halukoid human is something else."

I stretched my alien lips into a smile facsimile. "My tale

is next on the docket. But first, sir, you need to get on the horn and tell John Ellington to organize the emergency Rampart board meeting. Let's make it 1100 hours at Rampart Tower. And please caution your stooge very strongly to keep news of the gathering away from Fake Helly Frost. Otherwise, we might arrive at Rampart Tower and discover that all of the directors except the demiclone have disappeared."

"Leave it to me," said the 400-kilo gorilla. He took a phone from the inside pocket of his suit coat and began tapping pads.

During the hiatus, the back doorbell rang and Joanna went to answer it. She returned in a moment followed by a rugged elderly man wearing a white coverall labeled C'EST CHEESE CATERING SERVICE. The logo of a comical mouse in a chef's toque was embroidered on his back.

Karl Nazarian spotted me, did the predictable double take and said, "Aw, shit! Aw, *shit!* Is that you, Helly?"

"Yes."

"Shit," he said for a third time. He stood there for a moment with his face screwed into an expression of thunderous fury. Then he put down the sizable container and the garment bag he was carrying, came to the table, pulled me to my feet, and embraced me in a bear hug. "We'll get those Haluk bastards for this!"

"Yes," said Bea Mangan quietly. "We will."

I introduced Karl to the group. "I was just about to regale these good people with the adventures of Helly the Haluk. Now you can hear the story, too. What's in the box? Weapons?"

"They're outside in the van. This is something better." He opened the large container and began unloading it onto the table. "My girlfriend the caterer thought I might as well bring some of her great home cooking. Quiche, anyone? Six different kinds. Also pigs-in-a-blanket, croissants, brioches, walnut bread—"

"One of everything for me," I said. "I have a feeling I'll need to keep up my strength today."

By the time I'd finished telling my story and answering questions, it was nearly ten o'clock. We'd eaten all the food Karl had brought. Periodically, my narrative was interrupted by phone calls, some directed to members of the spellbound audience, some made by the audience themselves.

Sontag heard from his media liaison people. Superefficient Macrodur flacks were already demanding a lightning policy briefing in anticipation of the big show. Ef passed on information and gave orders.

John Ellington called back, informing his boss that he had organized the emergency Rampart board meeting. Eight of the twelve directors were in Toronto, constituting the necessary quorum. I would do my presentation before Gunter Eckert, my sister Eve, my father Simon, John Ellington, Chief Finance Officer Caleb Millstone, Chief Technical Officer Crista Wenzel, Small Stakeholder Representative Thora Scranton, and Chief Legal Officer Satoshi "Sam" Yamamoto.

According to Ellington, no one at Rampart Tower knew the whereabouts of the alleged Asahel Frost. He had not been seen in his offices for three days.

Prompted by my account of the Haluk leaders viewing me in the tank and discussing the Grand Design, Bea Mangan deduced—correctly—that Alistair Drummond was not a virtually perfect genetic replica of me as Fake Helly Mark II had been. Since Drummond had been in dystasis for only four weeks, he would retain substantial amounts of his own DNA. Bea downloaded Drummond's stats from her lab at ICS. At her suggestion, Adam ordered Macrodur sleuths to begin searching for a verifiable biosample of the impostor— as well as for Drummond himself.

When I described the pirate attack on Captain Schmidt's vessel, and mentioned that the demiclone Dolores da Gama had let slip the name of the Haluk base in Sagittarius, both Sontag and Stanislawski went into action.

The Delegate told his staff to subpoena the Sheltok Chief Operations Officer as a hostile witness during today's Assembly presentation. Ef planned to use the report on the incident that I'd sent to Karl; but even though that report was certified, it remained hearsay unless an independent source corroborated it. If the Sheltok COO did that, we'd have admissible evidence of Haluk hostility.

The Macrodur chairman ordered a fast, heavily armed cruiser belonging to his fleet to set off immediately from Katahdin in Zone 3. Its mission was to perform a secret scan of the supposedly abandoned asteroid way station called Amenti. It was unlikely that the recon of the alleged Haluk pirate base would be completed before the Assembly vote took place, but Stanislawski wanted the evidence anyhow— and he didn't trust Zone Patrol to obtain it.

I concluded my recital by describing my trip through the Dark Path of Toronto, together with an expurgated version of my reunion with Joanna, who smiled enigmatically. The others seated at the table burst into ironic applause at the end.

Adam Stanislawski said, "I never heard such a crazy yarn in my life. I believe every word of it."

I said, "Thank you, sir."

He said, "Call me Adam. What do you say we adjourn now, and let Helly get on with raising a shitstorm in the Rampart boardroom?"

"I'm coming with you," Joanna said to me. "To the tower and to the Assembly. And don't you give me that old-fashioned look, Citizen Stanislawski."

"Adam," he repeated, grinning.

"But Joanna—" I protested.

"Any political scientist would sell her soul to be present at these two events," she said. "Don't you understand that there's another *book* in this? Besides, I'll make a splendid character witness for Helly." She thought for a moment.

"Perhaps I'd better change into something more media-appropriate."

"Beat you to it," said Bea Mangan, rising from the table and showing off her handsome black suit. "And I'm going to Rampart Tower, too."

Joanna left us, and Bea began tinkering with her genetic assay equipment.

"Speaking of clothes," Karl Nazarian said, picking up the garment bag he'd brought and handing it to me, "here's the body armor and the Anonyme and the footgear you asked for. The new phone, too. But what in the world are you planning to do with the Joru costume?"

"Wear it into Assembly House later for the media conference," I said. "They wouldn't let me inside, wearing an Anonyme privacy screen. So I'll step into the galactic spotlight dressed as a shy, friendly alien, all muffled up. Whet the crowd's curiosity: Who he? Wasn't this conference supposed to be about Haluk? Then Ef gives the signal, I whip off the Joru cloak and hood—"

"Eek," said Bea.

"And take your place in show-biz history," Sontag said wryly. "I have to get back to my office. There are things that need doing, especially if we're to include that Sheltok piracy evidence in the presentation. The media conference is scheduled for 1315 hours in the rotunda, during the lunch recess. We'll be expected in the Assembly chamber exactly forty-five minutes later when the session resumes. Helly, you and Bea better not let me down—or I won't just have egg on my face, I'll have dinosaur doo."

"I'll get him to the church on time," Karl promised. "I have the catering van to drive him and Joanna and Bea from here to Rampart Tower. After the board meeting, one of my associates will be waiting in a hopper at the tower skyport for the trip to the Assembly."

"Cassius in his Tupo?" I asked Karl.

"He's rounding up the Over-the-Hill Gang even as we speak. They'll be ready if you need them."

"You seem very well organized, Citizen Nazarian," Adam said.

Karl shrugged. "I was VP for Spooky Projects at Rampart until Alistair Drummond fired my ass. Helly says I may be rehired fairly soon."

"I hope your van has room for one more passenger. I intend to go along to Rampart myself to keep an eye on the proceedings." The genial glint in Adam Stanislawski's eyes turned into something ice-cold. "And perhaps encourage a suitable outcome to the meeting." He passed out cards. "Here's my personal code, if any of you need to get in touch with me at any time."

I said, "You'd all better make a note of my new code, too. If you call the old one, you'll be talking to Alistair Drummond!"

Assorted humorous exclamations ensued. They really weren't all that funny to me.

Ef Sontag looked at his wrist chronometer. "I better call me a cab, then."

Adam offered a car key. "Take my little red Honda. It's parked out front. When you finish with it, just tell it to go home. Don't be deceived by its modest appearance. It's fully shielded and equipped with enough gadgetry to tempt the ghost of James Bond."

"Can it make a vente triple-shot no-foam latte?"

"In a New York minute."

Ef took the key, kissed it, and headed for the front door.

Karl Nazarian cocked his head in sudden bright-idea mode. "Chairman, I wonder if I could ask a favor. After today's Assembly session ends, Helly will need to get out of town quickly to avoid the media and . . . certain other people. Our friend Cassius Potter has offered his own private aircraft, but it's rather slow. And unarmed."

I saw what Karl was driving at. "My safe house is some distance away. Using a Rampart hopper isn't an option because of security considerations. If you have one I could borrow—"

Stanislawski poked a code into one of his cards with a cheap plastic stylus and handed it to me. "Go to the Assembly House skyport when you're ready to leave and give this to the dispatcher."

"Thanks very much."

"Would you like to tell me where you'll be staying?"

"Let's wait till I get there. I may have to change my plans."

Karl said, "Go get dressed, Helly. It's time to put this show on the road."

Adam smiled at Bea Mangan. "Why don't I help carry your equipment to the van, Chief Superintendent?"

"Not until I've done a DNA test of you and Karl." Both men stared at her, nonplussed. "We can't afford to take chances with *anyone*, can we?" she inquired reasonably.

I went upstairs to find Joanna, hoping there might be time for one last little inducement before the battle.

Chapter 9

Adam phoned John Ellington again as we drove south to the waterfront and the newly rechristened Rampart Tower, ordering his long-suffering minion to notify the Internal Security officers at the VIP skyway portal of our imminent arrival. In an unlikely vehicle.

I had to hand it to the Rampart guards. They didn't blink an eye as a catering van badly in need of a wash-job stopped inside the elegant portico on the 300th floor, where only executive limos and other prestigious rolling stock usually dared venture. One man opened the passenger door for me, while the other helped Joanna, Bea, and Adam alight from the rear. The guards courteously took charge of Bea's equipment, which was to be sent directly to the boardroom.

By then John Ellington himself had arrived to escort us to our rendezvous with corporate destiny. The vice chairman was a stocky black man dressed in a gorgeous three-piece Italian silk suit the color of aged bourbon, a green-striped scarf, and a golden brooch shaped like an African mask. The mask had tiny emerald eyes.

Stanislawski introduced Joanna and Bea by their formal titles, but pointedly left me incognito.

I said, "Vice Chairman, do you have the skyport access authorization code for Citizen Nazarian and the group that will arrive later by air?" Ellington shot me a nervous look. The privacy visor of the Anonyme hood has that effect on some people. Then he nodded.

"Give it to me, please."

I passed the card to Karl through the van's window and whispered, "Catch you soon, I hope!" We had already discussed contingency plans as we made our way through surface traffic to the tower. Karl gave me a little sardonic salute, then drove away into the down-ramp.

"Perhaps you'd like to leave your things in the visitors' cloakroom and freshen up before the meeting," Ellington said. He led us into a spacious lobby that contained enough potted tropical greenery to qualify as an annex of the Allan Gardens Palm House. A woman wearing the uniform of an InSec captain approached our group, looking grave, and addressed the vice chairman.

"I'm sorry, sir. But this . . . entity is armed." She nodded at me. "He will not be permitted to go further unless he relinquishes his weapon."

I carefully removed the small Ivanov Squire from the pocket of my dark gray anorak and held it out in harmless display. My Halukoid hands were concealed by dark gray matching mittens. "I prefer to keep the weapon."

"And he is wearing body armor," the captain pointed out. We'd all been scanned as we came in the door.

"Thank you," Adam Stanislawski said. "The gentleman will keep his gun and armor. That will be all."

The captain started to object, but Ellington made a curt gesture and she retreated to her desk. Adam and the two women went to doff their outerwear. The vice chairman was left standing with me.

"Looks like we're in for a change in the weather," I said.

"Are you speaking literally," John Ellington inquired in a snide voice, "or figuratively?"

A smartass. I wished I had managed to overhear more of Adam's conversation with him when they spoke on the phone earlier. How much did he already know?

"Are the Rampart directors present and accounted for?" I asked.

"Eight of us are here, including Chairman Eckert. As I told Adam, we have a quorum." He had moderated his tone to almost courteous. After all, I was here under the auspices of the gorilla.

I said, "I understand that Asahel Frost will not be joining us. Was he notified of the meeting?" A little double-checking never hurts.

"Following Adam's explicit instructions, I didn't invite him."

"Good. Tell the security captain, there, to alert all InSec posts in the tower. If Asahel Frost shows up, you are to be informed instantly. Then you'll inform *me* even faster."

He stared in frustration at my privacy visor, lips tightly compressed, before speaking very softly. "What the hell's going on here? Some kind of a palace coup?"

"Talk to the captain, John, and don't get uppity."

His dark eyes widened in outraged dignity. "Who are you?"

When I remained silent, he shook his head, went to the security desk, and did as I'd told him. A few minutes later the others joined us and we entered a very large, very elegant lift that had its very own potted palm. After Ellington plugged his card, we were whisked up another hundred stories to the top of what had once been Galapharma Tower, the most distinctive edifice on the capital skyline and the only one that had earned an obscene nickname.

Alistair Drummond's little joke. The same nickname had been applied to him.

I was gratified to see that the redoubtable Mevanery Morgan, executive assistant extraordinary, was still guardian of the corporate inner sanctum. She had relocated from the Seriphos office when Rampart attained Concern status. Morgan was not wearing her Gorgon Medusa pin today, but the dour, suspicious expression on her face made up for it.

Her new computer desk was even more awesomely equipped than the old one, situated at the center of the ante-

room like the tuffet of a controlling spider. Crimson carpeting with dramatic ocher spokes surrounded the desk. The
room's wall panels were satin-finish golden metal alternating with dark rosewood. There were no potted palms. The
sleek Braque sculpture, Simon's pride, that had graced the
former Rampart executive reception area hadn't made
the transition to the new digs; it had been supplanted by a
tortured assemblage of ruby glass tubing that looked like
the large intestine of some unfortunate marine mammal,
internally illuminated by glowing ordure. I wondered if
Rampart's new president had chosen it years ago to adorn
Galapharma Tower . . .

Mevanery Morgan greeted us solemnly and led us to the
boardroom door, one of four that opened into the anteroom.
None of the doors had anything so plebeian as an identifying sign. We trooped inside, ladies first. John Ellington went
to his place near the head of the long table, at the right hand
of Chairman Gunter Eckert. Adam Stanislawski sat down at
the table's foot without asking anyone's permission. Morgan
showed us lesser mortals to chairs on either side of Adam
and then went out, closing the door.

I noticed that Bea Mangan's genetic assay device and the
small Hogan truth machine had arrived ahead of us. They
rested on a stand beside the door.

The wall behind Gunter Eckert's chair had tall narrow
windows that overlooked the leaden, island-scattered waters
of Lake Ontario. Beyond the southern edge of the force-field
umbrella was a fuzzy blur that might have been either mist
or falling snow.

Eve and Simon stood near a refreshment bar at the far side
of the room, talking quietly together, their backs to the rest
of us. Caleb Millstone, the prissy CFO, Crista Wenzel, the
Chief Technical Officer, and Thora Scranton, who had represented Rampart's small stakeholders for over two decades,
sat at the boardroom table just below John Ellington, staring
at me. Three chairs on Gunter's left were empty. The fourth

was occupied by Sam Yamamoto, my friend and colleague in
Rampart's legal department, who had been my principal associate during the Galapharma trial. I was glad Sam had
been promoted into the Chief Legal Officer slot, wondered
what he was studying so intently on the recessed computer
display in front of him.

Gunter Eckert said, "Ladies and gentlemen, I'd like to call
this meeting to order."

Eve and Simon came to the table and sat down in the
chairs at Gunter's left, leaving an empty seat between
them—presumably in case President Asahel Frost showed
up after all. My sister did not condescend to notice those
of us at the foot of the table. She had always been a
clotheshorse, but today she was so perfectly groomed—
striking in an ivory sheath and large sapphire earrings, every
hair in her coiffure lacquered firmly in place—that she
might have been an android mannequin. A rather short one,
with an attitude.

Simon was a shocking contrast. Seven months had
worked a terrible change on my father. He had become
skeletally thin, his signature denim ranchman's outfit appeared many sizes too large for him, and his tooled leather
belt had been ratcheted to the last hole. Sunken rheumy eyes
darted restlessly from one person to another until they found
my incongruous figure and turned slitty with apprehension.

I thought: What in God's name have they done to you,
Pop?

But I knew the answer. No doubt Simon had refused to retire, and couldn't be forced off the Board of Directors, so
Drummond and his crew had dealt with him as they had Karl
Nazarian. Unless I intervened, the malignant virus was
going to live in my father until he died.

Gunter Eckert called the group to order, dispensed with
the reading of the minutes, and invited John Ellington to
present the first order of business.

"Before I do that, let me introduce our guests," Ellington

said. "You all know Adam Stanislawski, Chairman and CEO of Macrodur Concern. He requested this extraordinary meeting today. On Adam's left are Joanna DeVet, a distinguished author and professor of political science at Commonwealth University, and Chief Superintendent Beatrice Mangan of the Interstellar Commerce Secretariat's Forensic Division. The man seated at Adam's right has not been presented to me. Perhaps Chairman Stanislawski will do the honors."

Adam said, "The Chief Superintendent, Professor DeVet, and I are agreed on his identity. Those gadgets over there on the cart will verify it as well." He took me by the arm and rose to his feet, drawing me with him. "This man is the real Asahel Frost."

Murmurs of astonishment and indignant disbelief.

"No," Eve said. Her face had turned the color of ash.

Adam plowed on. "The person who has used Helly's name for the past six months is an impostor. A genetically engineered demiclone of the type described by Delegate Efrem Sontag in his committee hearings. This afternoon Delegate Sontag will present evidence of Helly's identity to the news media and to the Commonwealth Assembly."

"No!" Eve said again in a more emphatic tone. "That's impossible!"

Several of the others loudly voiced their agreement with her opinion. But Sam Yamamoto was smiling at me, and one of his eyes slowly closed in an unmistakable wink.

Gunter Eckert bellowed, "Adam, have you lost your bloody mind?"

Stanislawski turned to Joanna and Bea with an ironic smile. "Ladies? Have I?"

Bea said, "I tested this individual's DNA. He has been subjected to a genen procedure and his appearance has been altered. But he's Asahel Frost, beyond a doubt."

Joanna rose from her chair and stood beside me, one hand

resting on my shoulder. "I know him better than any person here. Better than Eve, better than Simon. This man is my husband."

I felt my chest constrict in sudden breathless joy, wanted to leap and shout and stomp and tell the Rampart board that I didn't give a hoot in hell what they thought—what the whole goddamned galaxy thought!—so long as *she* accepted me.

All the same, I didn't say a word, didn't move a muscle.

Eve regarded the lot of us with cool contempt. "I don't know what you're playing at, Adam, how you've managed to dupe these two women and Delegate Sontag, or brainwash them—"

"Let him prove himself," Thora Scranton demanded. "Use the truth machine."

"Machines can be rigged," said Gunter Eckert.

Bea Mangan said, "Then bring in your own psychotronic device and your own interrogator. Call the ICS and request another DNA examiner with another assay machine. This man will pass any identity test you can give him. He is the real Asahel Frost."

"No," Eve insisted. Her eyes were burning in her pale face and both hands were clenched into fists. "No impostor could have done the things my brother Asa did. He accomplished far more than the Rampart-Galapharma consolidation. He made himself my good right arm! He's kind and affirming and strong. He's never tried to undermine my authority. Thanks to him, Rampart has become a respected member of the Big Seven."

"Thanks to him," I said, finally speaking up in my altered voice, "trade with the Haluk is the bulwark of Rampart's prosperity. But it won't last, Evie. The aliens will take it all away. The impostor has inserted Haluk demiclones into Rampart corporate management."

"The Faceless One speaks!" drawled Crista Wenzel.

"And you'd better listen," Adam Stanislawski said.

Eve cried out, "This is ridiculous! Everyone in the Concern has been DNA-tested regularly since the Sontag committee started its flap in August. Including me. Including Asa."

"Who did the testing?" I demanded. "Rampart Internal Security?"

"Of course."

"Evie—"

"Don't call me that!" she shouted.

I said, "Madam Chief Executive Officer, if the Rampart president is a demiclone, don't you think InSec would be the first part of the Concern he'd subvert? . . . Have you forgotten our turncoat pal Ollie Schneider so soon? I know how devastating this revelation is. How shocking. Joanna showed me holovids of the impersonator in action. He's utterly convincing. A corporate team player—exactly the kind of man you and Simon hoped and prayed I'd turn into after the big trial, ready to fulfill the family hopes that I'd dashed over and over again in the past. But you know in your heart that the real Asahel Frost could never have become that man."

"I know nothing of the sort!" she said, but the conviction that had been so rock-solid before might have been faltering.

With the exception of Sam Yamamoto, who was whispering into the stylomike of his computer, the other directors were listening to Eve's and my exchange with expressions that ranged from blank puzzlement to sick uncertainty.

I asked her, "Would you be willing to have independent experts assay the DNA of every top Rampart executive? Including that of your so-called brother Asa?"

She lifted her chin and smiled coldly at me. "Of course. I'll authorize it personally—*after* the Haluk colony bill passes."

"The hell you will!" Adam Stanislawski exclaimed furiously.

"Don't try to bully me, Chairman," Eve snapped. "Rampart is my corporation, not yours, and I won't see its best interests compromised. If my decision doesn't please you, put your stake on the block and we'll buy you out."

Sadly, I said, "Oh, Evie. Are you willing to set aside all your past suspicions about the Haluk, all their treachery and the personal suffering you endured at their hands? Never mind that the Commonwealth of Human Worlds might also be in deadly danger—"

"There is no plausible evidence of a Haluk threat to humanity," she stated. Her voice was flat, almost without inflection. "The true Asahel Frost has proved that to our satisfaction."

"Under psychotronic interrogation?"

"Don't be idiotic."

Simon suddenly said, "Who is he?"

Everyone looked at my father, who pointed a trembling finger at me and spoke in an agonized rasp. "If you're Asa, then who's this crafty sidewinder who's taken us all in, played us for fools?"

"He's Alistair Drummond," I said.

Eve cried, "That's a lie!" The other directors seemed petrified.

Simon's gaunt face twisted with some devastating emotion. "Turn off your privacy visor, you! Right this fuckin' minute! I'll know if you're really my son!"

"Maybe not, Pop," I said. "The Haluk have worked me over in a dystasis tank." And to my sister: "Same as they did to you, Eve, once upon a time on the planet Cravat."

"Quit shilly-shallying, dammit!" Simon said. "Show us your face!"

"All right." I pulled off my constricting mittens and flicked the switch of the visor.

Pandemonium.

As the room erupted, I removed the anorak and handed it to Joanna, who still stood beside me, and whispered a few words to her.

She said, "Are you sure?"

"Watch him. Go over to the refreshment bar. I don't think there's any immediate danger, but don't take your eyes off him for a minute. I won't be in a position to do anything during the tests. I'll have to depend on you. Can you manage?"

She folded the Anonyme and held it tightly against her. "Yes."

Adam Stanislawski endured the uproar for only a few minutes before shouting, "That's enough!"

In the ensuing silence, Gunter Eckert said, "Chief Superintendent Mangan. Please use your machine to test this— this man's DNA."

Bea said, "Very well." She moved the equipment cart next to my chair and set to work.

Joanna was helping herself to coffee. Simon sat slumped in his chair, eyes closed, lips mumbling silently. Eve's expression was stubborn and aloof. Adam Stanislawski wandered up to the head of the table and spoke in an undertone to Gunter Eckert and John Ellington. Millstone, Scranton, and Sam Yamamoto waited with expectant faces. Crista Wenzel, the Chief Technical Officer, left her seat and took up a position where she could observe the DNA analyzer's display.

After a few minutes the machine confirmed my identity.

Wenzel said to me, "Now I'd like to use the psychotronic device to interrogate you briefly, if you please." She smiled minimally. "Or if you don't please."

I submitted to the hookup. When the truth machine activated, I felt an unpleasant sensation, as though an entire hive of nanobot bees had invaded my cranium. Wenzel asked only one question.

"Are you Asahel Frost?"

I said, "Yes, I am."

Zap. Momentary blankout. Pain.

Wenzel watched as Bea touched several control pads. The

CTO studied the display, nodded, and addressed the board. "This machine also confirms his identity. In my opinion we have no choice but to tentatively accept these test results, pending confirmation by an independent examining team. I so move, and call for a second."

"I second the motion of the CTO," said John Ellington.

Gunter Eckert said, "Those in favor, please raise your hands."

Ellington, Crista Wenzel, Thora Scranton.

"Those opposed."

Eve, Caleb Millstone, and—shit!—Sam Yamamoto.

I looked at him. He shrugged.

Gunter said, "Simon? Are you abstaining?"

The old man had tears streaming down his face. He said to me, "It'll destroy Rampart, you know. After everything we went through. The other Concerns will wipe us off the map for screwing up the Haluk trade."

"We're going to face some tough times, Pop," I said. "All of us, not only Rampart. The greed and stupidity of the Hundred Concerns have put humanity at terrible risk. I'm going to the media this afternoon to talk about it, and then I'll repeat my allegations before the Assembly. Whatever this Board of Directors decides, I don't intend to let Alistair Drummond and the Haluk win."

Simon's green eyes blazed at me with some of their old fire. "You gonna stick with us, then, afterward?"

I hesitated, knowing what he was asking. Sighed. "Yes, you blackmailing old coot. If I survive this fucking mess."

"I vote aye," Simon said.

Eve shook her head. "Oh, Pop. What have you done?"

"What I had to do," he said to her coolly. "What's more, you know it, missy! Rampart's not your child any more'n it's mine. And don't you forget it."

The virus hadn't sapped my father's old feistiness, or his common sense, either.

Gunter Eckert touched the computer display on the table

in front of him. "In the absence of our Corporate Secretary, I herewith record that the motion has carried." His eyes swept the group. "We now face a peculiar situation. Our election of the erstwhile Asahel Frost to the positions of president and syndic is nullified—"

"No, it's not," I said. "You elected Asahel Frost. I'm Asahel Frost. I hold the offices and I still have a seat on this board, by virtue of my quarterstake." Thus giving notice that any attempt to vote me out would fail for lack of the required stakeholder votes, I spoke to Yamamoto. "Do you agree with my position, Mr. Chief Legal Officer?"

"In my opinion, you're correct." Sam spoke blandly. "Although I doubt there's any precedent to support you."

"You can't do this!" Eve exclaimed. "You have no right!"

I ignored her, wondering how Alistair Drummond had managed to turn this intelligent, decisive woman into a deluded fool. Perhaps Simon was right about her thinking of the Concern as a person with a life of its own. Legally, of course, it was—but not morally. Trust a lawyer to make the distinction.

"As Rampart president," I said, "I exercise my right to relinquish the office of syndic, and appoint John Ellington to fill the vacancy. Do you accept, John?"

Almost inaudibly: "Yes."

"I instruct you to immediately contact those Delegates of the Commonwealth Assembly who represent our planets. You will urge them to vote against the upcoming measure granting the Haluk three hundred new Perseus colonies. If your persuasions fail, you may expect the gravest possible consequences."

"I understand." He threw a bitter glance at Adam Stanislawski. "I have every confidence that the Delegates will respond appropriately."

A silence.

"Is there any other new business?" Gunter Eckert asked formally.

Simon let out a cackle of laughter that hovered on the edge of hysteria. "The hell with business. Let's all get on over to the Assembly chamber and watch the friggin' fireworks!"

"It's my intention," I declared, "to request that ICS, CCID, and ECID teams immediately begin genetic profile comparison tests of every person in top-echelon management and every member of the Rampart security force. Eventually, each Rampart employee will be tested. In Toronto this action will be supervised by Chairman Gunter Eckert, as soon as his identity is verified by Chief Superintendent Mangan, and by Karl Nazarian, who has already been tested by her. Karl will resume his former position as Vice President for Special Projects at once, appointed by me. In our Seriphos outplanet headquarters, I will request that CCID personnel immediately test Zared Frost, Rampart Chief Perseus Operations Officer, and Matilde Gregoire, Vice President for Perseus Security. They will then supervise testing of Rampart executives in that region. In our Hygeia headquarters similar testing will be under the supervision of Orion COO Edison Vivieros and Orion Security VP Reinhard Fournier. Does any member of the board wish to move an objection?"

No one spoke. Eve was staring at her clasped hands.

I said, "Then I move this board meeting be adjourned."

"Second," said Thora Scranton. "Helly, are you giving out freebie tix to your media circus over at the Assembly?"

Good old Thora; we'd always been buddies. I showed my inhuman grin. "Anyone interested can join the party . . . after Bea Mangan tests their DNA."

"Except John," said Adam Stanislawski, "who has other business to take care of."

Ellington had already risen from his seat and started for the door. He said sourly, "Stop twisting it, Adam. I told you I'd convince the Delegates."

"I think not," said Sam Yamamoto. He stood up suddenly

at his place, a Kagi pistol in his hand. "Come back to the table, John. The rest of you, sit still."

Thunderstruck, Eve whispered, "Sam?"

Adam Stanislawski said, "Oh, shit."

"Is Alistair Drummond on his way, Sam?" I inquired archly. "Or did you just send out a general mole-call on your computer?"

"Guess."

"He's a demiclone," I said.

"Shut up!" Fake Sam shouted. He fired at me twice. The blue beams hit me square in the chest. The people at the table cried out in horror as I fell from my chair and landed in a heap on the floor, praying Sam wouldn't try a head shot. A sharp smell of ozone and burnt fabric filled the air.

I heard starchy Caleb Millstone call Sam an unexpectedly filthy name. Lying on my right side, I had a perfect view of the demiclone as he pulled Simon to his feet, pressing the muzzle of the photon gun into the old man's temple. "Everyone sit down and keep quiet! My people will be here in a few minutes and we'll sort everything out."

Eve said, "Oh, Asa . . ."

I couldn't see her face, but the changed timbre of her voice told me that she had finally accepted the truth. I hoped that it wasn't too late to matter.

John Ellington addressed the impostor. "Do you seriously think Mevanery Morgan is going to allow unauthorized persons access to the executive elevator?"

Fake Sam smiled. "She will, if the alternative is watching Simon Frost's brain go extra-crispy." He swiveled his captive around toward Gunter Eckert. "Call her in here, Chairman."

I wasn't hurt, of course. My body armor had saved me. I waited for an opportunity to make a move without endangering my father.

Eckert was hesitating, and it made the demi nervous. "Do it now, Gunter! Do it, damn you!"

He brandished the Kagi for emphasis, and it shifted mo-

mentarily away from Simon's head and pointed harmlessly
at the boardroom wall behind Eckert. I braced one arm and
leg and hurled myself crabwise at the legs of the two men—
—at the same time that Joanna, still standing behind Fake
Sam at the refreshment bar, shot him in the back with the
Ivanov I'd left in my anorak pocket.

I phoned Karl Nazarian, who was waiting with his gang at
the Rampart Tower skyport, and asked for his suggestions on
what we should do next. Our contingency plans hadn't included a demiclone on the Board of Directors who would tip
off his alien confederates inside the building.

Karl told us to call the cops.

CCID was clearly flabbergasted at receiving a request for
armed assistance from an Amalgamated Concern—big businesses always cleaned up their own messes—but Gunter
Eckert's authority was not to be denied. Inside of twenty
minutes Rampart Tower was sealed and swarming with
Criminal Investigation personnel corraling Rampart executives and security employees. Half an hour after that, forensic teams from ICS and half a dozen other government
agencies were administering DNA tests.

Only a handful of InSec demis offered armed resistance.
Even fewer managed to escape. All of the executives submitted meekly to the testing.

Karl and his crew came from the skyport to the boardroom for instructions shortly after CCID arrived. By the
time he reached us, Bea Mangan had already checked the
DNA of Gunter Eckert and the other members of the board,
as well as that of Morgan the Gorgon, who was vastly indignant that we should think a Haluk capable of impersonating
her. Everyone was legitimate except snoozing Sam.

I gave Karl custody of the unconscious demiclone, then
arranged for a CCID SWAT team to accompany him and his
associates to Rampart InSec's psychotronic lab. Karl had orders to commandeer the place and interrogate anyone in the

building whose DNA wasn't up to human snuff. I promised to check with him after the second act of the day's melodrama played out at Assembly House.

A felony theft-of-identity warrant was issued for the arrest of a human John Doe having the spurious iris-ID of Asahel Frost. Among other places, the APB was transmitted to· every starport on Earth. I hoped we weren't locking the barn door after the horse had escaped. One of the messages sent by Fake Sam had gone to my old personal code, so Alistair Drummond knew we were hot on his trail.

As we prepared to leave, Adam Stanislawski declared he'd had enough up-close-and-personal excitement for one day. He intended to watch the rest of the fun and games from the safety of his own private suite in Macrodur Tower. Cassius Potter dropped him off there before flying Bea, Joanna, and me to the media conference.

It took place pretty much as Ef Sontag and I had scripted it.

We appeared side by side, I in my concealing Joru robes, at a podium on a small improvised dais at the very center of the rotunda that fronted the Assembly chamber proper. Bea Mangan, her trusty equipment, and Joanna were poised just behind us, awaiting their cues. Experienced Macrodur flacks helped Ef's PR staff orchestrate the technicalities.

There must have been close to six hundred reporters crowded into the glass-domed circular foyer, all festooned with the tools of their trade. Huge holovid monitors had been set up in adjacent areas to accommodate the nonmedia audience, who numbered in the thousands. Displays in the Assembly dining rooms also showed the news conference live, at the request of interested Delegates.

I hoped the Servant of Servants of Luk and his entourage were paying close attention, too. A member of Ef's committee had reported that the Haluk were already in the building.

After Sontag greeted the journalists and made brief introductory remarks, I flung off my concealing black-and-white robes to dramatic effect, standing on the dais naked to the waist while the cameras went crazy. Ef told the crowd who I was, why I looked like a Haluk, and what I was going to talk about today inside the Assembly chamber.

Then Bea tested my genes and not only proved that I was Asahel Frost, but also demonstrated that I had been subjected to illegal demiclone therapy—presumably by the same entities whose superficial appearance I now wore. In a touching character-witness testimonial, Joanna declared once again that I was certainly her former husband, a man unjustly convicted of crimes and deprived of citizenship, whom she had never ceased to respect.

Connected to the Hogan truth machine and interrogated by Sontag, I told the citizens of the Confederation of Human Worlds how I had been kidnapped by the Haluk and cloned. I described how my Evil Twin had taken my place at Rampart so as to gain control of the genen vector PD32:C2, and how he had used my name and reputation to promote the Haluk cause. I disavowed the lies that had cast doubt on the evidence presented by Sontag's committee. I dared the impostor wearing my face to come before the media and get tested as I had been.

I did not identify the Fake Helly demiclone as Alistair Drummond.

The galaxy-wide audience heard a heavily edited version of the Rampart Board of Directors meeting and my reclamation of the office of Rampart president. Racked with pain from the continuing zaps of the nasty little Hogan machine, which verified my every statement, I described the measures being taken at that very moment to flush demiclone agents from Rampart. I urged other Concerns and Commonwealth agencies to be zealous in the DNA testing of their own personnel.

Another piece of intelligence I passed on was the demicloning of Sam Yamamoto. Where—I asked rhetorically—

was my real friend being held prisoner? Where were the other unwilling human DNA donors whose places had been taken by Haluk spies? Were they captives of the aliens—as blue and miserable as I—or had they been callously executed after they had served their purpose?

I told my listeners that the confessions being elicited from captured demis would probably come too late to be included in Delegate Sontag's Assembly summation. With luck, however, they might be released in time to influence tomorrow's vote.

Keep tuned for late news at 2200 and 2300 hours! . . .

The last thing Ef Sontag asked me was, "Are the statements you have made here today truthful?"

I said, "They are." And the psychotronic device socked it to me one last time, confirming it.

Then, while the media people called out questions and Ef responded to a favored few, Bea Mangan detached me from the Hogan machine. Joanna gave me a drink of water and some painkiller perles. She wiped my streaming alien eyes and mopped my sweaty azure brow.

"Delegate Sontag!" said PNN. "What reason would the Haluk have to spy on humanity with demiclones?"

"That matter will be addressed inside the Assembly," he replied.

"Do you have any evidence of demiclones infiltrating or influencing the Haluk Consortium of Concerns?" asked the *Wall Street Journal*.

"Not at this time. The matter is under scrutiny."

"Prominent Conservative party members have stated that the Haluk trade is vital to the continuing prosperity of the Hundred Concerns," said *The Times*. "Do you agree with that sentiment?"

"I do not."

Next, *20/20 Interactive* asked, "Will the Liberal party call for revisions in the Haluk nonaggression and trade treaties if the new colonies are voted down?"

"I can't speak for other Delegates. I will personally demand such revisions no matter how the vote goes."

He shook his head negatively as more queries were shouted.

"We have no more time for questions, ladies and gentlemen. It's almost 1400 hours and the afternoon session of the Assembly is about to begin. My committee and I will be presenting new evidence supporting a vast Haluk conspiracy against humanity. One of our witnesses will be the genuine Asahel Frost. After we've spoken, Delegates favoring the new Haluk colonies will summarize their position. A final vote on the measure will be taken tomorrow at 1000 hours Toronto time."

He paused, taking a breath, then burst into an uncharacteristically passionate peroration. "Citizens of the Commonwealth, I urge you to observe the upcoming Assembly session. Use the PlaNet to inform your own Delegate of your reaction to this media conference and to the Assembly vote. Powerful commercial forces have exerted pressure on your Delegates, demanding that the three hundred new Haluk colonies be approved. These forces wish to ensure that trade with that race will continue without significant human oversight or inspection of Haluk planets in the Milky Way. Do not let this happen. Tell your Delegate that the Haluk cannot be trusted. Tell your Delegate that you will not permit Haluk demiclones to infiltrate human institutions and undermine our economy. Citizens—tell them! . . . Thank you for listening."

"A little showboaty," I whispered to Ef as we left the dais surrounded by a wall of security personnel, "but it's been that kind of a day."

Politicians are often keen showmen. Ef Sontag, for all his natural reticence, was no exception. He decided it would bore our galactic audience—and the Delegates, most of whom had been listening avidly to the news conference one

way or another—to repeat my genetic testing and psychotronic interrogation inside the Assembly chamber. So Bea
and Joanna would not be asked to testify after all.

Ef arranged for the women to watch the proceedings from
the VIP gallery. Maybe they'd meet Simon or Thora Scranton or Crista Wenzel up there. The other Rampart directors
had declined to attend, either afraid of being cornered by the
media or engaged in damage control at Rampart Tower.

When the session warning-chime sounded, Ef and the six
Delegates of his committee led me into the chamber. I had
discarded the remnants of the Joru costume and was dressed
once again in Dan's track suit, complete with twin burn-
holes in the breast of the jacket. We took our places at small
desks on the central testimony platform—alias "the floor"—
that stood immediately before the Speaker's bench. Above
the bench was a representation of the Great Seal of the Commonwealth, and behind that rose a colossal holoscreen that
would show close-up images of persons addressing the Assembly.

Semicircular tiers encompassed the chamber; inset within
them were the shell-shaped carrels of the fifteen hundred
legislators. About three-quarters of the delegates were physically present, and the rest were participating virtually. The
spectator galleries and regular media boxes were packed. A
quick flick of my desk display panned the VIP section. I
didn't see any Rampart people, but Bea and Joanna had
good seats. Most of the alien visitors occupied special loges
at the front.

I searched carefully—and there he was: the Big Blue
Cheese himself, the Servant of Servants of Luk.

In honor of the occasion, he'd forgone frivolous human attire and was garbed in magnificent rainbow-hued formal re-
galia, topped off with the ostentatious platinum diadem
and ceremonial fossil jewelry. The SSL was surrounded by
somber figures in black robes that I took to be the Council

of Nine. No one seemed to know if their role was only advisory or if they enjoyed genuine authority. Other Haluk in handsome dress uniforms had to be a security force. There were at least two dozen of them crowded into the loge.

Another chime. Silence fell.

The Speaker, Aziza Alameri, called the session to order and invited those opposing the Haluk colony bill to give final testimony. There was some procedural backing and filling. Members of Sontag's committee presented a brief summation of their earlier arguments, then Ef himself called the first of only two witnesses who would be asked to support the summation.

"If it please the Speaker and this Assembly: in evidence of ongoing Haluk hostility toward the Commonwealth of Human Worlds, I call Citizen Hengpin Kang, Sheltok Field Operations officer. He will testify under subpoena via subspace communicator from his office on the planet Lethe in Zone 8."

The giant holoscreen activated, and the real show began.

SONTAG: Citizen Kang, have you been informed by Sheltok counsel of your legal rights and obligations relative to this Assembly subpoena?

KANG: I have.

SONTAG: Do you affirm that the statement you are about to make is completely truthful?

KANG: I do.

SONTAG: Are you aware that your statement may be verified *sub duritia*, by means of psychotronic interrogation, at the request of Assembly Delegates?

KANG: I am.

SONTAG: Very well. At this time the Assembly requires answers only to selected questions. We reserve the right to depose you in more depth at another time . . . My first question: Do you have personal knowledge of pirate attacks upon Sheltok transactinide carriers traversing the Sagittarius Whorl during the past twelve months?

KANG: I do.

SONTAG: Approximately how many such attacks have taken place during that time?

KANG: I have personal knowledge of thirty-four. Others may have taken place that were not brought to my attention.

SONTAG: How many of these attacks resulted in the hijacking of the carrier vessel or its unexplained disappearance?

KANG: Twenty-eight.

SONTAG: To which race did the pirate vessels belong?

KANG: It wasn't always possible to tell. Some of them were certainly Y'tata. We've always had trouble with Y outlaws in Zones 3 and 4, most of it relatively minor. But in the past year or so . . . Haluk corsairs have been positively identified in about half of the incidents, sometimes in company with Y'tata, sometimes not.

SONTAG: To the best of your knowledge, has Sheltok Concern deliberately concealed knowledge of these Haluk attacks from Commonwealth authorities, from the media, or from Sheltok stakeholders?

KANG: Our personnel received strict orders from Sheltok Earth management not to discuss the Haluk attacks with the media or the general public. I have no knowledge of whether stakeholders knew of them. Following regulations, my staff regularly reported hostile Haluk activity to Zone Patrol and to the Secretariat for Xenoaffairs.

SONTAG: Did official action result from your reports?

KANG: None that I was ever aware of.

SONTAG: In your opinion, why has this Haluk activity been concealed?

KANG: In my opinion . . . so as not to inflame the citizenry against the Haluk trade treaty and the Haluk Consortium of Concerns.

SONTAG: Is it true that, approximately seven months ago, the element carrier SBC-11942, *Sheltok Eblis,* under the

command of Ulrich Schmidt, arrived at the planet Lethe
and reported an attack by sixteen Haluk pirate ships?

KANG: This is true.

SONTAG: Is it true that Captain Schmidt's vessel was saved
from hijacking or destruction by the intervention of an
armed cruiser, human in conformation, whose identification was unknown?

KANG: This is true. Captain Schmidt reported that the unknown human starship destroyed sixteen Haluk bandits.
The cruiser commander identified himself only as Hugo.
Captain Schmidt assumed he was a Good Samaritan
smuggler, if you can imagine such a thing . . .

SONTAG: Thank you, Citizen Kang. You are excused. [*To the
Assembly*:] The next witness, Asahel Frost, will also address this incident. First, however, my committee and I
will ask him to provide background information on his
personal involvement with the Haluk.

Sontag read me the same caution that had been given to
Kang. At the pleasure of the Assembly I could be interrogated later, till my eyeballs popped and blood flowed from
every orifice. For now, I took a simple oath to tell the truth
and nothing but.

Then, with Ef and his fellow Delegates prompting me, I
began to relate my adventures with the Haluk, beginning
with the appearance of the titanic Haluk starship at Helly's
Comet, in support of Alistair Drummond's scheme to seize
control of Rampart Interstellar Corporation. I described my
horrific adventures on Cravat and Dagasatt. I deplored the secret collusion of the Hundred Concerns that had enabled the
Haluk to acquire advanced astrogation technology and other
embargoed human science—including the genetic engineering therapy that had illicitly eradicated Haluk allomorphy.

I didn't say a word about Emily's Mystery Mutant Exon,
or my suspicion that the eradication therapy might not be
permanent.

I removed my jacket and showed my Halukoid torso— monstrously magnified on the holoscreen behind the Speaker's bench—as evidence that the Haluk were continuing to create demiclones. I stated that my own DNA had been stolen, and a Haluk demiclone of me had been created for the purpose of gaining control of Rampart, the Perseus Spur worlds under Rampart Mandate, and the genen vector PD32:C2 necessary to suppress Haluk allomorphy. I stated my opinion that the Haluk intended to use their Spur colonies as jump-off points for a general invasion of our galaxy, and then gave evidence to support my belief.

I described my quixotic Barky Hunt, and what I had learned from Tregarth about the severe population crunch in the Haluk Cluster. It was hearsay, I admitted; nevertheless it provided a motive for the obstinate, even desperate, determination of the Haluk to migrate out of their home starcluster.

I admitted my personal intervention in the Haluk pirate attack upon *Sheltok Eblis*, confessing that I was Hugo. I had concealed my identity from Captain Schmidt because of personal notoriety and a desire not to compromise my search for Barky Tregarth. I stated that I was positive that the pirate ships were Haluk.

Ef Sontag entered in evidence the report on the pirate attack I had sent to Karl Nazarian, as well as Captain Schmidt's report to Hengpin Kang. The Delegates would be able to read the documents at their leisure.

I went on to tell how I was captured on Phlegethon, and how the demiclone agent Dolores da Gama had boasted to me that ultraheavy fuel elements were being stolen by the Haluk in order to cripple human starship capability and fuel an alien invasion fleet.

Finally, I told what I knew of the Haluk Grand Design to overwhelm humanity, gleaned while I eavesdropped on the Servant of Servants and Council Locutor Ru Kamik as I

floated in a dystasis tank in Macpherson Tower. I pointed a
blue finger at the Servant himself—sudden close-up of his
affronted face on the holoscreen—and invited him to submit
to psychotronic interrogation and affirm that his people did
not intend to use their Perseus Spur colonies as stepping-
stones for an invasion of the Milky Way.

Then I told Delegate Sontag and the Assembly that I had
nothing further to say, and I was excused.

Speaker Alameri invited the Servant of Servants of Luk to
comment on my testimony.

The Haluk leader declined the invitation to submit to a
truth machine. He consented to give a brief voluntary statement, should the Assembly care to receive it.

The Assembly did. So the Servant stepped onto an antigravity transporter that wafted him down to the floor, where
Sontag and his committee and I were still seated. I gave a little finger-twiddle of greeting. The Servant stonily ignored
me and delivered his speech in simultaneous translation.

"Respected Speaker! Delegates of the Human Commonwealth! This one calls upon Almighty Luk to endorse the
truths that follow, namely:

"This one strongly asserts the opinion that the person calling himself Asahel Frost is an egregious liar—a scoundrel
who attempts to vilify a noble race for evil motives of his
own. He has taken on a simulacrum of Haluk form solely in
order to mock and calumniate us. May Almighty Luk punish
this contemptible person as he deserves!

"Delegates of the Human Commonwealth Assembly: this
one asserts that no Haluk-human demiclones have been created since the signing of the Treaty of Nonaggression, which
specifically forbade it. None! If counterfeit humans exist
upon the planet Earth, they are agents created and employed
by persons unknown to the Sovereign Haluk Confederation.

"This one further asserts that, if Haluk corsairs are indeed
operating in the Sagittarian arm of the galaxy, they do so

without the authorization of our Sovereign Haluk Confederation. Any such ships are outlaws. We repudiate them and
are eager to cooperate in their extermination.

"In conclusion, this one pledges to the Human Commonwealth, and to the worthy Hundred Concerns that are the
bulwark of its economy, the eternal goodwill of all peace-
loving and law-abiding Haluk people. There is no sinister
Haluk Grand Design hostile to humanity. The Haluk do not
contemplate invading the Milky Way. Such a notion is illog-
ical. Orderly emigration has always been our objective. Your
galaxy is huge, with countless desirable worlds having
no sapient inhabitants. Haluk settlement of some of these
worlds can only enhance galactic harmony and prosperity.
The worthy Hundred Concerns concur in this belief.

"Delegates! We Haluk are eternally grateful to the Commonwealth of Human Worlds for permitting us to colonize
planets within your hegemony. We pledge to cooperate with
all just human laws regulating interstellar commerce and social intercourse. We look forward to receiving from this Assembly the three hundred additional planets so generously
proffered to us.

"The Servant of Servants of Luk thanks you for your gracious attention. And now, as a token of our outrage and sor-
row at the insult offered to us by the person calling himself
Asahel Frost, the Haluk presence will withdraw forthwith.
Wah!"

The Servant then proceeded to stalk out of the chamber
through the rotunda door. When I checked the gallery, the
other Haluk observers had also disappeared. Big symbolic
gesture, right?

I was mistaken. They had something else in mind.

Ef Sontag concluded his summation, then yielded the
floor to the pro-Haluk faction.

What followed was mostly a dreary anticlimax for me,
three hours confined in Ef Sontag's carrel, during which the

Conservatives tried to discredit or gloss over the new evidence presented by the opposition. The only good thing about their summation was the fact that Assembly rules prevented them from cross-examining me or Kang.

"We gave it our best shot," Ef said. He'd called for water and analgesics to soothe my splitting head. What I really wanted was a triple shot of Jack Daniel's, but booze was contraindicated following psychotronic torture—even the comparatively mild version inflicted by the Hogan machine.

"How did I *really* do, Ef?" I asked him anxiously. "The Haluk Servant implied I was pulling a hoax. Do you think any of the Delegates will buy that?"

He laughed. "You looked outlandish. No denying that. But your being blue helped our case. Only an idiot would believe that you underwent genen therapy and turned Halukoid in order to thumb your nose at the xenos and score political points. I can't say whether any of the pro-Haluk Delegates will be swayed by your testimony, but I guarantee that none of them will seriously entertain the notion that you're a hoaxer. You were impressive, Helly."

"Impressive enough?" I muttered. "The Servant's Big Lie routine didn't incite any hisses or boos. I was watching some of the ranking Conservatives during his performance. They weren't worried or even indignant. Those pocket pols think just like the Hundred Concerns that own them—they're confident they can sweep even the most dangerous and uncomfortable facts under the rug, and citizens will be too apathetic or fearful to do anything about it."

"This time, we might have a chance of beating the odds," Ef said. "Besides your own evidence of Haluk wrongdoing, there's Kang's deposition. And let's hope your people can wring something nice and damaging out of Fake Sam Yamamoto in time for the late night news posting. It would also help if a few more clones got flushed out of Rampart Tower and were positively ID'd as aliens."

"I'll check with Karl right away and see what's happening," I said, and also reminded him about the starship Adam Stanislawski had sent to reconnoiter the presumed Haluk base at Amenti. "There's a slim chance it might report in before the vote."

"I almost hope the ship finds nothing," he admitted gloomily. "The alternative is a really squirmy can of worms. A casus belli. I'm not ready for a war, Helly."

Neither was the Commonwealth. Zone Patrol was spread much too thinly, especially in the Perseus Spur. If the Haluk launched an attack, humanity's main line of defense would be the fleets of the Hundred Concerns . . .

I phoned Karl at Rampart Tower and requested a progress report, turning on the phone speaker so Ef could listen in. Karl said that Fake Sam was still zonked from the two stundarts Joanna had shot him with; he would be fully consciousness in three more hours, whereupon his interrogation would begin.

I said, "There are some important questions I want you to ask him." I enumerated them, then asked how things were progressing generally.

"The building's in a state of lockdown. The executives and security personnel are being held under guard in four employee cafeterias, pending genetic profiling. Lesser personnel were allowed to leave after being cautioned not to talk to the media under pain of job-loss and disenfranchisement."

"Ouch," I said. "Whose idea was that?"

"Eve and Gunter Eckert gave the order. The genetic profiling is moving along as rapidly as possible, but it'll probably take all night."

"Caught any blue fish?"

"So far, five demiclones had been confirmed among intermediate level InSec personnel. The big news is an exec named Amadeo Guthrie, a Galapharma holdover. He's Deputy Chief Fleet Dispatch, and he's a Haluk. We just finished his preliminary grilling. I didn't want to go to full interrogation before checking with you."

"Good one, Karl!" I enthused. "This bird will need special handling. Who's the CCID official in charge of the Rampart operation?"

"A Chief Super named Gleb Khabarov. Seems sensible and efficient."

"Ask him to witness the next phase of Guthrie's interrogation. You'll have to squeeze this mutt hard, and I want official corroboration of the gravity of the situation in case the clone dies on you. We need the names of all other demiclones working in top Rampart fleet positions, especially in the Perseus Spur. This is absolutely vital, Karl. We can't allow Haluk agents to have any control over our starships at this time. You're free to tell Khabarov that we're afraid of a sneak attack, particularly on Cravat or Seriphos. When you get the names, insist that Khabarov have the demis arrested by Spur CCID. If he gives you any back-talk, call Adam Stanislawski."

"You really think the Haluk might move before the vote?"

"I don't know what the bastards will do. Call me when you get something solid out of Guthrie. Is there any word on Alistair Drummond?"

"Nothing."

"Okay. Talk to you in a while." I broke the connection.

Ef said, "Scary stuff. But I think the Haluk will wait for the vote."

"I hope you're right."

I dozed for a while, overcome by reaction to the stress. Then I was suddenly wide-awake again, remembering something I'd forgotten to ask Bea Mangan. Fortunately, she and Joanna were still in the VIP gallery, sticking it out to the bitter end.

I phoned her and asked the question, keeping the speakerphone activated for Ef's sake.

She replied, "Yes, the six researchers did finish their experiments with the mutant telomeric exon. As far as they can determine, it's a powerful inhibitor that staves off sequence degradation. In layman's terms, it keeps one set of genes—let's call them bad genes—from turning off another set of good genes. Of course, the researchers had no notion of the precise function of the good gene/bad gene sequences. That was our little secret. Given the limitations of the experiment, the researchers couldn't provide me with precise timing of the turnoff. Or identify the sequence that would be affected."

"But we know what it has to be, don't we!"

"I can only presume that Emily Konigsberg didn't permanently eradicate allomorphism in the Haluk after all. I've been studying her notes for months. By inserting human genes, she intended not only to eliminate the trait in the engineered Haluk individual, but also in the individual's germ line, so that offspring of treated parents would be nonallomorphic, too. That's a complicated piece of work."

"Bea, I think Emily's therapy is already failing." I told her about the warehoused testudos I'd seen in Macpherson Tower.

"How interesting." On the phone display, Bea looked both thoughtful and apprehensive. "I wonder if the testudos will morph into normal allomorphic graciles on schedule? They might not, you know. They might not morph at all."

The implications of that hit me like a kick in the stomach. "Haluk technicians were watching the warehoused ones. Each testudo was being biomonitored. If they *don't* hatch . . ."

She smiled sadly. "If I were a Haluk who had undergone therapy, I'd be very pissed off at humanity. Paradise Lost, and all that. Do you have any idea how many Haluk have received the treatment?"

"Jesus. I think it started in a small way nearly eight years ago. Since the trade treaties went into effect, millions of them must have been treated. But wouldn't Haluk scientists have spotted the problem and called a halt to the therapy? I mean, my God—"

"Perhaps the reversion has only just begun," Bea said. "On the individuals who were among the earliest treated."

I was trying to remember something. "While I was eavesdropping on the Haluk in dystasis, the Council Locutor, Ru Kamik, made some derogatory remarks about Emily Konigsberg. The Haluk name for her was Milik. Ru Kamik said, 'This one has recently heard that some of Milik's work on the eradication of allomorphism has come under scrutiny.' The Servant of Servants denied that anything was wrong. But he would, wouldn't he?"

"You know, Helly, even if a renewed course of therapy reestablishes the nonallomorphic gracile state, the Haluk would still require periodic treatment all throughout their lives."

I said, "Yeah. From a limited supply of PD32:C2, harvested from one small Perseus planet. The stuff won't grow in the lab."

"I've heard rumors that Rampart is working hard to synthesize the viral vector," she said, "but so far without success. Haluk scientists are probably trying, too. Unfortunately, they aren't very experienced in the field of designer-virus construction."

Ef Sontag broke in. "But what does it mean, Bea, from a political standpoint?"

"Damned if I know," she said. "But we'll probably find out."

"Will the human demiclones revert also?"

"Unfortunately, no. The genes for Haluk allomorphy are completely eliminated by demiclone therapy—not merely suppressed, as happens in the much less drastic eradication treatment."

Ef said, "That could have ominous implications."

"I thought so," Bea agreed.

"What? What?" My brain was badly in need of rebooting. I didn't have the faintest idea what they were talking about.

"It's rather far-fetched," Bea said. "But if the Haluk discover that allomorph-eradication therapy is invariably fatal, they may be tempted to go the demiclone route. All it would require is the synthesis of PD32:C2 . . . and an unlimited supply of human DNA."

Finally, the interminable Assembly session adjourned. Ef's final call for a citizen referendum was voted down, as we had expected. But the gesture had been made and the stage set for a potential citizen veto.

When it was all over, he escorted me to the large skyport at the top of Assembly House. Bea and Joanna had agreed to meet us there, and Ef had mentioned that he intended to fly Bea Mangan to her home in Fenelon Falls. I assumed he'd see Joanna home as well.

He called for his private hopper and I asked dispatch to send the aircraft Adam Stanislawski had promised to provide for me. The skyport concourse wasn't very crowded yet and no journalists harassed us. They were busy doing reaction coverage downstairs, where every pundit in the capital would have opinions to express and predictions to make. Many of the Delegates were still conferring with their staff members or frantically consulting web pollsters to find out what kind of impact the day's sensational events would have on their constituents. No doubt the syndics of the Hundred Concerns—including John Ellington—were lobbying like mad to influence tomorrow's vote.

It was a scene neither Ef Sontag nor I wanted any part of. We'd had enough limelight for one day.

The two women finally emerged from the transporter and found us waiting in the ready-room. Bea Mangan was pulling an AG tote with her equipment, and Ef hurried to take charge of it and have it loaded aboard his hopper.

"Did you get lots of hot poop for your new book, Professor?" I asked Joanna.

"Today's action will provide at least two outstanding chapters," she said. "But the plot is still thickening."

"That's what I'm afraid of," I said wearily. "It can thicken without me."

A fast getaway was all I wanted right now, and after that the empty white silence of the Ontario north country, where I planned to hole up until I decided how to recreate my shattered life.

"Will we have time to stop and shop on the way?" Joanna asked me.

I looked at her without comprehending. "Shop?"

"Well, it probably wouldn't be prudent to go back to my town house for clothes and things."

When I persisted in stupidity mode, she smiled. "My dear, I'm coming with you to your hideout! There's so much more I need to know. The deep background of your anti-Haluk crusade."

"Your book's going to be about *me*?" I couldn't conceal my dismay.

"Of course! You're a public figure, a freelance provocateur, a cage rattler. Did you think you could do your thing and then slip offstage without anyone taking notice? Gunslinger comes to town, raises righteous hell, rides off into the sunset?"

"No, but—"

"Your story will personalize the controversy, catch the interest of nonacademic readers. As we say in the trade, you will be my hook. By the way, my publisher is very interested. I called her during your testimony. She was watching, of course. Along with almost everyone else having PlaNet access."

"A book sounds like a great idea," Bea said. "I'd download a copy."

I groaned. "Joanna, this affair isn't over. Political-science-wise, it's hardly begun."

"But your direct participation in it is done, isn't it?"

"God, I hope so. I'm so tired of tilting at blue windmills! Whichever way the vote goes tomorrow, I believe the Haluk are heading for a fall. Their demiclones will be exposed, along with the Sagittarian piracy and the other shit they've been pulling inside the Concerns. After the smoke clears, the Haluk treaties will be revised. There's no real possibility of a cover-up or a reversion to the status quo. Too many genies have been let out of the bottle."

Ef Sontag had returned from the baggage bot and was listening with approval. "A book that told the entire story would help ensure that," he said. "Joanna's right."

"Of course I am," Professor DeVet said serenely.

"What *are* your immediate plans?" Ef asked me.

"I'm going to kick back and take it easy. After the vote, who knows? Eventually I'll have to go back into the tank for a month or so to be restored, but God knows when I'll get around to doing it. If you need me, I'll be available for a few weeks, anyhow. I promised my father to help pull Rampart back on track, but I won't let that become a full-time job. During the Galapharma trial, I devoted nearly every waking minute to Rampart. That'll never happen again."

"Good," said Joanna. "You don't owe them that."

"I don't owe them anything," I said grimly. "They owe me. And if Eve or anyone else starts putting stumbling blocks in my way, I'll be out of there faster than a lobo with a knot in his tail, and Rampart can go straight to hell."

Ef was watching the overhead dispatch display. "Here's my hopper. Come along, Bea. Helly, Joanna, keep safe." The two of them went off.

I threw my former wife a look that mingled panic and confusion.

She smiled and put a hand on my shoulder. "If you really don't want me with you now, I'll respect that. I can take a taxi home."

"No! I mean—" What did I mean?

"The stress of the past days must be unbearable. I apologize for trying to intrude. If you need quiet time alone, we can talk about the book later."

The dispatch display showed that the aircraft for Helmut Icicle was ready.

I took her hand, pulled her toward the door leading to the hopper pad. "Dammit! I do want you to come. We'll watch the vote taken tomorrow, then see what comes down. You can tell me what it all means from a galactopolitical point of view."

She laughed. "All right. But I mean it about stopping for the clothes."

The ship was a big mean-looking Mitsubishi-Kondo that wore the white and gold Macrodur colors and the Big M corporate crest. It had full defensive shields, significant armament, a subspace communicator, an ultraencrypted phone link, and a well-appointed bedroom.

"How long did you say our trip would take?" Joanna inquired in a throaty purr.

I sighed. "Not long enough. Besides, I'm a useless wreck, babe."

"Then a holiday is just what you need."

"It won't take long to get where we're going, even if we stop and shop. This boat toddles along at three kay per. Adam lent us a lovely ride."

We settled in on the flight deck. "He seems like a very nice man," Joanna remarked. "He lives up to his reputation. No wonder the other Concerns hate Macrodur."

"Yeah. Imagine a businessman who doesn't put business first . . ."

We lofted into the air, moving slowly northward under the control of Toronto Conurb ATZ. The atmosphere was so thick with trapped mist that it was hard to distinguish one tower from another, but our hopper was not immediately vectored out from under the force-field. Instead, we came to a dead stop in midair, joining multiple stalled processions of other aircraft. A moment later the force-field's golden umbrella winked out. The mist that had been held beneath it was torn to bits by sudden wind, and snowflakes swirled around us.

"What the hell?" I murmured, and began querying the navigator.

"Helly, look!" Joanna exclaimed, pointing outside.

A train of starship gigs was descending out of the storm toward the city center. There must have been thirty or forty of them, large and beetle-shaped and decorated with cobalt-blue lights.

They began to touch down at the Macpherson Tower skyport.

"I'll be damned," I said. "The Haluk are leaving!"

I used the hopper's sensitive scanner to clarify the scene and was proved right. The aliens had somehow obtained permission to embark directly from their tower into Earth orbit, without using Oshawa Starport.

"But why?" Joanna asked in bewilderment. "Is this what the Servant meant by withdrawing the Haluk presence? Is it some formal expression of wounded dignity?"

"I hope that's what it is," I said. But a ghost-icicle had materialized at the back of my neck.

The aerial exodus lasted about forty minutes, while hopper traffic above Toronto remained totally paralyzed and the snowfall thickened, causing mild havoc on the streets below.

I surfed the news channels. The media were giving the amazing event a big play, even broadcasting satellite views of a monstrous alien starship waiting in low geosynchronous orbit for the return of its auxiliaries. It was the flagship of the Servant of Servants. I'd seen it myself twice before, under more ominous circumstances.

When the last gig vanished into the sky, the force-field umbrella was turned on again. Air traffic resumed its normal pattern. The capital of the Commonwealth of Human Worlds

went about its interrupted business and so did we, escaping
the restricted airspace of the conurbation and rising to our
cruising altitude in the ionosphere.

Had all of the Haluk gone away?

Absolutely not, the media reported breathlessly. Reporters' phone calls to the official Haluk embassy codes
were answered—curtly. No comments would be forthcom-
ing from Haluk sources until after tomorrow's Assembly
vote. The Servant's flagship was "on a meditative cruise."

Macpherson Tower was shielded against scanners, as were
most of the commercial and government buildings in the
central city; however, persons of Halukoid physique had
been observed moving in front of undraped windows. One
enterprising media snoop even analyzed water usage in the
upper half of the tower—and concluded that Haluk toilets
were being flushed. Lots of the aliens were still in there!

Hoppers carrying tabloid websters that attempted unauthorized landings on the Macpherson skyport were shooed
away, as always, by Haluk guards armed with riot-batons.
Elevator access was blocked, as usual, by Haluk security
personnel. Neither CCID nor the Enforcement Division of
Xenoaffairs attempted to enter the tower by force. Techni-
cally, the top two-thirds of it was still alien soil, and no
Commonwealth judge was empowered to issue a warrant to
search it.

Yet.

Half dozing in the command seat as we soared through
the sky under autopilot, I wondered whether my brother
Dan was still inside Macpherson Tower. Was Alistair Drummond hiding there, too, along with other blown demiclone
spies who had infiltrated other establishments in the capital? Minor genplas makeovers and iris implants would enable them to assume alternate identities. If they avoided
sensitive occupations, demis might easily be able to fade
away into the general population—especially on the freesoil worlds. All human beings had a genetic profile made at

birth, but retesting everyone would be prohibitively expensive.

It was more likely that both the Haluk and their demiclone agents were simply biding their time as we were, awaiting the outcome of the all-important vote.

Nothing of any importance, I believed, could happen until then.

Chapter 10

Now arriving Timmins Municipality ATZ. Please supply next routing.

I started awake at the sound of the navigator's voice. Joanna had also closed her eyes during the half hour or so it had taken us to travel the first leg of our journey. She yawned and stretched and looked out the side window of the flight deck.

We were in a holding pattern at ten thousand meters. We'd left the snowstorm behind, and the clear night sky blazed with stars; there was no moon. The total blackness of the land surface was relieved by widely scattered patches of twinkling lights that marked small communities, plus a single urban constellation of moderate size directly beneath us.

"Timmins, Ontario?" she murmured in disbelief, checking the navigation display. "This is your secret hideout?"

Timmins was a former mining center 180 miles north of Lake Huron, now a hub for an assortment of wilderness recreation areas.

"It's your one-stop shopping mall," I told her. "We're about halfway to our destination, a place called Kingfisher Lodge, another six hundred fifty klicks northwest of here. The lodge is a great big comfortable house that Rampart once used for corporate junkets and executive family holidays. Nice lake—although that'll be frozen over by now."

I said to the navigator, "Land at Timmins Municipal Skyport. Proceed to the general aviation terminal."

En route.

"Is the lodge very isolated?" Joanna asked.

"There's a little town called Central Patricia about ninety kilometers west of it, maybe four hundred souls. Otherwise, nothing but bush, a few trails and unpaved roads. No one lives in Kingfisher Lodge during the winter months, but it's always heated and maintained. Domestic robots keep it clean and in good repair. It has a storehouse full of staple foods and all kinds of other supplies. It also has an exceptionally good security system, which is the main reason I decided to stash myself there."

The hopper was plunging inertialessly toward the ground. We'd land within a few minutes. I gave Joanna the Macrodur corporate niobium credit card that I'd found waiting for me on the hopper's instrument console.

"Use this to buy whatever special edibles and winter clothing and personal items you think we might need. Keep my damned wasp-waist in mind when you buy my snow gear. And no gloves for me, either. My four weird fingers won't fit. Stick with mittens."

"I understand."

"Take as long as you like to shop. We're in no hurry. As a matter of fact, I need time to make a few important phone calls. The Timmins e-merchants and malle-armoire services will deliver right to the hopper. I'll stay out of sight while the stuff is stowed aboard."

"I wonder—does the lodge have equipment for cross-country skiing?" She smiled in reminiscence. "It might be fun for us to do that again . . . unless you think we should stay indoors."

"No, of course not. Why don't you buy skis and envirosuits for us. I know there are snowmobiles at the lodge. We can play with them, too."

We flew over Timmins at low altitude, heading for the skyport north of town. It was only 1935 hours and the place was wide-awake.

"I've never driven a snowmobile," Joanna said. "Is it risky?"

"Not if you travel at a reasonable speed and stay off thin ice. The snow won't be very deep this early in the season. Tell you what. Give me your phone. I'll program it with my own dex and links. That way you'll have instant access to all of Rampart's services in an emergency. And you won't end up locked outside the security perimeter or unable to access the in-house systems if I get stomped by a bull moose or something."

She gave me a sidelong glance. " 'Or something.' Are you talking about danger from the Haluk?"

"I'm just saying that in the wilderness, Mother Nature can get you if you don't watch out—or even if you *do*. It's only sensible to take precautions. As the for the Haluk . . . I suppose they could come after me, if they knew where to look. But I've covered our tracks pretty well. And now that the Helly-demiclone cat is out of the bag, they no longer have any compelling motive for shutting my mouth. Actually, after the Servant's denials in the Assembly today, it would be counterproductive for them to try it."

"True." But she looked troubled as she rummaged in her shoulder bag and handed me her phone. "I'm afraid it's just an inexpensive thing. It doesn't even have video."

I checked the instrument out. It was a real clunker, at least five years old. "We'll need a model with a bit more pizzazz. Why don't you pick up a Lucevera 4500 just like mine. I'll teach you how to make it do some great tricks."

She tucked the phone back into her bag with a sigh. "You probably think I'm a hopeless Luddite. To me a phone is just something for talking into, or accessing the odd bit of data when I'm away from my computer."

We were on the ground now—actually hovering just above it—drifting after a FOLLOW ME bot that led us to a parking bay. Timmins had a nice little skyport with heated pavement, but there was no force-umbrella and the air temperature was around minus-ten Celsius. I conversed with the general aviation desk and arranged for a short stay under-cover, then turned back to Joanna.

"Tell me the truth, babe. Are you having second thoughts about this jaunt? If so, you can catch a commercial flight back to Toronto in a couple of hours."

"No. I'm going with you," she insisted. "About our fresh food and wine: How long will we be at the lodge?"

I hadn't thought much about that. Besides the basic secu-rity considerations, I had a compelling need to put distance between myself and the chaos in Toronto while still remain-ing accessible for long distance consultation. Whether I'd be able to indulge myself depended on one of the phone calls I was about to make.

"How long would you like to stay?" I asked Joanna.

"We could try it for a week," she said softly, after hesitat-ing a moment. "I'll call my department secretary tomorrow and plead urgent family business. It's more or less the truth."

"Are we . . . a family, Joanna?"

She smiled sadly. "I don't know the answer to that, Helly. I don't know *you*—and I'm talking about the man inside the blue skin, not the captivating alien who had his wicked way with me."

My laugh, at least, was still human. "I beg your pardon, Professor. Who seduced whom?"

She gave a wry shrug. "I confess. You were irresistible." Her expression became somber. "But you've changed so much over the years we've been apart. I can sense it, even in the short time we've been together again. Those stories you told . . ." Her eyes clouded. "You're more driven, more adamant, less vulnerable. Perhaps it's a good thing." But she didn't sound convinced.

"I think I'm also a lot wiser than I was when I left you. It was the worst mistake of my life. But I was devastated by what had happened. I didn't want your pity. That, on top of everything else—"

"It wasn't pity I felt for you then! It was love."

I had to ask the question. "How do you feel about me now?"

"I don't know." She looked away.

"I love you. What I did—giving in to despair, not trusting you—was stupid and cowardly. I'd like to start again. This damned body of mine—"

"That's not a factor, Helly. It's only a distraction."

"What *is* a factor?"

She seemed to take a deep breath before plunging ahead. "For one thing, I was very disturbed when you said that you'd killed your Haluk demiclone in cold blood. It wasn't self-defense, then? Did you really mean what you said?"

"I meant it."

"Will you tell me about it?"

"I'd rather not." I had glossed over the incident when recounting it earlier.

"I'm not morbidly curious. I'm trying to understand."

Understand what goes on inside a killer's head . . .

"All right." I spoke slowly and calmly. My stiff Halukoid features were a useful mask to hide behind. "I woke in a kind of hospital room inside Macpherson Tower. There were alien medics tending me for a while, and then they went away. I didn't realize at first that my body had been transformed. When I discovered what had been done to me, and found the unconscious demiclone lying in a bed across the room, I knew what the Haluk were going to do with him. Even knew why they'd let me live. I was going to be forced to tutor my double in his role as *me*. I smothered him with a pillow."

She nodded slowly, unwilling to comment.

"It wasn't revenge, Joanna." But as I said it, I had to wonder. "It was mortal combat. An act of war against an enemy that intended to use my persona to further their conspiracy against humanity."

"But there is no war!"

"The Haluk Grand Design is equivalent to war. And demicloning is a weapon. I had a right and an obligation to prevent that weapon from being used against us. Fake Helly had no right to live, any more than a dog infected with rabies has. There was no way I could cure the demi of his . . . condition. All I could do was prevent him from using it to harm the Human Commonwealth."

She spoke calmly. "You killed him because he stole your identity and was going to insinuate himself into Rampart. Not because you believed he was going to harm anyone."

"I admit that those notions were in my mind. But there were larger considerations as well. You don't know the Haluk as I do, the monstrous things they've done. What they intend to do. And you have no idea of my real feelings about Rampart. I don't love the Concern or live for it, the way Eve does. And I certainly would never kill for it."

But it wasn't my motivation that distressed Joanna so much as the state of my conscience.

"When you killed the clone . . . didn't you feel *any* remorse?" Her tone was now almost desperate. I knew the reassurance she wanted, but I couldn't give it to her. She had a right to the truth.

"What I felt was revulsion," I told her. "Regret that the actions were necessary. But I had no sense of doing wrong and certainly no remorse. I wasn't sorry then and I'm not sorry now. Do you remember my telling you and the others about the two hundred demiclones in the secret lab on Dagasatt? I killed them deliberately, too, because it seemed necessary at the time. I've had nightmares about it for years, and I'll probably dream about snuffing Fake Helly when my overloaded brain gets the incident fully processed. I killed because I had to, Joanna. If you can't bring yourself to accept that—"

She lifted her hand, touched the side of my alien face. Tears welled in her eyes. "I'll try. I'll do my best to try to understand. When I see what the Haluk did to you—your poor face, the lost smile that I loved so much, the rest of your body—I'm so *sorry*, Helly! I didn't intend to make it worse for you." She threw her arms around me, buried her head in my chest. "But it's hard."

Hard to love, easy to pity.

I said, "Let it alone. Put it out of your mind, at least for a week. Please, Joanna."

"All right," she said, drawing away, trying to smile. "I'll begin by applying woman's sovereign remedy: shopping."

While she was inside the terminal, I retreated to the hopper's bedroom to make the first of the phone calls. After engaging encryption, I programmed the data-strip to identify me by my real name, sans code ID. I left the video option engaged, then buzzed my old pal and political antagonist Geraldo Gonzalez, the lone Delegate of the Reversionist party. Our conversation was brief—with a predictable preamble when he saw my face.

"Gerry, it's Helly."

"Jesus! . . . Oh, man! I watched the news conference and nearly had a heart attack. And then your performance in the Assembly—"

"What did you think of it? Was I credible?"

"*I* sure as hell accepted your story. You know why? Because one of the first things the impostor did when he mysteriously returned from Sagittarius was cut off Asahel Frost's financial support of the party! You and I haven't always seen eye-to-eye on political strategy, but I couldn't believe you'd abandon us without an explanation. That asshole absolutely refused to meet with me. All he'd say was that he'd had a change of heart."

"That was true enough, metaphorically speaking."

"So he was a Haluk impostor! Did you manage to nab him?"

"The demiclone has vanished," I said, not correcting his error of fact. "God only knows what kind of a mess he left my financial affairs in, but I wanted to assure you that my funding of the Reversionist cause will be restored as soon as possible. Meanwhile, I'll see that you get a generous string-free contribution directly from Rampart."

"Thank you . . . Helly." He was still uncomfortable connecting the identity to the blue face. Couldn't blame him.

"I'm back on the Rampart board," I told him, "and I've taken over as Rampart president. We're weeding Haluk demiclones out of the Concern with the help of CCID, and we'll release their names and their confessions as soon as possible. I intend to do everything in my power to show up the Servant of Servants as a roaring bullshit artist."

Gonzalez was nodding his agreement. "Yes. Yes. Throw that lying speech of his right back in his teeth! Jesus God— how many Haluk spies do you suppose we're going to find hiding in the woodpile?"

A good question. "Gerry, have the Assembly Delegates ever submitted to DNA profiling?"

"Sontag proposed it in mid-September, when his committee hearings were really raising a media stink. The measure was voted down. A few Liberal Delegates followed Sontag's example and were tested anyhow. There were also rumors that your man Nazarian did some clandestine testing six months ago and found zip."

"I put him up to that. But a lot could have happened in half a year."

"Fuckin' A. After today you can bet your life the DNA testing measure will be reintroduced by constituent demand. Maybe I can do it myself! My office is being deluged with mail from worried citizens—and most of them aren't even Reverse voters. I'm not the only Delegate getting an earful, either. The Liberals I've talked to say the volume of negative comment is unprecedented. The Conservatives are keeping mum and looking worried."

"Good. That's what I wanted to hear. Well, I'll let you go now. I just wanted to reassure you about my commitment to the party and its principles."

"Umm . . . you should know that we've taken a slightly different direction since the Sontag committee hearings began. The push for preindustrial Insap rights lost its popular appeal with the disclosure of the Haluk demiclone threat. We switched our emphasis to the corrupt influence of the Hundred Concerns—especially the Haluk Consortium—on Commonwealth political decision-making. We blame them for letting the Haluk situation get out of control, pushing those ineffective treaties through. Our current push is for prompt treaty revision."

"I agree one hundred percent. We'll talk later, Gerry."

I touched the End pad, thinking that the Reversionist party wasn't the only one that would have to rethink its strategy during the days ahead.

Especially if the Haluk colony vote went the way I feared it would.

I tapped out Karl Nazarian's code. It was several minutes before he answered. He looked calm and assured, and somewhere along the line he'd ditched the incongruous caterer's coverall and donned an elegant business suit that would have done John Ellington proud. Both men had about the same build. Maybe the vice chairman had shared.

"Do you have time to give me a progress report?" I asked. "I'm on my way to the safe house. With Joanna."

"I see." The old security man kept a perfectly straight face. "Are you going to reveal your secret bolt-hole to me?"

"Kingfisher Lodge. Don't tell anyone else."

Karl nodded his approval. "Yeah, that might be just about perfect. God knows none of the paparazzi websters will find you up there. We pretty much shut the lodge down after Dan's abduction, but there was no important damage to the physical plant, and the fritzed security system was repaired. Do you have portable weapons?"

"The hopper Adam loaned me has a locker full of top-drawer assault gear. Supplying computers to the Commonwealth must be dangerous work."

Karl chuckled. "High-paying, anyhow. You want me to let Stanislawski know where you are?"

"I'll tell him myself. What's happening in Toronto? Any trace of Drummond? I figure he's either hiding in Macpherson Tower or else the Servant of Servants took him away in the Haluk flagship for some strenuous debriefing."

"Maybe not. *Makebate*'s gone."

"Shit—I didn't even realize the ship had survived Phlegethon!"

"Fake Helly drove her back to Earth, claiming he'd been held captive by Y'tata corsairs for six weeks. Since then Drummond has taken the ship all over the galaxy, overseeing the Rampart-Gala consolidation. He's even been to Artiuk, the Haluk GHQ in the Spur. No telling where he's headed now if he's driving that dazzle-boat of yours. A Macrodur security team checked *Makebate*'s berth at Oshawa Starport and found her gone. She jumped the line and lifted off for an unspecified destination just before noon. That would have been shortly after Fake Sam called Drummond's code from the boardroom. The ship manifest listed a pilot named Helmut Icicle."

"That wiseass! Thumbing his goddamn nose at me . . . I'm surprised he didn't wait to see if Fake Sam regained control of the boardroom situation."

"Probably figured it wasn't going to happen," Karl said. "Think about it."

"Yeah. Well, it's probably for the best if Drummond just drops out of sight. We certainly don't want to bring him to trial. Let the galaxy believe that an anonymous Haluk was my double."

"There's no trace of *Makebate*'s fuel signature within a hundred light-years of Earth. He's had all the time in the world to make a clean break. Zone Patrol's on alert, and Rampart has put a hefty price on the head of the John Doe perp who stole the starship. *Makebate* is so distinctive that

Drummond won't dare take her to any important human world."

"Let's hope he ends up on Bumfuck-Beta in the Crab Nebula," I grumped. "What's the situation now in Rampart Tower? Have you been able to question Fake Sam?"

"Yes. The Haluk Grand Design is just what you suspected: a plan for conquest by subversion. Demiclones were supposed to infiltrate Commonwealth government agencies and the Hundred Concerns over a period of years. According to Sam, they already have a fair number of maggots inside the Concerns, but relatively few in the government."

"Did you ask him about Assembly Delegates?"

"Yes, but he had no information. I suppose it figures. Most espionage systems are compartmentalized."

"Tell me more about the Grand Design."

"No real surprises. While the demiclone insertion continued, Haluk colonies in the Milky Way were supposed to expand as rapidly as possible. They'd build up their starship fleets, their scientific and technical establishments, and their heavy industry, with help from unsuspecting humanity. Eventually the Commonwealth authority structure would be so riddled with alien subversives that it would fall without much of a fight. Sam didn't know the precise Grand Design timetable. That's in the hands of the Haluk Council of Nine."

"Not the Servant of Servants?" I was surprised.

"Sam said the SSL concocted the original scheme, but he ultimately answers to the Nine. Their offices are hereditary and they act as repositories of racial wisdom and conscience. They don't overrule the Servant very often, though. He receives his authority directly from the Haluk common people—hence his title."

"Interesting. Did Fake Sam know whether an imminent attack on humanity is being contemplated?"

"No. He isn't privy to military strategy. He was trained in human corporate law and only assumed his position a couple of months ago. It was fortuitous that he went to Rampart rather than some other Concern. It's not easy for the Haluk to insert ringers in really high places without arousing suspicion, so they're forced to wait until an appropriate opportunity presents itself. The real Sam Yamamoto was granted an extensive leave of absence not long after you took off for Phlegethon, with the understanding that he'd be promoted and raised to the board on his return. It was a perfect setup for the Haluk to plug in their man."

"Did you find out what happened to the real Sam?"

"The demi says he's locked up in Macpherson Tower. The Haluk kept him alive for what the fake called 'coerced consultation.' There are nearly three hundred other DNA donors being held prisoner there for the same reason. Not all from Rampart."

"Christ! . . . Karl, we've got to do something about them before the Haluk decide to eliminate incriminating witnesses."

"I've already got Hector working on it. There's no way short of a declaration of war that CCID or ECID can search an alien embassy without permission. But embassies have been stormed by inflamed mobs of citizens before. I guess it all comes down to the principle you quoted in your infamous *Wall Street Journal* interview: we can do whatever we please, so long as we don't give a damn about the consequences."

"Helly's Rules," I murmured, "come back to haunt me. Okay. Do it! Just have Hector and his hooligans wait until after Toronto's 2300 hour newscast . . . Did Fake Sam give you the names of other demi agents inside Rampart?"

"So far we have Amadeo Guthrie, our biggest fish, thirty-six Internal and External security people ranging from colonel to grunt, and forty-five relatively low-ranking personnel in the Finance and Data Processing departments. Sam also named twelve high-ranking executives working for other Haluk Consortium Concerns. They were the only outsiders he could recall offhand. I've already passed that information on to CCID and ICS. We'll get more names out of Sam during the next interrogation session when we go to deep-probe. He's resting now."

"Right. Now tell me about Amadeo Guthrie."

"Pure gold!" Karl grinned triumphantly. "He opened a secret file in his personal computer that listed over sixty demiclones in crucial Rampart fleet positions on Seriphos, Tyrins, Hygeia, Asklepios, and Caduceus. Dispatchers, Fleet Security starship officers, even an Assistant Maintenance Chief at Seriphos Starport. With luck, they're being rounded up right now. We're getting the situation under control."

"Karl, I want the names of all Rampart demiclones in custody released to the media in time for tonight's late news posting. We need to arouse public opinion—make the invasion of Macpherson Tower morally justifiable."

"I can't release the names myself, Helly. I don't have the authority. If I leaked them anonymously, only the tabloids would pick them up. You need the information posted on legitimate media sites."

"All right, I'll talk to Eve about it. You pass the names on to her immediately, along with any other confession material that might make a splash. Just one last question: When your gang did the secret DNA testing of the Assembly Delegates, did they find any ringers?"

"Not a one. We tested a fair number of staffers, too. They were all human seven months ago."

"Okay. Keep up the good work. And let me know how Hector's plan to storm the embassy shapes up."

I ended the call, got myself a cup of coffee from the hopper's tiny galley, and drank it down scalding, cursing the impossibility of having a real drink for at least two more hours. I could have used some Dutch courage before making the call to Eve, which would determine whether Joanna and I continued on to Kingfisher Lodge or returned to Toronto.

Under normal circumstances, even with the Haluk out to

fry my fanny, I'd probably have stayed at Rampart Tower and worked with the others on damage control, at least until after the Assembly vote. But I wasn't normal—not mentally and certainly not physically. I was walking wounded and desperately in need of a timeout. Trouble was, I was afraid my older sister might be, too.

She picked up on the third buzz.

"What is it?" Her face was haggard but her hair was still perfect. She recognized me instantly and didn't flinch.

"I'm on my way to a safe house. I plan to stay undercover for a while until I'm certain the Haluk aren't still gunning for me. I'll keep in close touch with you and with Karl Nazarian and Adam Stanislawski."

"Gunter Eckert will also want to confer with you," she said crisply. "Will you let me have your phone code?"

I gave it to her. "Tell Gunter I'll talk to him tomorrow, after the vote. Till then I'm incommunicado unless the world falls down. I've got a serious case of combat fatigue, and if I want to function tomorrow, I'll have to get some sleep. How are you holding up, Evie?"

Her eyes were focused firmly on mine. "I'm coping . . . Asa. The police action in the tower has quieted down. Simon has retired to his tower suite. The other members of the Board of Directors are still here, helping to normalize the situation in whatever way they can. John Ellington will be wire-pulling and whip-cracking all night. I've spent most of my time talking to Cousin Zed and Matt Gregoire on Seriphos. Rampart ExSec starships are cooperating with Zone Patrol to organize interstellar surveillance over the Haluk colonies. Matt suggested we evacuate all civilians from Cravat as a precaution, and I agreed."

"We'll have to set up a heavy blockade around the planet. The best ships we have."

"They're already on their way. I understand the situation. Now."

"Evie—"

"You can trust me, Asa. I fully accept what you told us at the board meeting. I was duped and I feel humiliated and angry, but I'm not dysfunctional or in a panic. I'll survive this mess and so will Rampart. Just don't expect any warm gushes of sisterly sentiment for a while. At the moment, my emotions are on hold. There's too much work to be done."

"I agree. And it sounds like you have things well in hand. One thing I need you to take care of personally is the release of the names of all Rampart demiclones to the media. Do it in time for the *Late Night Toronto* newscast on PNN. Karl Nazarian will give the information to you right away."

"May I ask why you want to do this?"

"Have you been keeping in close touch with Karl?"

"He sends me hourly progress reports. I've only skimmed the latest one. The Perseus situation has occupied most of my attention."

"The Sam Yamamoto demiclone confessed that around three hundred human DNA donors—the real people who were exchanged for Haluk agents—are alive and being held prisoner inside Macpherson Tower. They look just like me."

"Oh, dear God."

"I want you to tell that to the media, as well as announcing the names of our missing people. Demand that every single one of the captives be freed immediately, unharmed. Warn the Haluk that dire things will happen if those people are killed or taken away. After the newscast, call up the Haluk embassy and formally reiterate your demand. Insist that it be forwarded at once to the Servant and the Council of Nine. If you can manage it, convince other Concern CEOs to do the same. A lot of those captives aren't Rampart people."

"But the Haluk will deny—"

"To hell with them! We want to arouse public opinion. Make our citizens receptive to the notion of a rescue raid on Macpherson."

"Asa, you can't!"

"It'll be a mob of outraged citizen protesters or some such thing," I said. "Nothing to do with Rampart. Would you rather have the captives dead?"

"No, but—"

"You have to do your part. Those people had their DNA stolen, just as I did. They've lost their human appearance and their identities. Alien interlopers have taken their places at work, lived in their homes, invaded the lives of their families . . . Can I count on you to issue the statement, Evie?"

"Yes," she said, with no more hesitation.

Her old self.

"Thank you. There's one final thing you should know about." I told her how Karl had been deliberately infected with a debilitating virus by Haluk agents, and my suspicions about Simon. "Ask Karl to refer you to the doctor who was able to cure him. It's imperative that Simon no longer be treated by Rampart medical people."

"Those bastards," she hissed. "Those fucking blue bastards! I'll have Pop taken care of right now."

She cut me off.

I sat on the edge of the bed with my head in my hands, overcome with abruptly released tension, trying not to vomit up the coffee I'd drunk. Thanking God that Eve was charging ahead with her usual efficiency. That Karl and Hector and the others would continue to fight the good fight without me. That I didn't have to return to Toronto.

Joanna and I could continue on to the tranquil solitude of Kingfisher Lodge. Deliberately, I programmed my phone to accept only Cosmic Priority emergency calls. Then I lay down to catch a few winks.

We arrived at our destination in the Eastern Kenora region of Ontario just after 2115. With only starlight for illumination, it was difficult to see any details on the ground, so while we were still at cruising altitude I turned on the wide-scan terrain viewer with false color enhancement to give Joanna an idea of what lay beneath us.

It was a beautiful, forbidding landscape of rolling, snow-covered boreal forest, laced by rivers and streams and strewn with icebound lakes. To the south, beyond the arterial Albany River, lay the vastness of Nipigon Wilderness Park, a rugged outdoor playground in summer, nearly uninhabited in winter. Northward and to the east the land flattened into dense boggy thickets of black spruce and tamarack that extended without a single track all the way to Hudson Bay. To the west was the little town of Central Patricia, where only administrative personnel, service and transport people, and traders lived all year round.

We descended to a little over 2000 meters and hovered in preparation for landing. I switched to a close-up view of Kingfisher Lodge itself. The rambling one-story building was constructed of sturdy plascrete with an attractive faux-log veneer. It was situated on the shore of a moderate-sized body of water called Caddisfly Lake, frozen solid now and smoothly covered with snow. Dense stands of balsam fir and white spruce surrounded an open compound about three hundred meters wide. I knew that the defensive perimeter extended another 400 meters into the forest and the lake.

Aircraft casually overflying and scanning Kingfisher Lodge would think it was deserted, buttoned up for the season. The compound had no ground-based dissimulator, external force-field, or any other detectable high-tech defenses. The Kagi emplacements and less lethal intruder deterrents were well-camouflaged among the lake rocks and brush, as were the multiphase alarm sensors. No interior lights were visible from the air. Two of the fieldstone chimneys gave off narrow plumes of vapor, indicating that the heating system was functioning, although the thermostat was probably set at a temperature level too low for human comfort.

In addition to the main lodge, which had at least ten bedrooms, the establishment included a guard tower disguised as a backwoods food cache, an equipment building, a couple of utility structures, and a boat shed. Between the rear out-buildings and the main house was a snow-covered circular area about ten meters in diameter, a lidded hopper lift that gave access to an underground hangar carved from the solid granite of the Canadian Shield. A tunnel led from the hangar to the house. Not part of the original design, hangar and tun-nel had been added during Dan's year-round confinement, for the convenience of the resident staff.

"Now let me show you how we get inside our rustic fortress," I said to Joanna. "Since this is a Macrodur hopper, it doesn't carry any of the lodge's system links, so we'll use your new phone."

She took the instrument out of the inside breast pocket of her suit coat and I showed her how to call up the lodge-exterior command menu, deactivate the antiaircraft sensors and photon weaponry, and roll back the door covering the el-evator platform of the underground hangar.

While I guided the hopper's manual descent, she took care of the landing preparations. Then she accessed the lodge-interior menu and tapped more pads to switch on room lights, crank up the heat, awaken the housebots so they could deal with our baggage, turn on the mattress-warmer in the master suite, and start a couple of hot baths.

"This is absolutely decadent," she said, laughing. "A backwoods technocottage! Look: I can light a fire in some-thing called the master-suite snuggery. Doesn't that sound cozy? And the phone even wants to program the stereo. Would you prefer classical or jazz?"

"Both. How about the *Undercurrent* and *Intermodulation* albums with Bill Evans and Jim Hall. Then maybe *Eine Kleine Nachtmusik*."

"Perfect."

I reengaged the perimeter defenses. We were hovering

now at a little over tree height above the underground hangar entry, which was over a hundred meters from the house. I turned on the Mitsubishi's emergency landing spot and saw something dash across the snowy ground and disappear behind one of the outbuildings. Joanna saw it too.

"What was that?" she exclaimed. "It looked like a bear."

"Small one, maybe. Funny. I'd have thought bears would have hibernated by now." Something else was odd about the presence of the animal, but I was too maxed-out mentally to make sense of it. "Okay, babe, down we go. Hit the pad to roll back the hangar elevator door."

"I thought I already did," she said, frowning.

"The lid's still closed. Give me the phone and I'll recheck the menu."

A blinking red telltale. I queried it and the display read HANGAR DOOR IS LOCKED. PLEASE GIVE PASSWORD.

Well, damn. The thing wasn't supposed to lock until I fed it my own new password. I tried the override and reboot, but the maneuvers didn't succeed. The circular opening remained sealed shut.

"Rats. Could be a computer glitch. Or maybe some jerk forgot to purge the old password when the staff left. Well, we'll do things the old-fashioned way for now, and I'll check the lift machinery tomorrow."

I touched down in an open area less than twenty meters from the back of the house. The night was windless and pitch-black after I doused the hopper's spotlight, the snow depth modest, and the temperature minus-twenty Celsius.

We spent a few minutes in the cargo bay sorting out clothes and toiletries for our immediate needs and stuffing them into a large duffelbag. I pulled a couple of guns out of the weapons locker—a holstered Ivanov to discourage wandering bears, and a big ugly Talavera-Gerardi 333 actinic blaster with an autotargeting scope, in case the Haluk slammed the perimeter defenses and started besieging the

house. The rest of the supplies and weapons could wait until
tomorrow.

"Why don't we slip into the envirosuits instead of carrying them," I suggested to her. "It's pretty cold out there and
the snow's deep enough to ruin your nice shoes."

So we did that, hauling the lightweight coveralls over our
regular clothes and donning heated overboots and helmets. I
strapped on the Ivanov, slung the heavy Tala-G on my back,
and carried the duffel and a heavy-duty flashlight. Joanna
had her purse and a plastic grocery sack that contained the
makings for a late supper of scrambled eggs, Nova Scotia
smoked salmon, French bread, fresh Tasmanian strawberries, and Veuve Cliquot champagne.

I used a remote-control gorget hung around my neck to
open the hopper's cargo door and deploy the steps. Said,
"Mush, you huskies! That means you, Professor DeVet."

She giggled and we disembarked into shin-deep snow. I
used the gorget to close up the aircraft and turn on its security system and environmental shield. Then we stood side by
side in an immense dark silence roofed with overarching
stars. It was every bit as beautiful as Arizona.

I was about to make a romantic remark when Joanna said,
"What's that smell? Could it be the bear?"

A very faint disgusting odor hung in the icy air and penetrated our helmets. It wasn't the familiar skunky perfume of
bear scats, though; this stench was as offensive as the reek
of the Y'tata, although composed of different molecules.
And I knew what kind of creature had produced it.

"Not a bear, a wolverine. That's what we must have seen
moving below the hopper."

I turned on the flashlight and found a line of prints that
made a beeline across the compound. We went to look at
them. They were nearly as long as a human hand but much
wider. Big guy. The animal had stepped neatly in its own
tracks, placing the hind foot where the front foot had pressed

down the snow, so that each print seemed to have a double row of five stout claws.

"That's strange," I murmured. "The perimeter defenses let small animals and birds get through without getting zapped. But something as large as a wolverine should have triggered a painful warning shot from one of the Tazegard units, then a lethal Kagi blast if the beast kept on coming. I wonder if part of the perimeter is down?"

We paused while I unzipped my suit and asked my phone to run a system check. All the defensive units were on-line. The obvious explanation eluded my fuddled brain. "I can't figure it. But I hope the critter managed to escape the lodge perimeter while we were landing. We sure as hell don't want a wolverine loose inside the compound."

"Why?"

"They don't hibernate, they're powerful enough to kill a moose, and they like to break into wilderness houses and smash things for the fun of it. Then they spray the bits and pieces like a giant skunk and . . . sometimes deface the scene of the crime in other unpleasant ways."

"Good grief! I've never seen a wolverine. Are they very large?"

"A big specimen can weigh nearly 30 kilos and be more than a meter long. I've only seen one in the wild. It had reddish-black fur and looked like a small bear. They're notoriously fierce and have the worst temper of any North American wild animal. You don't ever want to meet a wolverine."

"Well, I guess not," said Joanna, looking apprehensively over her shoulder.

Instead, we were about to meet something a whole lot worse.

We had unlocked the lodge's heavily secured back door before leaving the aircraft, so we entered easily into a warm, brightly lit mudroom where we were able to take off our envirosuits. I hung the hopper gorget and the pistol belt with the Ivanov on a handy peg beside my suit.

Joanna was still wearing the handsome camel-colored wool ensemble and blue silk blouse she had chosen for the earlier festivities. With her shining hair pulled back into a braided coil, and a discreet string of pearls at her throat, she looked like every randy student's dream of a female academic.

Mine, too.

I was still clad in Dan's perforated athletic garb, although I had shed the body armor right after the media conference. I looked shabby and ridiculous and felt like a sack of azure ordure.

A domestic robot appeared, one of those faceless yard-high jobs with umpteen recessed grab-arms and finicky cleaning accessories. It said, "Good evening! May I carry your baggage?"

Someone had pasted a label on it that read: ROBERTA. Clever. Half the domestic bots in the Commonwealth were named Roberta. The rest were called Robbie.

Nevertheless, I gratefully handed over the duffel and the weighty long gun. Joanna kept the groceries.

"May I know your names, sir and madam?" the machine inquired.

"I hate these things," I muttered. "So pushy. Mom and Pop would never have them in the house."

"Don't hurt its feelings," Joanna admonished me. "It's only trying to do its job." To the machine: "I'm Joanna. He's Helly. Please follow us with the things, Roberta. Don't make any gratuitous remarks or offer helpful comments unless we ask you to do so."

"Yes, Joanna."

The three of us moved into the kitchen, which wouldn't have shamed a small hotel. Joanna began opening cabinets and inspecting appliances.

I said, "I'd love to cook for us, but I don't think I could boil water tonight. Can you manage?"

"Poor baby. Of course I can. Why don't I get our little supper ready now. The lodge has a servitron robot. It can bring the food and wine to us when we want it. Meanwhile, you go unpack our things and relax. Just tell me how to find our room—"

"Master suite," I corrected her. "Go down the long hallway until you get to a living room the size of the Commonwealth Art Gallery. The suite's on the opposite side of the living room, down another hall that leads into the guest-bedroom wing. Remember that your bath awaits, madame! I'm going to have one that's lavender-flavored."

The bot and I trundled off, while Bill Evans and Jim Hall played "Angel Face" on the global stereo.

When my brother Dan was in residence, *he* had inhabited the master suite—the family wanting to make him as comfortable as possible. I'd tell Joanna about Dan's incarceration when our stay in the lodge was over. Why infect the ambience for no good reason?

The decor was luxuriously backwoodsy, with floors of heated stone flags relieved by large rag rugs. Walls of dark-glazed pine were decorated with watercolors, limited-edition photoprints of outdoor scenes and animals, and Indian carvings. Not a stuffed critter head in the place. Officially, no one was allowed to hunt out of Kingfisher Lodge. All the windows were covered by armored shutters disguised as wood. I decided I'd roll up the ones in the bedroom so we could enjoy starlight on snow. If the wolverine came around, we'd show him a thing or two.

With Roberta trailing after, I passed a breakfast room, the main dining room, a game room, a huge library, a room devoted to fly-tying paraphernalia and fishing tackle, and a full bar with a baby grand piano and other musical instruments. Beyond that was the main entry hall, with one set of closed doors opening into the living room and another, heavily secured now, leading to a large sunporch that was used only during warm weather. A third door led to the service wing.

I opened the doors to the living room and said, "Follow me, Roberta."

It kept quiet. No gratuitous conversation.

The chamber was cavernous, with a high beamed ceiling and a hideous chandelier made of discarded caribou antlers that for some reason had not been turned on. Most of the room was deeply shadowed. The bot and I went about halfway across the room, to where half a dozen leather settees were grouped around a huge fireplace fashioned of granite blocks. The only light came from gas flames flickering among faux paper-birch logs, and a Tiffany-style bridge lamp standing near a liquor cart full of decanters and glassware. The stereo speakers in this room were playing some Germanic opera that Joanna certainly had not programmed.

She hadn't ordered the huge living room fireplace turned on, either, or requested the liquor cart.

"Stand perfectly still," he said, from somewhere behind me and to my right. "It would be a great pity if I had to double-dart you before we had an opportunity to talk. We've never really had a decent conversation, you and I. It's an appropriate time, don't you think? On the brink of events that will stagger the galaxy."

It was my voice, but overlaid with an intonation that was British or Scottish. No trace of a cowboy twang. The theatrical diction was *way* wrong.

He stepped out of the shadows holding an Ivanov MS-120, a model that fired darts with extra sleepy-juice. Two shots would put an adult human out for twelve hours. I saw a tall, husky man with breadcrust-colored hair and a prominent widow's peak. His eyes were mean green and his mouth thin-lipped and wide. He wore knife-creased brown slacks, a tan wool Pendleton shirt, a cream neck scarf, and Gucci loafers. The duds were nice, but hardly my style.

He said, "Are you armed?"

"Only the Tala-G the bot's carrying. Left an Ivanov in the mudroom."

"Let's make sure. Strip down."

"Aww—"

"Do it!" God, he was an ornery-looking devil. Is that what people had seen when they looked at *me*? "Don't bore me with false modesty, laddie. I've watched you floating in the tank. And a gratifying sight it was."

He made me give my phone to the bot and tell him where the remote control for the hopper was. As I removed my clothes, shook them out, and then immediately got dressed again, my fatigued mind was putting it all together. Too late.

His own aircraft was inside the locked hangar, secured by his password. Not *Makebate*, which was much too large to fit, but her orbiter gig, with the starship herself parked in space, concealed by the powerful dissimulator.

The wolverine had snuck into the compound when he lowered the lodge defenses for landing, then found itself trapped.

His own "Asahel Frost" personal phone, programmed with virtually all of the data in my own instrument, would have given him access to the lodge. And of course he'd been here before, during Dan's abduction. He'd know what a superb hideaway it was.

Two great minds with but a single thought . . .

He told the robot to withdraw to the opposite end of the room, after instructing it to accept commands only from him. "As for you, lad, please be seated. We'll wait for your lovely wife." He indicated a couch opposite the liquor cart. "I was surprised to see her at your side during the media conference. Her loyalty was touching."

"Joanna never had anything to do with you," I said. "Let her go. Do whatever you like with me."

He poured amber liquid from one of the decanters into a cut-glass tumbler and sipped it, still standing, without offering me any. The Ivanov was tucked in his belt, its two-shot ready-lights glowing. I didn't have a prayer of rushing him, even if I'd been fit.

"I'll do whatever I like with both of you," he said. "Your wife will be just as valuable a negotiating piece as you. When I came here to the lodge, I could conceive of only one way to save my neck. Now, thanks to you, I have two alternatives—and the second is much more attractive than the first. After tomorrow's Assembly vote—"

Joanna screamed, "Helly! Oh, God, Helly!"

She had entered the darkened room and seen him illuminated by the Tiffany lamp and the flames. The man with my face.

I rose from my seat. "No. It's not me."

She stood transfixed, staring incredulously at the two of us, clutching the strap of her shoulder bag as though it were a lifeline.

"Let me introduce myself, Professor DeVet. My name is Alistair Drummond. I am the former chairman and CEO of Galapharma AC. Please come and be seated beside your former husband."

She obeyed, moving like a sleepwalker, unable to take her eyes off him. He had put down his drink and taken the Ivanov from his belt, holding it negligently, apparently without threat.

"Please empty your purse onto the coffee table," he said. She complied and he stepped closer to inspect the contents—a card wallet, a cosmetics case, a computer notebook, several stylomikes, a flat-key folder, a handkerchief, a tiny tin of peppermint Altoids, and a phone. He scooped up the computer and the phone and tossed them into the darkness.

"Roberta! Pick up the two items I dropped. Take them and the other things you're carrying to the communication room. Leave the things there and secure the door with my password."

"Yes, Citizen Drummond," said the machine. No facile familiarity with *los domesticos* for our Alistair. "I was instructed by Joanna not to offer helpful comments. Will you rescind that order?"

"Yes," Drummond said. "What d'you have to say?"

"A servitron containing cold champagne and hot food prepared by Joanna is waiting in the kitchen. Shall I summon it?"

A brilliant smile broke over Drummond's face—my face. I heard Joanna gasp. She'd always loved my smile.

"Yes," Drummond said to the robot, "I'm feeling a bit peckish. Good of you to've obliged, Professor."

Joanna glared at him.

"Only two place settings have been included," said the robot. "There are adequate amounts of food and wine for three. Do you wish an extra place setting?"

Drummond laughed. "Yes, by all means, Roberta. And now you are dismissed."

"Damned fink-bot," I growled. "God, I hate those things."

So we ate and drank, Joanna and I sitting side by side, Drummond lounging on the couch opposite us. He was only slightly inconvenienced by having to keep us covered with the stunner while shoveling down eggs and lox and hogging most of the strawberries. He was in excellent spirits and seemed eager to talk. Maybe megalomaniacs aren't really happy unless they have an audience.

As Karl had suspected, Drummond knew the game was up as soon as Fake Sam informed him that Helly the Haluk had been accepted by the Rampart Board of Directors. Even if Sam's demiclone security officers had been able to take control of the boardroom and its distinguished occupants, there was no possible way for Sam to salvage the situation. Murdering the directors would accomplish nothing. Taking hostages was an even more useless option. Realistically, all Sam could have hoped to do was retreat, taking the Rampart demi contingent with him.

Sam had urged Drummond to immediately take refuge in

Macpherson Tower. Not bloody likely! The Scotsman was crazy but not stupid. The brilliant stratagem he had conceived was totally buggered, and in his Fake-Helly demiclone condition, he was a dangerous liability to the aliens. If he entered their embassy, he would never emerge alive. Free, he might think of a way to blackmail the Haluk into financing a new life for him on some comfortable freesoil world. But where could he hide while waiting for events to ripen?

He remembered Kingfisher Lodge.

Taking a Rampart hopper there would have meant almost instant capture—either by Rampart or by the aliens. Every corporate ground vehicle, aircraft, and starship had a monitoring chip in its navigator that sent a coded data stream directly to Fleet Security and from there to the bean-counters in Finance. Haluk demiclones were present in both departments.

The only Rampart ship exempt from monitoring was *Makebate*. I had made sure of that.

Drummond was reluctant to leave Earth for the reasons I had already noted. He was a wanted man; *Makebate*'s ultraluminal fuel-trace was easy to identify, given enough people looking for it, as was the ship herself; he had no outplanet hidey-hole ready to receive him; and he wanted to stay close to the action in Toronto so he could judge his options accurately. Therefore he did the only practical thing—took off in the starship using ordinary sublight drive, parked in geosync orbit, then returned to Earth immediately in the gig, staying outside the air traffic control network.

I said, "But you must have suspected that the day would come when the aliens wouldn't need you anymore. Didn't you whomp up some sort of insurance policy, the way Ollie Schneider did when he was your mole?"

"No," he said quietly. "It wasn't necessary."

Oh, boy. Maybe escape hatches and fallback maneuvers were too mundane for hubris-loaded nutcases: every contretemps a fresh challenge. Even now he wasn't planning a getaway. He was mulling over a new scam involving Joanna and me.

I could hardly wait to find out what it was.

Joanna said to Drummond, "May I ask you something?"

That damned smile. "You may *ask*." He poured the last of the champagne into his own glass.

"How in the world did you escape from the landslide at the Arizona gold mine?"

"By following rattlesnakes." He threw me a humorous look. "Spare me the obvious comment, lad. The mine was riddled with old tunnels and shafts. I had my little penlight, which I tied to my head with my scarf, and I had my Lanvin actinic pistol. There was water to drink. So I coped."

He had crept and crawled inside Copper Mountain for nearly three days. A couple of times he nearly died in rock-falls. One of them cut him off from returning back the way he'd come. (And convinced searchers that he must be lying dead beneath it.) On the third day, weak from hunger and with the penlight battery starting to give out, he began following what seemed like a moving stream of air, thinking it might lead to an exit. It only brought him into a dead-end gallery.

"At that point I thought I'd had it. There seemed nowhere else to go. I set about exploring a jumble of large rocks and suddenly put my boot right into a rattler nest. The snakes were rather small, but they were striking at me viciously and I knew they were venomous. I shot at them with the Lanvin and fried a few—but the rest fled into a crevice among the rocks that I hadn't noticed. Every single snake disappeared. I checked out the crevice and discovered the source of the wind. It was rubble-choked crawlway too narrow for my body, with sunlight at the end. I blasted rocks until the charge in the Lanvin pistol was exhausted, and shifted the pieces with my hands. I got out. I climbed down the mountain and followed a dirt track fifteen kilometers to a highway. I hitchhiked to Phoenix in a ranch truck and contacted Tyler

Baldwin, the demiclone Galapharma security chief . . . and told him about the idea I'd conceived while lost inside the gold mine. He took me to the Haluk leaders. I think you can imagine the rest."

"That's amazing," Joanna said.

"Do you really think so, Professor?" He'd told the story directly to her, and as he spoke his eyes had toured her leisurely from north to south, with several scenic detours that had made me grit my teeth in fury.

Before she could reply, I said, "You got lucky. But the Haluk aren't going to give you a third chance at the jackpot, so what's your new game plan? Holding us for ransom?"

Reluctantly, he shifted his attention from Joanna to me. His voice was quite courteous. "A variation on that theme. Following the Assembly vote tomorrow—whichever way it goes—you will invite Adam Stanislawski and the seven members of the Rampart Board of Directors presently in Toronto to confer with you here at the lodge. The meeting will be conducted under conditions of the utmost secrecy, with no other persons present—"

"I won't do it," I said.

His gaze flickered to Joanna. "I think you will, given the proper incentive."

"It'll never work. You can't hold hostages here. The security's not good enough. Remember how you grabbed Dan. Others know Joanna and I came to the lodge. They'll be suspicious—"

"We and our guests won't remain here," Drummond said airily. "We'll all be aboard *Makebate*, one of the fastest starships in the galaxy. And one that is very well armed. A deal will be struck. I guarantee it. If not—" He shrugged, cocked his head and listened to the edgy music. "—at least the denouement will be appropriately Wagnerian."

He gave us a mocking toast and tossed down the last of the champagne.

Joanna was staring at him with an expresion of objective interest. Her voice had taken on a clinical tone. "That's what you really want, isn't it? A dramatic ending. To destroy Helly and Adam and the Rampart leadership, because they defeated you twice over."

Alistair Drummond put down the empty champagne flute and lifted the Ivanov. "You're a very lovely woman, Joanna. I'd like you to share my bed tonight."

"No, thank you," she said politely. "I'm afraid I've just started my period."

"You lying bitch!" Drummond snapped.

"No, it's true. Why don't I clear away these supper things into the servitron?" She rose from the couch, picked up a china plate, and suddenly scaled it expertly at Drummond like a Frisbee, missing his head by only a few centimeters. The plate smashed against the granite fireplace.

Drummond shot her in the breast with the Ivanov. Two darts. She fell back against me. "Lying bloody bitch!" he shouted.

I struggled to shift her body and get at him, but it was useless. He popped me twice in the shoulder and I felt the world dissolve into a red-black abyss.

The last thing I remember was Drummond calling, "Roberta! Clean up!"

She was sitting beside me on the edge of the king-sized bed, fully clothed, wiping my face with a damp towel. When I made an inarticulate noise she lifted my head and held a glass of water to my lips.

"Careful, dear. Just take small sips."

I did. My mouth felt like week-old straw in a mule stall.

She took the water away. "Thank God you're finally awake. We've got to act quickly before he comes, and I'm not sure how to work the damned thing."

"What?" I struggled to sit up. We were in a beautifully appointed bedroom. A clock on the nightstand said it was 1333 hours. What was going to be the most memorable day of my life was already half gone.

I stretched my arms, flexed my legs. Except for a sore spot on my shoulder where the darts had penetrated, I felt almost good. Maybe I'd send the Ivanov people a testimonial.

Joanna had left me and gone to a large pottery vase on a low dresser that held an ornamental arrangement of dried grasses. She rummaged around in it. "I hid it in here, in case he came in before you woke and decided to . . . search my clothes."

She pulled out the new Lucevera 4500 she'd bought in Timmins and handed it to me.

I said, "Jesus Christ!"

"It was in my inside jacket pocket all the time. Drummond never thought that I might have been carrying two phones. Thank heaven he shot me in the opposite boob." She made a face. "Incidentally, the dart wound still hurts like hell. I was afraid that if I used the phone to call the Rampart emergency code, the call would register somehow on Drummond's own phone. That's why I waited for you to wake up."

"No, it wouldn't. He and I have separate phone codes. All we share is the computer data and system-links. But I'm glad you waited. We'll call Karl instead of arguing with ExSec. They're likely to be kinda uptight and antsy at this point in time."

The armored shutter on one window was open. Outside, fat snowflakes fluttered straight down in a winter wonderland. I climbed out of bed and checked the compound. The Mitsubishi-Kondo was gone.

"He's moved the hopper," I said. "He must have put it into the garage out of sight. Along with the orbiter gig."

She said, "The door of our suite is locked and it's not ordinary wood. I think it's made of the same armor as the shutters. The glass in the windows looks very thick, too."

"They're unbreakable and laser-proof. This suite was designed to be ultrasecure. A good thing, too. We're going to lock Alistair Drummond out of here, then make some big botheration."

I began tapping pads.

"What are you doing?" Joanna asked apprehensively. "Won't he know if you access the lodge systems?"

"Not unless he's looking at the phone display. Pray he's got it stowed in his pocket . . . Hah! Gotcha. The original code for the secure-suite lock was deactivated when the lodge was shut down. A new one hasn't been installed. That means Drummond must have used his simple password to engage the lock. The dumb galoot even gave the password to that idiot robot."

Tap tappety tap tap tap.

"I don't understand," Joanna said. "Secure suite?"

"Never mind. Look." I showed her the phone's data-strip. It said:

LIST PASSWORDS: GLASGOW 1/1

"He didn't encrypt it. Why should he? Anytime we want, we're out of here, babe. But not yet. Definitely not yet!"

I installed a new code for the lock—encrypted, of course—killed the Glasgow access, and locked us in. Then I closed the window shutter that Joanna had opened.

"We're going to make sure our fish doesn't get away," I said. "Then we call for help. Crawl under the bed."

While she gaped at me in stark disbelief, I summoned another menu. This one was for *Makebate*'s gig. I explained: "Both Drummond's and my phone have links to the nav-autopilot system of the starship gig. If I park the gig somewhere, or even leave it inside the starship, I can call it to come pick me up—just like a car or a hopper."

"But the gig is already here," Joanna protested. "In the underground hangar along with the Macrodur hopper."

I took her arm and urged her onto the floor. We both slithered under the bed. "I'm going to send the gig home to *Makebate*. Unfortunately, I'm going to forget to open the garage door first."

"Oh . . ."

"The lodge is a very sturdy building," I reassured her. "We should be all right. Ready?"

I pressed the pads that would light up the gig's engines. Did the requisite preflight rigmarole. Then I told the orbiter to lift off. The phone began to shriek like a banshee. I could hear a tinny computerized voice saying, *Danger. Danger. Overhead obstruction* scanned. *Liftoff aborted. Liftoff aborted.*

No doubt Alistair Drummond heard it, too.

I told the phone, "Override alpha-three-one-one. Go!"

The concussion did not lift the house off its foundation, nor did it break the armor-glass windows. The hangar was carved out of bedrock and the major force of the fuel blast was directed upward, with a secondary shockwave rushing along the subterranean tunnel, where it severely damaged the deserted staff quarters wing.

We clung together while bits of demolished machinery rained down on the ceramalloy roof like a hailstorm from hell. The bedframe had leaped off the floor and thumped down harmlessly. A tall chest of drawers and a bookcase had toppled and scattered things. The ceramic bedside lamps had crashed, and so had the vase with the grasses, a couple of large framed pictures, and a passel of nameless sundries that had fallen off shelves and out of cabinets in the adjacent bathroom.

"Are you all right?" I asked Joanna.

"Yes. My God, it was just like a bomb!"

"Exactly like one." The clinging was very nice. "Did you really start your period?"

"It's a standard antirape ploy. Men are so squeamish."

"All the same, I'm glad you threw the plate . . . On your feet, babe."

We crawled out into the mess. I opened the shutters on all three bedroom windows. A tall column of smoke swirled from the hangar hole in the middle distance. Not much debris was visible; it had sunk out of sight in the deepening snow.

Next order of business: I called Karl Nazarian's personal code.

"It's Helly, at the lodge. Alistair Drummond's here. I've destroyed the transportation. Send a SWAT team fast. He's armed with a Tala-G and God knows what else. Joanna and I are barricaded in Dan's old secure-suite. We'll be okay."

"I copy your emergency," said the cool old cucumber. "Hold while I talk to ExSec and dispatch the team."

I waited.

Joanna said, "I hear something at the door."

Scratching sounds. Then the sharp yelp of a photon gun, one with less power than my Tala-G, perhaps a Claus-Gewitter, weapon of choice for serious meat-hunters. Maybe Drummond didn't know how to operate the more esoteric combat piece.

Cheeow cheeow.

I muttered, "Give it up, sucker. You and your Haluk goons couldn't blast your way in here when you came for Dan. You had to torture two guards to death to get the lock-code."

Joanna's eyes were wide with horror. "Helly . . .?"

Another photon blast, then silence.

"I'll explain later," I told her. Karl was back on the phone.

"The team'll fly out of our Oshawa facility inside of half an hour," he said, "five hoppers and thirty personnel. You're looking at a ninety-minute ETA. They'll try to take Drummond alive."

"Goody. Did the Macpherson Tower raid come off?"

"You haven't heard?"

"Drummond was waiting for us when we arrived. Joanna and I have been stunned-out for over twelve hours."

"Well, shit. You missed some crazy action. Eve made her

pitch to the media and then to the Servant, who denied everything in a rebuttal newscast. Couple hours later a mysterious armed hopper shot sleepy-gas grenades into every floor in the top half of the tower. Toronto Public Safety and ECID were shocked. Shocked."

I laughed. "Let me guess. The hopper escaped. The cops entered in force to assess damage to the embassy and injury to the poor alien occupants. They found the Halukoid folks."

"All safe, all removed to Toronto General Hospital—including your brother Dan, the only human being in the place who actually looked like one. There were no demiclones in Macpherson. They must have all been evacuated. Of course the media had a field day. And the Servant filed a formal protest with Xenoaffairs, claiming the cops had kidnapped innocent Haluk, not transformed humans."

I snorted. "Stick with the Big Lie, right to the edge of the Grand Canyon drop-off."

"The vote!" Joanna exclaimed. "What about the goddamned vote?"

"Did you hear the professor's respectful query?" I asked Karl.

He said, "The Assembly approved the three hundred new Haluk colonies by a margin of forty-six votes. The Speaker invited a Citizen Veto Poll. The PlaNet hits are still being tabulated and verified, but it looks like the veto won."

Joanna and I cheered.

"What's more," Karl said, "there's a groundswell growing for the recall of the Delegates who voted for the Haluk colonies. Some Reverse spokespersons are demanding top-to-bottom reform of the Assembly to eliminate the influence of the Hundred Concerns. We're living in interesting times, my friend."

"And here *we* are," I lamented, "sitting it out on the sidelines with a homicidal maniac."

"I'll be on my way to the lodge myself after I talk to some

people. Turn on your holovid and catch up on what's happening in the universe. Sit tight till the cavalry arrives, and don't do anything stupid."

"Have I ever?" I asked, and ended the call.

Joanna was already examining the holo projector in the adjacent snuggery, prodding its remote keypad without result. "Nothing but a blank blue field," she mourned. "The projector seems all right, so I suppose the antenna was damaged in the explosion."

The phone buzzed. I looked at the display. The instrument was in intercom mode.

I said, "Hello, Alistair. Did you enjoy the fireworks?"

"It's not over," he said softly.

"Yes, it is. Tell you what. I'll see that you get your real body back before they chain you to the bed in the funny farm."

"I'm leaving now, Frost, but we'll meet again. I doubt that the pleasure will be mutual. I intend to have something very special waiting for you—and for Professor DeVet. Dream about it." He ended the call.

Leaving?

Something medium-large sped past the windows, then reappeared and cut a sharp right turn, kicking a rooster tail of snow against the glass.

Cursing, I ran to check it out. The snowmobile's track led from one of the outbuildings to the lodge. Drummond had deliberately buzzed our suite. Now he was heading directly toward us at low speed, the twin headlights of the sleek Ski-Doo haloed by floating ice crystals.

The machine was classic yellow-and-black with nice scarlet flashes. The helmeted figure in the saddle lifted a hand with two gloved fingers extended. Peace? . . . V for victory? . . . Nope. In the British Isles the double-digit salute had another meaning.

Fuck you.

An instant later a portable force-field shield enveloped the Doo in a hemisphere of golden sparks. Drummond did a 180 and headed straight out onto the frozen lake at maximum speed, leaving a huge white cloud of powder snow in his wake.

I dug in my pocket for the phone, frantically called up the lodge-exterior menu and switched on the defenses he had deactivated. Too late. The damned sled was traveling at nearly 200 kph and it was already outside the perimeter and gone away.

I rushed to the door of the suite, spoke the unlock code, and began galloping down the hall. Joanna was right behind me as I crossed the living room—where there was remarkably little damage from the blast—came into the entry and took a detour into the service wing. The com room door was wide open. My Talavera-Gerardi lay centered on a small table, neat as a display in a gunshop.

I swiftly checked the weapon out. It seemed completely undamaged, the barrel was clear, and the ready display said FULL CHARGE. I slung the piece over my shoulder.

Joanna said, "What are you going to do?"

I pushed past her, heading for the mudroom. Our enviro-suits, helmets, and overboots were still there. The Ivanov was gone. I propped the long gun against the wall and began to dress.

"I'll need to take the phone," I said. "You'll have to make a note of the door code so you can lock yourself in the secure-suite."

"But—"

"Drummond might double back. The exterior defenses are useless because he can access them. When I'm gone, get back into the suite and stay there until the SWAT team arrives."

"You can't go after him!" she stormed. "Don't you understand? It's what he wants you to do! He's not trying to escape. He'll be waiting for you out there."

I tinkered with the helmet, establishing the phone link and the system feed with the suit and boots that I hadn't bothered with during the short trip from the hopper to the lodge.

"Find something to write the code on, Joanna."

"Wait," she said tightly. She went into the kitchen and returned with a recipe e-book.

I read out the alphanumerics, tucked the phone inside my suit, and zipped up.

She said, "Don't do this, Helly. Not if you love me. Don't go after that man to kill him." Her face was very pale, with an odd hectic flush on the cheeks that had nothing to do with makeup. She clutched the little book tightly in one hand, holding it at her side like a missile ready for throwing.

"I'll bring him back alive if I can."

Speaking in a strained whisper: "The SWAT team can do that better than you. Stay with me. Please don't leave me alone again."

"I can't let Drummond get away. If he reaches Central Patricia, he could commandeer a fast Park Service hopper and fly down to Thunder Bay Conurb. There's a starship shuttle service at the skyport—"

"He's not trying to get away." Her eyes were bright with moisture. "He left your weapon when he could have taken it himself or destroyed it . . . And I'm sure you'll find an operable snow machine waiting out in the equipment building. If Drummond wanted to escape, he'd have disabled it. He's playing a game with you, Helly. An insane game!"

"Will you kiss me goodbye? I love you, Joanna."

She let me embrace her, passively accepted my hard lips, the alien tongue we'd laughed about and enjoyed. When we broke apart her tears had overflowed.

"Goodbye, Helly," she said, and turned and walked away.

Of course Joanna was right about Drummond planning an ambush. I knew that his chance of escaping—even as far as Thunder Bay—were infinitesimal. The SWAT team would

nab his ass as easily as a pack of Ontario timber wolves running down a crippled caribou. Unless I got him first.

And I intended to.

I'd ignored my wife's good counsel, confirmed her doubts
about my character, maybe torpedoed any chance of a permanent reconciliation. One part of me was kicking the other
part and cursing it for a prideful fool. But I couldn't do anything else.

Cowboys . . .

As Joanna had predicted, there was another shiny Ski-Doo
waiting for me. Two toys were evidently all Rampart had
sprung for to entertain the troops, but the Concern hadn't
stinted on quality. The Formula 12K-XC was the primo
back-country trail sled. Its frame was scandium alloy—the
same stuff that catalyzes trans-ack starship fuel—stronger
than titanium and lighter than aluminum. To make the machine ride even lighter—and get you out of holes when you
bogged down—it had inertial stabilizers and optional antigravity enhancement. Its powerful engine was whisper-
quiet. The console was loaded with nifty gadgets, including
com equipment, a terrain scanner with warm-body capability, global positioning, an emergency beacon, and a buddy
beacon. Drummond would deactivate the latter feature, and
so would I. Buddies we weren't.

Other goodies included a retractable bivouac enclosure
that you could shelter in if you broke down or got trapped in
a blizzard, an independent heater, trail rations, survival kit,
and first-aid unit. My sled did not have a defensive force-
shield. That particular item is not among the luxury accessories offered by the Ski-Doo folks. Drummond had either
brought his own umbrella or swiped one from the Macrodur
hopper. The Doo did have a swingaway hunter's gun-mount
with a weatherproof stretch-sheath that was barely adequate
to cover my ultramacho Tala-G. I installed the weapon, fired
up the engine, and eased out of the barn.

I hadn't been on one of these machines for nearly ten

years, but I didn't anticipate much difficulty driving. I was in
no hurry. Alistair Drummond would wait for me in the backwoods arena of his choosing.

I hoped to arrive at a time, and from a direction, that was
not of his choosing.

The snow was coming down heavier. It was now impossible to see the opposite shore of the lake, six klicks away. I
checked the scanner to be sure my adversary wasn't lurking
anywhere in the immediate vicinity—or circling the compound to catch me from the rear. Even with a tree-filter,
there was a lot of clutter on the screen. It showed only a single warm body blip, sans machine accompaniment, moving
at a brisk galumph through the woods on the other side of
the lake. An animal. The data strip said:

SPECIES: WOLVERINE—WT: 35.5 KILOS

"Go away, beastie," I murmured. "Other game is afoot."

I called up the positioner map, selected a twenty-kilome-
ter radius, and studied the bright terrain-proper display. A
number of narrow tracks webbed the forest and bogs surrounding the lodge, illegally zapped a couple of years ago by
bored security guards whose duty it was to nanny my unfortunate brother.

During warm weather the trails were probably horrific
even for iron-butt backpackers or anglers—muddy, rough
with burned-off stumps, and mosquito-plagued. In winter,
after the snow attained a reasonable depth, they'd be handy
little corridors for snowmobilers and game poachers, hence
the gun-mount on my sled. Nothing like a rack of venison or
a moose-muffle to liven up the staff menu. Nothing like a
running target to sharpen rusty marksmanship skills.

I expanded to a 50 km overview, then 100 km. The last
display included the hamlet of Central Patricia ninety klicks
to the west. A single trail, beginning at the far side of Caddisfly Lake, twisted and twined and ended up there. I won-

dered briefly what attractions the lonely men had found in the tiny outpost. A bar with live music and friendly local ladies? Hey, in their shoes it would have appealed to me.

I highlighted the C-Pat Trail, then returned to the large-scale map and called up a holographic topo display. To check for high ground overlooking that trail—preferably not too far away from the lodge.

There wasn't much. The most likely—very nearly the only!—ambush spot I could find was a sparsely wooded granite ridge only 29 meters above the surrounding terrain. It was situated about nine klicks from the western lakeshore. The ridge was relatively steep and treeless on the southern side, above the trail, and sloped gently to the north, where the forest was thicker.

The stretch of the C-Pat Trail next to the ridge was fairly wide and straight, inviting a sledder to travel at speed. A couple of klicks west of the high ground, a branch trail came in on the right. This was a much narrower and more convoluted path leading back to the lake, paralleling a short creek that drained a pond. Its termination was about five kilometers north of the C-Pat trailhead.

If I were Alistair Drummond, I'd drive across the lake and go west on the C-Pat past Granite Ridge to the Creek Trail junction. Turn right. Trend back eastward a klick or two behind the ridge. Leave the trail and drive my sled ever so carefully south, upslope through patchy trees and rocks to the overlook.

Hunker in. Wait for Helly to come bombing along the C-Pat down yonder, gung ho to catch up with the fleeing miscreant. Pot him like a ptarmigan.

Unless the intended victim entered the forest on Creek Trail instead, and snuck up behind the sniper.

I sped diagonally across the lake. The ice was freeway flat and the scanner came up dead empty. From the shore the Creek trailhead was almost invisible, clogged with brush

and a tangle of downed birch saplings. I punched the antigravity and hopped over them, then started along a winding
path that was barely wide enough for a single machine. The
air temperature was minus-five. My snow-depth indicator
read 34 cm. Ten of that was fresh powder, and there'd be lots
more before long.

Nearly an hour had passed since I'd spoken to Karl Nazarian. The SWAT team would be arriving soon. I cranked the
throttle and drove as fast as I dared. The engine was a tiger-
purr, muffled by the falling white stuff.

Twenty minutes later I was behind Granite Ridge. The irregular ground upslope showed no trace of a warm body. I
could only presume he was on the other side of the crest,
where broken rock formed a natural redoubt above the C-Pat.
If I went farther along the Creek Trail, looking for his sled
tracks to verify that he had, in fact, chosen this spot for the
ambush, there was a chance he might scan me or hear me. I
opted to climb the ridge on foot. The scope of my Tala-G had
a thermal targeter three times more sensitive than that of a
Ski-Doo—or a Claus-Gewitter blaster.

I called up a compass on my visor display and took a
rough bearing on my objective. The vantage point was about
a mile and a quarter southwest. There would be adequate
cover until I reached the ridge top, where only small clumps
of trees had found a footing in the frost-fractured granite.

My boots had a nifty feature: deployable miniature bear-
paw snowshoe webs. I spread them and started mushing. The
blood singing in my ears was the only other sound in the
winter fastness. I still didn't have my old stamina, but I made
the climb without too much difficulty in the relatively shal-
low snow, doing a sweep with the scope every dozen meters,
finding nothing warm—and no shield ionization signature,
either.

Just below the ridge crest, sheltered by a group of jack
pines, I rested and turned off the heating system of my envirosuit. Every little erg counts. Then I began to creep toward

the overlook, which I estimated was about 200 meters away, snaking through tall snow-covered rocks, taking advantage of every bit of cover, sighting through the gun scope every other minute, praying that Drummond was up here and that he was concentrating his attention on the C-Pat Trail, not scanning the ridge to his left.

In the scope, two blips of warm.

I flattened, sinking into the snow behind a white-capped chunk of granite the size of a car. Changed the scope mode to amplification, peeked out.

I saw a crouching figure holding a long gun at the ready. His Ski-Doo waited close by, slightly downslope among the trees. No force-field hemisphere, of course. You can't shoot a blaster through a simple portable shield.

I pulled off my right mitten so I could operate the trigger and targeted Alistair Drummond, the man wearing my body. Range, 156.2 meters.

Don't do this, Helly. Not if you love me. Don't go after that man to kill him.

I'll bring him back alive if I can.

Rats.

I switched the gun to manual fire and blasted a pine snag six meters away from him. He fired down at the C-Pat Trail, then sent another wild shot to his right, decapitating a small balsam fir. He hadn't found me with his scope and the snow made it impossible for him to judge my position.

I waited. Willing him to do it.

He fired again, coming nowhere near me, then made a dash for his snowmobile. Boarded, flicked on the shield. Safe from my photon weapon beneath his sparkling dome, he started his machine and headed downhill toward Creek Trail, weaving feather-light through the spindly pines. He'd turned on the antigravity enhancer to maximize his speed on the fluffy powder.

I surged to my feet, clambered on top of the rock, and began to mow down the trees ahead of him, blasting the trunks near the base so they dropped like jackstraws. Some bounced harmlessly off the force-field, others fell to either side as I continued to aim in front of the scuttling, turtle-shaped mass of golden sparks.

He had nearly dropped below my line of fire when I nailed him. A perfectly felled pine came down right across his path and the sled hit it head-on. The force-field projector cut out as the power died. I watched the yellow-and-black machine do a nose-flip right over the log and begin rolling down the steepening slope. Drummond was still in the saddle.

The Ski-Doo disappeared in the snow. I hopped off the rock and began floundering after it. I found him a few minutes later, under the broken and twisted machine. It had fetched up against a tree. Both of his legs were grotesquely entangled in the skid-frame. There was not much blood.

I dug the snow away from his head and opened his visor and looked into my own face, twisted in agony. Alistair Drummond was fully conscious.

He said, "Damn you. Damn you."

"There's no way I can winch this thing off without hurting you," I told him. "I'll have to go back to the lodge and find a cutting tool."

"Why didn't you shoot me on the ridge?" he asked.

"I killed myself once in Macpherson Tower. Once is enough."

The first-aid unit and survival kit were intact. I wrapped the parts of his body that I could reach in mylar foil blankets. Did my best to inspect his shattered legs without removing the remnants of his envirosuit. It was still producing warmth.

"There's bound to be a medic in the Rampart SWAT team coming up from Toronto. It should arrive soon. I'll put up the survival tent to keep the snow off you. Would you like a drink of water?"

"Go to hell."

He turned his head away and didn't say anything else. His

eyes were closed. There was a pulse in his neck, so I figured he'd either fainted or gone into shock.

Time to move along. I flicked the emergency beacon, erected the tent, and turned on its heater. Then I hiked back down Creek Trail to my own machine and returned to the lodge.

Joanna and I were still trying to find a cutting torch in the shambles of the workroom, which was in the damaged staff wing, when five blue Rampart ExSec hoppers landed in the compound. The team leader was an Amazonian black woman named Captain Sarah Marcus.

She had the medical personnel and the equipment necessary to free and evacuate Drummond. She had the good sense not to argue when I said I was going along.

Two aircraft landed in the creek bed, the only open space available. Captain Marcus supervised loading the gear on AG totes, but I was the one who led the way as we snowshoed through the cold white woods to the place where Alistair Drummond awaited rescue.

"What the hell is that stink?" Marcus said.

I said, "Oh, shit," knowing.

We found the tent torn to bits and bloody snow trampled by clawed feet and a body with its throat torn out, defiled with foul-smelling musk.

"There it is, Cap!" one of the troops cried, whipping out his Kagi sidearm and taking aim. "Looks like a goddamn bear!"

I knocked his gun arm up and the blast went harmlessly into the trees. A bulky dark form bounded out from a tumble of rocks and dashed downhill with surprising speed. In a moment it had vanished into the storm.

"Not a bear," I said. "A wolverine. Leave it alone."

Captain Marcus said, "It killed this man. We can scope it out and burn it later, when we're airborne."

"No," I told her firmly. "We'll let the animal be. It's a wild thing. It acts naturally, following its own rules. It has a right to do so. Do you understand?"

"Yes." She turned her back on me and began giving orders to the others, and I tramped away downhill into the clean white falling snow.

Epilogue

The scout ship that Adam Stanislawski had sent to Amenti, in the Sagittarius Whorl, reported that the asteroid was the home base of an estimated two hundred Haluk corsairs. Shortly after the incident at the Haluk embassy was reported by the media, the Macrodur chairman dispatched a fleet of Concern cruisers to clean out the pirate nest.

Following the destruction of their starships, the Haluk declared war on the Commonwealth of Human Worlds.

A force of consisting of eighty heavy warships and 160 light starfighters lifted off from Haluk colonial planets at the tip of the Perseus Spur and headed for Seriphos, Rampart's local headquarters. The attackers were intercepted in deep space by Rampart starships and Zone Patrol. Eventually they were annihilated, although the outnumbered defenders suffered heavy casualties. Seriphos itself was left unscathed.

Immediately after this engagement, a second enemy fleet of equal size left the Haluk worlds and began to encircle Cravat, sole source of the genen vector PD32:C2. Rampart forces had been siphoned away from Cravat to defend Seriphos, and the tide of battle began to turn toward the aliens.

At the same time, Rampart's powerful Fleet Scanner Satellite at Tyrins detected nearly four thousand alien vessels en route from the Haluk Cluster to the Perseus Spur.

I consulted with the Rampart Board of Directors, then ordered the Rampart defenders to incinerate every landmass on Cravat with antimatter bombs.

Virtually every armed Concern and Commonwealth starship in the galaxy, including that of Captain Guillermo Bermudez Obregon, based on Kedge-Lockaby, was mobilized to defend the Milky Way Galaxy. I drove *Makebate*.

After sixty-one days of fighting in intergalactic space outside the Perseus Spur, the aliens surrendered.

Mimo, who was once again in excellent health, personally accounted for eighty-four ship-kills. He threw a celebratory luau at his Eyebrow Cay home, and some three dozen lowlife starship commanders who had distinguished themselves in the late conflict attended.

So did I. I was still blue, but no one minded. I had popped 166 of the bastards.

The defeated Haluk deposed the Servant of Servants and imprisoned him in a monastery of Anointed Elders, where he was to undergo corrective meditation for the rest of his life.

The surrender agreement was eyeballed by Locutor Ru Kamik and the Council of Nine. In it they abjectly disavowed the Grand Design and begged the Human Commonwealth to have mercy on the Haluk people.

Magnanimous in victory, the Commonwealth agreed to sponsor a massive research program—contracted out to Rampart Concern—synthesizing the vector virus PD32:C2. If, after five years, the aliens demonstrated that they embraced peace and abandoned the pernicious philosophy of uncontrolled population growth, the vector manufacturing process would be made available to them, gratis. Human inspection teams and family-planning counselors were to be welcomed in the Haluk Cluster, as well as the Haluk colonial worlds. Normal trade relations would be reestablished. If all went well during the five-year period, the Commonwealth would consider systematically granting limited numbers of Milky Way planets to the Haluk, until their population pressures eased.

Until then they were stuck with allomorphy and the worlds they already inhabited.

The flawed allo-eradication therapy developed by the late Emily Blake Konigsberg would be studied by human experts during the interim, and tweaked to eliminate the relapse factor. Fortunately, treated Haluk individuals who had reverted to the testudomorph state did emerge from their chrysalids as healthy allomorphic graciles.

In another condition of the surrender, the Haluk agreed to round up all Haluk-human demiclones, toss them into dystasis tanks, and change them back into normal Haluk. A few genetic transforms, including the woman known as Dolores da Gama, eluded the dragnet and are said to be blissfully enjoying the human condition on obscure freesoil worlds.

Nearly ten thousand human DNA donors were rescued from the Haluk colonies, in addition to the higher-status individuals imprisoned in Macpherson Tower. Some of the former had floated for years, and had had five or six alien copies made of themselves. After memory reprogramming, over half of the donors regained their mental health, found employment, and resumed their interrupted personal lives. The others were cared for by the Commonwealth at Haluk expense.

The Haluk promised to eschew mining transactinides with convict slave labor. In another CHW-sponsored project—contracted out to Sheltok Concern—human mining engineers traveled to the Haluk Cluster to instruct the aliens in more civilized technology. The Haluk were apt pupils. In time Sheltok would find itself purchasing more efficient machinery for the Sagittarian mines, designed by Haluk—just as Bodascon Concern would adopt certain Haluk starship innovations.

The aliens were hardware hotshots but abysmally unskilled in biotechnology and computer science. The new trade treaty allowed them to buy all the human goods they wanted, with the exception of certain armaments.

Enormous quantities of Macrodur computers were sold to the Haluk. The manufacturers of ticklesuits and Japanese kimonos also did a roaring business.

Meanwhile, back on the planet Earth, a political upheaval was in full swing.

Many Conservative Delegates were recalled and Reversionist candidates elected to take their places. Geraldo Gonzalez matured into a statesman of major stature. Together with Efrem Sontag, he sponsored Assembly bills that eventually eliminated the longstanding domination of CHW politics by the Hundred Concerns.

Pocket Delegates disappeared into oblivion. Syndics found other jobs. Corporation finks were immediately purged from the Secretariat for Xenoaffairs, the Interstellar Commerce Secretariat, and Zone Patrol. Over the next decade, legislation was enacted that reformed many areas of the human governmental structure.

The *Conlegius* statutes, which had given Concerns far-ranging independent police powers, were abolished. At the suggestion of Delegate Sontag, Karl Nazarian was appointed to a new CCID task force overseeing Concern security reorganization.

The Commonwealth Correction System was also revamped, eliminating the penalty of disenfranchisement except for capital crimes. Throwaways were invited to reapply for citizenship and carefully screened. The scandal-ridden Coventry penitentiaries were closed down.

Corporate ownership of the stars would persist for a long time, as the Assembly slowly whittled away at the entrenched hegemony of Big Business and enacted new tax measures to finance the reforms. Rome wasn't built in a day, and neither was a galactic democracy.

Nonstargoing Insap races were granted just wages and given educational options. They did not become corporate stakeholders and share in the profits of their exploited worlds. Their consciousness raised, some of the natives became predictably restless. But the majority didn't give a damn, so long as the human invaders brought in plenty of trade goods.

Beer was an especially big hit among carbon-based life-forms.

After the brief Haluk War, I spent time in dystasis and emerged with my previous body, buffed up a little here and there. Joanna was present for my rollout, and so were Simon—healthy as a horse—and Eve and Beth and even Cousin Zed. Karl Nazarian and his Over-the-Hill Gang were on hand, along with Mimo and my old comrades Ivor Jenkins and Ildiko Szabo.

Daniel Frost pleaded a previous engagement with his psychotherapist. He now lived quietly with his wife in a secure house in the Ontario Cottage Country and steadfastly denied that he had done anything wrong.

Fulfilling my promise to Simon, I now serve as a part-time Rampart executive. Most of my work is tedious troubleshooting. I have moments when I sincerely wish I were a beach bum again.

I did manage to implement Reversionist principles on many of the planets in the Perseus Spur, but the ex-Galapharma worlds in the Orion Arm fought my radical notions tooth and nail. Their reform may have to wait until the Commonwealth Assembly does the job for me.

I myself have no desire to seek public office, although I still give generous donations to the Reversionists. A political cowboy is a sorry thing.

One of the charitable foundations that I manage is dedicated to alleviating the lot of the denizens of the Dark Path. Sadly, numbers of them want nothing more than to continue on exactly as before; the trogs are always with us. A sizable majority have been assisted by my foundation to make new lives under one sun or another.

Mama Fanchon Labrecque became head of the Visiting Practitioner Service of Kedge-Lockaby's new Katje Vanderpost Memorial Hospital.

Mohammed al-Wazan is in medical school and hopes someday to join Mama. The sadistic executive creep who used him as a boy-toy was mysteriously shanghaied and is now a permanent maroony, in charge of toilet-cubicle maintenance in the asteroid Phlegethon.

Santa Claus still lives beneath Toronto. If there is profound symbolism there, I haven't been able to figure it out.

The rest of the Grange Place Tribe have returned to their families and are doing as well as can be expected.

Professor Joanna DeVet teaches political science at Commonwealth University for three terms each year. Her book was a popular smash and provoked unseemly jealousy among certain of her academic colleagues, even though she donated the proceeds to charity.

We were remarried a week after I emerged from the tank. We have a house in the Kawartha Lakes region and an apartment in Rampart Tower. Neither one has domestic robots.

We vacation at the Sky Ranch and on Kedge-Lockaby. She loves my yellow submarine. I love the way she sits a horse.

Joanna is still trying to understand me, and claims that the natural history of the wolverine offers significant insights into my character. I call that piffle.

She has also tells me that she sometimes misses Helly the Haluk.

I don't.

Don't miss
*The Galactic Milieu
Trilogy*

by Julian May

JACK THE BODILESS

DIAMOND MASK

MAGNIFICAT

Published by Del Rey Books.
Available in bookstores everywhere.

If you haven't read the first two installments in the Rampart Worlds Trilogy, don't miss:

Perseus Spur

◆

Orion Arm

Part 1 and 2 of
The Rampart Worlds Trilogy

by Julian May

Published by Del Rey Books.
Available in bookstores everywhere.

DEL REY® ONLINE!

The Del Rey Internet Newsletter...

A monthly electronic publication e-mailed to subscribers and posted on the rec.arts.sf.written Usenet newsgroup and on our Del Rey Books Web site (www.randomhouse.com/delrey/). It features hype-free descriptions of books that are new in the stores, a list of our upcoming books, special promotional programs and offers, announcements and news, a signing/reading/convention-attendance calendar for Del Rey authors and editors, "In Depth" essays in which professionals in the field (authors, artists, cover designers, salespeople, etc.) talk about their jobs in science fiction, a question-and-answer section, and more!

Subscribe to the DRIN: send a blank message to
join-drin-dist@list.randomhouse.com

The Del Rey Books Web Site!

We make a lot of information available on our Web site at
www.randomhouse.com/delrey/

- all back issues and the current issue of the Del Rey Internet Newsletter
- sample chapters of almost every new book
- detailed interactive features for some of our books
- special features on various authors and SF/F worlds
- reader reviews of some upcoming books
- news and announcements
- our Works in Progress report, detailing the doings of our most popular authors
- and more!

Questions? E-mail us...

at delrey@randomhouse.com (though it sometimes takes us a little while to answer).